Praise for the novels of Sheila Roberts

"No one writes emotionally satisfying, warmhearted tales of small-town life quite like Sheila Roberts."
—*Booklist*

"What better place to start over than Moonlight Harbor, where new friendships and new beginnings await?... Moonlight Harbor is a great place to lose yourself for a few hours."
—*The Romance Dish* on *Beachside Beginnings*

"An irresistible story that will have readers wondering until the conclusion...Lighthearted and full of colorful, quirky characters and surf-side warmth, this latest foray into Roberts's picturesque coastal world is sheer delight and will appeal to romance and women's fiction fans alike."
—*Library Journal* on *The Summer Retreat*

"Roberts does an excellent job of creating sympathetic and relatable characters with real-life problems in a small-town setting."
—*Library Journal*

"Roberts kicks off her new Moonlight Harbor series with this delightful story of family, friendship and new beginnings. The vividly drawn coastal Washington setting comes alive."
—*RT Book Reviews* on *Welcome to Moonlight Harbor*

"The plot takes several unexpected twists and turns on its way to a delightful ending. see what life has in store for Jenna at Moonlight Harbor."
—*FreshFiction.carbor*

"*Welcome to Mooture your attention as e.com*

Also by Sheila Roberts

CHRISTMAS FROM THE HEART
ONE CHARMED CHRISTMAS

Moonlight Harbor

WELCOME TO MOONLIGHT HARBOR
WINTER AT THE BEACH
THE SUMMER RETREAT
BEACHSIDE BEGINNINGS

Icicle Falls

CHRISTMAS IN ICICLE FALLS
STARTING OVER ON BLACKBERRY LANE
THREE CHRISTMAS WISHES
HOME ON APPLE BLOSSOM ROAD
CHRISTMAS ON CANDY CANE LANE
A WEDDING ON PRIMROSE STREET
THE LODGE ON HOLLY ROAD
THE TEA SHOP ON LAVENDER LANE
THE COTTAGE ON JUNIPER RIDGE
WHAT SHE WANTS (also published as
ROMANCE ON MOUNTAIN VIEW ROAD)
MERRY EX-MAS
BETTER THAN CHOCOLATE (also published as
SWEET DREAMS ON CENTER STREET)

Look for Sheila Roberts's next novel
A LITTLE CHRISTMAS SPIRIT
available soon from MIRA.

SHEILA ROBERTS

sunset on moonlight beach

mira

If you purchased this book without a cover you should be aware
that this book is stolen property. It was reported as "unsold and
destroyed" to the publisher, and neither the author nor the
publisher has received any payment for this "stripped book."

Recycling programs
for this product may
not exist in your area.

ISBN-13: 978-0-7783-3175-9

Sunset on Moonlight Beach

Copyright © 2021 by Roberts Ink LLC

All rights reserved. No part of this book may be used or reproduced in any manner
whatsoever without written permission except in the case of brief quotations
embodied in critical articles and reviews.

This is a work of fiction. Names, characters, places and incidents are either the
product of the author's imagination or are used fictitiously. Any resemblance to
actual persons, living or dead, businesses, companies, events or locales is entirely
coincidental.

This edition published by arrangement with Harlequin Books S.A.

For questions and comments about the quality of this book, please contact us
at CustomerService@Harlequin.com.

Mira
22 Adelaide St. West, 40th Floor
Toronto, Ontario M5H 4E3, Canada
www.Harlequin.com

Printed in Lithuania

MIX
Paper from
responsible sources
FSC® C021394

For the Sheila Girls. Love you all!

sunset on moonlight beach

One

You have a great life, Jenna Jones told herself as she took the glass of champagne her sister had given her. She was living proof that if you waited long enough and worked hard enough, you could turn a shipwreck into a new life.

She looked around the crowded living room of her great-aunt's beach house. It was filled with friends and family, all celebrating the fact that Jenna was now a member of Moonlight Harbor's city council, thanks to a special election in March to replace a councilman who'd resigned due to health problems. It had been a hard-fought battle, but she'd won and she had high hopes of accomplishing great things for the town, including getting support for building a convention center.

A town with a city council, it was a little odd. Moonlight Harbor didn't really have the population to qualify as a city, but the powers that be thought they were close enough, so why split hairs?

"We're all so proud of you," said Jenna's mother, Melody Jones, putting an arm around Jenna's shoulders.

"Yes, we are," put in Aunt Edie, the woman who had made Jenna's new life possible.

"Yes, we are," echoed Jolly Roger, the parrot, from his cage. "Give me whiskey."

"We're not serving whiskey, Roger," said Jenna's sister, Celeste. "You have to ask for champagne. Say, it Roger. Give me champagne, give me champagne."

"Say it, Roger. Give me champagne," said the bird, bobbing his head and stepping back and forth on his perch.

"Poor Roger. Nobody ever gives him anything to drink," Celeste joked.

"Poor Roger," said Jolly Roger, making several of the guests chuckle. "Give me champagne."

Celeste and Brody Green, Jenna's ardent admirer and campaign manager, circulated about the room, refilling glasses with champagne or sparkling cider. Jenna's daughter, Sabrina, pouted when Brody poured more sparkling cider in her glass, and muttered, "I'm eighteen now."

"Which is a long way from twenty-one," Jenna reminded her, and she rolled her eyes.

Once everyone's glass had been filled, Celeste performed the toast. "To Jenna Jones, the most successful woman I know. Moonlight Harbor is lucky to have you."

"Hear, hear," echoed Brody.

Ellis West, friend and fellow businessman, said, "I'll drink to that." Ellis owned the Seafood Shack, the popular fast food restaurant next to the Driftwood Inn.

"So will I," Jenna said and smiled.

Successful. A few years ago she would have never used that word to describe herself. She'd come to Moonlight Harbor, newly divorced, with a wounded heart and an angry daughter, towing their worldly goods in a rented trailer. She hadn't been sure how she was going to pay the spousal support the court had allotted her cheating ex, the starving artist, and keep a roof over her and her daughter's heads until she'd gotten Aunt Edie's invitation.

Aunt Edie had offered Jenna a home and a job running the Driftwood Inn along with the future security of knowing someday the vintage motel would be hers. It had been a run-down dump when she arrived, but she'd turned it into a charming bit of nostalgia and the motel was actually doing well.

So was her daughter. Sabrina had been anything but cooperative when the unwanted change had been dumped on her, but she'd eventually found her feet (along with the love of her young life) and, like her mother, had put down roots in the beachside town. There'd been plenty of room for them in Aunt Edie's beach house, and the older woman enjoyed having them with her.

Jenna looked at the trio of women who were the pillars of her life. Her mother, Melody (Mel to her friends), in her early sixties and still slender and beautiful, was standing next to Ellis, whose eyes had lit up the moment he saw her. She was happily holding her two-month-old second grandchild. Next to her stood Jenna's younger sister, Celeste, sneaking an appetizer to her dog, Nemo. She was curvy and cute, the life of the party, now married and responsible for that second grandchild. Then there was sweet Aunt Edie, still perky at almost eighty-six. She was proudly wearing an orange Elect Jenna Jones T-shirt that clashed horribly with her hair. It was a shade of bright cherry red that made her head look like a lost Christmas light, but she'd sported that shade for years and refused to be budged from it, in spite of the best efforts of her friend Pearl at Waves Salon to switch her to something slightly more subdued. Her coral lipstick added yet another interesting color to the palette that was Edie Patterson. In short, she was adorable.

Yes, Jenna thought, looking at them and all the people who had come to mean so much to her, what more could a girl ask for?

Sex. Getting a sex life sometime before she died would be great. She'd been divorced for almost four years. Surely she was ready to take a chance on love again.

And who better to take it with than tall, blond, blue-eyed Mr. Gorgeous, Brody Green? Successful, charming, well-off, he was Moonlight Harbor's catch of the day, and Jenna had caught him the first time they met. Most people already considered them a couple, friends with benefits.

Except there weren't any benefits, hadn't been anything beyond a couple of hot kisses, one of them fueled by alcohol and moonlight when she first came to town. Brody was more than willing to offer benefits, and waiting patiently for her to say the word. So far she hadn't been able to.

Her eyes strayed to Seth Waters, who'd been renting a room at the motel ever since he hit town and started his mold removal business. Dark, swarthy, pirate Seth Waters, who knew how to make the sparks fly. She'd tried his lips on for size, too, but that relationship was stalled. No, more like stuck forever right where it was.

Aunt Edie was a big fan of both men, but Brody had been her buddy for years and he was her favorite. "I don't know what you're waiting for," she'd said to Jenna when another Valentine's Day came and went and her left-hand ring finger was still bare.

"You're waiting because the time isn't right yet," her mother said when Jenna had repeated Aunt Edie's words. "When it strikes the hour for love, you'll know."

Jenna was beginning to wonder if her love clock was broken.

Nothing wrong with her appetite though. She popped another one of Annie Albright's bacon-wrapped dates in her mouth.

Annie had her own catering business and a food truck. She'd come a long way from the days of waitressing at Sandy's Restaurant.

"What's going to be your first order of business now that you're on the council?" Ellis asked Jenna, catching her in mid-chew.

The others all looked at her expectantly.

After revamping the Driftwood, she'd felt ready to change the world. At least the world of Moonlight Harbor. Not that her town needed much changing, but she did have ideas.

"I'm sure going to be pushing for looking into building a convention center. It would be great for our local businesses if we could bring tourists to town all year long, and a convention center would help us do that. Then we could hold our winter festival indoors."

The first Seaside with Santa festival had been a disaster, and even though the chamber of commerce had tried again, moving it to earlier in December, luring people to the beach when the weather was iffy was still a challenge. Tourists could be such wimps.

"A good idea," Ellis approved. "I'm not sure you'll get everyone in town on board with it though. It costs money to build convention centers and people might not want to make that big of an investment."

"Yes, but if we all make more and benefit in the long run it will be worth the pinch in the short run," Jenna argued.

"Good luck with even getting to that," said her friend

Nora Singleton, who owned Good Times Ice Cream Parlor as well as the fun-plex and go-cart track next to it. "People are more concerned with having more sidewalks in town and solving the deer problem."

"They're only a problem for our local gardeners," said Jenna's pal Courtney. "The tourists love 'em."

So did Jenna.

"I love them, too," said Tyrella Lamb, who owned the hardware store. "In venison stew. I hope you're listening, Councilwoman."

"I won't be able to get a law passed that you can run around town with a rifle, shooting deer," Jenna said to her.

"Who needs a rifle? They walk right up to you, the stupid things. I could club one to death."

Sabrina gasped. "That's terrible."

And out of character for a woman who was normally so kindhearted.

"No, terrible is what they did to my rhodies last spring," Tyrella said. "They aren't even supposed to like rhododendrons and they ate every bud."

"But they're so cute," protested Sabrina.

"And they were here first," Courtney added.

"First come first served...on a platter," Tyrella retorted, unrepentant. "The population is out of control. You all just wait. If something isn't done pretty soon we're going to start seeing cases of Lyme disease down here. You've got power now, girl," she said to Jenna. "You need to use it."

"Yeah, to save the deer," said Courtney. "They're God's creatures, Tyrella. Don't they teach you to have love for God's creatures at church?"

"I love God's creatures," Tyrella insisted. "But I eat hamburgers. Don't you?"

"See what I mean?" Nora said to Jenna. "I think we'd

better take up a collection and buy you a suit of armor. Now that you're on the city council you're going to need it."

Good grief. What had she gotten herself into?

She said as much later when it was just her and her family, seated around the living room, finishing up the leftover appetizers from the party.

"Nothing you can't handle," Celeste assured her. She burped baby Edie and handed her over to her daddy.

"Pretty thankless job," said Celeste's husband, Henry, as he took the baby.

"Some jobs need to be done, whether we get thanked or not," Mel said. "I'm proud of you for taking this on."

"I'm looking forward to it," Jenna said. "Moonlight Harbor is my forever home and I want to do my best for it."

"It does my heart good to hear you say that, dear," Aunt Edie said. "I can rest easy knowing the Driftwood will be in capable hands after I'm gone."

"You're not going anywhere for a long time," Jenna said firmly. "You're going to live to be a hundred."

"Who knows?" Aunt Edie said, just as Pete Long, the motel's not-so-handy handyman walked into the dining room, resplendent in dirty jeans and a shirt in need of patching at the elbows. As usual, the old coot needed a shave and his chin was a bristly white mess.

He stopped at the little dining room table to help himself to a cupcake. "You've got lots of good years left in you, Edie, old girl," he said.

"Pete, you missed the party," Aunt Edie scolded.

Which meant that there had been enough food for all the guests. Pete was a two-legged locust and about as useful.

"Yeah, I hear congrats are in order," he said to Jenna.

"She won by a landslide," Celeste told him.

"Fourteen votes is hardly a landslide," Jenna said.

"It is if there's not that much land to slide down," Celeste argued. "Moonlight Harbor isn't exactly Seattle, and it's not like everyone gets out and votes."

"True, but the ones who really care did," said Aunt Edie.

"I voted," Pete said, leaning against the archway. He stuffed half the cupcake in his mouth.

"Who did you vote for?" Celeste asked him.

"Jenna, of course," he said around a mouthful of cake.

"Did you, really?" Jenna asked, surprised.

He half frowned. "Sure. Why not? You whipped the Driftwood into shape. I guess you can do the same for this town. Anyway, keeping you busy with Moonlight Harbor business will keep you off my back."

"The real reason," she said with a knowing nod. Pete needed constant nagging.

"A win-win," he said, then gobbled up the last of the cupcake and returned to the refreshment table to forage for more goodies.

He stayed long enough to finish off the last of the appetizers plus two more cupcakes. Then he left to go hang out at The Drunken Sailor, the town's favorite watering hole.

Baby Edie was soon fussy and tired, and Henry took her over to the motel room where he and Celeste were staying to put her down for the night and work on the final edits for his latest thriller novel.

"Take the dog with you," Aunt Edie said.

Nemo, not feeling the love, whined, but he followed his master out of the house. Then it was just the women and time for girl talk.

"What did you think of Ellis West?" Aunt Edie asked Mel.

Mel's cheeks turned seashell pink. "He's very nice."

"And he's very successful," said Aunt Edie. "Plus he's good-looking."

"Looks like he's interested in you, Mom," Celeste said.

The pink got darker. "He was just being friendly."

"I think he'd like to get a lot friendlier," Celeste insisted.

Mel blew it off. "Oh, nonsense."

"Melody, I think you've forgotten how to read the signs when a man is interested," said Aunt Edie.

"Interested and friendly are two different things," Mel told her.

"Yeah, friendly says, 'Hi, nice to meet you. You from around here?' then wanders off to talk to someone else. Interested wants to hear the story of your life, never leaves your side and hurries off to fetch food for you," Celeste said. "How many times did Ellis get you more canapés?"

Now the pink was sunset-vivid. "Oh, honestly," Mel said in disgust.

"He's a really nice man, Mom," said Jenna.

"He is, but I'm not interested. There will never be another man for me but your father."

"Now, don't go getting all sentimental and rule out possibilities," Aunt Edie scolded. "You can love more than one man in a lifetime."

"I doubt it," Mel said. "Anyway, I'm too old for him. He's still in his fifties."

"Not for much longer," Jenna said. "I think he's fifty-eight."

"Age doesn't matter at this point in life," Aunt Edie argued.

"I read somewhere that since men die younger than women, a woman should marry a man seven years younger than her," Jenna said. "And what are you always saying to me? Don't give up on love."

"You girls," Mel said, her face still red. "You obviously don't have enough to do."

"We've got plenty to do, trust us," Celeste said. "But we're never too busy for you, Mom."

"That's sweet," Mel said, smiling at her. "You just work on helping your sister get her love life sorted out. Let's see her find her happy-ever-after. That's what I want."

"Me, too," said Celeste. "When are you going to figure out what you're doing?" she asked Jenna. "I'm ready to start planning your wedding."

"You'll be the first to know," Jenna said.

"After me," put in Mel.

"And me," said Aunt Edie.

"And me," said Jolly Roger. "Give me champagne."

"A good idea," said Jenna, and went in search of the last bottle. Her love life was enough to drive her to drink.

"Okay, I've got problems," Courtney Moore said to Annie Albright the next morning as they sat at their kitchen table, fueling up for the day with coffee and some of Annie's Portuguese doughnuts, fresh from the stove.

She and Annie had shared Courtney's beach house and the rent ever since Annie left her alcoholic husband. It was only a matter of time now until Courtney moved out and took her relationship with fireman Jonas Greer to the next level, letting Annie have the place to herself.

It would be the end of an era. She and Annie had become like sisters, encouraging each other through a lot of ups and downs. Of course, that would continue no matter where they both lived. Hopefully, one day Annie would meet someone wonderful who could step in and be the husband and father her ex had never been. Meanwhile, though, they enjoyed their weekly chick flick nights with their pal and former roomie, Moira King, and encouraged each other in their business pursuits.

Annie's food truck had been an instant success. It did a hot business during tourist season, and during the slow winter months, she was able to pay the bills by catering parties. She was already booked to cater a wedding in June in nearby Quinault, and had an upcoming anniversary party to cook for as well.

Courtney continued to sell her clothing designs at the upscale Oyster Inn, and supplemented that income with helping out on the reception desk at the not quite so upscale Driftwood Inn. Having clothes for sale at the Oyster Inn was great, but she dreamed of having her own clothing boutique. Somewhere, somehow she'd make it happen. But for the moment she was doing okay.

"What problems could you possibly have?" Annie asked her, not looking up from the grocery list for the Friends of the Sea fundraiser she was catering later in the week.

Courtney motioned to the Moonlight Harbor Firefighters calendar hanging on the wall. "Do you know how many women are thirsty for my Mr. March? They've been coming out like termites ever since we flipped the calendar. I actually overheard someone in Beachside Grocery telling a friend she'd start a fire at her house if it meant she could meet him. Sick."

Annie snickered. "They'll never be able to compete with the one you had."

"Very funny," Courtney said with a frown. So cooking wasn't her forte. She had other skills that Jonas appreciated much more than making fried chicken. "We can't all be chefs."

"Don't feel bad. You make a great tuna sandwich," Annie teased.

"You've got to admit, my brownies are pretty good, too."

"There you go. Brownies from a box and tuna sandwiches. Stir in all your other talents and no woman can compete with that."

"I don't know," Courtney said.

"You're not serious."

"I am, a little. Look at him."

"He is a fire starter."

Yes, he was. Big, brown eyes, that perfect nose that Courtney always envied, a fine, strong chin, just enough wave in his hair to make a woman want to tiptoe her fingers through it. She looked to where she'd hung the calendar on their kitchen wall. There he was, washing the fire truck in his fire britches, but shirtless, of course, and aiming the hose at the camera, pretending to squirt the photographer.

"All those fired-up women, wanting to check out the size of his hose," she said with a scowl.

"The calendar is a big moneymaker, and the money all goes back to the community," Annie reminded her.

"I know, I know. The kids' Halloween party, the annual Easter egg hunt at the park."

"Not to mention the free emergency kits they give to low-income families and seniors."

"It's March, for crying out loud. You'd think those calendars would stop selling by now," Courtney grumbled. "Beachside Grocery's had to restock twice." She frowned. "We ran into Rian LaShell there last night and she was practically purring over Jonas."

"You don't have to worry about her. Everybody knows she's crazy about Brody," Annie said.

"Well, that's a lost cause. He's with Jenna."

"Yeah, but is Jenna with him?"

Good question. Jenna and Brody looked like a couple,

but Jenna was keeping them stalled out as buddies. She was perched on the edge of the dock, afraid to dive into the Sea of Love.

It wasn't hard to figure out why. Seth Waters. He was there on the dock, too. Courtney had advised Jenna on more than one occasion to slip over to his room at the Driftwood and suggest some moonlight skinny-dipping in the motel pool, but Jenna always replied, "It's complicated."

Courtney didn't buy that. Either you loved someone or you didn't. Of course, sometimes your loving someone complicated things for others. She'd managed to complicate Moira's life pretty good.

Then she'd met Jonas and all the relationships that never worked out, that never even got off the ground, faded to nothing. Everyone should dive into the Sea of Love. The water was great.

But nobody had better come paddling up to her man or Courtney would drown her.

"Jonas is crazy about you. You don't have to worry," Annie assured her. "I'm glad you finally found a keeper."

"His cousin in Seattle might be a keeper, too. You know Jonas is more than willing to set you up." It was a waste of pretty to see Annie, with her delicate features and freckles, with no man but a lousy ex-husband in her life.

Annie shook her head. "No, thanks. I'm not ready. In fact, I don't know if I'll ever be ready. I think Greg soured me on men."

"Not all men are losers."

"Enough of them are. Anyway, between Emma and my business, I don't have time."

"Everyone has time for love." And Emma was ten, not two. She was old enough to understand if her mother got a boyfriend.

"I make time for love. For my daughter." Annie picked up her grocery list and took one last swig of coffee. "I've got to get going. I'll see you tonight."

"Okay."

"You're in charge of the snacks," Annie called over her shoulder.

"I'm on it," Courtney assured her, and started collecting the dirty dishes.

The house was silent except for the sound of rain pattering against the windows as she went into the living room with a second cup of coffee and plopped on her couch with her sketch pad. She loved the beach house they rented. She could step outside her front door and instantly be on a path to the water. She'd painted the walls a soft blue and had hung vintage fashion posters on them. Her cable spool coffee table gave the living room an artistic flare and distracted from her funky old couch. She'd replaced the fake Tiffany floor lamp she'd once had with an antique white nautical one with anchor for its base. Actually, Moira had replaced it—an unnecessary but kind gesture born of guilt, since the old lamp got broken when she was in a struggle with her abusive ex.

Exes. It seemed like when it came to men everyone Courtney knew had an ex story.

But there was no better place to heal and hit Restart than Moonlight Harbor, with its lovely beaches and supportive residents.

Well, most of them were supportive. Thank God Courtney had found a way to escape the old sea serpent who owned Beach Babes Boutique. Talk about just plain nasty. Susan Frank was a human red tide. She could probably count on one finger the number of friends she had in town, but she persisted in hanging around, poisoning everyone with her crankiness and sour attitude.

And her shop was a joke. Its collection of overpriced ugly drew very few tourists, and Susan herself didn't exactly inspire loyalty. She sure hadn't inspired it in Courtney when she'd worked at Beach Babes. The constant criticism and snapping had been soul-crushing.

Even Edie Patterson, who had once been a loyal customer, never went in there anymore, thanks to Susan dissing Jenna. You didn't mess with Edie's family and get away with it.

What a waste of good retail space. Many a time Courtney had jealously eyed that shop with its prime location. It was smack dab in the middle of two rows of cute little brightly painted cabana shops, right next to Beachcomber, a tourist magnet that sold beachy home decor and candles.

Courtney knew her creations would jump off the racks. They did in the Oyster Inn gift shop, and she would be forever grateful to Grande Dame Patricia Whiteside, its owner, for giving her a place to start. But that little cabana shop would be perfect. Unlike many business malls, the setup for this one was unique. The shop owners owned the land collectively and their buildings individually, plus, of course, their inventory. It was the business equivalent of condominiums. Susan's inventory was worthless but the building…oh, lust.

Yeah, well. Dream on.

Meanwhile, Courtney had work to do. She started sketching, working out ideas for the last pieces of her spring and summer line. She'd found a great jersey knit cotton in sea mist green that she was going to give a wispy chiffon overlay—scarf-like layers to drape in the front and create a dropped-tail hem at the back. She'd do capped sleeves and give it a V-neck to show some skin. Edge the neck with embossed clam shells? No. Too much. She'd go simple on this. Ooh, but what about a chiffon shawl of the same color to wear over a simple white dress? That could be embossed with clam shells. Yes. She liked that idea.

The day slid by and before she knew it, Annie was back and her daughter Emma was home from school and wanting to see what Courtney had designed. And then asking what fabulous snack she was making for when Moira came over for a chick flick night. Annie was careful of what Emma was allowed to watch, but even when she wasn't allowed to stay for the movie, she always got to share the treats.

"Oh, my gosh. I completely forgot we were doing that tonight. I'd better get to the store," Courtney said, and went in search of her purse.

She'd just found it when her cell phone rang. "Hey there, beautiful," said her favorite fireman. "What's on the menu for chick flick night?"

Beautiful. She loved that. Courtney had never considered herself beautiful. She'd managed striking, thanks to long, dark hair, nice eyes, great makeup skills, and a damned good figure (if she did say so herself), but she didn't have the pretty round face and perfect little nose her friend Jenna had. Jonas didn't seem to care and she adored him for it.

"I'm creating something," she told him.

"Yeah? Gonna duplicate it for me when I'm off?"

"Of course. You'll love it."

"I love everything you do. You know that. What is it?"

"Something sweet."

"Like dessert?"

"Pretty much."

"All right. I'm off tomorrow, so how about coming over to my place and making it for me?"

"Absolutely," she said.

"I'll pick up a pizza. But let's have dessert first. And not the stuff you're making."

"Good idea," Courtney said. Her lacy black bra and matching panties were on standby and ready to go.

She said goodbye and hurried to the store to pick up the makings for her treat. She was just about to get in the checkout line when her cell phone rang again. This time it was Jenna.

"Do you need me tonight?" Courtney asked. It wasn't a regular work night for her, and she hated to miss out on chick flick night, but if Jenna needed her at the Driftwood she'd be there.

"No, but I have some interesting news. I just went to pick up Aunt Edie from Waves. Susan Frank was in earlier and told Pearl she's thinking about selling Beach Babes."

"No way."

"You might want to stop by the shop and see what she's asking."

"Thanks. I will."

There was that business lust again. If only. She wasn't exactly rich and she couldn't picture Sherwood Stern over at Harbor First National giving her the VIP treatment.

Still, it couldn't hurt to ask how much Susan wanted. Maybe, just maybe they could work something out.

Courtney stopped on her way back from the store and wove past the other shops to Beach Babes, her former dysfunctional home away from home. Most of the cabanas were painted in happy Florida colors—peach and yellow and minty green. They were a welcome lift on rainy, gray days like this one. Susan's shop, however, was a slate blue...which had perfectly matched Courtney's mood when she used to work there.

No customers were browsing the racks of frumpy sweat-shirts and slacks and off-brand rain slickers. Rain boots and galoshes were fashion statements everywhere in the country but here. The ones Susan was selling looked as exciting as a trip to the dentist. And not a pair of stylish jeans or pants to be seen.

There, sitting behind the cash register, was the Queen of Ugly herself, an underweight, middle-aged woman whose smiles were as thin as her hair. She had a crossword puzzle book in front her. Susan was great at crossword puzzles. People were a puzzle she'd never mastered though. She had no idea how to create a friendly atmosphere in her shop.

The jingling of the bell over the door made her look up. No welcoming smile on her face, and at the sight of Courtney in her dripping raincoat, Susan's lips actually slid down at the corners.

"Courtney, what are you doing here? Don't tell me you've come to ask for your job back. I thought your clothes were selling so well over at the Oyster Inn," she taunted.

Good to see you, too. But Courtney was hardly sur-prised by the reception she was getting. Susan hadn't been welcoming when she joined the chamber of commerce and avoided her at every meeting.

"They are," Courtney said.

"Then why are you here?"

"I heard you might be selling your business."

Susan's lips turned so far down at the corners it was a wonder they didn't slide off her face. "Who told you that?"

Jenna wasn't exactly a favorite of Susan's, either, so Courtney stayed vague. "I just heard it somewhere."

"I haven't decided for sure," Susan said, at her huffiest. "But if I was going to, you can be sure I wouldn't sell to you, you ingrate."

Ingrate! Just because Courtney had quit and found a place to sell her clothing line. As if she should have been grateful for the way Susan had treated her when she was employed there. This shop was misnamed. It should have been Bitch Babes.

"You can't discriminate against people," Courtney informed her.

"I'm not discriminating. I haven't decided. But if and when I do, I can assure you, you won't be able to afford it."

"Maybe I can."

"Of course you can't."

She'd like you to give up and slink away. Don't do it.
"What are you thinking of asking?"

"More than you can afford. Now, really, I don't have time to sit and talk to you. I'm very busy."

Doing your crossword puzzle.

To prove how busy she was, Susan got up and parted the curtains to her back room and disappeared behind them. Negotiations over.

"Yeah? We'll just see what I can and can't afford," Courtney muttered as she marched out the door.

Really, Susan was probably right. Those cabana shops were prime real estate. Courtney could never get Beach Babes without financial assistance. Getting a loan from the bank would require the use of hypnosis, and she was sure it would be beyond the scope of a Blue Moon grant, as well. Those grants were in place to aid Moonlight Harbor entrepreneurs but they didn't stretch to the point of buying real estate for them.

"It sucks," she said later to Annie and Moira as the three friends sat eating her dessert creation.

"But you have a shop," said Annie's daughter, Emma. She swirled the butter cookie crumbles and Caramelo M&M's topping into her serving of sand pebble cream ice cream from Good Times Ice Cream Parlor.

"It's not mine. I only sell some things there." Courtney leaned over and squirted more whipped cream on Emma's dessert, earning a grateful smile.

"Why won't Mrs. Frank sell you her shop?" Emma wanted to know. "Doesn't she like you?"

"She doesn't like anyone," Courtney said. "And no one likes her."

"I wouldn't want no one to like me," said Emma.

"You don't have to worry," Moira assured her.

"Be kind and you won't have that problem," her mother added.

"Isn't Mrs. Frank kind?" Emma asked.

"Not even close," Courtney said, stabbing her ice cream with her spoon.

"Why?"

Who knew? "Because when she was a baby, the cow that gave out the milk of human kindness ran dry and there wasn't any for her bottle," Courtney said with a frown. "I truly hate that woman."

"Mommy says you shouldn't hate people," Emma said.

"Your mommy's right," Courtney said. "I shouldn't." But she did.

"It's too bad you don't know how much she wants for the business," Annie said.

Courtney sighed. "Whatever she wants, it'll be too much for me. I'm stupid to even think about it."

"You're not stupid," Moira said. "You're one of the

smartest women I know. If you want that shop you'll find a way to make it happen."

There had to be a way. How and where was she going to find it?

Two

Melody Jones drove home from the grocery store where she'd worked for the last twenty years, sadness sitting next to her in the passenger seat. The ax had finally fallen. Soon she would have no job.

Her carpal-tunnel-afflicted wrist was happy and so were her feet. But her heart, not so much.

There'd been rumors circulating for months. The chain had been bought and mismanaged and the store would be closing. She hadn't believed them. Hadn't wanted to. Wasn't ready. Wasn't ready even after she and her fellow employees got the official announcement. Now, ready or not, the sixty-day notice had come.

Not that she hadn't thought of retiring. Jenna had been urging her to quit and move to Moonlight Harbor for the last two years.

"You'd love living down here, and if you really still want to work I'm sure you could always get a part-time job at Beachside Grocery. Or better yet, you could help out at the Driftwood," Jenna had said.

Mel loved visiting her daughter and granddaughter and Aunt Edie, but move? She'd lived in her house her whole adult life. This community was the webbing that had held her life together for so many years. It was where she'd worshipped, socialized and worked.

Work would soon be a thing of the past though. She and her coworkers would be scattering, finding new jobs who knew where.

She'd started applying at other grocery stores but so far no one had called. Was it an age thing? Probably. Would potential employers be ignoring her if she was forty? Fifty?

She turned in to the driveway of her two-bedroom house. A tract house, built in the late sixties, it was nothing special. But it was special to her. She loved the place. She and her husband had bought it when they first married. Over the years she'd painted the bedrooms, gotten new carpet, swapped out the carpet for laminate flooring, and redone her countertops. She'd mourned the loss of her husband in this house and struggled to figure out how she was going to raise two small girls on her own with little college education and no job training. The Bluebirds and then the Camp Fire Girls had met in this house, friends had stopped by on Christmas Day. It was where her grown daughters always came when they needed to talk over problems. It was home.

Still, home was where family was. Yes, Celeste lived only half an hour away, but Jenna and Sabrina were in Moonlight Harbor. And Celeste was making noises about moving there. If she did, Melody would be here alone.

No, not alone. All her friends were here.

Still, she could make new friends. She'd already had enough contact with the women in Moonlight Harbor to know they'd welcome her with open arms. Thanks to the high prices of houses anywhere near Seattle she could sell hers, make a nice profit and have money left over to live on.

But all the memories in this house were woven into an invisible cord wrapped around her heart, staking her where she was.

"You'll have to figure it out," she said to herself as she pulled into the garage.

The house seemed quieter than usual as she walked into the kitchen and set down the bag with the few grocery items she'd bought after her shift. She docked her phone and streamed some classic rock on Spotify. Linda Ronstadt started crooning about going back to Blue Bayou. Mel loved that song, but this night it made her teary-eyed and she skipped it. Going back. If only she could.

She brewed herself a cup of rooibos tea, took out the crackers and cheese and a Seattle Chocolates bar she'd bought before leaving the store. A perfect meal for one.

None of it tasted very good, not even the chocolate, which was the best around. It was going to be a long night. Good thing she'd also picked up a new Melinda Curtis romance novel.

She felt better by the time she turned out the lamp on her nightstand, but by morning better was gone and melancholy was knocking on the door. She refused to let it in. She'd had a good life for many years. There was no reason to think it was going to turn bad. This was simply a crossroads.

"What are you going to do?" her coworker Angie asked her the next day as they sat in the employees' lounge, eating their lunch. Angie was dieting again, determined to lose forty pounds. She was eating yogurt but eyeing Mel's ham and provolone sandwich jealously.

"I'm not sure," Mel confessed.

"By the end of May we'll be out of jobs," Angie said bitterly.

"Yes, but maybe something even better is waiting. Every storm brings a rainbow."

"You still have to get through the storm," Angie argued.

Money management had never been Angie's forte, and she and her husband lived from paycheck to paycheck. It could prove hard for her to find that rainbow.

"I've applied at Haggen, IGA and Safeway," she said. "None of them are hiring. Now—" she shook her head "—Brit and Doug were smart. They saw the writing on the wall and got out while the getting was good. She's starting as a checker at IGA next week, and he got on at Safeway." She dug into her yogurt. "This sucks."

"At least Carl's still working," Mel pointed out.

"We can't live on his paycheck alone."

Maybe they couldn't, not with the way Angie spent money. To be fair, she had three teenagers to provide for. It was more expensive raising a family than it had been back when Mel was raising her girls. Still, Angie's family would have an income, which was more than Mel could say. And they had each other.

It had been hard raising children without her husband. The grandparents had been a godsend after Mel was widowed, but so many times she'd wished John was with her, both to see the girls' progress and to help her make decisions. All she'd had of him were memories. Memories couldn't fix leaky sinks or change the oil in the car. Memories couldn't pay the bills.

But memories could remind you that you'd lived more in a few short years with your wonderful man than many women lived in a lifetime with theirs. Memories couldn't warm your cold feet at night but they could warm your heart.

Mel had managed. She'd manage now, too. So would Angie.

"Things will work out," Mel assured her.

She said as much to herself when she got home. She had some money saved. She'd be fine.

Her neighborhood book club met later that week at her house to discuss the first work of fiction by Muriel Sterling, a nonfiction author they all liked. The story was about a group of women helping each other through difficult circumstances, titled *The Way Home*. Mel had rooted for the characters as they fought through health issues, divorce and a scandal or two.

She was sure her next-door neighbor, Amanda, who'd been divorced twice, would sneer at the neatly wrapped happy ending, and Ellen, who lived on her other side, a connoisseur of novels, would find it trite. But Roberta, Caroline and Holly, like her, would be happy to see things work out for the characters. Real life was already hard. It was satisfying when the pretend version ended well.

"What are you going to do now?" Amanda asked Mel when the discussion was done and the conversation turned back to what was going on in their lives.

"I wish I knew," Mel said, and helped herself to more cheese and crackers.

"I think it's a shame the store is closing," said Roberta. "And it's so sad to be losing your job after all these years."

"Yes, but you've been there forever. I think, like Birdie in the book, it's time for you to have a new adventure," Holly chimed in. She was the youngest member of the group, a redhead with a husband who loved to travel. Birdie had been her favorite character.

"I don't see any adventure that glamorous in my future," Mel said. "Birdie got to go to Paris."

"Everyone should go to Paris," said Roberta. She was their oldest member. Her husband had been in the navy and she'd been all over the world.

"Or Moonlight Harbor," said Ellen. "Maybe it's time to move. Of course, you know we'd hate to see you leave."

"But we'd come visit you," Roberta added.

People often said that, but time had a way of swooping in and erasing old friendships. It had happened to Mel when she married and moved away from her home in the city. She'd seen it happening with Jenna, who was hearing less and less from her old friends. It was the nature of things. She liked to think it would be different with these women.

But if it wasn't...

"Zelda might have someone interested if you decide to sell your house," said Caroline. Caroline's daughter, Zelda, was a real estate agent.

They were already moving her out of their lives. Mel tried to smile and look appreciative.

"I'll keep that in mind," she said.

That night she dreamed Jenna was in her old Toyota, parked in Mel's driveway, the window on the driver's side down. She was crying. Mel stood next to the car, patting her daughter's shoulder, trying to console her.

"It'll be okay," she kept saying to Jenna.

"It'll never be okay again," Jenna sobbed.

"Yes, it will," Mel insisted. "Look how much you've gotten through already."

"I can't this time, not without you."

"I can't leave your father," Melody said. She looked to where John stood on the front porch.

"But I need you," Jenna protested.

"But I need him."

John was big and solid, filling the doorway. He had such broad shoulders. He used to love to ride Jenna around on them when she was a toddler. He began waving. Waving goodbye to Jenna, of course.

Then he began to fade. No! Mel turned and ran back to the house, but by the time she reached the front porch he was gone. There was only the front door, shut.

She walked back down the driveway and got into the Toyota's passenger seat. "Okay, let's go," she said to her daughter, and they sped down the driveway. They turned onto the street and Mel didn't look back.

She awoke feeling both unsettled and determined. She hadn't dreamed about John in over thirty years. And the part her daughter played in that dream was disturbing. But the message was clear.

She took a deep breath. "All right. I'm going."

"Owww," protested Nora from the massage table as Jenna worked another knot out of her right calf.

"Sorry," Jenna said, and eased up.

"Don't be. I need this," Nora said. "I have got to retire."

How many times had Nora said that in the last few years?

"What would you do with yourself?" Jenna teased, stretching the muscles.

"I'd sit for a month. Watch TV, read. Then I'd finally start on all those craft projects I've been talking about. The boys are capable of running the ice cream parlor and the funplex. What am I waiting for, anyway?"

"Good question," Jenna said.

"I mean, am I going to keep talking about all the things I want to do or am I going to do them? Life's too short."

"You have plenty of life left in you."

"I do, and I want to do something with it other than scoop out ice cream. Not that I haven't loved owning the parlor. But it's time to move on."

"Once you really do decide to make it official, we'll have a party to celebrate," Jenna promised. "A wine night at Crafty Just Cuz. I bet K.J. and Elizabeth can come up with a perfect party project."

"That sounds like a great idea," Nora said. "I love those MacDowell sisters. Of course, we don't have to wait until I retire to get together there."

They shouldn't. No matter how much she talked about retiring, Nora never got around to setting a date for it. She and Good Times Ice Cream Parlor were like pumpkin pie and whipped cream, a matched set.

"Okay, I think you're good to go," Jenna said as their hour session came to an end.

"Good for another week, anyway. You are a massage genius. I'm so glad you moved here."

"Me, too," Jenna said.

Another year of working as a massage therapist and then her five-year sentence of spousal support would come to an end and she'd be done forking over money to her ex the leech. Much as she liked her work, she was ready to cut back. The Driftwood Inn was doing well, and now that she was on the city council, she was busier than ever. She was ready to cut back her work schedule and spend more time on the other aspects of life. Including love.

Her thoughts were interrupted by howls of agony coming from the front hall.

Jenna tore out of the spare downstairs room she used for her massage business to find her daughter bursting through the door, tears streaming down her face. Oh, no.

"Sabrina, what's wrong?"

It was as far as she got. Her daughter hurled herself into Jenna's arms. "He broke up with me."

Well, crap.

Still, Jenna wasn't surprised. Sabrina had been a freshman in high school when she met Tristan. He'd been a senior, already accepted to the college of his choice. Long-distance relationships were hard, especially when one member of the couple was a teenager still in high school and one had moved on to college. College changed things. Still, the relationship had lasted longer than she'd thought it would.

"I'm so sorry, sweetie," Jenna said, hugging her sobbing daughter.

"He f-found someone else."

Which was what Jenna had suspected would happen. Oh, how it hurt when the one you gave your heart to found someone else. She thought of Damien, her ex, and his someone else and fought the urge to grind her teeth.

"They're engaged even. He's been cheating on me!"

Tristan was so lucky he wasn't anywhere within strangling range. "He doesn't deserve you," Jenna growled.

Truer words were never spoken. Her daughter had outgrown her teen brat phase and turned into a sweet young woman.

Alas, at a time like this, words held little comfort.

Aunt Edie, who had been puttering in the kitchen, came into the hall, wiping her hands on a dish towel. "Oh, no. What's happened?"

Nora was dressed again, and she, too, joined them.

"Tristan broke up with her," Jenna explained.

"He was my true love," Sabrina wailed.

"I know, baby." Jenna walked her into the living room

and settled her on the couch, the other two women following.

"How could he do this to me?" Sabrina looked at Jenna, her blue eyes red and teary, lower lip trembling.

As if Jenna had an answer. How could Damien have dumped her after how hard she'd worked to support them all while he pursued his career as an artist? The human heart was a mystery.

She shook her head. "Do you want it straight or do you want it sugarcoated?"

Sabrina swallowed. "Straight," she whispered.

"He found someone he thought was a better fit for him."

"But we were so happy," Sabrina protested on a fresh sob.

"I know you were. And I'm sorry," Jenna said. She put a hand to her daughter's cheek. "This is not really about you. It's about him. You are fabulous."

"If I'm so fabulous, why wasn't I a fit? I thought I was a fit. I thought we fit together perfectly."

"I thought I was a fit," muttered Jolly Roger from inside his cage.

"Oh, Roger, do be quiet," Aunt Edie snapped. "I'm going to make you some hot chocolate," she said to Sabrina. "That will make you feel better."

"Nothing will make me feel better. Ever," Sabrina insisted. "It's not right."

It never was. "I know," Jenna said, and put an arm around her. "I know."

Nora dug a tissue out of her purse and handed it over. "The love of my life broke up with me when I was about your age," she said as Sabrina blew her nose.

Sabrina sniffed and looked at her hopefully. "How did you get him back?"

"Get him back? Are you kidding? Why would I want someone back who didn't have enough good taste to appreciate me? I got my hair done, bought some new clothes and stood up in my homeroom class and announced that I was taking applications for a new boyfriend."

Sabrina managed a weak smile at that.

"And?" Jenna prompted.

"And none of them were good enough. I didn't find the real love of my life until I was in college. But he was worth the wait."

Aunt Edie returned with a steaming mug of instant hot chocolate and handed it over to Sabrina. "This will turn out. You'll see. Every storm brings a rainbow."

Jenna smiled at that. It was her mother's favorite saying. Maybe she'd learned it from Aunt Edie.

Eventually Sabrina was soothed and went to her bedroom to text her girlfriends with details of Tristan's perfidy and plan for how she would get on with the rest of her forever ruined life. Aunt Edie returned to the kitchen and Jenna let out a sigh and leaned her head against the couch cushions.

"Another crisis survived," Nora said with a smile as she dug the money she owed Jenna out of her purse. "I guess I'll go on home now."

"Thanks for the words of wisdom," Jenna said. "You saved the day."

"It's hard being young and in love."

It was hard being in love at any age. Or, in Jenna's case, being confused. How could you love two men at the same time, for crying out loud?

She should just make a decision, she thought after Nora left. It was obvious. She needed to grab Brody and say,

"Let's do it. Let's go to the courthouse right now and get married." He was a great fit for her. He'd raised kids and he was always able to empathize with whatever she was going through with Sabrina. He was fun and he made her laugh.

Then there was Seth, who could set her hormones sizzling. He had a depth to him that called to her, and whenever problems arose he'd always been there for her in his quiet, unobtrusive way. But he had a past, and he wasn't going to ever let the scars completely heal so he could move on. She knew he wanted her, wanted to be with her, but he wouldn't let himself.

Brody had no such reservations. He'd made it plain he wanted her ever since she'd moved to Moonlight Harbor. His kids liked her and she liked them. Sabrina had always liked Seth but she'd also come to accept Brody's presence in their life. So, really, there were no obstacles to them getting together.

Still, she hesitated. She had one divorce to her credit already. She didn't want to make a mistake the second time around. She cared for Brody. A lot. But did she care enough for them both to be content and happy together for the rest of their lives? If only she could get clarity.

Maybe she never would.

Now, there was a cheery thought.

Her cell phone summoned her. Mom. How was it her mother always seemed to know to call just when she needed to talk?

"Mom, am I glad to hear from you."

"What's wrong?" Mel asked, sounding concerned.

"Don't worry. Nobody's died or anything. But we have had some drama. Sabrina's boyfriend broke up with her."

"Oh, our poor girl," Mel said, instantly sympathetic.

"I must say, though, I'm surprised they lasted as long as they did."

"Same here," Jenna said. "Still, it hurts. He was actually seeing another girl."

"Well, then, he certainly wasn't a keeper."

Just like Damien. His betrayal had felt like a fatal wound at the time. And even though the wound had healed, it still stung occasionally.

"Needless to say, it's been a traumatic afternoon." Jenna sighed. "I sure wish you lived down here."

Not that she couldn't talk to her mother on the phone when she had a problem. But Mel was a calming presence, and with juggling work, motherhood, managing the motel and keeping Aunt Edie, the hazard behind the wheel, from sneaking off with her car, Jenna sometimes felt overwhelmed and in need of calm.

"Actually, that's what I called to talk to you about. Our layoffs finally happened and I'm thinking of selling the house and moving to the beach."

"Oh, Mom, that would be awesome!" Her mother right there with her. She'd been pushing for it long enough.

"I assume your friend Brody could help me find a house."

"No need to find a house. You can stay here with us."

"No, you're crowded enough as it is."

She did have a point. "Well, then, stay with us until you find a place. I don't mind sharing my room. We'll put in twin beds."

"I am not going to do that to you." Mom sounded horrified at the thought.

"It would be great to have you living with us."

"We'll see," her mother said, not committing to anything.

"It's time you moved here. And once Celeste and Henry get a place we'll all be together." Her whole family at Moonlight Harbor, it would be perfect.

"I guess I'll give Caroline's daughter a call and see about putting the house up for sale then."

"She'll jump at the chance."

"I must admit, it's going to be hard to leave," Mel said. "So many memories."

Yes, there were. Jenna remembered all those slumber parties in the house, she and her girlfriends stretched out across the living room floor in their sleeping bags, talking about boys, eating chips and her mother's home-baked peanut butter cookies, getting crumbs everywhere. The Bluebirds had held their meetings there and then the Camp Fire Girls.

She and Celeste and the neighbor kids had played softball out in the street and freeze tag on the front lawn. She still remembered being in charge of welcoming the neighbors every year when her mother hosted her annual Christmas open house. That red velveteen dress with the lace trim, how she'd loved it.

How she'd loved growing up where she had with the mother she had. Yes, the place was a treasure trove of memories. But...

"You take your memories wherever you go, and we'll make new ones here."

"Yes, we will," Mel said. "There comes a time when you have to move on, and for me it looks like that time is now."

"Aunt Edie will be over the moon to have you with us. Come on down weekend after this and tell her."

"All right," Mel said.

Meanwhile, this weekend would be a quiet one with her daughter gone. Damien would be showing up to haul Sabrina away to spend time with his family.

Jenna could hardly wait until her daughter's graduation. Seth was fixing up a car Jenna had found through a private seller, and once Sabrina had her own wheels, she'd be able to drive to Seattle to see her dad, and there'd be no shuttling her back and forth, which would give Jenna a break from having to see Damien.

He arrived to pick Sabrina up late Friday afternoon, wearing jeans and a suede jacket over a stylish white shirt, loafers on his feet. No socks, even though it was cold. His hair was pulled back at the nape of his neck in a short ponytail and he looked ready for a photo shoot for *GQ*. He was still long and lean and beautiful.

Snakes were long and lean, too.

Jenna had been doing some paperwork in her little massage room. She'd heard the knock on the front door and had come out to answer in time to see Aunt Edie opening it.

"Oh, it's you," Aunt Edie said, looking him up and down with disgust, as if his arrival was an unpleasant surprise.

Aunt Edie was sweet as caramels, but she did have a feisty side, and she had no problem bearing a grudge against anyone who hurt her family.

"I came to pick up Sabrina," he said.

"Sabrina, your mother's ex-husband is here to kidnap you," Aunt Edie called up the stairs. Then she shut the door in his face.

"Aunt Edie," Jenna chided.

Even though he didn't deserve to be invited in, he was

Sabrina's father. For her daughter's sake she needed to stay civil.

"We can't leave him standing out there on the porch." In spite of the fact that the idea of Damien standing in the cold March rain was an appealing one.

"Why not? It's covered."

"He is Sabrina's father, so for her sake?"

Aunt Edie gave a snort of disgust and marched off toward the kitchen. "Don't let him sit down. He's all wet."

Jenna opened the door and let the viper inside. He was, indeed, wet, water dripping off his nose. She didn't ask him to sit down.

"I don't like her," he said, nodding to where Aunt Edie had disappeared down the hall.

"That's okay. She doesn't like you, either."

"She's got a mean side. I hope you're still in the will."

Jenna's hackles went up. "What's that supposed to mean?"

He shrugged. "Only that you ought to get something out of all this."

Like she was some kind of buzzard, waiting around for her aunt to die. She knew who the buzzard was. If she inherited anything while she was still paying spousal support, Damien would be right there with his beautifully sculpted, greedy hands held out, asking for more.

"I already do get something out of all this. I get a place to stay so I can afford to pay you," she said, smiling over clenched teeth.

That brought a scowl. "I was within my rights."

"Legally, but not morally, and you know it." Yep, being civil. She waved away the resentment. "Never mind." Only a year to go and he'd have to stop leeching off of her. "Have you sold any more pieces?" The last big commission he'd been promised had fallen through. He was doing art shows and occasionally selling a piece, but so far he wasn't making any kind of splash in the art world. Not even so much as a drop. Unrecyclable detritus was his medium. Junk to art, made by a man who was human junk.

At least he was making an effort at being a good dad.

Sort of. If not for his parents wanting to see Sabrina, how much would she see him? Really?

"Some," he said in answer to Jenna's question.

A nice, evasive answer.

"Hi, Daddy." Sabrina came bounding down the stairs, her backpack slung over one shoulder, a smile on her face. How quick children were to forgive their parents.

He ditched the frown he'd had for Jenna and gave his daughter an answering smile. "Ready to go?"

"Yep," she said. Then, to Jenna, "I'll see you Sunday." She gave Jenna a quick hug and was out the door.

Damien turned to follow her.

"Don't forget," Jenna began.

He held up a hand to stop her. "I know already. Back by early evening. Jeez, Jenna."

"Just making sure we're on the same page," she said in her own defense.

He shook his head. "This is why I left."

"This what?" she demanded.

"This nagging. You always were so damned controlling."

"Yeah, silly me. Wanting to be able to pay the bills." She'd worked hard to keep them afloat. But there was more than one way to sink a marriage.

"You never understood me," he grumbled, and started down the front steps.

"No, I didn't," she said with a sigh.

Not until it was too late. Too bad she hadn't realized what a narcissist he was before they got married. Before she got pregnant. But then she wouldn't have had Sabrina. Like Mom said, every storm brought a rainbow.

Another year and she'd be free of him.

It couldn't come soon enough.

Three

"I'm so glad you called me," Caroline's daughter Zelda said to Mel as she stepped through the front door of Mel's house. "You know I'll work like crazy to make sure you get top dollar, Mrs. J."

Once upon a time, Zelda had been a skinny little girl with buck teeth and a big voice. She and Celeste had practically been inseparable growing up. Now she was svelte and professional, spoke with softly modulated tones and had a big bank account. She was wearing stylish black pants and black heels and a black blazer over a gray ribbed top. The outfit showed off her dark coloring beautifully. Small gold hoops in her ears, a gold bracelet on her wrist and a gold chain with a swing of freshwater pearls dangling from her neck completed the outfit. Zelda was the number one salesperson in her office and she dressed accordingly.

"I know you will," Mel said. Top dollar, that was a good thing. Moving…she still had mixed feelings about it.

"Mom's sure sad you're leaving," Zelda said.

"I am, too, but it's time."

"I hear you're going to be down at Moonlight Harbor

with Jenna. That sounds fabulous. Beachcombing, kayaking, windsurfing."

Beachcombing, yes. Kayaking, maybe. Windsurfing, definitely not.

"And clam digging. I remember going there with you all when I was a kid. It was so much fun doing that."

"You're welcome to come dig clams any time," Mel told her.

"If I ever get time. Between work and the kids I barely have a minute to breathe."

"You are in the busy years," Mel said.

She was busy, too. But that would have ended with her last day of work, and she'd have been stuck with time on her hands, unsure what to do with it. It was a good thing she was relocating to the beach. With everything going on down there she'd find plenty to do. Yes, this was the right move for her.

"We'll want to ditch those," Zelda said, eyeing the blue velvet wingback chairs that had belonged to Mel's mother.

"They're still in beautiful condition," Mel pointed out.

"Yes, but they're dated. Let's move out the sofa and love seat as well. I can bring in some things that will look more neutral."

Mel reminded herself that Zelda wasn't judging her taste in furniture, only thinking in terms of how best to show off the house.

In the kitchen, Zelda said, "If you can clear everything off the counters, that will be great." She pointed to the vintage cookie jar, a fat little lady pig with a red-trimmed skirt and red bow on her head. "I remember raiding that with Celeste. You made the best oatmeal cookies ever."

"Maybe we should keep that out," said Mel.

Zelda shook her head. "No, go ahead and pack it." She

looked through the row of cookbooks in a corner of the counter and picked out the Williams Sonoma one. "Keep this out. We'll leave it open on the counter."

"Wouldn't the cookie jar be more interesting?" Mel ventured.

"Too distinctive. We want the house to look impressive but neutral. You'll attract more buyers that way."

They walked down the hall to the bedrooms, past the family picture gallery. "These all need to come down," Zelda said.

Mel nodded. Of course. The place had to be scrubbed of all such personal treasures, changed from a home to a property. After someone bought it, it would once more become a home, and a new family would put their own stamp on it.

By the time they got to the bedrooms she already knew what she had to do. More pictures would have to be taken down. Lose her mother's old slipper chair and the hope chest that had been her grandma's, make the room look bigger.

"This house will sell right away," Zelda predicted as Mel signed the listing agreement. "I wouldn't be surprised if we have a bidding war. I'd like to hold an open house next weekend if you're okay with that."

"That will be perfect. I'll be at the beach," Mel said. Making new memories.

When Celeste heard their mom was coming down the following weekend she decided to come down, too, and make it a girls' weekend.

"You'd better bring Little Edie, then, so I can get my auntie fix," Jenna had told her.

"Of course," Celeste had replied. "Edie loves coming to see her Aunt Jenna."

The baby didn't know who Aunt Jenna was yet, but that didn't matter. She was all smiles and coos and great fun to cuddle.

The weather wasn't about to cooperate, and the Friday Jenna's mom and sister were due to arrive brought gray skies spitting rain and nippy temperatures. But who cared? The beach was always a great place to gather, no matter what the weather.

Mel was the first to show up, pulling in early in the afternoon. Jenna always worried about her mother making the long drive down to the coast by herself, especially in bad weather, and was relieved to see her fifteen-year-old Honda pull in. It would be so nice when she was in Moonlight Harbor for good.

She hurried out to the car with an umbrella to help Mel bring her things into the room at the Driftwood that they'd reserved for her. "I'm glad you made it down okay," she said as they walked to the room.

"I always do," Mel said.

"I know, but I worry."

"Darling, I'm not that old yet. Haven't you heard? Sixty is the new forty."

Mom was past sixty now, but Jenna decided not to point that out since she wasn't that far past.

"Did I beat Celeste down?" Mel asked as Jenna unlocked the door.

"Yes. But I heard from her just a few minutes ago. She's in Aberdeen now so she'll be here in another forty minutes."

"Is she sharing the room with me?"

"I've got her in the house," Jenna said. "Easier for feeding Edie. Anyway, you don't want to be woken up when it's time for that two in the morning feeding."

"Maybe not," Mel said with a smile.

Once her overnight bag was dropped on the bed, mother and daughter walked across the parking lot to Aunt Edie's house. It was a welcoming two-story number, painted blue to match the motel, with a long porch running across the front and a porch swing where Aunt Edie could sit and watch Driftwood Inn guests come and go.

"It's been killing me not to tell Aunt Edie and Sabrina you're moving down," Jenna said.

"If I sell the house."

"You'll sell it. I bet you'll get an offer this weekend."

"Here's a lovely surprise," Aunt Edie said when Jenna brought her mother into the kitchen, where Aunt Edie was busy making an orange cream pie. "What brings you down here, Melody?"

"She needed a beach fix," Jenna answered for her mother.

"You need to move down here," Aunt Edie said, pointing her mixing spoon at Mel, and Mel and Jenna exchanged smiles.

Celeste drove in right when Jenna predicted she would, bringing a bundled-up baby Edie with her. "Look," she said to the baby as they walked into the kitchen, "here are your three favorite women in the whole wide world."

Edie's face puckered up and she let out a cry.

"We can tell," Jenna cracked.

"She just woke up. She's cranky," Celeste explained.

"Here, give her to Grammy," Mel cooed, holding out her arms.

Celeste handed Edie over, and she and Jenna went to bring in all the baby paraphernalia.

"What's Henry doing to keep from being lonely while you're down here?" Jenna asked.

"More book edits still. I swear, his career consumes him. When he's on a roll he's up writing until midnight. There's a deadline lurking around every corner. And if he's not on deadline he's editing. If he's not editing he's online promoting the book or doing a book signing. I swear, I'm never going to see him."

"The price of success," Jenna said, refusing to feel sorry for her sister. She had a great guy and a baby, and she loved going to Henry's book signings. Much more than he did. "And you're crazy proud of him."

Celeste smiled at that. "Yes, I am. He's so talented. He's dedicating this next book to Edie. How sweet is that?"

"Very," Jenna said. Life was good in Celeste's corner of the world.

It was good in Jenna's too. But she could make it better…if she'd quit stalling Brody.

Sabrina was delighted to come home from hanging out at Beans and Books to find her aunt and grandmother there.

"Nobody told me you were coming," she said to Mel, who was giving the baby a bottle. She bent to kiss her grandma's cheek and cooed a hello to the baby.

"Surprise attack," Jenna said, pouring herself a second cup of tea.

"Don't feel you have to stay home if you had plans," Mel said to her granddaughter.

Sabrina's face clouded over and she plopped onto a chair. "I don't have a boyfriend anymore."

"You can have plans even without a boyfriend, darling," Mel said gently.

"And we are going to party all weekend," said Celeste. "So that counts as plans."

Now that they were all together it was the perfect time for the big announcement. "It looks like we'll be able to keep that party going," Jenna added, looking to her mother. "Right, Mom?"

"I'm moving down," Mel announced.

Celeste had been standing at the counter, chopping celery. She whirled around. "What?"

"Seriously?" Sabrina asked, perking up.

"I put the house up for sale," Mel said. "Zelda's doing an open house this weekend."

"OMG! That is lit," Sabrina cried happily.

"It will be wonderful to have you here," put in Aunt Edie.

It would also be helpful. Jenna hoped the house sold right away.

Pete arrived in time for dinner, as usual, and joined the women for clam chowder and French bread.

"Melody's going to be moving down here," Aunt Edie told him. "Isn't that exciting?"

"Guess you're gonna retire then, huh?" Pete said. "The medical down here sucks."

"It does not," Aunt Edie argued.

"Nearest hospital is Aberdeen," he said.

"Well, who needs a hospital, anyway?" Aunt Edie argued.

"I might," he said. "I'm not in the best shape, you know. My back."

Ah, yes, the legendary bad back. Jenna rolled her eyes and helped herself to another piece of French bread.

After dinner Pete left to go hang out at The Drunken Sailor. Sabrina got an invite to an impromptu party from her best friend, Hudson, and left with her grandmother's blessing, promising to stick around all day Saturday.

Then it was just the four women and the baby. Jenna built a fire in the woodstove and they settled in the living room with Aunt Edie's beach sandies and hot chocolate to continue visiting.

"An open house already?" Aunt Edie said, bringing them back to the subject of Mel's big life change.

"Zelda doesn't waste any time," Mel said, staring at the flames crackling behind the glass door of the woodstove.

"Funny. Sometimes it's hard to think of her as a successful real estate agent," Jenna mused. "She wasn't all that ambitious in high school."

"She had other interests," Mel said diplomatically.

"Yeah, boys," Celeste said, and smiled down at baby Edie, who was in her lap, regarding her with great interest.

"Like you," Jenna teased.

Her sister had been much more interested in the social aspects of school than the scholastic ones.

"Yeah, well, I remember reading a couple of interesting passages in your journal," she shot back at Jenna.

"Touché," murmured Aunt Edie.

"But I actually did my homework," Jenna said.

"So did I," Celeste insisted. "Eventually."

And she'd done well enough to go on to college and get a teaching degree. Along with a nice collection of student loans it had taken several years to pay back.

"We all end up finding our passion in life sooner or later," Mel said. "I'm glad Zelda found hers."

It seemed like, eventually, if a woman looked long and hard enough, she did. Jenna was glad she'd finally found her passion in fixing up and running the Driftwood Inn.

But had her mother ever really found hers? Sometimes it seemed to Jenna that her mother had spent much of her life watching everyone else have adventures. She'd been on the sidelines, coaching her daughters, consoling and encouraging them. But she'd never jumped back into the game.

"Zelda's hoping for a bidding war," Mel said, returning Jenna to the moment at hand.

"A bidding war," Aunt Edie said in disgust. "What happened to the days when you saw a house you loved and made an offer and it was accepted?"

"I'm sure that still happens down here. But it's a hot market where Mom is," Jenna said.

"It still doesn't seem right. It should be first come, first served," Aunt Edie said with a frown.

"I won't complain if there's a bidding war," Mel said. "That will give me more money to live on."

"You don't need to worry about having money to live on," Aunt Edie told her. "You'll be with us."

"That's kind of you," Mel said to her, "but I think I'll see if I can find a little place of my own."

"No need to hurry," Jenna reminded her. "We can put your things in storage and you can stay here."

"My kitchen is your kitchen," Aunt Edie added.

"It will be lovely to all be together," said Mel, not committing one way or the other.

More than lovely. It would be perfect.

"You've got to be excited for what the rest of the year's going to bring," Celeste said to Mel the next morning as the women all sat at breakfast.

"Making a new start can be exciting," Mel said, but she sounded like she only half meant it.

The mention of new starts made Sabrina's lower lip wobble.

"For you, too," Celeste said to her. "You'll see."

"See what?" asked Pete as he walked in the kitchen door.

"What a good year it's going to be," Celeste said, smiling encouragingly at her niece.

"I'm never going to find anyone like Tristan," Sabrina said, and helped herself to a cinnamon roll to console herself.

"Let's hope not!" Celeste said. She put baby Edie on her shoulder and began patting her back. "You don't need to start collecting jerks."

"Women can be jerks, too," said Pete, pouring himself a cup of coffee. "Believe me, I've known some in my time."

"We're not talking about the women you've known. We're talking about Sabrina," Jenna snapped.

Honestly, what had she done to deserve having grumpy, useless Pete in her life? The scruffy old two-legged barnacle refused to let go and drift off to make someone else nuts. *Why me, God?*

Maybe Pete was in her life to teach her to be more tolerant and kind. If that was the case, she wasn't learning her lesson very well.

"Just pointing out that it's not always the men who are bad," he said. "Too much male bashing these days, if you ask me."

Not that anyone had.

"There are a lot of good men out there," Celeste said.

"You certainly found one," Mel told her.

"Yes, I did," Celeste agreed. "I just wish he wasn't so cheap. I swear, sometimes he acts like we're going to be out on the street any minute."

"The writing profession is a tough one," her mother pointed out.

"Henry's doing great," Celeste insisted. "He made the New York Times bestseller list, for crying out loud."

"It never hurts to be cautious," said Aunt Edie.

"Yeah, well, you guys try living with cautious and see how you like it," Celeste retorted.

"I lived with the opposite and look where it got me," Jenna said to her. Damien had never had a problem spending the small amount of money she earned.

"Henry will be happy to hear that you all side with him," Celeste said irritably.

Jenna couldn't help laughing at that. Celeste the drama queen. Her sister had always had a steady salary. Maybe not the biggest salary in the world, but one she could live on, even with student loans to pay off.

Unlike her big sister, she had no idea what it was to live close to the edge financially.

Jenna had never shared just how bad things had been, especially after her divorce. Aunt Edie had saved her.

"Just because I've been spending a little more than usual," Celeste continued.

There was an understatement. Celeste had never been a spendthrift...until she became a mom. Now Mel and Aunt Edie were giggling.

"What?" Celeste demanded.

"Little Edie is probably the best-dressed baby in Washington State," Jenna said.

In addition to clothes and a ton of baby paraphernalia and toys, Celeste had been buying out her local bookstore, reading every parenting book she could get her hands on. Then there'd been the matter of new clothes for the new mommy. Poor Henry was probably in sticker shock.

"Women. You have no idea how hard a man works," Pete said in disgust.

Pete, the hard worker. That made everyone, including Sabrina, laugh.

"There's too much estrogen in this room. I'm going fishing."

"After you finish painting room number six," Jenna said sternly.

"Don't you worry. It'll get done," he said.

"Sometime in my lifetime?" she called as he went out the door.

"He'll get it done, dear. Don't worry," Aunt Edie said, patting her hand. "Pete's got a good heart."

Hidden under all those lazy bones. Out of respect for her aunt, Jenna kept the thought to herself.

"What are we going to do today?" Sabrina asked, and it was enough to turn Jenna's focus in a more positive direction.

"Something fun," she said.

They spent the afternoon at Crafty Just Cuz, enjoying family time painting tiles. Elizabeth MacDowell, one of the shop's owners, had painted some with gorgeous day and night beachscapes and had them on display. After seeing how hers were turning out, Mel begged to buy them.

"The craft gene skipped me and went straight to my daughters," she explained to K.J., who was Elizabeth's sister and the other owner of the shop.

"But you have the kindness gene," Jenna said to Mel. Her mother truly was the sweetest woman she knew, and her inspiration.

They'd barely gotten home and started making dinner when Mel got a call from Zelda.

"Oh, my goodness," Mel reported. "Three offers and the top one is ten thousand more than I was asking."

It was really happening. Mom would be moving to Moonlight Harbor. Jenna felt light as a balloon.

"That is fabulous," said Aunt Edie.

"Yay, Mom!" Celeste said. "And once Henry and I get a house down here we'll all be together."

"Here's to being together," Jenna said, raising the cup of tea she'd just made herself.

"To new beginnings," Aunt Edie echoed.

"To new beginnings," Mel murmured. Her smile looked a little sad. Until she added, "And to making new memories."

"We're going to make some wonderful ones," Jenna promised the next afternoon as she and the other women in the family all walked her mom to her car.

"Yes, we will," Mel said, and hugged each of them.

"Call me when you get home," Jenna said as Mel dropped into the driver's seat. Silly to worry. Unlike Aunt Edie, the terror of the streets, her mom was a good driver. Still, it was a long way and her car was far from new.

"I will," Mel promised.

They stood and watched as she backed up and then drove out of the parking lot with one final wave.

"I can hardly wait 'til she's down here full-time," Jenna said.

"I hate that I won't have her close, but I'm glad she's going to move here. It's the perfect place to retire," said Celeste.

"It's the perfect place to live, whether you're retired or not," Jenna said.

Celeste nodded. "You're right. Now I really want to get down here. I want to raise Edie in a small town, surrounded by her family."

"How does Henry feel about that?" Jenna asked. "He loves his houseboat."

"So did I when we were first married, but we've got a baby now. We can't live on a houseboat forever. We need a bigger place and we're going to need a yard."

There was nothing Jenna would have liked better than

to have her whole family with her in Moonlight Harbor, but she hesitated to encourage her sister in this idea if Henry wasn't in agreement. He sure wouldn't thank her for it.

"Henry can write from anywhere," Celeste continued, "so it's not like we have to stay in Seattle."

They went back inside, played a game of Hearts with Aunt Edie and Sabrina. Then Edie woke up from her nap and it was time for Celeste to go home.

"I wish you didn't have to leave already," Aunt Edie said to her.

"We'll be back for Memorial Day," Celeste promised. "Maybe sooner, if I see a great place for sale."

"It's a good thing her husband is doing so well," Aunt Edie said after she left. "Our girl is definitely on a spending spree."

"If they've got it to spend, she has my blessing," Jenna said. "She's waited a long time for her happy-ever-after. I'm glad she found it."

"Now we just need you to find yours."

Jenna knew where this conversation was going. Aunt Edie was determined to see Jenna properly settled, as she called it, while she was still alive.

"I'm very happy," Jenna assured her.

"You could be happier," pointed out Aunt Edie.

"Don't worry. I'll sort things out," Jenna promised.

That night, as Brody drove her home after the usual Sunday evening line dancing, sorting looked pretty darned easy to do. They'd been doing things together for so long that she felt a little bit like an old married couple. They were in his slick convertible—top up since it was still cold at the beach—and the heat was on. Adele was crooning softly in the background. Jenna could smell his cologne and it smelled good.

"Guess that takes care of your exercise for the week," he said as they pulled into the Driftwood Inn parking lot.

"When are you going to be brave and go out on the dance floor with me?"

He smiled at her. "When they do the kind of dancing where I can get my hands on you. Maybe then I can convince you to take what we've got to the next level."

Right then she wanted nothing better than to grab him and kiss him. But once she started she wouldn't want to stop. And if she didn't stop, then they'd be at the next level, a couple for sure. It was the difference between writing their names in the sand and writing them in cement.

"You know I want to, but I have to be sure."

He slipped a hand through her hair, drew her toward him. "I can convince you."

His breath was warm on her cheek. His cologne tickled her senses. Every little girlie hormone in her body started jumping up and down in anticipation. *Here we go. Finally!* Her eyelids fell shut and her lips began to tingle even before his got to them. And once they arrived it was party time. His mouth moving against hers, his fingers in her hair. Then his hand sliding down her neck, tracing her collar bone. Oooh. This was good. This was more than good. This was heaven.

If she said the word, heaven could be hers all the time.

He ended the kiss. She opened her eyes and saw him smiling at her. It was the cocky smile of a man who knew he was irresistible.

"Come on Jenna," he murmured. "What are you waiting for?"

"I don't know," she said. What, indeed? She grabbed him by the face and went back for a second helping. And then a third.

The windows were getting pretty steamy and she was getting even steamier when car headlights shone at them. Her daughter returning from church youth group.

"Oh, my gosh," Jenna said, and pushed him away.

"What?" He looked up with glazed eyes.

"Sabrina's home."

"Oh." He pulled back.

"I'd better go."

"Wait," he said. "We can go to my place."

It was sign. They'd been interrupted for a reason.

She shook her head. "I can't do this yet."

He blew out a frustrated breath. "You're killing me here."

"I know. I'm sorry," she said, then jumped out, trying to pull herself together and look as innocent as possible.

Sabrina got out of the car as Brody zipped out of the parking lot. She was smirking.

"Did I interrupt something?" she teased.

"Don't be smart," Jenna said irritably.

Sabrina fell in step with her and slipped her arms around one of Jenna's. "It's okay, Mom. You're allowed to fall in love again, even if it is with Brody. He's okay."

Okay. Did that describe their relationship? Was that what they'd have if they became serious, something that was only okay?

Those kisses had been more than okay, that was for sure.

Crap. She was a mess.

She had a hard time sleeping that night. Brody waltzed into her dreams, dressed in a tux and carrying a long-stemmed red rose. "Dance with me," he said, handing it over.

She was dressed for dancing at a wedding, wearing a bridal gown, her hair caught up in a rhinestone clip. She was just about to let him sweep her into his arms when she heard Jolly Roger squawking, "Call the cops!"

She turned and saw Seth Waters approaching. He was dressed like a pirate and Roger was sitting on his shoulder.

"Don't be stupid, Jenna," he said. "You don't belong with him."

"Who do I belong with?" she demanded.

"Me," he said. Then he pulled out a sword and whacked off the train of her wedding gown.

"You're wrecking my gown," she protested.

"It's better than wrecking your life," he said.

"I don't have a life!" she yelled. "I want a life."

She was still muttering, "I want a life," when she woke up. She was tangled in her sheets, wrapped up like a mummy.

Which was what she was going to turn into if she didn't make a decision soon. Seth wasn't doing anything and Brody wouldn't wait forever.

And she wouldn't blame him. It wasn't fair to keep him dangling.

But after that disturbing dream he'd have to dangle for a little while longer, she decided as she got ready for the day. She had to be sure.

She had no massage clients booked until the afternoon, which meant she was free to putter around the office in the morning and make sure Pete finally got that room painted. She'd planned to remind him at breakfast but he wasn't in the kitchen when she came down.

"Have you seen Pete?" she asked Aunt Edie as she poured herself a cup of coffee.

"He was in before you came down and I gave him some eggs. He's gone back to his room though. His back's bothering him."

"I just bet it is," Jenna said with a frown. She made herself a piece of toast and then went in search of her useless handyman.

Her new maid was already at work, bustling to room twelve with her cleaning cart. She called a cheery hello to Jenna and Jenna called hello back. The girl was going to the nearby junior college and was a hard worker. Jenna hoped she'd at least be able to keep her for a couple of years.

She knocked on the door of the motel room Pete got, supposedly in exchange for his work. No answer.

She knocked again. Still no answer.

She went from knocking to banging. "I know you're in there, Pete. Your car's outside."

"Okay, okay," came the muffled voice. A moment later a bent-over Pete opened the door, a pained expression on his face and one hand on his lower back.

Jenna pretended not to notice. "I want room six painted today. You've stalled long enough."

He glared at her. "Did your eyes stop working?"

"No," she said. "In fact, I can see right through you."

"My back's killing me. I could barely get off my bed to open the door."

He'd managed to get to the kitchen for breakfast.

"Not that you care," he added.

"Playing the guilt card won't work," she informed him. That only worked when her daughter did it.

"I'm not playing," he growled. "And I'm not painting today. I'm in pain. It'll have to wait," he said, and hobbled back to bed. He let out a nice loud groan as he lay down.

"Oh come on, Pete. How stupid do you think I am? Your back only acts up when I need you to do something you don't want to do."

"That's a coincidence," he said. "If you want your damned room repainted you're gonna have to wait 'til I feel better."

The man was so irritating. "You'd better not feel better in time for dinner," Jenna warned as she shut the door on him.

Wait for Pete's back to get better? That was a joke. She'd be waiting until the thirteenth of Never.

She'd offered to give him a free massage once when he was claiming to be near crippled and he'd turned her down. "Lie there in my skivvies and have some strange woman pawing me?"

"I thought men liked getting pawed," she'd said.

"Only by certain women and in certain circumstances," he'd informed her, and that had been that.

She sighed, resigned to her fate. A few moments later, wearing an old T-shirt and jeans, she fetched the stepladder. Like the little red hen her grandma had read about to her when she was a child, she'd have to do the work herself.

The ladder was an unwieldy metal thing, and she banged her shin hauling it out of the storage room. She hated ladders. They were scary, especially to someone with a fear of heights.

But she didn't have to go that high to repaint a wall. It wasn't like she had to get up on a roof. She'd been there and tried that. Never again.

Maybe it was just as well Pete wasn't doing the painting. At his age, even falling a few feet could result in something getting broken.

Seth usually picked up the slack when Pete failed her, but Jenna didn't feel right always bugging him to do things. Unlike Pete, he paid rent for his room. Anyway, she was a capable adult. She could do this. She sure wished she didn't have to though.

Wishes were useless things. She got to work.

The day was far from balmy but at least the sun was out. She left the door open to bring in fresh air. Then she spread plastic on the floor against the wall opposite the bed and set up the ladder. She grabbed the paint bucket that had been sitting by the door for the last few days over to the ladder. She pried it open and poured some into the paint tray. It was the same light blue she'd used in some of the other rooms and would look lovely with the beachy bedspread and lamp with the blue crab vase she had on the nightstand. It also offset the very dark blue carpet, making the room appear a little bigger.

Like the carpet in the rest of the rooms, this one was a remnant she'd gotten on sale when she first refurbished the motel. It didn't show the dirt like a lighter carpet would and worked well with the lighter color on the wall.

Two of the walls in the room had taken a beating, especially the one she was starting with. One young guest had created a work of art in permanent marker. Another family had managed to dent the drywall in places. Pete had at least gotten around to filling in and sanding the damaged spots. She supposed she could be grateful for that.

She went up the ladder, balancing her tray of paint and paint roller oh so carefully. Then she settled the tray in place.

There. Ladders weren't so bad, she decided as she started in with her roller. Look at her, the painting queen. She was all the way to the top and not even fazed. Piece of cake.

Until she reached a little too far. Suddenly she was about to be airborne. *Noooo.*

She tried to right herself, but in her panic she wound up catching hold of the paint tray instead of the ladder itself. The ladder stood its ground but both she and the tray went down. She landed on her padded end with little enough harm done beyond a momentary owie. The tray, however, had flipped and gone sailing, raining blue as it went and then landing at the edge of the plastic sheet.

"Oh no!" She dove for the edge of the plastic, trying to stem the river from overflowing onto the carpet. Too late, of course. It had already seeped over.

"A new artistic expression?" asked a deep male voice from the doorway.

She knew that voice. There stood Seth Waters, looking like he'd just stepped free of the cover of a romance novel. Jeans and boots, a pec-hugging T-shirt under his favorite old leather bomber jacket. Where Brody was tall and blond, he was short and dark, compactly built with muscles in all the right places. He was one of those men who always seemed to do everything perfectly. Seth Waters would never fall off a ladder.

"Very funny," she said, irritated at being caught looking stupid even more than she was by his comment.

He shook his head, came over and helped her contain the river, then pushed her hair out of her face so she wouldn't have to touch it with her paint-splotched hands. "What do you think you're doing, anyway?"

"Pete's job, of course."

"I thought we'd decided you weren't going to go up on ladders anymore," he said as he set the paint tray outside the door.

"I don't think I ever said that," she hedged.

"If you didn't, you should have."

He carried the ladder out of the room while she attempted to fold up the plastic without spilling any more paint.

"Here, let me help you," he said as he came back in.

"Thanks," she said, wiping her hands on her jeans. "And thanks for not laughing. I feel like a character in a sitcom."

"Wouldn't dream of it. And why are you doing Pete's job? Wait, don't tell me. His back is bothering him."

"He's practically a cripple."

"Oh, yeah. I forgot." Seth looked down at the paint-ribboned carpet. "You got enough left over from when you remodeled to replace this?"

"Maybe I can manage to clean it up," she said.

"Maybe, but it might be easier to replace the whole carpet."

Probably a good idea. Jenna had noticed it was looking a little worn in places.

"I can get on it tomorrow. You're not booked solid yet, right?"

"Not until Memorial Day weekend."

"Then no problem."

That was Seth, always ready to help, not only her but anyone who had a need. Seth Waters to the rescue. Did she take advantage of that?

Probably. "I'm always bugging you."

"It's not bugging if I don't mind. Anyway, that's part of the deal with me staying here."

"You pay rent."

He gave a snort. "Pretty minimal. I've got enough saved. I should find a rental. The house peddler would be glad to find me one about ten towns away."

There was no love lost between Seth and Brody. They'd taken an instant dislike to each other the moment they'd met.

"Don't do that," Jenna protested. "What would we do without you?" She couldn't imagine him not at the Driftwood, not in her life in some way.

"You'd manage. I see you were out with him the other night."

"Were you watching from your window?" she teased.

Speaking of, had he seen them steaming up the windows in Brody's car? Whoo, boy. Talk about steaming. She could feel her face getting warm.

"I was looking for the Easter Bunny. You getting a diamond ring in your Easter basket?"

"From the Easter Bunny?"

Seth frowned. "Don't be stupid."

"From you, then?"

He focused on rolling up the plastic sheet. "You don't want a ring from me."

"How do you know?"

"Maybe because you're always with him." He sounded almost surly.

"That's because he asks."

Seth shrugged. "Just as well. Pick the sure bet, Jenna. You deserve it."

"What about you? What do you deserve?"

"I'm happy enough."

"You could be happier." Maybe they both could.

He just shook his head.

"Why are you trying to make it so easy for me?" she demanded.

He wanted her, they both knew it. He should fight for her, give her a reason not to choose his rival. It made her mad that he wouldn't, made her mad at both him and herself. Because really, he'd made the choice obvious. And she still hadn't made it.

"I'll finish cleaning up here," he said. "I can get the carpet torn up tomorrow after work."

"Thanks. And nice way to change the subject, by the way."

"It needed changing," he said as he picked up the plastic.

"You are such a chicken."

The man was so frustrating. He'd fight off a sea serpent if her life was in danger, but handing over his heart was another matter entirely.

"We all have to be good at something," he said, her petty name-calling bouncing off his armor.

She returned to the house, grinding her teeth.

At least the day ended well. Jenna and Aunt Edie were relaxing on the couch, Jenna reading the latest business book she'd found at the library and Aunt Edie knitting, Jolly Roger perched on her shoulder, when Sabrina came home from school all smiles.

She plopped in between them and announced, "Scotty Rarig invited me to the Spring Fling."

"Is that like the Highland Fling?" Aunt Edie asked.

"It's the last big dance before prom," Sabrina explained. "Hudson told him that Tristan and I broke up. He told me he was sorry I got hurt but he was glad I wasn't with Tristan anymore. He's been wanting to ask me out all year."

"Everything comes to he who waits," said Aunt Edie.

"He who waits," echoed Roger.

"He's so cute, Mom," Sabrina said, all wiggly with excitement. "He's the student body president and he's on the football team. And he's a member of the honor society."

"So, not just a pretty face," Jenna said with a smile.

"He's really nice. I've liked him for a long time. As a friend," Sabrina quickly clarified.

"Friendship is a great basis for a relationship," said Aunt Edie.

"As long as he's a good guy, that's all I care about," Jenna said to her daughter. "Someone who thinks about others and not only himself."

Someone who thought only of himself. Gee, who did that remind her of? Jenna had heard it said that when it came time to marry, boys wound up looking for their mother and girls their father. She certainly hoped that wasn't true for Sabrina. One Damien in their lives was more than enough.

"He does," Sabrina said. "He's nice to everyone at school, even Loyola Burns, who nobody likes."

"Why doesn't anybody like her?" Aunt Edie wanted to know.

Sabrina shrugged. "She's weird."

"We're all a little weird when it comes right down to it," said Aunt Edie.

This was the first Jenna had heard of Loyola Burns. "I hope you're nice to her."

"Of course I am," Sabrina said, shocked.

"Good, because everyone deserves kindness."

Sabrina rolled her eyes. "I know that, Mom. Sheesh." She hopped up from the couch. "I have to go text Hudson and Taylor."

"It looks like our girl's heart is healed," Aunt Edie observed as Sabrina raced up the stairs.

"I'm glad," Jenna said. "I thought it would take a lot longer."

"The young heal fast."

"I guess so." Once you hit your forties, the healing process sure slowed down.

At least they were finally out of reality show mode. Hopefully, life would stay calm for a while.

Setting things to rights in room six was a good beginning. Jenna insisted on helping Seth pull up the carpet and he insisted on Pete helping him paint. Funny how Pete never gave Seth grief about doing things around the place.

Once the room was painted, Seth enlisted the help of a friend who worked as a carpet layer to help him put down the new carpet. Mysteriously, Jenna didn't get a bill.

Which was fine with her. It was still their slow season and she was all about saving money wherever she could.

That didn't mean she took a helping hand for granted. The day after room six was restored, she put together two thank-you baskets, one for Seth and one for his pal, of IPA brews and various bags of munchies, along with gift cards to The Drunken Sailor. Once she saw Seth's truck in the parking lot she went to his room to deliver them.

"A thank-you to you and your friend for laying that carpet," she said once he'd opened his door.

She'd caught him freshly cleaned up, his hair damp from the shower, barefoot in jeans and a T-shirt. Those pecs! Don't drool. She forced herself not to stare, moving her gaze up to his face.

That was when she caught him staring. Juggling the two gift baskets had put a strain on her V-neck tee and it was dipping down her chest, showing off the top of her left boob. He looked back up and saw he was busted and his cheeks turned russet.

He cleared his throat and took one of the baskets. "Here, let me help you."

He set it on the bed, then turned to take the other one

and found her right next to him. There they stood, kissing-close. She remembered a certain New Year's Eve kiss they'd shared, back before he'd made a resolution to leave her alone. The very memory of that kiss was enough to start the tingles going. If one of them moved just a little closer...

Now he was looking at her lips.

She swallowed hard. Okay, pivotal moment here.

But the moment didn't pivot. He actually grimaced.

"You need to hurry up and get engaged," he said.

Disappointment swept over her. "Maybe I do."

She turned to go and he caught her arm. "It's not that I don't care," he said softly. "You know that."

"Rejecting me for my own good. What a guy," she said bitterly. She pulled her arm away and started for the door.

"Don't go away mad," he pleaded.

"Just go away."

She sounded angry and resentful. What a coincidence. She was. She was sick of him being so stupid and noble, driving her away and not even giving them a chance. Nobility was overrated.

"You really do make me so mad," she growled.

"And you make me crazy," he said with a half smile, "so I guess we're even."

"Do you want to be even?" she demanded in disgust.

He frowned. "I need a beer. Go back to the house, Jenna."

And she needed to break one of those beer bottles over his stubborn head.

She pointed a finger at him. "You know, life is all about choices. You make a dumb one and you're going to have to live with it."

His face shut down and he swung the door wide, his invitation for her to leave loud and clear. "I know all about choices, and some of them have nothing to do with what you want."

Of course he did. One of his choices, noble as it was, had cost him years of his life, landing him in prison for something he hadn't done.

"I'm sorry," Jenna said, instantly penitent. "That was a stupid thing to say."

He shrugged, forgiving her, but said nothing, just stood there by the door, waiting for her to leave.

"But your life's not over," she added.

"Neither is yours. Quit wasting time, Jenna."

She wanted to say more, but he ended the conversation with, "Thanks again for the basket," and began to shut the door.

Short of pushing it back open, there was nothing to do but wrap her pride around her shoulders and leave.

Okay, fine. If Seth wanted to make it easy for her then she'd let him. Brody was a great choice, and he not only wanted her, he wanted to be with her. And she was just fine being with him. She was done wasting her time.

Jenna slapped the platonic label on her relationship with Seth and moved on, and life settled into a quiet, drama-free routine. Gray clouds began to give way to the occasional blue sky.

Easter Sunday was a blue sky day. After church and Easter dinner, Jenna held an egg hunt on the beach for a bunch of Sabrina's friends, hiding plastic eggs, some filled with candies and others with gift cards in small amounts to favorite places such as Beans and Books, the funplex, and of course, Good Times Ice Cream Parlor.

She met the amazing Scotty and was pleased to see that

he was, indeed, a nice kid. The proof? He gave the Beans and Books gift card he found to Sabrina.

Brody came over bringing a bouquet of spring flowers and hung around. He even took part in some of the games the kids were playing, including spoons, a competition that involved cards and diving for a spoon. There was always one less spoon than there were players, and whoever wound up with no spoon on enough rounds was out of the game. It was teen-level competitive and Brody finally wound up getting elbowed in the eye by Scotty as they wrestled for the last available spoon.

"Man, I'm sorry, Mr. Green," Scotty apologized. "Are you okay?"

"Oh, yeah, I'm fine," Brody assured him. "Think I'll quit while I'm behind."

"Probably a good idea," Jenna said as she gave Brody ice to put on it.

"If I hadn't about lost my eye I'd have gotten that spoon," he insisted.

"Maybe it's just as well you're out of the game. You don't want to end up with two black eyes."

The fight for spoons kept going among the kids, and Jenna and Brody retired to the living room to join Aunt Edie.

"That was one of Ralph's favorite games," she said as Brody and his ice pack settled with Jenna on the couch.

"And ours growing up," Jenna said.

"Did you play that aggressively?" Brody asked. "Oh, wait. Never mind. Dumb question. Of course you did."

"There's nothing wrong with being determined," she said.

"No, there's not," he agreed. "I'm pretty determined myself," he added, the expression on his face telling her exactly what he was determined about.

Later, after the kids had left, and it was just him and her standing in the doorway, he drew her to him. "How about coming over to my place for a while?" he murmured.

Jenna knew where that would lead. "That's a little too tempting," she said. Although why she was hesitating to move things along between them, she had no idea. It really didn't make sense in light of the fact that she had, finally and firmly, categorized her relationship with Seth as a no-go. Brody was ready to go. She should be, too.

"I really am okay waiting as long as you tell me I'm not waiting for nothing."

"You're not," she said. "Once I get Sabrina graduated then I can think about myself."

"Good. That'll make two of us thinking about yourself," he said with a grin.

Then, to keep her thinking about him, he kissed her. The man knew how to kiss, that was for sure. It was stupid not to move their relationship to the next level. Come summer, she decided. Then she'd give Brody a thumbs-up and enjoy some summer sizzle.

She was smiling when she went to bed. Now her love life was all resolved.

Until Seth Waters showed up in her dreams again, this time in a gondola, dressed like a gondolier. There she stood, on the beach of a desert island, still in that same gown she'd worn in her last dream, holding the same long-stemmed rose. It was wilted now.

"What do you think you're doing?" he demanded, his boat bobbing on the waves.

"I'm waiting for Brody. You remember him, the man who's actually committing to me."

"Him? Don't be stupid."

"You're always saying that to me but you're the one who's being stupid and I'm tired of waiting for you. Anyway, I love Brody."

"As much as you do me?"

"Absolutely. And he's a better kisser."

"Oh, yeah?"

Instead of hopping out of the boat and proving her wrong, he paddled away.

"Come back!" she called, but he ignored her.

She awakened with a frown. "You are a chicken," she muttered. "Even in my dreams."

Too late for him, anyway. She'd made up her mind and she'd made the right choice.

There. Her love life was settled and the rest of her life was falling into place beautifully. Calm waters ahead.

Until the council meeting. Jenna had gone to the mayor's office a couple of days before, pushing for a chance to bring up the idea of a convention center. She found Parker Thorne looking both mayoral and chic in a dark blue suit with a pencil skirt and heels. She wore a tiny pin shaped like a half moon on the lapel, to signify her loyalty to Moonlight Harbor. Her smile was as polished as her look, and she kept it in place as Jenna made her case. Of course, with Parker that didn't necessarily mean she was in agreement. It simply meant she was a good politician.

"It would really benefit the town," Jenna concluded.

"I'm sure it would," said Parker. "Let's wait to put it on our agenda. Right now, as you know, we have many pressing matters to deal with."

Couldn't they deal with those matters and introduce the topic of the convention center, too? Jenna asked as much.

"People can only take in so many things at a time, Jenna.

We have other business we must deal with first. We need to make a decision on where to add new sidewalks. We don't have much money budgeted for that this year so we can only pick two locations. Then there's the business of rounding up the artists to paint the fire hydrants and deciding on what theme we're going with."

"Isn't that already decided? I thought we were going with a beach theme?"

"We still need to vote on it, and we'll have citizens who want to speak to that before we cast our votes. And we have the issue of the deer."

Ugh. When would her convention center ever become a priority?

"That convention center would be a great benefit to Moonlight Harbor, and if you got on board with the idea it could ensure your re-election," Jenna pushed, sure the mention of re-election would serve to inspire.

"It would also be costly and require issuing bonds, and, as you know, many of our residents are retired and on a fixed income. I'm not sure people will go for it."

"They might if they hear how we'll all benefit from it," Jenna said.

"Until our citizens learn how much it will cost." Parker gave her a condescending smile. Jenna half expected Parker to pat her on the head like she was a precocious child. "I know you're enthusiastic and anxious to serve our fair city."

Town.

"But let's take this slowly, Jenna. Really do our research before we present the idea. One step at a time."

That was Parker Thorne, always careful where she stepped. Jenna left her office frowning.

She stopped at the grocery store for milk and eggs and

got more than she'd bargained for. Florence Peterson, head of the Moonlight Harbor Garden Club, was in the checkout line ahead of her, talking with Maisy the checker.

"Something had better get done about the deer problem tomorrow night at the council meeting," Florence said. "The city council needs to deal with this problem."

"I agree," Maisy said. "My neighbor got giardia. You know what it turned out to be from? Watering her lawn in her bare feet. Deer pee had seeped into the lawn."

"That's disgusting," said Florence.

Jenna decided to find a different checkout line. She turned to leave only to see she'd been hemmed in by a tall white-haired man.

"I'm with you, Florence," he said. Then, looking at Jenna, he added, "I'm sure our newest member of the council will advocate for us."

Jenna's right eye began to twitch.

Florence whirled around. "Jenna Jones. You came to my house, doorbelling."

"I did," Jenna admitted. *Blink, blink.*

"Mine, too," said the tall man. "We know you'll do the right thing."

"Just what is the right thing, Bob?" demanded a new customer who'd come up behind him. "Many of us happen to appreciate the deer. And they were here first."

"Well, now they need to be somewhere else," snapped Florence.

"The population is out of control," put in the tall man. "If the council doesn't do something about it, we're all going to end up with Lyme disease, mark my words."

"And it will be on your heads," put in Florence, pointing a finger at Jenna, whose nervous tic was now in full bloom.

"You people need to get a grip," the newcomer said to Florence.

Jenna needed to get out of there.

"We'll all be at the meeting to express our views," Florence said to her. "And you'd better listen well."

"We'll do our best," Jenna replied, and realized she wasn't even remotely looking forward to her first city council meeting.

Four

Jenna's first city council meeting was memorable, and not in a good way. She'd barely been welcomed onto the council when the fireworks started. Before the council members got down to business and passed ordinances, the floor was open to the local citizenry to express their feelings. This evening they came loaded for bear...or, rather, deer.

First up to the mike was a plump little lady edging toward her sixties, wearing jeans and an I Heart Moonlight Harbor sweatshirt. As was required, she stated her name for the record. Mildred Morrison.

"I heard the council was considering rounding up the deer and killing them all," she said, her tone of voice accusing.

"Go for it," said Tyrella Lamb, who was sitting on the opposite side of the aisle.

Yes, Tyrella disliked the deer, often referring to them as cloven-hooved rats, but this animal violence streak she'd begun displaying seemed out of character. Jenna had always thought of her as an animal lover. She had a cat and only recently adopted a rescue dog, a cute little Labradoodle she'd named Michelle, in honor of the former first lady. She gave money to PAWS, watched the *Kitten Bowl* on TV every year, and was always posting cute pet pictures on Facebook. When had she turned into Cruella de Vil?

"Let's have one person at a time speak," Parker Thorne said, looking sternly at Tyrella.

"It's wrong," Mildred continued. "Those poor, defenseless animals have just as much right to live as anyone else in Moonlight Harbor. It's animal cruelty."

"No one is talking about rounding up the deer population," Parker said.

"I should hope not!" Mildred said, and took her seat.

The next person waiting in line behind her was the tall white-haired man from the grocery store, who gave his name as Bob Wilson. "Mayor, members of the council, I've been doing some research, and statistics show that in areas where the deer population has increased, so has the incidence of Lyme disease. I'm sure we don't want that for Moonlight Harbor. One way we can cut down on the exploding deer population is by making it illegal to feed the deer. By feeding them we extend the rutting season and that increases the population."

Mildred popped up from her seat. "But how will they survive?"

"On leaves, like they're supposed to," Tyrella said.

"If anyone wishes to speak, please get in line to use the microphone," Parker said in her most authoritative mayor voice, and Tyrella clamped her lips shut.

Bob left and turned the microphone over to Florence of the garden club, who Jenna also remembered from the grocery store. She'd been dancing around behind him like a four-year-old in need of the restroom.

"Florence Peterson," she said. "This is not the first time we've come before the city council expecting you all to do something and you haven't. Meanwhile, the deer are devouring everything in our yards and running amok. I want to know what you people are going to do about this. We elected you to be public servants. You need to serve us!"

"We are, of course, doing our best to serve everyone in Moonlight Harbor," Parker replied.

"You don't need to be serving the deer. They don't pay taxes. And they don't vote! Next election we're going to remember who did what," Florence threatened and stamped back to her seat.

Can't we all just get along? Jenna thought. Good grief. With all the seriously bad things going on in the world, was this what everyone chose to get worked up about?

The next person in line wanted to point out how bad it was to feed the deer apples, everyone's treat of choice, including the deer's. "Washington State Fish and Wildlife states that feeding the deer things like apples actually messes with their digestive system and gives them deer diabetes. So, in kindness to the deer, we should at least stop people from feeding them."

Mildred popped up yet again. "I don't believe it! The deer love those apples."

"Well, you shouldn't be giving them to 'em," Tyrella called from her side of the aisle. "It needs to be made illegal and there should be a stiff fine."

"My eighty-year-old mother loves to feed the deer. Would you fine her?" shot back Mildred.

"Yes," Tyrella retorted, her voice rising. "I don't believe in age discrimination."

"People, please. The microphone," begged Parker.

Another man was on his feet, a hefty specimen in jeans and a camo T-shirt. He pointed a finger in the general direction of the council members. "If you don't do something you're nothing but a bunch of useless wimps!"

The woman next to him got to her feet, too. "We want action now!"

"That's right. We're sick and tired of not being listened to," roared Mr. Camo Tee. "We've been talking about this long enough. No more screwing around!"

"Sir, if you don't calm yourself I'll have you removed," Parker snapped, and the policeman present, who just happened to be Victor King, everyone's favorite cop, made a move in his direction.

The angry citizen sat back down and shut up. And glared at each member of the council in turn.

"The council will look into this and then make a decision," Parker promised. "Jenna Jones, will you please research this issue and report back with a recommendation at our next council meeting?"

The angry man in the camo tee glared at Jenna, as if to say, *You'd better do what I want or I'll bean you with an apple.*

Oh, boy.

And here came her nervous tic. Her right eye began to twitch. "M-m-me?" she stuttered. *Blink, blink.*

"Yes. The council will hear your report and then vote on this matter."

Fine, throw the new kid under the bus.

The mayor was talking. Jenna barely heard her. New business. Something about new business.

Fellow council member Kiki Strom began talking about the proposed painting of the fire hydrants. Local artists were encouraged to participate. Moonlight Harbor residents would have the opportunity to cast their votes for their favorite once the fire hydrants were complete, and there would be a cash prize of two hundred dollars for the creator of the winning hydrant.

"Fire hydrants," scoffed Mr. Camo Tee just loud enough to be heard. "Who gives a shit?"

"These will be yet another way to enhance the charm of Moonlight Harbor and will be good for tourism," Parker continued as if she hadn't heard him.

"The deer are good for tourism, too," said Mildred Morrison, also just loud enough to be heard.

So are convention centers, Jenna thought, and sighed inwardly. And to think she'd actually wanted to serve on the council.

She finally dragged herself home a little before ten to find Aunt Edie on the couch, happily crocheting a granny square for the latest afghan she was working on. It was to be a graduation present for Sabrina, who had picked out the colors—shades of blue and teal. "Like the ocean," Sabrina had said.

"How'd your first meeting go?" Aunt Edie asked.

Jenna fell onto the couch. "Remind me again why I wanted to be on the council."

"To serve Moonlight Harbor," Aunt Edie said. "And I'm sure you're going to do a wonderful job."

"If half the town doesn't kill me first. People feel so strongly about the deer issue, no matter what we decide it won't be popular with someone."

"You can't please everyone, you know that," Aunt Edie said calmly as she worked her crochet hook in and out of the yarn. "As council members you all have to do what you think is the best for the town."

"Yes, and guess who's supposed to do the research on the issue and come up with a recommendation."

"You'll figure it out," Aunt Edie said placidly.

"I hope so. You should have been there. For a minute I thought we were going to have a riot."

"People get worked up about things. You should have seen some of the fights back in my day."

"What were they fighting over then?"

"You name it. How big residential lots should be, whether we should allow chain stores to come in. A lot of people were not happy when McDonald's arrived. They were the first and, other than a couple of small brand name hotels, the last. Somehow, we all survived."

"I guess we'll survive this, too." Jenna sighed. "I don't know when we're ever going to get to talk about the convention center. Other things always seem to get in line ahead of it."

"When the time is right," Aunt Edie assured her. "Rome wasn't built in a day."

"I guess Moonlight Harbor won't be, either."

Aunt Edie tied off the yarn and put the finished square in the basket next to her. "Well, dear, I think I'll head off to bed. I'm feeling awfully tired."

"You do too much," Jenna told her. "Let Sabrina and me take over the cooking."

"Then what would I have to do with myself?" Aunt Edie countered.

"Relax. Read more. Crochet."

"I already do that, dear. No, I need to feel useful. I can't just sit around and take up space."

"We like the space you take up," Jenna said with a smile.

Aunt Edie smiled back at her. "You are a darling. Here now, kiss me and then I'm off to bed."

Jenna gave her a kiss on the cheek. Her skin was soft and she smelled like her favorite fragrance, Chantilly.

She pushed off the couch, using both hands to help herself get up, then headed for the stairs.

She's getting frail, Jenna thought, watching her go. Aunt Edie had slowed down considerably in the last year. Lately she'd starting gripping the banister to half pull herself up the stairs.

How many more years would they have her? Many, Jenna hoped. Aunt Edie had been the anchor keeping her life stable ever since she came to Moonlight Harbor. She simply couldn't lose her anchor. The very thought depressed her.

She sighed again. She was tired. She always turned melancholy when she was tired. "Go to bed," she instructed herself.

Good advice. She had massage clients in the morning and had research to do. She turned off the lights, checked to make sure the back door was locked, then followed her aunt upstairs.

As she climbed into her bed she gave herself one final instruction. "No dreaming."

Her subconscious didn't listen. She dreamed that she was on the beach, in the middle of a line of does. They were on their hind legs, wearing fancy cancan dresses with layers of brightly colored ruffles and doing a deer version of the famous French dance for the city council, who were all sitting on logs, watching them. Jenna was in the chorus line, kicking up her heels, too. In addition to her fancy dress she wore deer antlers on her head.

She was laughing and happy until someone threw an apple at her. Tyrella.

The deer scattered, their little deer tails sticking out from their ruffled skirts, leaving Jenna all by herself in her cancan dress. Tyrella launched another apple, hitting Jenna's antlers and knocking them askew.

"If you don't get rid of them, we can't be friends," she yelled.

Here came the guy in the camo tee, holding a bow and arrow. Fortunately for Jenna, instead of a tip, the arrow had a giant suction cup on the end of it. But it still made her yelp when he hit her in the thigh with it.

"We should never have voted for you," he hollered.

"Hey, give me a break. I just got on the council," she yelled back, pulling the arrow off her leg.

Tyrella threw another apple at her. "Deer lover!"

"I do love the deer," she yelled back, dodging as Florence of the garden club showed up and threw an apple. She had an entire basketful of them.

Meanwhile, all Jenna's fellow council members were doubled over laughing. "We needed a scapegoat," called Parker Thorne.

Mildred Morrison had arrived on the scene with several other women, and they were all dressed like Valkyries, wearing helmets and bearing broadswords. "Protect the deer," she cried, raising her sword, and began to run toward the apple throwers.

"No!" Jenna shouted, holding out a hand to stop them. "We can't let something like this divide us."

Next thing she knew, a big buck was by her side. "Get on," he commanded.

She hopped on and the deer galloped off down the beach with her bouncing around on his back and holding on to his antlers. At least someone still had antlers. Hers had fallen off.

He galloped her up to an entire herd of does and they all

crowded around her. "We know you'll do the right thing," said Mr. Bambi.

"I'm going to try."

"Do more than try." Who knew deer could growl?

"Otherwise," said one of the does, "we'll have to hurt you. Our hooves are very sharp, you know."

"I'm new on the council," she protested.

"You'd better do what's right," said the doe. "You've been warned."

"I'll try," Jenna said. "I just want to make everyone happy."

"You can't please everyone," said the buck.

"I know," she said, wringing her hands. "I know, I know."

The conversation got no further. She woke up.

She finally got back to sleep and her subconscious left her in peace, but she didn't wake up feeling very rested.

"You look awfully tired, dear," Aunt Edie said when she shuffled into the kitchen in search of coffee. "Didn't you sleep well?"

"Not really," Jenna said. "I need caffeine."

"Coffee's ready. And I've got a nice egg casserole."

As if on cue, Pete entered through the back door, looking bristly and scruffy as usual. At one point he'd had a key to the house but Jenna had put a stop to that. Not that it helped any. Aunt Edie always unlocked the door first thing every morning to give the mooch full access to the kitchen.

"Something sure smells good, Edie old girl," he said.

"I see your back's better," Jenna said to him.

Pete frowned. "It's hasn't quit bothering me since you had me painting that room before it was even healed."

"The bathroom lights in rooms five and twelve need

changing, and the sink in room ten needs to be snaked, like I told you yesterday. Think you can handle that?"

"Think we can do without the sarcasm?" he retorted.

"Pete's wonderful with clogged sinks," Aunt Edie said, stepping in to smooth the old rooster's ruffled feathers.

"You're out of light bulbs," he added.

"I'll get you some today. Meanwhile, that sink needs to be taken care of."

"I'm on it. Don't get your knickers in a knot."

"See that you do," Jenna said, determined to have the last word. She took her coffee and left to get the massage room ready for her first client.

As she left she could hear Pete saying to Edie, "That girl is wound too damn tight."

Yes, and who was it who wound her up? People thought the deer were a pain. They should have to deal with Pete Long on a regular basis.

On her lunch hour, Jenna went to the hardware store. She walked in feeling some trepidation over seeing Tyrella, who owned the store and was always either at the cash register or helping her employees stock items.

Today she was at the register. "I was hoping you'd come in," she greeted Jenna.

Great. Here came the first citizen assault, and by her good friend, too.

"I meant to call you," Tyrella said. "I should have."

"About the deer?" She'd already made her views plain.

"No, about me."

"You?" Jenna looked at her, puzzled.

"My behavior. I was a stinker last night and I'm sorry." Jenna blinked in surprise.

"It's a lot of work being on the council and I didn't do anything to make your first meeting very easy."

"Nobody did," Jenna said.

"They handed you the dirty job, too. But I know you'll do what's right."

Good luck with that, Jenna thought.

"Thanks," she said, and moved off to get her light bulbs. "I'm hoping Pete will actually earn his keep and replace the burned-out ones today," she said when she returned.

"The man truly is a thorn in your side, isn't he?" Tyrella said as she rang up the purchase.

"He is, but Aunt Edie loves him so I'm stuck with him. One of life's little irritations," Jenna added with a shrug.

"Little irritations everywhere. I guess when you look at the big picture, though, most of them aren't even enough to take up one corner of it."

Very philosophical. Jenna hoped if the council voted on measures that weren't enough to satisfy the deer haters, Tyrella would remember her own words of wisdom.

"Where would you say the deer fell in that picture?" she asked, thinking it the perfect opportunity to prime the tolerance pump.

"A small corner," Tyrella admitted, handing over the purchase. "If worse comes to worst I'll just have to get a greenhouse and build the fence in the backyard higher to protect my raspberries and blueberries. 'Cause it's not keeping them out and the netting sure isn't stopping them. I think they use it for dental floss."

"I guess you could always get Michelle to chase them away."

"Oh, no. You never heard what happened to Betty's little cockapoo? It went after a doe that came in Betty's yard and the thing beat the poor dog nearly to death with its hooves."

"Seriously? I thought deer were timid."

"I guess not always, especially in spring if there's a fawn around."

"So the deer was protecting its baby," Jenna said. That was understandable.

"There was no fawn anywhere in sight when this happened."

"Maybe it felt threatened."

"Maybe," Tyrella conceded. "But ever since I heard that, I haven't let Michelle out in the backyard by herself."

Jenna had never had a strong opinion about the deer one way or another. She enjoyed seeing them, especially the fawns. But then she didn't have to deal with their eating habits. There were no tempting edibles, either at the motel or Aunt Edie's house—only boxwoods at the corners of the house and some juniper along the front, which weren't attractive to deer. They had no berries or fruit trees to guard, no roses to lose, so obviously she wasn't feeling the local gardeners' pain. On the other hand, many people loved the deer and the tourists were charmed by them. She could only hope she'd be able to present a recommendation that would somewhat pacify everyone.

"At least they don't eat my daisies and lavender in the front," Tyrella finished, sounding resigned. Until she added, "But I still want to see them gone."

Speaking of going. "I'd better get back," Jenna said and scrammed.

Just in time, as Bob Wilson was entering the store. Jenna changed her exit route, detouring past some shelves of garden tools, then ducking out the door before he could spot her.

Back at the inn, she restocked the storeroom with light bulbs, then went to the motel office to post some new pictures on the website. She had some fun beach shots of people flying kites and, ironically, a picture she'd taken of a couple of does grazing on some grass by the entrance to town. The perfect tourist lure. *Come one, come all. See the cause of the Moonlight Harbor civil war.*

Pete actually earned his keep by doing what Jenna had asked of him. Then he shocked her by stopping by the office after and asking if she needed anything else done. Would wonders never cease? She thanked him and let him have the rest of the day off.

The next few days brought sunshine along with some chilly April breezes, and Jenna took advantage of them to air out some of the rooms during the day. There was nothing like fresh air to make a room smell good.

She got a total of six new bookings for Memorial Day weekend, which, counting the room she was saving for Celeste and family, put the Driftwood Inn at full capacity.

All was quiet and calm and happy.

But not for long. Late Friday afternoon, Jenna had just returned from the store where she'd picked up wine and some chocolate-covered almonds for Aunt Edie's weekly Friday night party, when Celeste blew in.

"Hey, there. What are you doing here?" Jenna greeted her sister as she walked through the door holding baby Edie in one arm and the diaper bag in her other hand. Nemo came in next to her, wagging his tail. Something was missing from this picture.

Jenna looked past Celeste but saw no sign of her husband. "Where's Henry?"

Celeste's brows dipped into an angry V. "Henry's home. And I don't want to see him again until Memorial Day... of 2080."

Uh-oh.

Five

Henry was the perfect man for Celeste, solid and practical. He adored her and it had looked like they were going to have one of those marriages other people envied. So what had happened?

"What's going on?" Jenna asked as she followed her sister into the living room. It was all she could do not to add, *Please, I've had enough drama over the last few years. No more.*

"Henry's being a jerk, that's what's going on." Celeste dumped the diaper bag on the floor, then took the baby out of her carrier. She perched on the edge of the couch and began to remove Edie's pink fleece jacket.

"Call the cops," advised Jolly Roger from his cage.

"Good idea," Celeste said. "911-Jerk."

"So you guys had a fight and you walked out?"

Good grief. What could they possibly have found to fight about? Silly question. Every couple found something.

"We had a disagreement and I left."

"Like I said."

"I told him I needed some sister time and he needed to think."

Oh, boy.

Aunt Edie entered the room, drying her hands on a dish towel. "Celeste, dear, this is a nice surprise."

Under the circumstances, *nice* was the wrong word.

"Where's Henry? Is he parking the car?" Aunt Edie asked.

Nemo trotted up to her, tail wagging, and she pushed him away. Only somewhat diplomatically. Aunt Edie and Nemo had never really bonded, thanks to Nemo about scaring the feathers off poor Jolly Roger when Sabrina and Celeste first adopted him.

"Come here, Nemo," Celeste commanded, and the dog trotted back to her and settled at her feet with a doggy groan.

Henry's dog training had worked wonders. It looked like his husband skills hadn't.

"Henry's not with me. On a lot of things," Celeste added irritably.

"Oh, dear," Aunt Edie said, and sat on the nearest chair.

"Okay, spill," Jenna commanded.

"He's being completely unreasonable. I found what could be the perfect house for us on Zillow and he refused to come down and look at it. And now's the time to buy, while prices are still affordable."

"What's his objection?" Jenna asked.

"He wants to wait until we have more money in savings."

"That sounds practical," said Aunt Edie.

"Well, it's not," Celeste insisted. "We can't keep living on a houseboat, Auntie, especially when Edie starts walking. Jenna, you've seen what those rails are like. Once she's mobile she'll be able to climb right over them and fall in Lake Union."

"Henry could adapt them," Jenna suggested.

"And the windows open completely, including the screens. That boat was fine for just the two of us, but now that we've got Edie, we need to change our lifestyle. Besides not being safe for a toddler or preschooler, it's too small. There's barely room for all her things."

Baby Edie had everything a baby could possibly need and a first-time mama could ever want—baby crib, stroller, changing table, toys, highchair (which she didn't even need yet since she was too young to sit up), playpen (ditto), portable baby picnic chair (ditto again), humidifier (pink), and enough clothes to stock a baby boutique. Then there were the lotions, potions, and stacks of baby diapers. All the baby paraphernalia had taken up most of their living space, and Jenna could see how her sister would be ready to move to someplace larger. But they had time.

"We're camping out and I'm tired of it," Celeste continued. "I want Edie to have a nursery."

"If you don't have the money—" Aunt Edie began.

"We have enough for a down payment," Celeste said. "And if we sell the houseboat we'll have plenty. Plus we can easily qualify for a loan. Henry's just being cheap."

"Or cautious. You know, writing isn't the most stable career," Jenna pointed out. "Anything in the arts," she added, thinking of her ex and his far from flourishing career.

Except there was really no comparing Damien and Henry. Damien was a narcissist with not enough talent to justify his narcissism. He'd had no problem spending money, even when they didn't have it and had left Jenna to do all the heavy financial lifting. He was still sponging off of her. Henry, on the other hand, was both humble and responsible. *Jerk* was not the word that came to mind when she thought of her sister's husband.

Celeste gave a snort. "Henry's career is going great. His publisher wants to make him the next Lee Child. Plus he already had money in savings even before he got his contract."

"Wanting and making can be two different things," Jenna said. "You can't blame Henry for looking out for your future and trying to keep an eye on finances. Somebody needs to."

"What's that supposed to mean?" Celeste demanded.

"Well."

"I don't spend that much. So I get a mani-pedi once in a while. So I keep my hair looking good." She looked pointedly at Jenna's hair.

Her highlights weren't so high anymore and she really needed to get to Waves and have Moira do something. But years of penny-pinching had become ingrained and old habits died hard. She always put off going to the salon as long as possible.

"He keeps telling me I have no concept of money. As if I didn't manage my money and pay my own bills when I was single. And pay off my student loans. Sheesh. It's not as if I spend money like I won the lottery, for crying out loud."

"Who are you kidding?" said Jenna, the voice of reason. "You've been on one giant spending binge ever since you married Henry."

"I was working part-time subbing," Celeste said, offended. "I wasn't just blowing through his money. Anyway, it's our money. That's what he's always saying. We're a team."

"Maybe he wants you to be more of a team player, dear," Aunt Edie suggested.

Celeste cuddled the baby to her. "Edie's part of the team,

too. He needs to be thinking about her future, our future as a family."

"It sounds like that's what he's doing by making sure you all are on solid financial ground," Aunt Edie told her.

"I want to be living on solid ground, period. That houseboat is not safe, and we could have a place to live right here…if he'd just come down and look. Honestly, I thought you two would be on my side."

"We're on both your sides," Jenna said.

"You can't be this time. You have to pick one," Celeste informed her.

"Well, stay with us this weekend," Aunt Edie said. "The girls are all coming over tonight and I know they'll love seeing you and the baby. Here, I'll hold her while you bring in the rest of your things."

"Just the weekend? That was subtle," Celeste said as she and Jenna walked to her car. She picked up the portable crib and Jenna grabbed her overnight bag. "Will you go look at the house with me tomorrow?" she asked. "I thought Brody could take us."

"What's the point if Henry isn't ready?" Jenna replied.

"Maybe if Brody thinks he can negotiate a deal, it will change Henry's mind. I can send him pictures."

"He didn't see pictures online?" Jenna asked.

"He did. But he says you can doctor pictures to make a dump look like a castle. This one I saw is no dump, though, and it's not going to last forever. It's got three bedrooms so Edie could have her nursery and Henry could have an office. Two-car garage. Perfect for us. Plus it's on one of the canals."

As if beachfront weren't enough, the town also boasted two lakes and a network of canals, perfect for kayaking and paddle boarding. A house on one of those canals sounded great.

Except, "You were worried about Edie falling off the houseboat. She could fall into the canal, too, you know," Jenna pointed out.

"First she'd have to get out of the fenced backyard. Henry should be jumping all over this. We could get a little fishing boat or one of those party boats."

Jenna gave a snort. "Sure. Why not? You know how expensive those are? Someone had theirs for sale at a garage sale I went to last summer. They wanted ten thousand dollars for the thing."

Celeste's eyes got big. "Oh." But she recovered. "Well, then, a rowboat."

"I don't think the canal is a good idea," Jenna said. "Why don't you try and find something like what Courtney's in? Not on the water but a quick walk to the beach."

Celeste nodded, considering. "That could work."

"Only if you can convince Henry," Jenna reminded her. And Henry could be stubborn when he thought he was right.

"Let's call Brody and see if he can find something," Celeste said eagerly as they walked back in the house.

"All right," Jenna conceded. "But if Henry's not on board, this will be a frustrating waste of time."

"No, it'll be fun," Celeste predicted.

Doing just about anything with her sister was fun. Still, it sure wouldn't be fun if Henry got mad at her for encouraging Celeste to pursue something they didn't agree on. "Don't let him know I'm going with you. I don't want to be named as a co-conspirator," Jenna said, and Celeste chuckled.

Come seven in the evening, several of the women of

Moonlight Harbor gathered in Aunt Edie's living room to drink wine, eat chocolate and other fattening goodies and encourage each other in their various business pursuits. Present were Tyrella Lamb, Annie Albright, Nora Singleton, who'd brought ice cream from the ice cream parlor, Patricia Whiteside, Cindy Redmond, proud owner of Cindy's Candies, and Courtney Moore, who started overloading on chocolate early on.

"So, it's a no-go on buying Beach Babes from Susan?" Tyrella asked her.

Courtney dug another mint truffle out of the candy bowl on the coffee table. "No. She'd rather stay here forever and be miserable than sell to me."

"That's so wrong," said Tyrella, who'd laid claim to the baby and wasn't looking like she'd be giving her up anytime soon.

"That's Susan for you. I wish I was some kind of rich criminal with a shell corporation so I could buy the place," Courtney said.

"What about applying for a Blue Moon grant?" asked Celeste. "It sure helped Jenna."

Courtney shook her head. "I thought about it but I'd need more money than the grant could give me."

"It would be a great investment if you could get it," said Patricia.

"Of course, the value is in the building, not the inventory," put in Tyrella.

"For sure. None of the inventory is anything anyone would want," Courtney said. "I think I'd feel guilty even donating those clothes to a nonprofit shop."

"Once upon a time, when she first opened, her clothes were in style," Patricia said. "She did a fairly good business."

"Styles change," Courtney said. "Adapt or die," she added, showing no mercy. "I know I could make that shop a roaring success." She gave a half-hearted shrug. "Oh, well. It looks like I'm not going to get it. Susan's said she'll never sell to me. She'll price it too high."

"That woman," Nora muttered, shaking her head in disgust. "She never appreciated what she had when you were working for her. It's foolish not to encourage talent."

"Yes, it is. She could only have benefitted by selling your designs," said Patricia. "Like I did," she added, smiling at Courtney. "By the way, don't worry about any sour grapes from me if you get a chance to move on and move up."

"Thanks," Courtney said. "You are a class act."

"All our Moonlight Harbor business mavens are," Jenna said, thinking of Aunt Edie and Nora. They were all an inspiration to the entrepreneurs coming along behind them. "Something will work out somewhere," she assured Courtney. "Meanwhile, you're doing all right where you are."

"Her creations fly out the door of my gift shop," said Patricia.

Courtney did smile at that. "I owe you big time for taking a chance on me and letting me sell my clothes at the Oyster Inn."

"Women love them," Patricia said.

Courtney sighed. "I really want to expand. I thought Beach Babes would be perfect."

"You can always sell online," Cindy suggested.

"I've got some things on Etsy," Courtney said, "and I'm looking into Amazon. So, really, why do I need a shop here?" She said it so wistfully.

"Because this is your hometown," Annie said. "And those shops are really cute. We get it."

"We sure do," said Nora, helping herself to another piece of the chocolate bark Cindy had brought.

"Don't give up. Miracles still happen," said Tyrella, and passed the plate of chocolate bark to Courtney.

Courtney smiled at all of them. "You guys are the best when it comes to encouraging people. Thanks."

"That's what we're here for," Tyrella said.

"Here's to friends," Courtney said. "Wait a minute. My glass is empty. How can I toast with an empty glass?"

"Let's take care of that," Jenna said, and fetched the bottle of her favorite white wine from the dining table.

Courtney filled it. "Okay, now. Here's to friends."

"To friends," everyone echoed.

"You have such an awesome support group down here," Celeste said to Jenna later when it was just the two of them in the living room, visiting.

Baby Edie was tucked in her portable crib up in Jenna's room, which she and Celeste were sharing for the weekend. Sabrina was spending the night with her friend Taylor, and Aunt Edie had gone to bed shortly after the last guests left.

"It is great."

"That's another reason I want to be down here. Where do you find this kind of community?"

"All over America, I'm sure."

"Probably. But Moonlight Harbor is special."

"Yes, it is. I can't imagine living anywhere else," Jenna said. "Thank God for Aunt Edie."

Celeste's smile shrank a little. "Is it my imagination or is she looking more frail these days?"

Jenna let her concern escape in a sigh. "She is getting up there."

"Lots of people live to be ninety. I hope she turns out to be one of them. Maybe if we got her to slow down a little."

"Don't think I haven't tried."

"Let's lock her in her room," Celeste said with a grin.

"She'd probably pick the lock."

The sisters were silent a moment. Then Celeste said, "I really want to be here with you. I could help if we were."

"Hopefully, we'll have Mom for that soon."

"Another reason to be in Moonlight Harbor," Celeste said sourly. "My whole family's here."

"At least you can come visit."

"Or I can move down and Henry can come visit."

"You know you wouldn't really do that."

"Maybe I would," Celeste said, lifting her chin. "Darn it all. He needs to figure some things out."

"It sounds like he's trying," Jenna said. "And you have time. Edie isn't even crawling yet."

"I don't want to wait 'til the last minute. I don't understand what he doesn't get about that."

"He probably gets more than you think. Knowing Henry he'll come up with a plan." Celeste said nothing, and Jenna continued. "Have a little faith in him. You've got a good man."

"I know." Celeste examined a perfectly manicured fingernail. "So, you think I'm being…"

"A brat?" Jenna supplied, and Celeste frowned at her. "It's a strong possibility."

"Maybe I should call him."

"Maybe you should. I heard your phone ping several times when the women were here." And saw her shut it off.

Celeste's famous mischievous smile came back full force. "It's good to make him sweat a little."

Jenna shook her head. "I don't know how he puts up with you. You're so spoiled."

"Baby of the family," Celeste said with an unrepentant

grin. She sobered. "I guess I can be patient a little longer. But I still want to look at houses, so call Brody."

"Are you sure that's a good idea? I mean, what are you going to do if you find one you like?"

"Convince Henry to come down and check it out."

Back to square one, Jenna thought. Poor Henry. He was married to a steamroller.

Celeste went upstairs to have a conversation with her long-suffering husband, and Jenna put in a call to Brody.

"Hey there," he said. "Is girl time over?"

"Yep. How would you like to have some girl time tomorrow?"

"With my favorite girl? Sure."

"And her sister."

"Celeste's down?"

"She wants to look at houses."

"So she talked Henry into taking the leap, huh?"

"Hardly. Right now she's the only one leaping. She came down by herself."

"Showing houses when only one half of the couple is on board doesn't usually go real well," Brody said.

"I know. I think she's sure if she finds a bargain she can convince him to go along. You don't mind, do you?"

"No, not at all."

"Even though she's just a lookie-loo."

"Some of my best customers started out as lookie-loos," he said. "That's the nature of the business. People have to look around to get an idea of what they want."

"She knows what she wants. Got to have three bedrooms so the baby can have a nursery and Henry can have an office."

"On the beach?"

"Not necessarily, but near it. Kind of like what Court-ney's in."

"I've got a couple. One needs some TLC, but it's a bargain."

"Henry would like that."

"Another just came up a couple blocks away from Court-ney's. Three bedrooms and an easy walk to the beach. Motivated sellers."

"Sounds great."

"Okay. I'll do some checking and see if I find anything else. I'll pick you two up at ten thirty."

Even if Celeste didn't wind up buying a house, it would be fun to go looking. Fun to be with Brody.

When was it not fun to be with Brody? The man was good-humored and easygoing, a good listener and her number one fan. And he wanted to commit to her. Yep, he was the right choice.

Sabrina was summoned home the next morning to baby-sit and Brody picked the sisters up promptly at ten thirty. He'd even gotten lattes for them.

"Curbside service," he said with a smile.

"You are such a keeper," Celeste said, beaming at him.

"That's what I've been telling your sister," he said and winked at Jenna. "So, got three places to show you. The first one, the price is right but you need to keep an open mind." He handed over printed sheets with pictures of the houses along with pertinent information.

Celeste looked at the top one and her brow wrinkled. "You're kidding, right?"

"It needs a little a work," he said glibly.

There was an understatement. They pulled up in front of a two-story house near the beach that had not been loved for a long time. The garage door was rusted, and the siding on one side of the house had slid off and was lying on the ground.

"An easy fix," Brody told Celeste. "I bet you could get Victor King to take care of that in his off hours. He loves projects."

"Projects," Celeste echoed weakly as they followed him up the walk.

"It's got potential," Jenna said.

Celeste said nothing.

The inside of the house was also a mess, with a kitchen that had been built in the seventies. The dirty orange carpet on the living room floor had little mushrooms growing in one corner.

"Maybe there's hardwood underneath," Jenna said. She went to one corner where the carpet was frayed and coming up, pulled it back and little and checked. Nope. No hardwood. "Never mind."

Celeste sniffed and made a face. "That smell."

"They had pets," Brody said.

"We've got a pet too, and our houseboat doesn't smell like this," she said, disgusted.

"You can get it for a song."

"This is one song I don't want to sing," Celeste said, and turned and walked right back out the front door before they could see any more.

"Really?" Jenna said, cocking an eyebrow at Brody.

"You said she wanted a bargain."

"The only person getting a bargain out of this would be the seller," Jenna said.

"Okay, on to the next one."

The second house was the one Celeste had seen online. The kitchen had been remodeled, which she loved.

But there was a problem. The hallway leading to the bedrooms tilted at a slant.

"I think I'm getting seasick," Jenna said.

"Sometimes houses settle. You might have to jack up the foundation," Brody said.

"Jack up the foundation?" Celeste repeated weakly. "That doesn't sound good."

"It's not that big a deal," Brody said.

"Maybe not to you," she muttered. She poked her head into the first bedroom. "Gosh, it's small."

"It could work for Edie," Jenna said. "But that hallway."

"I guess it's a good thing Henry didn't come down," said Celeste.

"For sure." Jenna could envision what Henry would have had to say about buying a house that had dropped its siding or one with possible foundation issues.

The last house was a different matter. It was near Courtney's street, and both sisters fell in love with it at first sight. It was more expensive than the first two, but a good example of the old saying that you get what you pay for. With two stories and a bay window in the living room, it was white with blue trim and had a picket fence around the front yard. The front porch held two white wooden rocking chairs and a wicker basket filled with sand dollars. It had laminate throughout, and the kitchen had been updated with quartz countertops.

"This is perfect," Celeste said, taking pictures as they passed through the various rooms. "And Henry could use that little area between the two bedrooms for his office."

"Not a bad price," Brody said. "Motivated sellers, so I think they'd be willing to come down in price a little."

Celeste was already calling Henry. "You have to come down and see this," she told him. "It's perfect for us. Two bedrooms and an office area, two-car garage. Nice neighborhood. The beach is a five-minute walk from here." She was silent, listening. Then, "Brody says the sellers are motivated. We might be able to get it for less than the asking price." Another pause. "Asking price?"

Jenna could picture Henry's frown as her sister shared the price. It was a fair one and the house would be a great starter home for them.

"Henry," Celeste said through gritted teeth, "nobody's giving away houses these days."

Whatever Henry said, it wasn't, *You're right, dear.* Celeste ended the call and growled.

"Not interested?" Jenna guessed.

"He wants to wait until his next advance check comes at the end of the month. This house will be gone by then, I know it."

"Houses come on the market all the time," Brody said to her as he locked the place back up.

"Yes, but not that one. It's perfect for us."

"You'll find something, I promise," he said easily. "And if it's any consolation, everyone has a story about the dream house that got away. You'd be surprised how many dream houses are out there."

"I guess," Celeste said. "I think I'm going to poison my husband."

"She's kidding," Jenna said to Brody, who was looking shocked.

"Sort of," Celeste added.

They started back to the car and Jenna said, "Speaking of finding dream houses…"

"You in the market?" Brody asked in surprise.

"No, I love where I am. And actually, this isn't a house.

It's a shop. Did you hear that Susan Frank is talking about selling Beach Babes?"

"No. Is Courtney going to buy it?"

"Not if Susan has anything to say about it."

"You can't discriminate."

"She'll find a way around that," Jenna said. "She as much as told Courtney she'll either price her out or not sell at all."

"That woman is a blight," Brody said in disgust.

"I wish I could afford to buy it," Jenna said. "I'd resell it to Courtney. Think I could swing a business loan?"

"From Sherwood?" Brody sounded dubious.

Sherwood Stern at Harbor First National hadn't exactly rolled out the red carpet to help Jenna when she was fixing up the Driftwood Inn.

But, "I've turned things around since the last time I was in to beg, er, see him. Maybe he'd give me a loan."

"Maybe," Brody said. "But I wouldn't hold my breath if I was you."

"It doesn't seem right," Jenna said with a sigh. "She's the perfect one to own that business."

"Think she could make a go of it? I suspect Susan's just hanging on by a thread. No pun intended."

"I'm sure she could. She's talented and ambitious. She just doesn't happen to have a lot of money."

"It always comes back to that, whether you're buying a house or a business," Brody said.

It wasn't exactly a chatty ride back to Aunt Edie's. Celeste was disappointed and her bubbly personality had gone flat.

"Thanks for taking me to see the house," she said to Brody before she got out of the car. "Sorry I wasted your time."

"Hanging out with the prettiest sisters in Washington is never a waste of time," he told her with a smile.

"You are so…right," she said, and managed a smile in return. "I'll leave you two to sit here and sizzle for a while," she added, then got out, shut the door and went back into the house.

Brody waggled his eyebrows at Jenna. "Wanna sizzle?"

"Maybe," she said. "How about tomorrow after Celeste goes home?"

"Fine with me. I'll buy you dinner before line dancing."

"Good," she said, and started to let herself out.

He caught her arm and gave her his thousand-watt Brody Green smile. "How about a little something to tide me over?"

"Haven't you heard? Waiting makes the heart grow fonder."

"I don't think my heart could grow any fonder of you," he said softly. "Come here."

Well, what was a little sizzle between friends?

And boy could he sizzle. Before she knew it, Jenna's lips were on fire and so was the rest of her. "You make me dizzy," she said after a couple of long and lovely kisses.

"That's just a sample. Wait 'til we really get down to business."

Get down to business. She knew what that meant. But jumping into bed with Brody was the ultimate commitment, and as far as she was concerned that meant taking a chance on marriage again. The fire she'd been feeling got a little smaller.

"Promise me you won't rush me," she said.

"We haven't exactly been rushing things, Jenna," he pointed out.

She bit her lip. "I know. It's just… I don't know what's

wrong with me." She'd made her choice. She should be more than ready to act on it.

"I do. You're afraid. I get it. But not every man is like your ex."

She nodded. "I know." And Brody had proved himself to be trustworthy.

"But no rushing," he promised. "Just a little nudging," he added with a wink.

Maybe a little more nudging was all she needed.

By the time she got in the house, Celeste had a bottle and was feeding the baby. Good smells were coming from the kitchen.

"Aunt Edie's making grilled cheese sandwiches for lunch and she made brownies," Celeste said. "Maybe it's for the best we're not down here full-time. If I'm around her baking for long, I'll end up gaining ten pounds."

"You'll find the right place when the time is right, I'm sure," Jenna said.

"I guess. And maybe once Henry gets that next chunk of money, he'll feel better about taking the leap and getting a house. I'll just have to be patient."

"Patience pays off. Remember how long it took you to find the right man," Jenna said.

Celeste rolled her eyes. "Don't remind me."

"But it was worth it. He really is great."

"I know." Celeste looked down at her baby. "I guess I should be glad I have such a cautious man for a husband. He's only trying to make sure we don't end up in over our heads financially."

"That's very insightful of you," Jenna said. Not something her sister would normally say.

"Those aren't my words. It's what he said. He's right,

though. How can I stay mad at him when he's trying to look out for us?"

Jenna smiled at that. "I guess this means you'll be going home tomorrow?"

"I guess you're right. Sister time is over."

Celeste put the baby over her shoulder and began to pat her back. Jenna remembered doing that with her daughter. Unlike Celeste, she hadn't had the luxury of being a stay-at-home mom for long. Someone had needed to bring in a steady paycheck.

"You're lucky to have such a good man," she said.

"I'm thinking you're getting pretty lucky these days, too. Have you finally made a decision?"

"I have," Jenna said.

"Brody's a great guy." Celeste studied Jenna. "But are you sure?"

"I think I am."

Thinking she was sure. Was that the same as being sure? Who knew?

One thing she knew. A little sizzle on a cold spring night would sure feel good.

Six

"Was it my imagination or was Brody's car getting pretty steamed up out there in the parking lot?" Courtney teased when Jenna stopped in at the office Monday night after a date with Brody to make sure all was well.

Even though Courtney was busy creating designs and her clothes were selling well at the little shop in the Oyster Inn, she still needed the extra money. Jenna was glad for the extra help. It was a win-win.

"Talking steams up windows, you know," Jenna said. There'd been some talk. And some nudging. On top of the nudging Sunday night she'd been good and nudged.

"Right," Courtney said with a knowing smile.

They should never have gone to the Monday night special at the little movie house. A remake of *Pride and Prejudice* had been playing. Romantic movies always left her feeling mushy.

"You can probably pack it in for the night. I don't think we'll hear much from our remaining guests," Jenna said, changing the subject. The last of the weekend guests had checked out that morning and only one couple remained, a retired pair, newly married.

"Haven't heard a peep out of the lovebirds," Courtney said. "You got two new bookings through the website for June. Putting up that picture of the deer was a good idea."

"The deer. Don't remind me. The next council meeting will be here before I know it and I still have a bunch of research to do."

"You should have told me. I could have done some of that tonight."

"No biggie. I'll get it done tomorrow. Did you sketch any new designs?"

Courtney whipped out her sketch pad and showed Jenna a design for capris and a top that was both sophisticated and playful.

"I'd buy that outfit in a heartbeat," Jenna said. "You are so talented."

Courtney shrugged. "Yeah. Look out, Marc Jacobs."

"Would you be crushed if you didn't become world famous?" Jenna asked.

"Oh, I don't know. I think really, I'd be happy making a splash right here. Maybe whoever takes over Beach Babes will have some vision and want to sell my clothes there."

"That would probably be better in the long run than you owning the shop," Jenna said.

A frown settled on Courtney's face. "I know. It's stupid to want to buy it. But I do. Don't ask me why."

"Well, now I have to ask. Why?"

"I guess I'd like to really feel like a legit member of the chamber of commerce. I'd like to have something concrete that I own. Even back when I was working for Susan, I saw so much potential for Beach Babes, so many fun things you could do there, like fashion shows and classes on style. I saw it as kind of a hub for the women here, a little like what Waves is." She shook her head. "Maybe I've watched too many movies."

"You never know. Maybe you'll still end up putting on fashion shows there, only without the headache of owning the business."

"Hey, I still have a business and the headache. It's just not a very big one yet."

"Your business is going to grow," Jenna assured her. "You're too good for it not to. And then, when you get really big and famous, we'll lose you. You'll go off to New York or live in Paris."

"No, everything I really want is right here in Moonlight Harbor."

"You mean everyone," Jenna said.

That made Courtney smile. "Yep. Life's good at the beach." She sobered. "I wish I could find a way to make it even better."

Jenna couldn't see how Courtney would be able to make buying Beach Babes happen. She wished she could afford to buy the business and resell it to her friend. Darn, but sometimes it came in handy being rich.

Everything Courtney wanted was, indeed, in Moonlight Harbor, including Beach Babes Boutique. Feeling nothing ventured, nothing gained, she took a chance and went to see a loan officer at Harbor First National Bank.

Okay, so much for nothing ventured, nothing gained. She left feeling like a loser. Why had she bothered? She'd known it was a losing proposition before she walked in. But she'd been desperate and grasping at the proverbial straws.

So she didn't make a ton of money. She was employed, though, and her business was growing. She'd taken along her spreadsheets to prove it. What were banks for if not to loan you money?

Not that she'd known exactly how much she needed. That probably hadn't impressed the loan officer, even though she'd explained that she was just putting out feelers. It was hard to say how much money you needed to buy a shop when the woman selling had no intention of telling you what she was asking. Did Susan want to sell Beach Babes or didn't she, for crying out loud? And really, what did she care who bought it if she wanted out? Why was she being so stubborn?

Pride, of course. If Courtney, her former employee and now competitor, took over and made a success of the shop, it would kill the old sour lemon. She'd probably find someone to make a deal with on the sly. That way she couldn't be accused of discriminating against anybody.

Still, Courtney had hoped that if she could float a loan, she'd be able to wave a wad of cash under Susan's nose and change her mind. What little mind the woman had left.

If only she knew somebody with a lot of money who wanted to take a risk on her. Her parents would have in a heartbeat, but they'd recently gotten a home improvement loan to put on a new roof and redo their kitchen, and they didn't have any money to spare. Her sister had bought a house and was also on a tight budget. Jonas was always supportive and encouraging, but he'd recently used his savings for the down payment on his place.

There had to be someone. Sadly, she couldn't think of anyone.

"You don't need Beach Babes, anyway," Jonas said to her when she was grumbling her way through their lunch date at Beachside Burgers. "You've got plenty of work to keep you busy already, right?"

"I could be busier," she said. "I'd like to do this full-time at some point and not have to be working part-time at the Driftwood. Not that I don't like working for Jenna, but I want to build my own empire."

He took a gulp of his milkshake. "I get that. It's about doing what you were put here to do."

Jonas was definitely doing what he'd been put on earth to do. He loved his job, especially loved it when he actually got to fight a fire. Most of the time work consisted of cleaning the fire truck, working out or doing school visits.

That was fine with Courtney. She didn't like to think of him risking his life, even if it was for her fellow Moonlight Harbor residents. Firefighters faced more than a fierce blaze when they went to put out a fire, thanks to increased use of plastics and synthetic materials in home construction. She'd read the studies that linked firefighters' on-the-job exposure to chemicals and toxins in urban blazes with an increased risk of cancer. At least the Moonlight Harbor Fire Department was on the ball, providing a chemical detox sauna for their men. Still, every time they got called out, they put their lives on the line for the people in their community. Noble work.

"I'm not exactly saving lives like you," she said.

"You save my life every time we're together," he said with a grin. "And what you do is cool. It's like art. It makes people happy."

"Women at least."

"And guys. I like seeing you in the stuff you design. It's hot."

"You're biased."

"I don't think so," he said, and took a big bite of his hamburger.

She pushed hers away, half-eaten.

"You not gonna eat that?" he asked.

"It's all yours." She didn't have that much of an appetite. Thank you, Susan Frank.

"Something will work out. Hang in there," he advised. "Doors have a way of opening at the right time. Look at me. I was a volunteer for three years before I finally got my job here."

"That was definitely the right door," she said.

"Yeah, 'cause I met you."

There was something to be grateful for.

After lunch, Jonas left to get ready to go to the station, and she went home to work on another dress to sell at the Oyster Inn. "You're doing what you like and people are buying your clothes," she lectured herself. "Don't be such an ungrateful bitch."

There. Lecture completed. *Now, get happy.*

She didn't make it to happy. Didn't make it to contented either. Until Jonas's day off when they spent the whole day together and she wound up tangled in his sheets and his arms later that night. Okay, life wasn't so bad.

A couple of days later she was in Beachside Grocery in the cookie aisle and heard voices in the next aisle over. Susan Frank and Kiki Strom.

"I won't be at the next chamber of commerce meeting," Susan said to Kiki. "I've got too much to do. I'm moving. I'm going to live with my daughter in Oregon. The beaches there are much nicer than here."

"I don't know. I think our beaches are pretty special," Kiki said. "But it will be nice to be with your daughter. What about your business?"

"I sold it."

Sold it. Courtney felt like she'd just been doused with ice water. Sold. To who?

"Oh, did Courtney buy it?"

"Her? Certainly not. I wouldn't sell to that cocky little upstart if my life depended on it."

Courtney clamped her lips together. Better to be a cocky little upstart than a dried-up lemon. She grabbed a package of Oreos. Extra filling.

"Then who?" Kiki asked.

"Someone who knows a lot about business. He appreciates what I've been providing all these years."

Someone who appreciated ugly, outdated styles?

"He wants to see Beach Babes keep going."

It would have a better chance of that with Susan out of the picture, for sure.

"Well, who is it?" Kiki pressed.

"You'll see," Susan replied coyly. "This buyer paid cash, gave me asking price, no dickering. Now I can leave town happily, knowing the shop will be in good hands. I just put the house up for sale yesterday."

"My, that's fast."

"When the time is right, the time is right," Susan said.

Courtney grabbed another package of Oreos. The time obviously hadn't been right for her. It had been a pipe dream, anyway, but still. This sucked. This really, really sucked.

Damn it all, who had bought Beach Babes?

Seven

Courtney kept telling herself it wasn't meant to be, but that didn't make knowing someone else had bought Beach Babes any easier.

"That sucks," Jonas said when she called him with the news.

Great minds thought alike. "That's what I say," she said miserably.

"But hey, whoever bought it will probably sell your stuff there. That's the main thing, right?"

"It is," she admitted. Maybe she only wanted the shop for the same reason Susan didn't want her to have it. Good old pride.

"Let it go," she told herself as she drove to the Driftwood on a late Monday afternoon to take the evening shift for Jenna. That was the healthy thing to do. Sadly, she couldn't seem to pry her emotional grip from the place.

Jenna was still in the office, paying some bills online, when Courtney came in clutching her cookies, her hair drippy from the rain. Her smile died at the sight of her friend walking into the little room behind the reception desk.

"What's wrong? Did you and Jonas break up?"

There. That put it in perspective. At least, it should have.

"No, we're good," Courtney said. "Somebody bought Beach Babes."

"Oh, no. Who?"

"I don't know."

"Then how do you know somebody bought it?"

"Because I overheard Susan telling Kiki Strom when I was at the store." She pulled out the cookies she'd bought and opened the package. Held it out to Jenna. "Want one?"

"No, thanks. With all the goodies Aunt Edie bakes, I'm already turning into Jabba the Hutt. Nothing fits."

Courtney frowned and dumped the package in the wastebasket. "Good point. Anyway, sugar won't help. My sorrow is too deep."

"I'm sorry," Jenna said. "I wish you could have gotten it. If I had the money I'd have helped you."

"I know you would," Courtney said. She heaved a sigh. "I guess I'll have to wait 'til I'm rich and famous to set up my own clothing store here in town."

"You won't need to. You'll be selling to major outlets all over the world."

"I don't know," Courtney said. "I guess if I wanted that kind of success I'd have moved to New York long ago. I think I just want to be the big fish in the small pond. Best of both worlds that way, because Moonlight Harbor has my heart." And so did Jonas.

Jenna nodded. "I hear you. You can put down roots in a hurry here."

"You sure did. Ever see yourself leaving?"

Jenna shook her head. "I've got the motel and Aunt Edie, all my friends. Got Mom moving down and Celeste, too, probably. And Sabrina's going to go to the local community college and expects to live at home. My roots are too deep now."

"Who'd have thought roots could grow so deep in the sand," Courtney said.

"I know, right?" Jenna backed out of the program she'd been using and pushed away from the desk. "Guess I'll get over to the house and try to convince Aunt Edie to let me help with making dinner."

"Good luck with that," Courtney said. Edie Patterson was practically welded to her stove. There'd be no pulling her out of the kitchen.

Jenna left and Courtney settled down to read the new Jill Barnett historical novel she'd loaded onto her phone. There were no guests due to check in, and the few that were still in the motel had already enjoyed Edie Patterson's cookies, so they wouldn't be back. It would probably be a quiet night. Just Courtney and her book and her misery.

She dug the package of cookies back out of the wastebasket. Her sorrow may have been deep but she'd paid for the cookies so there was no point in wasting them.

She was halfway through the package and feeling slightly ill when she heard a car pull up outside. People sometimes came in without reservations, hoping for a room, but usually not this early in the year.

She left the office and went to the reception desk to see who was venturing out on a rainy spring night. It wasn't a guest. It was Brody Green.

"Jenna's at the house," she told him when he dashed into the office, brushing rain off his windbreaker.

"Actually, I'm here to see you," he said.

"Me?" Why on earth would Brody want to see her?

"I just bought a business and I'm thinking it might have been a mistake."

"Mr. Wheeler Dealer? When it comes to business you never make mistakes."

"I think this time I have."

"Can't you back out of the deal?"

"I paid cash. It's a fait accompli. Everything will be final in a week. But it's really not me."

"Okay, I'm dying of curiosity. What the heck did you buy?" she asked.

"Beach Babes."

"B-Beach Babes? You bought Beach Babes?" Brody Green bought Susan's business and he didn't even want it? Life was so not fair.

"I'm thinking you might want to buy it," he said, helping himself to one of the three remaining cookies on the plate that Edie kept filled every day.

"Wait a minute," Courtney said suspiciously.

"We can work out a deal. You can make monthly payments."

"Brody Green, did you really want that business?"

"No, but I heard you did," he said, and flashed that gorgeous grin he was famous for among all the women of Moonlight Harbor.

"Oh, my gosh. You did this for me?" If he did, Brody was the world's best Good Samaritan.

His face reddened and he shrugged. "I heard you were having some trouble negotiating with Susan."

"Negotiating? Susan doesn't know the meaning of the word."

"So, want to talk business?" he asked.

Did she! Excitement was bubbling up in her so fast she was sure she'd explode.

"You bet." Except. "How much did you pay for it? Maybe I can't afford it."

"I'll carry the contract and we'll make sure you can. Let's crunch some numbers."

She led him into the back office and they did the number crunching. Brody had paid a fair market price and Susan had been happy to take the deal. Now he was offering it to Courtney for considerably less than he paid for it.

"I can't do that," she protested, horrified. "It wouldn't be right."

"It would for me. I need a write-off. So, how about you manage it for me for the first six months. Then I'll sell it to you and you can start making payments. Whatever profit above your salary that you bring in during that time can go toward paying for the shop."

"Sounds like a good deal for one of us," she said.

"It's a good deal all around," he said easily and held out a hand. "Shake on it?"

"You bet!"

They shook hands. Then he said, "Once my deal with Susan goes through I'll get the papers written up and we can sign our agreement."

"You are something else," Courtney said gratefully.

"So I hear. See you later."

Then he was gone, leaving Courtney half wondering if she'd dreamed what had just happened. But no, she hadn't. There'd been three cookies left on the plate. Now there were two.

She grabbed her cell phone and called Annie, who was home prepping to cater a Kiwanis luncheon the next day. "You'll never guess what just happened," she said breathlessly.

"What?"

"Brody Green bought Beach Babes and he's going to resell it to me for dirt cheap."

"Oh, my gosh. Seriously?"

"Seriously. I am so shook."

Annie chuckled. "So much for Susan not wanting to sell it to you."

"So much for Susan, period."

"Pretty funny," Annie said. "Here she thinks she's been so clever and really Brody's made a total fool of her."

"Not to her face. I'm going to be managing it for the first six months with the option to buy. By the time it's mine Susan will be long gone."

"So no pouring salt in the wound."

"I don't need to," Courtney said. "Karma will get the old sour lemon without any help from me. I don't need to be part of that."

"You're right. You don't. I'm glad for you. But are you going to have enough inventory to fill the place?"

"It'll take a while. I'll have to stock it with some other brands as well. And I'll have to tell Patricia I won't be selling in her gift store anymore."

"She'll miss that, but I know she'll be glad for you, too," Annie said.

"I still can't believe it," Courtney said happily.

"Really generous on Brody's part," said Annie.

"He's something else."

No wonder Jenna had finally settled on him. Maybe they would be a good match. They both sure had a lot of heart.

Courtney ended the call, hugged her sketch book and twirled around. "My own shop!" Now the beach really did have everything she'd ever want.

Cinco de Mayo came, bringing another birthday for Jenna. Forty-four. She was getting old.

"I remember when I used to like having birthdays," she said to Aunt Edie.

"You're just a baby," Aunt Edie scoffed. "You have lots of life left to live."

Aunt Edie was right, but it was hard for Jenna not to focus on how much of hers had already slipped away. Not to mention how much of it she was still wasting by keeping herself in love limbo.

Courtney tried to ease the pain by planning a surprise party for her at Sandy's, where they were offering specials on mojitos. Celeste came down and brought Mel, and all Jenna's friends from the chamber of commerce showed up. She received enough chocolate from everyone to put her in a diabetic coma, along with flowers from both Seth and Brody. Brody's bouquet was bigger.

Not big enough to hide the fact that she was another year older. Ugh.

"You're not getting older, you're getting better," he assured her later when it was only the two of them, parked in his car at the beach, watching the moonlight dance on the water. "According to scientists, you're hitting your peak sexually. I may not be able to keep up."

That made her laugh. "Yeah, right, I'm believing that."

"But I'll try," he added, and kissed her. Oh, yes, the man had more sizzle than a pan full of bacon. "You're killing me," he said when she broke away before clothes could start getting shed right there in the front seat. "Come back to my place and let's make this worth our while. You know you want to."

She did. And yet something kept holding her back.

Fear. She gave Seth such a bad time about being a chicken, but it turned out he wasn't the only clucker in Moonlight Harbor.

"Just a little more time," she said. "I need to be sure."

He looked hurt. "Seriously? What are we doing, then?"

"Making sure. I know I'm being a flake but…" Her voice trailed off. How long before you recovered from a divorce, anyway? "I keep thinking, what if something goes wrong?"

"I'll make sure it doesn't." He slipped a lock of hair behind her ear. "I get it, Jenna. I really do. Your ex did a number on you. But I promise I'm not him. How long do you want to stand in the doorway watching the party instead of joining it?"

"Good point."

"So then, let's go back to my place."

"Soon."

He smiled ruefully. "Did I mention I hate cold showers?"

"I'm sorry." And she really was. It wasn't fair to keep the poor man hanging. "You should give up and go find someone else."

"I don't want anyone else. I want you. And I don't give up easily."

That was obvious.

Since he'd paid cash, Brody's deal with Susan closed in record time, and by the Saturday after Jenna's birthday party, Courtney and Annie and Moira were in the shop, busy boxing up the ugly clothes that had once defined Beach Babes. They'd actually found a thrift store willing to take them. Proceeds went to a women's shelter in nearby Aberdeen, and the store owner was more than happy to take both the clothes and the donation Courtney had given her.

"So, basically, you bribed her to take them," Annie said.

"Something like that," Courtney said.

"Somebody might want them. They're not all that bad," put in Moira.

"They're not all that good, either," Courtney said. "But hey, if the shop owner is happy, so am I."

"We need to paint this place," Moira said, looking at the ugly brown walls. "This color is way too dark. Something neutral, like a cream."

"Good idea," Courtney said. "I want the walls to enhance the clothes, not compete with them for attention."

"I wonder if you could find one of those old-fashioned mirrors to stand in one corner," Moira continued. "You know, the ones where you can tilt the mirror. What are those called?"

"Cheval, I think," Annie said.

"Cheval," Moira said, trying out the word. "That would be cute. Paint the purchase counter white and stencil some blue fish on the front of it," she continued, "to give the place a beach feel."

"And add a sign on the wall that says Life's Good at the Beach," added Annie.

Yes, it sure was. "I like that. Maybe I'll see if I can find a glass-top table to display socks on."

"Did you order some fun, funky ones?" Moira asked.

"Of course," said Courtney.

Moira pulled out her cell phone and began scrolling through it. "I was thinking about you yesterday and saw the cutest wallpaper. I thought you could put it in your changing booths." She turned her phone so Courtney could see the screen.

"Oh, my gosh, flip-flops. I love it! I swear if you weren't so good with hair you could become an interior decorator."

"I love making things pretty," Moira said.

She'd certainly done that for Waves Salon, which she

was now managing for Pearl Wellman. Pearl wasn't around much anymore. She had a man in her life and had spent the winter at his digs in Palm Desert.

"I really appreciate both of you taking time to help me with this place," Courtney said.

"You helped me when I needed a place to stay," Annie reminded her. "I'm glad I can finally do something for you."

"You're the best, both of you," Courtney said.

It was Saturday morning. Annie had a party to cater that evening and Moira would have to leave for the salon soon. Both women were busy with their own careers but still taking time to help her. And Jenna and Brody were coming over in the afternoon to help haul the boxes of clothes to the thrift store. Tyrella had offered Courtney a twenty percent discount on anything she might need from Beach Lumber and Hardware. Talk about good friends! Courtney had found treasure at the beach more valuable than anything any pirate could ever imagine.

"So when do we paint?" Moira asked. "I could help tomorrow. Victor's off, too."

"I can do tomorrow," Annie said.

"Then let's paint tomorrow," said Courtney. "I'll hit the hardware store after this and pick up some."

"This is going to be so amazing when you get it done," Moira said. "Have you thought about when you want to have your grand opening?"

"Memorial Day," Annie said. "You should shoot for that. We'll have lots of visitors in town."

"That hardly gives me any time," Courtney said, thinking of all the things she needed to do—what she still wanted to order. And make.

"You've been ordering things since the minute you

struck the deal with Brody. And Patricia's giving you all the clothes you had in her gift shop, right?"

"Yeah, but I still need more than that," Courtney said, fearful of running out of merchandise.

There was so much to opening up a boutique. She'd known that in her head, but the reality of it was overwhelming. At least she already had some of what she needed—hangers, mannequins, shopping bags—and she didn't have to worry about coming up with the money to stock the shop. Brody had given her carte blanche. Still, she'd eventually be on the hook for material she'd bought and all those extra purchases, and she was trying not to go crazy and overstock. It was a fine balance between having enough and having too much.

"Annie's right. You should shoot for Memorial Day weekend," Moira said. "We can help you get set up. Ooh, and you could have a fashion show on that Saturday afternoon as part of your grand opening. That would really bring in people."

"A fashion show?" On top of pulling together the shop. Her head would blow off.

"It doesn't have to be like New York Fashion Week, you know," Moira said. "Just a small one."

"Would you be one of my models?" Courtney asked her. With her pretty face and that long hair gleaming iridescent like a pearl, Moira would be striking.

"Sure. I'll close the salon for a couple of hours. I wouldn't have anyone coming in anyway. Everyone will want to be at your grand opening."

"I'll give you a discount on whatever outfit you choose."

"Me, too?" Annie asked.

Annie was, by nature, shy, but catering had been bringing her out of her shell. And getting her hair done for free in exchange for being a hair model when Pearl had her grand reopening of Waves had given her a taste for bartering.

"Absolutely," Courtney said.

Maybe Jenna would model, too. And if her sister was in town, Courtney knew she could be counted on as well.

"We'd only model your clothes, though, right?" Moira asked.

"For sure."

A fashion show featuring her designs—who said dreams didn't come true?

"Still, it's a lot to pull off in a short time."

"You can do it," Moira assured her. "We'll help make it happen."

A sudden angry rapping on the shop window made Courtney jump. She had a sign up telling shoppers they were closed for renovation. Who the heck?

She looked up to see Susan Frank standing at the door, looking angry enough to chew her way through the glass.

Eight

Courtney's heart did a sick flop. "Just what I wanted to see, the wicked witch of Moonlight Harbor."

Susan's mouth was moving and they could hear muffled but not specific words. It was a sure bet whatever she was saying it wasn't *Courtney, good to see you.*

"Don't let her in," said Annie.

"If I don't she'll stay out there, glaring at us and yelling through the window," Courtney said.

Although she'd have liked nothing better than to ignore Susan. If she ignored the sour lemon long enough, maybe she'd give up and go away. Sure. In a parallel universe.

Susan rapped again. Her mouth was moving rapid fire and her face was crab shell red. She jabbed at the door handle. She looked like an out-of-practice wizard trying to get lightning to shoot from her fingers.

Courtney took a deep breath, went to the door, unlocked and opened it. "What can I do for you, Mrs. Frank?"

"You can tell me what you're doing here in my shop," Susan snapped as she marched inside. She was wearing a mix of ugly styles—the elastic waist jeans she favored and a windbreaker with a purple-and-pink geometric design that she must have had since the eighties. Her hair was done up in a pink scarf styled to look like she'd stepped out of an episode of *I Love Lucy*, and she'd accented the outfit with a nice big frown.

Her shop, huh? "Painting," Courtney replied.

"I can see that. But why are you here? This isn't your shop."

Not yours, either. Courtney lifted her chin. "I'm managing it for Brody."

"Managing," Susan sneered. "So you got your hooks into him, did you? I suppose you're going to sneak in some of your silly designs."

"No sneaking needed." This woman was poison on legs. "I thought you were moving." *The sooner the better.*

"I am. I'm going someplace where the people are friendlier."

She'd have a hard time finding a place friendlier than Moonlight Harbor. "Well, good luck with that," Courtney said. She had so had it with this woman.

"Are you being disrespectful of me?" Susan demanded.

Courtney had tried to be the ideal employee. She'd bitten her tongue so many times when she worked for Susan it was a wonder it was still whole. But she didn't work for Susan anymore and she'd taken about all the abuse she was going to.

"No, not yet. But if you stay here insulting me much longer, that's going to change. You had your chance with this shop and with the people here and you blew it. You'll have to live with that."

Susan took a deep, offended breath. "Of all the nerve."

"Maybe it's time somebody had the nerve to tell you what you need to hear," Courtney said. Not meanly, just firmly. Okay, maybe a little meanly.

Susan swelled up like a cartoon villain, and Courtney

half expected her to sprout into a twelve-foot-high monster. "You… You manipulative, ungrateful… I gave you a job."

"And I earned every penny you paid me, so we're even. Okay?"

Judging from Susan's expression, it wasn't.

"Wherever you end up, maybe you'll be able to make more friends than you did here," Courtney said.

"I hope you fail," Susan spat.

"Thanks for the warm wishes. I'll be sure to pass them on to Brody," Courtney said, keeping her voice light. Inside she was a blazing inferno. If Susan didn't scram soon she was sure she'd set the old bat's hair on fire.

Susan whirled around and stormed out of the store, and Courtney locked the door behind her.

"Wish you the worst," Courtney said, flipping her off.

Not that Susan could see. Still, it made Courtney feel better.

"She's got issues," Moira said.

"She gives the rest of us issues," Courtney said in return.

"Did you know that her husband left her for another woman when she was pregnant with their daughter?"

This was news to Courtney.

"How did you learn that?" Annie asked.

"I've been doing her hair, remember? Everyone talks to her stylist."

"I can't picture Susan talking about that," Annie said. "Not to anybody."

"It sort of came out one day. I was saying how glad I was that I'd got away from Lang. We started bonding over rotten men."

"In Susan's case, I can understand why he left," Courtney said, refusing to feel sorry for her former boss.

"You never know," Moira said. "Sometimes the meanest

people are just people who've been hurt really bad." She fell silent a moment, looking at the box of ugly clothes in front of her. "I feel kind of sorry for Susan."

"I don't," Courtney said. "Everyone gets hurt. That's no excuse for passing it on."

"I guess. But maybe she doesn't know how to be any different."

"You are too softhearted," Courtney said.

"Maybe I am. Sometimes I actually feel sorry for Lang."

Courtney was shocked. "Are you kidding? After the way he treated you?"

"He's paying for it now."

"We all pay for our mistakes, one way or another," said Annie, whose ex-husband Greg was still struggling with his own demons. "I feel sorry for Greg sometimes, too."

"You guys are too nice," Courtney said. As far as she was concerned, the Susans, Langs and Gregs of the world deserved what happened to them. They were all drowning in pools they'd filled themselves.

But that didn't mean she had to stand poolside and gloat. "Well, Susan's history now. Wherever she goes, I hope she figures out how to smile more." And that was all the thought she was going to give to Susan Frank's future. "Meanwhile, I'm going to prove to Brody that he didn't make a mistake being a superhero and making this happen for me by turning Beach Babes into a huge success."

"You will," Annie predicted.

Damn straight she would.

Jenna was in Brody's real estate office, dropping off a batch of cookies Aunt Edie had made for him, telling him how noble he'd been to buy Beach Babes for Courtney, when Susan Frank walked in.

"Susan," Brody greeted her, wearing his diplomatic, friendly real estate agent expression.

She cut right to the chase, not bothering to return his greeting or give one to Jenna. "What is that woman doing managing my shop?" she demanded.

Brody's brows pulled together and he shook his head, the picture of confusion. "Your shop?"

"Don't you play dumb with me. You know what I'm talking about," she said, wagging a finger at him. "I was just over there and saw Courtney Moore inside, boxing up all the clothes."

"She's going to manage it for me," Brody said. "Surely you didn't think I'd do that myself. I don't know anything about women's clothes."

"Neither does she! This is wrong."

"Susan," Brody said firmly. "Did I or did I not offer you a fair deal?"

"That's beside the point," Susan said, her jaw jutting out at a pugnacious angle.

"No, that is the point. I offered you a fair price and you were happy to take it. I've also gotten a good price on your house for you."

Susan suddenly wasn't looking him in the eye. "I probably could have gotten more."

"Then you shouldn't have accepted the offer," he said reasonably. "Although I can tell you now you wouldn't have gotten more."

Susan's lower lip began to wobble. "You're all against me."

Susan Frank never cried, and Jenna found the sight of an approaching tear storm unnerving. "Susan, you know that's not true," she said.

Actually, maybe it was. Susan, with her negative attitude and general crankiness, didn't exactly inspire warm thoughts, let alone loyalty.

Brody put an arm around her. "Susan, you can't look back. You know that. You've got a new life ahead of you and a good nest egg to begin it with. Who cares what happens in Moonlight Harbor now, right? It's in your rearview mirror."

Susan bit her lip and sniffed. "It's not right, that's all."

"It's going to be okay. Beach Babes, the business you started, will keep going, and that's the important thing."

"Well," she said, considering his words. Reluctantly.

"It's all good," he said, walking her toward the door. "Your house should close in another three weeks, and you'll be walking away with a nice profit. This Memorial Day you'll be in Oregon with your daughter, having fun shopping instead of working. Time with your family, no stress. Be glad you're out of the rat race."

Susan nodded. Sniffed again. "I am tired of working so hard."

"Well, there you go," he said easily.

"But you shouldn't let that woman run your shop. She'll ruin you."

"I'll take my chances," he said.

"Then you'll deserve it," she said, reverting to the Susan they all knew and didn't love. Then, without another word, she left.

"No good deed goes unpunished," Jenna teased.

"Or unrewarded," he said, holding up the tin of cookies and making her smile. "How about you? Are you going to reward me?" he asked, moving close and doing that silly thing with his eyebrows.

"Virtue is its own reward," she said.

He frowned. "If you ask me, virtue is overrated."

He was ready to prove it later. They went out to dinner, then wound up at his beach house, sharing a bottle of wine, with Brody doing most of the sharing and Jenna doing most of the drinking.

He opened another bottle and refreshed their glasses. Gewürztraminer, her favorite.

Jenna took a sip and sighed happily. It was a gorgeous night, the sky a dark canvas for the stars…which were starting to spin a little.

"I love it here," she said, lying back against the lounge chair they were sharing on his back deck. "With you," she added, smiling at him.

"I'm glad you moved down," he murmured, taking her glass from her.

Wine, a beautiful night at the beach, and Brody—what a powerful combination. Of course, she had to let him kiss her. And kiss her. And kiss her.

"You're steaming me up like a pot of clams," she said.

"Mmm," he said back, and took a little nibble of her neck. "You taste better than clams." He undid a button on her blouse and slipped it down her shoulder, ran his lips along her collar bone. *Ooooh.*

Another minute or two of this and she'd be in hot water. Except hot water was a good thing. Hot baths, hot springs, hot times. She giggled.

He stopped his nibbling and frowned. "What?"

"I'm buzzed. Did you get me drunk so you could seduce me?"

"You think I'd have to get you drunk to do that? You think so little of my seduction skills?"

"I think your seduction skills are amaaazing."

He pulled away and studied her. "Oh, boy. You are drunk. What was I thinking?"

"Even my nose is buzzing."

He slipped her blouse back up her shoulder.

"What?" she protested.

"I don't know where my brain was, giving you so much wine."

"It was on my boobs," she said, and snickered.

He got up and held out a hand. "Come on, Cinderella. The ball's over and it's time to take you home."

"What if I don't want to go home?"

"We'll finish this later, when you're sober."

"Well, I like that," she grumbled. She took his hand and let him pull her up. *Whoa.* "Who moved the deck? Are we having an earthquake?"

"No, no earthquake. You're fine."

"I know," she said, and giggled again. "Not as fine as Celeste. She's the pretty one."

"You're damn hot yourself, and you know it," he said, walking her back into the house. "Come on, where's your purse? Let's go."

"I thought you said virtue was overrated."

"So I lied. If we're going to do this I want you sober."

She draped herself over him. "You are a wonderful man. You know that?"

"That's what I hear. Come on."

He drove her home with the top down on his convertible, and the brisk ocean air helped her sober up.

"I did have a good time tonight," she said once the car had stopped. "I always have a good time with you, Brody."

"We'll have a lot of good times in the future," he predicted.

Good times in the future. She liked the sound of that. She'd had enough crummy times in the past to last her a lifetime.

He opened the car door for her, then escorted her back to the house and up the stairs. She was weaving only slightly. He gave her a soft, sweet kiss, then said, "Okay, in you go."

"You truly are an amazing man," she informed him.

"Yes, I am," he agreed. "I hope you'll remember what you said once you're sober."

"I'm sober enough."

That remark obviously deserved a thank you kiss. And the thank you kiss deserved a thank you for the thank you kiss.

"Don't make me wait too much longer," he whispered before she went in the house.

She shouldn't. She wouldn't.

Everyone was in bed when she stumbled up the stairs. She tried to be quiet brushing her teeth, tried not to literally fall in bed and wake up her mother, who was staying for a few days to house hunt and sharing her room with her since there were no vacancies at the Driftwood.

The last thing she heard before oblivion was her mother saying, "He's a very nice man, Jenna. Hurry up and marry him."

Hurry up and marry him. What was she waiting for, anyway? She wished she knew.

The following afternoon she had other things to think about, like the looming city council meeting. She got busy at her computer, finishing up her research on the deer issue.

Most of the websites she visited warned against making the wildlife dependent on humans for their food, even in winter. It only took an hour for her to gather enough information to make even the most determined deer feeder reconsider. Feeding the deer was bad for their digestive systems and could sicken them and even cause death. It also made them lose their fear of humans, turning them into a potentially dangerous species thanks to those hooves and antlers. Also, as Bob Wilson had said, it messed with their reproductive systems, increasing the population—something the town's gardeners would certainly not want. Stopping people from feeding the deer would help slow down the out-of-control population and, in the long run, be a kindness to the deer already wandering around town.

If the goal was to keep everyone happy, then making it illegal to feed Bambi was the way to go, and she said as much when the mayor called on her to give her report and recommendation at the May council meeting.

"According to one wildlife biologist's post, feeding wildlife threatens humans, pets and our wildlife," she concluded, trying hard not to blink.

The council voted and the decision was unanimous. It would no longer be legal for residents of Moonlight Harbor to feed the deer anywhere within the town limits. An ordinance would be drafted and signed.

"That was the right decision," Tyrella said to Jenna after the meeting finally broke up. "I think we can all live with it."

Mildred Morrison wanted to talk with Jenna, too, and not to thank her. "The deer were one of the reasons I moved here. I love feeding them and you've taken that away from me."

"I'm very sorry, Mrs. Morrison." *Blink, blink.* "But we want to do what's best for everyone, don't we? Even the deer."

"They'll starve next winter and it will be your fault."

Whoa, wait a minute. She'd signed up to serve, not to be abused.

"Mrs. Morrison, I recommend you go online and do some research yourself. If you do, then you'll realize that if you break the law and feed the deer, they'll get sick and die and it will be your fault," Jenna said without so much as one eye twitch.

"Well, I never," Mildred huffed as Jenna turned her back and started for the door.

"I hope you never," Jenna muttered.

If Mildred decided to break the law, Jenna sincerely hoped she'd get caught. There would be a fine and Mildred would be a very deserving recipient.

When Jenna got home, Aunt Edie and Sabrina were both waiting to hear what had happened, watching an episode Sabrina was streaming of her latest teen drama series and keeping themselves fortified with popcorn and root beer.

"What happened?" Sabrina asked, handing her mother the popcorn bowl.

"It will no longer be legal to feed the deer. We're going to keep our wildlife wild." Jenna took the bowl, plopped onto the couch in between the two of them and dug in.

"I'm glad that's settled," said Aunt Edie.

"It's settled but not everyone's happy about it."

"It is kind of sad," Sabrina said. "People like feeding them. Taylor's grandma always buys apples for the deer that live in the thicket on the empty lot next to her house."

"She won't be able to anymore," Jenna said. "And it really is for the best. In the long run it doesn't help the deer." She dug out another handful of popcorn. "Maybe now we can move on to other things."

"Like a convention center?" Aunt Edie said.

"Like a convention center, which I hope will be the next order of business…after whether or not to make a leash law."

More controversy. If people got upset about the deer, she

hated to think how they were going to feel on the issue of whether to leash their dogs or let them run free.

"It seems mean to make dogs always have to be on leashes, especially on the beach," Sabrina said.

"Yes, but dogs running free can also mean dogs getting hit by cars, and getting into fights with the owners not being able to separate them," Jenna said. "That can cost hundreds of dollars in vet bills."

"But there's plenty of room on the beach," Sabrina said. "Poor Nemo would hate being on a leash when he's down here."

"We all have to make sacrifices. Even dogs," Aunt Edie said.

Yep, and here was a glimmer of what lay ahead at the next city council meeting. Fun times.

Nine

There were no housing developments in Moonlight Harbor. When it came to building houses, everyone had always done their own thing and still did.

Some styles popped up around town a lot. Craftsman beach bungalows with front porches were popular, and many houses had lookout towers that enabled owners to see over the ones between them and the beach. Some were on stilts with parking underneath, ensuring the house would stand just in case a tsunami ever visited the Washington coast. Some were ultra-modern and some had been modern back in the sixties.

There was plenty to look at. The town was exploding with new construction everywhere, especially along the various canals, which had been put in by the Army Corps of Engineers back when the town was first being developed in the sixties and movie stars like Pat Boone were being lured out to play on the golf course. Some houses in town were beautifully maintained. Others had clearly been neglected, and rust was forming on their garage doors and mold on the siding.

"You can get some bargains," Brody had told Mel. "I've bought a couple and flipped them and made a nice profit."

Mel had smiled when he said that and told him she wasn't interested in profits. "All I want is a modest home where I can cook for my family."

To that end, with Jenna riding shotgun, he took Mel to some properties he thought would interest her. One was on the largest of the town's canals, which bore the grandiose name of the Grand Canal. It had two bedrooms, a large back porch and a dock.

"You could get a kayak and explore the canals. We have twenty-four miles of them winding around town," he said.

"It is nice," Mel said.

Jenna knew what that meant. Her mother was being polite but wasn't interested. Melody Jones had never been what one would call a sporty woman.

"Did you say you had something else?" she asked.

Brody got the message and moved them on. To a really tall house that was three stories high. Right on the beach, though, and the view was stunning. The kitchen and great room were all on the top level. The space was beautiful with hardwood floors and a fireplace at one end of the room. The kitchen was nicely updated with gray quartz countertops and stainless steel appliances. The best feature was the never-ending view of the ocean. Three bedrooms. Mom could have her friends come down and stay.

"Wow," Jenna breathed. "Think of the gorgeous sunsets you could enjoy from here."

"It's lovely," Mel said, "but I don't know if I'd want to carry my groceries up three flights."

And, moving on.

They saw two more houses before her mother fell in love. The house that captured her heart was a small two-bedroom cottage, painted coral, right on the beach at the far end of town, not far from the pier. No endless ocean view here as they were now across the bay from Westhaven. But the water was gorgeous and the beach was sandy.

"You'll see the fishing boats going out in the morning and coming back in at night," Brody said as they stood on the little back porch.

"I love it," Mel gushed. "And it's under my budget."

"It's kind of small," Jenna said.

"There's only one of me," her mother replied. "And the kitchen's big enough for me to cook in." She looked out at the water. "This feels like home. I want to make an offer. Full price, Brody. I don't want to lose this."

"All right," he said. "Your wish is my command."

He walked off with his cell phone, calling the real estate agent who had the listing, and mother and daughter sat down on the steps and admired the sand dunes and the waves beyond.

"Can you imagine waking up to this every morning?" Mel said.

As they had a view of the beach from Aunt Edie's house, it wasn't hard to imagine. "You're going to love it. I think this place will be great for you," Jenna told her.

"And with the extra bedroom, I can have some of my friends down. The dining area's big enough that I can fit all of you around the table. And at night I'll be able to hear the waves hitting the shore."

"It'll be great," Jenna said. Her mother had worked hard for so many years, struggled as young widow, and raised her daughters on her own. She deserved to be happy.

She also deserved to find love. Maybe Ellis West, who'd taken such an interest in her at Jenna's election win party, would become a frequent visitor. Mom would need help moving in. Jenna was sure Ellis would be more than happy to oblige. *Heehee.*

Since Mel was offering full price, it didn't take long to get a yes from the sellers, and twenty minutes later, Brody shared the happy news that Mel's offer had been accepted. He'd run them home, then get busy putting together papers to sign.

"I'm so excited I hardly know what to do with myself," Mel confessed when they were back at the house and had shared the news with Aunt Edie.

"We need to celebrate," Jenna said. "Let's go out for lunch. I know the perfect place."

"Not someplace expensive," said Mel. That was her mom, always money-conscious. Even when she no longer needed to be. With what she was making from the sale of her old house, she was in good shape.

"I know just the place. Let's go to the Seafood Shack," Jenna said.

"Oh, yes, a good idea," said Aunt Edie. "They have the best fried clams anywhere in Moonlight Harbor."

"You two go on over. I'll be right behind you," Jenna said to them.

She watched as her mother and great-aunt made their way across the parking lot to the little fast food building with the giant wooden razor clam on its roof, then selected a number from the contacts in her phone. Ellis West answered on the third ring.

"Ellis, my mom just bought a house down here at the beach. We're going over to the Seafood Shack to celebrate. Are you overseeing the kitchen help today?"

"No, I was just finishing up waxing my car. Maybe I'll take it for a spin."

"Good idea," she said.

A new house and a new love. Life at the beach was going to be good for her mom. She was going to make sure of it.

The three women had just settled down with fish and chips and the famous fried clams when a red classic convertible from the fifties pulled up outside. Ellis West and his pride and joy. It was freshly waxed and shiny with white wall tires and a white top, which was down to take advantage of the warm day.

"Look who's here," Jenna said innocently.

Her mother turned her gaze to the window and her eyes got big.

The man behind the wheel looked just as cool as the car he was getting out of in his jeans and golf shirt and aviator shades. Ellis was a big, sturdy specimen with a barrel chest, a superhero jaw and silver hair. A true silver fox.

He spotted them in the window and waved.

Jenna and Aunt Edie waved back, and Mel eyed her daughter suspiciously. "Did you know he was going to be here?"

"How would I know that?" Jenna hedged.

"Hardly surprising," said Aunt Edie, "since he owns this place. When he's not working in the kitchen he's always stopping by just to make sure his staff is behaving. You have to keep an eye on these kids."

"Not the ones he hires," Jenna said. "They all love him. A couple of them are going to the local community college and he's paying their tuition."

"That's very generous," Mel said, obviously impressed.

"He believes in helping kids," Jenna said. Points scored for Ellis.

He sauntered into the place, had a greeting for the girl working the counter, and then made his way over to them. "Hello, ladies. Welcome to my humble establishment."

Jenna, who'd made sure the seat next to her mom was vacant, waved him over. "Join us."

"Thanks," he said and slid in next to Mel, whose cheeks were turning seashell pink.

"We're celebrating. Mom just bought a house here," Jenna said to him as if it were fresh news.

"Where'd you buy?" he asked Mel.

"Down by the pier," she said.

"It's right on the beach and it's so cute," Jenna added.

"Tell me more," Ellis said, and that was all it took to start the conversation flowing smoothly between the two of them.

Jenna took a sip of her iced tea to hide her smirk. Dang but she was good.

They lingered in the restaurant, people coming and going, with Jenna observing how things were progressing between her mother and Ellis. She was aware of Aunt Edie doing the same thing. It was a wonder her mom didn't feel like she was in a zoo.

Brody called, suggesting they make their way over to the office and sign the necessary papers.

"How about going for a drive with me later?" Ellis said to Mel as he walked out with them. "I just got my baby all waxed and pretty."

"I think we'll be too busy finishing up this deal," Mel said. As if it would take hours to sign some papers.

Oh, no. Her mom wasn't going to get out of a date that easily. "You could go tomorrow afternoon, after church."

"Oh, I—" Mel began.

"It's not like you have to hurry back to go to work," Jenna continued. "Stay until Monday."

"Well."

"Weather's supposed to be nice tomorrow," Ellis said.

The expression on her mother's face was almost enough to make Jenna laugh. She looked like she'd been told to walk the plank.

"You really want to see more of your new hood," Ellis said.

"Well, all right. That's very nice of you," she said, and Jenna and Aunt Edie exchanged grins.

Her mom wasn't exactly grinning after Ellis drove away. "Really, Jenna. I can make my own decisions."

"You did," Jenna said. "Didn't she, Aunt Edie? Did you see me saying yes for her?"

"I certainly didn't."

"You put me on the spot. What else could I say?"

"Take a hike, you handsome man. I like being alone."

"That's not funny," Mel said huffily.

So Jenna tried not to chuckle.

Papers were signed on both sides, and later that evening Brody took the whole family out to celebrate, including Sabrina and Scotty, who held hands as they walked into the Porthole. Jenna was glad to see her daughter happy again. Now to see her mother happy.

"Brody, you shouldn't have," Mel said to their host after he'd picked up the check for dinner as well as a bottle of champagne.

"Just my way of thanking you for your business," he said. "I think you're really going to enjoy being in that house."

"I know I am," she told him. "It's the perfect size for me, and I love the view."

Funny, she'd always thought her old house was perfect, but now she was realizing it didn't fit her the way it once did. It was, indeed, time to move on. That house needed a family, needed to collect new memories. And this little house at the beach…it was a new build. It didn't have any memories yet and it was waiting for some. Every house should soak up more than sunshine. This one was ready and waiting to be filled with laughter and conversation. Maybe even an argument or a tear or two. It was ready to be lived in and she was ready to live.

She thought of Ellis and their planned drive for the following day. She wasn't sure she was ready to live that much.

But a drive would be nice. She couldn't simply depend on her daughters for her social life.

As if to prove it, they all returned from dinner and her family began to scatter. Pete stopped in and convinced Aunt Edie to go to The Drunken Sailor and root for him while he competed in a darts tournament. Sabrina and Scotty went off to a party, and Jenna and Brody took a walk on the beach. Then it was just her and Jolly Roger the parrot. But Aunt Edie had put Roger to bed for the night, covering his cage, so there wasn't even a peep out of him.

That was all right. She was used to being alone. No matter how much you went out and how many people you saw socially, when you were a widow, this was how you finished your day. This was your natural state.

She liked her own company. She could do alone just fine. She only wished she'd brought down the book she'd started.

There was always the TV. She rummaged through Aunt Edie's DVD collection and finally pulled one out. *Moonstruck*. She hadn't watched that in years. And she loved Nicholas Cage. Those eyes.

Ellis had eyes like Nicholas Cage.

Never mind him. She fetched a plate of Aunt Edie's oatmeal cookies, then settled in to watch the movie. A widow reinventing herself and ending up with a handsome man—had this been a subconscious choice?

She found herself sighing when Ronny Cammareri and a new and improved Loretta Castorini met at the Lincoln Center to see Puccini's *La bohème*. Then she found herself crying. Puccini could do that to you.

But it was more than Puccini, it was more than a romantic scene in a movie. It was a yearning, a need long suppressed. It ached and it cried to be acknowledged.

This wasn't the movies though. This was real life. She'd had her moment for love. She'd had that fairy-tale romance.

She didn't finish the movie. Jenna and Brody returned and they all played a game of cards. It was enough. Really.

Still, somewhere between that night and the next afternoon, Mel's earlier attitude got lost and she found herself looking forward to that drive with Ellis. True love was a once-in-a-lifetime experience, but friendship was another matter. She liked Ellis. There was no reason they couldn't become good friends.

"You look lovely, Mom," Jenna approved, taking in Mel's white capris and flowing turquoise top. "You could be a model."

Mel knew she was an attractive woman, but she never took compliments too seriously. Beauty wasn't anything a woman accomplished on her own, so it was silly to take credit for it. Still, she always tried to honor it as she would any other blessing, taking care of herself and dressing nicely. Her husband had appreciated it.

Not that you're dressing nicely for Ellis, she reminded herself. *This is simply a friendly drive and an opportunity to see some beautiful scenery.*

Still, she couldn't help but feel pleased with his appreciative smile when he came to pick her up. "Pretty as a picture," he said when she met him at the door.

He made a pretty good picture himself in his jeans and plain gray T-shirt with the black windbreaker over it. What was it about a man with broad shoulders that always set a woman's heart skipping?

She murmured her thanks but didn't return the compliment. She couldn't have him thinking she was interested in him for anything other than friendship, especially with her daughter and her aunt hovering in the living room archway.

"Have fun, you two," Jenna said as Mel grabbed her sweater and purse.

"We will," Ellis said, then followed Mel off the porch and down the stairs.

It was the kind of spring day that inspired poets and songwriters—azure sky, warm sunshine and a cool, gentle breeze. Perfect for a ride in a classic convertible.

"This is quite the car," Mel said as he opened the door for her.

"It was my midlife crisis car," he said. "But I called it an investment. They don't make 'em like this anymore. This T-Bird is worth a pretty penny now."

"A T-Bird," Mel repeated. How her husband would have loved to own a car like this one.

"Your daughter once called it a Caddy, but I forgave her," he said with a grin once he was behind the wheel.

"I didn't do a very good job of educating my daughters on cars," Mel said.

"You did a great job of raising them to be good people and that's what counts. Jenna's the best thing that's happened to Edie in a long time."

"The same can be said about Aunt Edie for Jenna. Funny how things have a way of working out," she mused.

"Yes, it is." He smiled at her, then started the engine and put the car in gear. "I thought you'd like to see Pacific Beach. It's a really nice one. Afterward I have reservations at the Ocean Crest restaurant. I hope you're not in a hurry to get back."

"I'm not," she said. It felt good having no schedule to keep and no money worries. After paying for her new house she'd still have enough money left to invest and live comfortably if frugally. She was free. No responsibilities. It was almost like being a teenager again.

"What kind of music do you like?" he asked.

"Gosh, almost anything. Except jazz. I'm not too fond of that."

"How about some good old classic rock and roll?"

"That sounds good," she said.

"Righteous Brothers?"

"Oh, yes."

"Carole King?"

"Her, too."

"How about Linda Ronstadt?"

"I love her."

"Got the perfect mix for you, then," he said. "I'm not such a purist that I had to keep the original radio in the car. This is a mix of some of my favorites. Sounds like you'll like it."

Carole King began to sing about the earth moving under her feet. "Oh, yes, I remember this song," Mel said. She found herself tapping the armrest in time to the music.

Carol finished and on came Linda Ronstadt, singing about how easy it was to fall in love. Ellis began singing along. He had a rich baritone voice and he knew how to sing harmony. So did Mel and she took the third part. She and Ellis and Linda made a great singing team.

Next came Linda singing "Blue Bayou," and again they both harmonized. Mel closed her eyes and let the music wash over her while the wind played with her hair. It was one of those moments you wanted to bottle so you could hold on to it forever.

"This is lovely," Mel said. "Thank you for inviting me."

"Thanks for joining me," he said. "You know, when I first bought this car four years ago, I regressed to my teen years. Pictured myself driving down the road with a beautiful woman next to me. 'Forget the woman,' I told myself, 'and be glad you got the car.' But now here I am with the whole package. You made my day."

Mel could feel her cheeks burning. Compliments always embarrassed her.

"You're certainly making mine. It feels good to be out just having fun, being carefree," she said, trying to keep both the conversation and herself on an even keel.

"Jenna said something about you not having to hurry home to work. You can't be old enough to retire yet."

"Trust me, I am," Mel said. "But I'd been working until recently. I guess you could say I got forced into retirement. I was a checker at a grocery store near Seattle and the store closed."

"Are you sorry about that?" he asked.

"I was at first. It was…unsettling. I'd been there for years, knew everyone in the neighborhood. Losing my job was hard. So was having to sell my house. I'd raised my girls there."

"That would be hard," he said.

She sighed, watched as they flew past evergreens fencing off miles of beach, and thought of how quickly life changed. Her time with John had ended far too soon.

"I've been through worse."

She'd just said that out loud. To someone she barely knew. She wasn't sure if she sounded like she was bragging over her toughness or looking for pity. It was neither, really. It simply was what her life was.

"But then, everyone's been through hard things, right?" she said, trying to keep her tone of voice light.

"True. But losing a spouse is probably the hardest. Jenna told me that you lost your husband when your daughters were young. Pretty rough."

"It definitely toughened me up. He was the love of my life." There, she'd said it. Best to get that out up front.

Ellis nodded. "I lost my wife ten years ago. Heart attack. The day before our thirty-ninth anniversary."

"I'm so sorry." So Ellis, too, knew the pain of sudden loss.

"It hurt."

"At least you had many good years together," Mel said, and felt a little envious.

"True, but when it comes right down to it, there's no good time to lose your other half."

"How did you cope?"

"At first? I shut myself up like a hermit. I swore. I kicked the furniture. When I put a hole through the bedroom wall I knew I had to find a better way to deal with it. Got some counseling, put things in perspective. We all die sooner or later. Some of us go earlier than we want. Those of us left behind have to figure out how to hit Restart. For me, it was finding a new community to be part of. Bought my fast food place, got a nice house on the beach, made some good friends." He shrugged. "Came back to life, I guess. I still miss my wife, but I'm also glad to be here."

"That was well said," Mel approved. "I'm glad to be

here, too. I love seeing how well my girls are doing, and I love having another grandchild."

Ellis smiled. "Life is good."

It certainly was in this moment. They parked the car at Pacific Beach and went for a walk. The sand and the water all stretched on forever. Surprisingly, except for another couple, small in the distance, they had the beach to themselves.

"There's something comforting about all this, isn't there?" Mel said. "I look at those waves and can't help thinking about God. What an awesome being to have created all of this."

Ellis looked out at the waves. "I was mad at God for years."

"Are you still?"

He shrugged. "No. What's the point?"

"It's still hard to accept bad things, though, isn't it?"

"The good balances it out." He smiled at her and then pulled a cigar out of his windbreaker pocket. "Does cigar smoke bother you?"

"Not in the great outdoors."

He bit off an end, spit it out and lit up. "I'm cutting back. My daughter's been on me to."

"A good daughter," Mel observed.

"She is. Got a son, too, living in DC. A couple of grandkids. There's always something positive to balance the bad. Today piles a lot of positive on the scales," he added, and smiled at her.

And she smiled back. He was so right.

He took her to the dining room in the nearby Ocean Crest Resort. The resort itself was a midcentury motel set on a bluff overlooking the beach. In addition to the million-dollar view, its dining room offered five-star meals and wines from the best boutique wineries in Washington.

"What looks good to you?" he asked as they read over their menus.

"Everything," she said, trying to find something cheap. "Maybe I'll have a salad."

"I hope you're not trying to save me money," he said.

"The food here is awfully pricey."

"Some things are worth the price. Pick what you want."

They dined on Kalamata rosemary bread, citrus-cumin-glazed prawns and charbroiled steelhead, and Mel tried not to feel guilty over how much he was spending.

With evening, the temperature dropped. Ellis put the top up on the car for their drive home, turned on the heat a little, got the music going again. Mel relaxed against her seat, mellowed out by the wine and the food, feeling like a little girl who'd just been taken to the county fair and allowed to go on all the rides.

"This has been lovely," she said to Ellis. "Thank you so much."

"No, thank *you*. I've enjoyed your company a lot."

"I've enjoyed yours, too," she said.

"I hope you'll let me show you more of Moonlight Harbor once you get moved down."

"I'd like that."

She'd missed having someone to do things with, someone with a voice lower than hers. The Righteous Brothers were singing now. "Unchained Melody." A feeling of longing for what she'd had so many years ago with John swept over her like a sneaker wave. She wondered if Ellis was experiencing similar feelings. He was now as silent as she.

The Righteous Brothers left and in their place came the Monkees, singing "I'm a Believer." The music lifted her up, bringing back a happy, carefree vibe. She started singing along. Ellis joined her for the chorus.

She was a believer. Love had happened to her, the fairytale kind. She had much for which to be thankful.

The sun had set by the time they returned to the house. She had the house key out before they even got to the door. Fumbling with a key was a sure signal that a woman wanted to be kissed, and Mel didn't think that was a good idea. But what if Ellis was expecting one?

She suddenly felt like a kid again, only this time a thirteen-year-old girl sitting on the couch in the basement with a boy at a party after someone had turned out the lights. What was expected of her? Should she offer a friendly hug? And if she did, would that be the same as a kiss?

Would it send a conflicting message? She herself was feeling conflicted. She really liked this man. And deep inside her was the longing for what she'd once had with her husband.

But she couldn't go down that road again. It no longer existed.

Start with the basics. "Thank you again," she said.

"My pleasure," he replied, and smiled at her.

That smile. That look in his eyes. Mel had been out of circulation for years, but not so long that she couldn't tell when a man wanted to kiss her.

Oh, dear, decision time.

Ten

The last man Mel had kissed had been her husband and that was many years ago. She probably couldn't even remember how to. She felt vulnerable and silly. Her palms were suddenly damp and her mouth was dry and her heart was speeding up as if she was running down the beach.

She and Ellis were going to be friends and that was all. No pressure, no possibility of hurt or heartbreak or loss.

She held out her hand to shake.

He took it. "I won't bite, you know." He pointed to his cheek with his other hand, turning his face to give her easy access.

She could handle a friendly kiss on the cheek. Surely it wasn't the same as a kiss on the lips.

It was almost an adventure touching her lips to his face. She could smell his aftershave—something fresh and a little spicy. Masculine. It reminded her of her husband's favorite in the eighties, Paco Rabanne's Sport.

She pulled away, tears in her eyes.

Ellis looked at her in concern. "Melody, are you all right?"

"You smell like my husband."

"Is that a bad thing?" he asked softly.

She shook her head. "I...don't know. It was kind of you to show me around," she said. Then, before he could speak again, she slipped inside the door.

Mel was relieved to find no one waiting in the living room to grill her about her drive with Ellis. Jenna would be off with Brody. Sabrina had obviously gone out and Aunt Edie was nowhere to be seen, which meant she'd gone to bed to read.

She knew she was only off the hook for the night. Come morning, her daughter and her aunt would both want to know how her time with Ellis had gone.

It had gone wonderfully, but he wasn't John. And she wasn't Ellis's dead wife.

What was the woman's name? She'd never asked. How thoughtless.

He hadn't said much about her. Maybe, unlike Mel, his heart wasn't anchored in the past. He'd obviously worked hard to move on.

She had, too. She'd built a life, a small life that she'd guarded to keep safe.

She remembered her words to her daughter back when Jenna was so determined to never let another man in her life. *Love hasn't given up on you.* What if it hadn't given up on her, either? She'd been as she was for so long, she had no idea how to answer that question.

Sabrina was still asleep but Jenna and Aunt Edie were both awake when Mel finally showed up for breakfast. She'd played possum, not even stirring when Jenna awoke and got out of bed. What a faker. Jenna knew her mother was a light sleeper.

At the sight of them, Mel moved forward with a casual

smile on her face as if she had nothing to share. "It looks like we have coffee ready. Have you two already eaten? I'm sure you have a full day ahead of you, darling, so don't let me keep you," she said to Jenna.

Nice try, Mom. "I'm not in that big a hurry," Jenna said as her mother headed for the coffee maker. "How was the drive?"

"It was good," Mel said, and pulled a mug out of the cupboard.

"Did he kiss you?" Aunt Edie wanted to know.

"It was only a drive," Mel said.

"No kiss?" Jenna asked in surprise.

Mel kept her face turned toward the cupboard, a sure avoidance technique. "He's a very nice man, but I'm not interested in any kind of serious relationship. I'm happy just as I am."

"You could be happier, dear," Aunt Edie said.

"Yes, Mom," put in Jenna. "You worked so hard raising Celeste and me. It's time you had a second chance at love."

"Why would I want that?" Mel argued, staying focused on getting her morning coffee. "My first chance was wonderful."

"That doesn't mean you can't have another go-round," Aunt Edie argued.

Mel shook her head. "You know what Shakespeare said, the world's a stage. The ones who belong on it are the young. They're the show. The stage is no longer yours when you get old. Instead you step off and watch the show."

"Oh, pooh," Aunt Edie said in disgust. "Haven't you heard the saying the show must go on? That doesn't mean only for the young ones. While we're here on earth we're all part of it, so why not take a good role and be happy?"

"I am happy," Mel told her. "I'm perfectly happy being the supporting cast for my daughters."

"Well, then, you're going to miss out on some wonderful love scenes," Aunt Edie said.

"What love scenes?"

The three women turned to see Sabrina. She wore a long sleep tee. Her hair (these days a shimmering mix of lavender and silver thanks to the genius of Moira at Waves Salon) was still mussy and her skin fresh and wrinkle-free. Slender and healthy-looking, she was the perfect illustration of what Mom had just been saying. The stage was waiting for her, the spotlight ready.

And yet Jenna was with Aunt Edie. What woman wanted to pack in those love scenes and miss out on the thrill and romance of a kiss, of feeling a lover's arms around her? There was plenty of room on that stage.

"Never mind, honey," Mel said.

"Your grandmother is a big coward," Aunt Edie said.

"Aunt Edie, I think we can move on to some other subjects," Mel said firmly. "Do you have any massages scheduled today?" she asked Jenna.

Yep, subject closed. Jenna and Aunt Edie exchanged looks. *What can you do?* You could lead a woman to a moonlit beach, but you couldn't force her to meet up with a man there if she didn't want to. Cupid had his work cut out for him.

Memorial Day weekend brought blue skies and tourists, and the little cabana shops were doing a brisk business. Beach Babes, celebrating its grand opening, was packed, with both locals coming to wish Courtney well and visitors lured in by her fanciful beach wear on display in the window.

"Wow," she said to Jenna, who was helping by ringing up sales. "I can't believe this."

"I don't know why not. I knew you'd be a success," Jenna said.

Courtney half wished old sour lemon Susan Franks was there to see how packed the shop was. But then she'd have found a way to ruin everyone's good time, so it was just as well she wasn't.

Courtney's mother approached the checkout counter, her arms laden with clothes. "Looks like your mom's going to buy out the store," Jenna said.

"She's going to try," Courtney replied.

"Ring 'em up," Mom said to Jenna. "These all look wonderful on me." Modest as always.

Courtney's mother was what some people would call larger than life. Not in size. She was a fourteen, which Courtney thought was darned good for a woman who'd just turned fifty-six and loved to bake. Her hair was as dark as Courtney's thanks to regular visits to the salon, and her nails had been freshly done in varying shades of pink. Mom had been a model once. "Department store only," she used to say, but Courtney had always thought that was cool.

The only thing that had embarrassed her was her mother's habit of saying whatever was on her mind, whenever. She still cringed thinking about the time Mom had told her first real out-in-a-car date to try and remember that she'd be with them in spirit, but if they stopped on the way home at Golden Gardens to park she would show up in person and slap him.

Today she was her usual outspoken self. "That's all you're getting?" she asked the woman who'd come up beside her.

"Mom." Where was Jonas when you needed him to put

out a fire on your face? Clear on the other side of the shop, keeping Dad company.

"I mean, how can you have such self-control?" Mom continued, ignoring her.

"It's not easy," the woman said.

"My daughter designed everything in here," Mom bragged.

"Well, almost," Courtney amended. "Once I've gotten my production up and running, everything will be my own designs."

She'd hired a couple of local women to sew for her, but even with that she was quickly learning that designing clothes and producing a few items for a little boutique shop in an upscale B&B was very different than stocking an entire store. She'd almost had a nervous breakdown getting enough clothes on hangers.

"I love your things," the woman said. "The store is so different from what it was when I was down here last year."

"We're under new management," Courtney said.

"My daughter owns the store," Mom explained.

Well, almost. She would own it out-and-out eventually, thanks to Brody.

"You can be sure I'll be back," said the woman.

Jenna pointed to the clock on the wall, set in an oversized blue water agate, and said to Courtney, "You've got five minutes 'til show time."

Show time. Her heart did a happy skip. Her first fashion show featuring her own designs.

She nodded, then stepped to the center of the store, where they'd squeezed in several seats. "Everyone, if I could have your attention."

The excited burble of voices died down and a crowd of faces looked her direction.

"We're going to start our fashion show in just a moment here, so if some of you can find a seat. Sorry we don't have enough for everyone. I didn't expect such a crowd," she admitted.

"Why not? We all love you," called out Tyrella, who had gone crazy with her credit card.

"Thanks. I never thought I'd see this day. This is a dream come true. Jenna, could you start the music?"

Jenna nodded and cued up Courtney's playlist on her phone, which was already propped up on a speaker. The first song to play had been an oldie Mel had suggested, "The Girl from Ipanema." Wherever that was. It was perfect, though, and set the tone.

The first model was Moira, and she came out from behind the backroom curtain, looking like a mermaid with her long, shimmering rainbow hair and the dress she wore draping in layers of teal. Tiny seashells dangled along each layer, dancing as she moved. Courtney had accented it with one of the pieces of the sea-themed jewelry she'd purchased to sell, a teal-colored beaded bracelet with a mermaid charm. To complete the look, Moira wore sandals adorned with a butterfly on the toe.

Her appearance was greeted with a chorus of oohs and ahhs, and women watched appreciatively as she walked the route that Courtney had outlined for her models.

"I was thinking cocktail party when I designed this dress," Courtney said after describing it. "We're pretty casual here at the beach, but we still like to dress for those special occasions."

Next came Celeste, who was down visiting her sister for the weekend, wearing a pair of pastel-blue-and-white tie-dyed lounge pants topped with a cropped light blue sleeveless blouse with appliqued white spiral shells along the bottom. The outfit accented her curves perfectly.

"I love that," Courtney heard one woman say to her friend. Music to her ears.

"You can dress this either up or down," Courtney informed her customers as Annie, looking self-conscious, showed off a pale green dress that went so well with her fair coloring.

Rian LaShell, who owned Sandy Claws, the town's pet supply store, looked elegant in a silver top and white capris, silver earrings shaped like sand dollars dangling from her ears. She had a slender figure and moved like a cat on the prowl. She not only captured the attention of the female customers, she had the few men in the shop paying attention as well. Including Jonas. He and Courtney would have a little talk about that later.

Jenna had changed into her outfit—light gray shorts and a filmy black blouse with a white sea turtle print. It had a low-cut ruffled V-neck. She looked beautiful in it and Courtney could imagine the look on Brody's face when he saw her. And Seth's. If that outfit didn't make Seth Waters get off his butt and do something before it was too late, nothing would.

Next came Rita Rutledge, who owned Beans and Books, followed by Laurel, the hostess at the Porthole, and Piper Lee, who worked for *Beach Times* writing articles for the Living Section. But it was Kiki Strom, super senior citizen and owner of the town's favorite tourist shop, Something Fishy, who stole the show. She showed the older women present how they could rock a look when she came out in a white jacket over a blue V-neck T-shirt and a long tapered skirt layered with little bits of iridescent chiffon that looked like fish scales.

"I call this my mermaid skirt," Courtney said, and Kiki with her slim, petite figure looked darling in it.

Who needs New York? Courtney thought, watching as the customers applauded when her little fashion show ended. It didn't get any better than this.

The patrons continued to shop, buying up everything that had been modeled in every size available. Crowds always attracted crowds, and more people continued to funnel in, curious to see what all the fuss was about.

"You are going to have to restock ASAP," Jenna said when the last customer finally left and Courtney was able to turn the sign on the door to Closed.

"No shit, Sherlock," Courtney said, looking around.

Many of the clothing racks were empty, and she was pleased to see that those were the ones with her own designs and label, Beachside by Courtney.

"That was awesome, Court," said Jonas, who'd stayed until the end.

"The models or the clothes?"

He frowned at her. "The clothes, of course."

"Okay. I could have sworn I saw drool on your chin when Rian slinked past you."

"I save my drool for you. You're amazing."

He put an arm around her and smiled down at her like she really was the most amazing thing in the world. Ha ha. Boy, did she have him fooled.

"My feet are killing me," Jenna said. "And I'm pooped. I don't think I want to be in retail."

"This was an unusual day," Courtney told her. "Grand opening, Memorial Day weekend. Normally it probably won't be this busy."

"I wouldn't count on that," Jenna said. "Word's going to get out."

"If she's right, I hope I can keep up," Courtney said to Jonas after Jenna had left.

"You will. You've got everything in place to make this work, got your elves sewing away. It's all good." He checked the time on his cell. "When are we supposed to have dinner with your parents?"

"Six."

"It's only five. Want to go back to my place and relax?"

She knew what that meant. His place sounded good.

"Absolutely," she said.

Jonas had champagne in the fridge and had ordered a small cake from the bakery. It was shaped like a dress, frosted blue, and had Congrats, Courtney scrawled across the top in red icing.

"Aww, that is so sweet," she said, and took a picture with her phone. "You are the best."

"Yes, I am," he agreed, and pulled her to him. And then the cake was forgotten.

Almost an hour later she said, "We'd better get over to the house. I'm sure Mom's wondering where I am."

"I bet she's figured it out." He traced a finger along her collarbone. "Guess we may as well take the cake and champagne over there."

"Good idea. We can have it after dinner."

They got to the house to find her mom and stepdad in the living room, visiting with Annie and Emma.

"Cake," Emma squealed at the sight of the bakery box. "Can we have some?"

"After dinner," Annie said firmly.

"Speaking of dinner," said Dad. "Let's go. I'm starving."

They wound up at Sandy's, Courtney and Jonas's favorite casual dining restaurant. Even though it wasn't right on the beach, it reminded customers that the beach was nearby with a mint-green lifeguard chair posted outside over a makeshift sandy beach complete with shells. Inside, a net hung on one wall, holding starfish and a glass float. The place was already two-thirds full, with more people coming in.

"Must be a good place," said Dad, looking around.

His theory was that good food always attracted a crowd. He was sure right in the case of Sandy's. Although, really, she couldn't think of a single restaurant in town that wasn't good.

"It's really nice of you to include me," Annie said to Courtney's parents once they were all seated.

"You're like a sister to our girl. Of course we have to include you," Mom told her. "Anyway, we can always use another child."

"Oh, thanks," Courtney said, pretending to be offended.

Considering what a pain she and her older sister had been, two should have been enough, but Mom was ready for more, especially grandkids. Courtney's older sister, Angela, hadn't done her duty and provided them. Neither had Courtney. Mom had been thrilled when she first got married and then horrified when she got divorced.

Until she learned that Courtney's ex was a cheater. Then she'd been ready to hunt him down and tie him to a telephone pole with a sign that said Cheater hanging from his neck.

"I'll provide the rotten tomatoes to throw," she'd said. "Or better yet, grenades."

Fortunately for the loser ex, Courtney had reminded her mother that living well was the best revenge.

"When does that include a new man?" Mom kept asking.

Then Jonas came along, and her parentals had met him and given him their seal of approval, and Mom started asking a new question. "When are you two going to get married?" This was usually followed by, "I want grand-children before I die. And you're not getting any younger."

Her stepdad, God bless him, kept his mouth shut and stayed out of those conversations.

They ordered—fish tacos for Jonas, popcorn shrimp for Emma, and Crab Louie for the ladies. And a steak for Dad, who wasn't all that fond of seafood. As they ate, the conversation mostly centered on the successful launch of Courtney's boutique, but there were also questions for Annie on how her catering business was coming and how her food truck was doing.

"The food truck is doing great," Annie said. "I've hired some part-time help, and she worked this afternoon for me so I could be there for Courtney."

"Our daughter's a lucky girl to have so many good friends in her corner," said Dad.

"And such a nice man," added Mom, smiling at Jonas.

Courtney suddenly had a feeling that her mother was about to say something embarrassing. She could always tell by the way Mom kind of cocked her head. *No, Mom. Please don't.* The head was still cocked and now there came that sly smile. *Oh, no. Brace yourself. Here it comes.*

Eleven

"So when are we going to see a ring on Courtney's hand? I'm ready for grandchildren."

Jonas choked on his Coke and Courtney glared at her mother. "Mom."

Mom shrugged. "Just wondering. Anyone with eyes can see you two are crazy about each other."

"We're not in a hurry," Courtney said, anxious to let Jonas off the hook.

He kept himself on there. "Your daughter's the best thing that ever happened to me," he said.

Mom waggled a playful finger at him. "Then you don't want her to get away."

Jonas looked at Courtney, his polite smile turning into something more serious. "You're right. I don't."

"Plenty of time. Don't rush the kids," Dad said to Mom.

Courtney smiled at him. *Thanks, Dad.*

Her mother frowned, but she dropped the subject, and they finished the rest of the meal with no more embarrassment. The evening went well once they got back to the house also, with everyone enjoying the cake and champagne Jonas had provided, followed by a rousing game of charades with Annie and Emma.

After Emma was sent to bed, the grown-ups enjoyed more conversation about both Courtney's and Annie's businesses, and Courtney figured that was the end of the embarrassing subject of marriage.

But it wasn't. Mom started the conversation out innocently enough. Stealth tactics. "This has been quite a day. I sent pictures of your fashion show to both grandmas and Aunt Marlys. They're so proud of you. And so are we."

One thing Courtney would say for her parents, they'd always been there for her.

"You're doing such big things with your life. Unlike your mother, who only went to college to get her MRS degree," Mom said.

"You raised Courtney and her sister," put in Annie. "I'd say that was doing something great."

Mom smiled and nodded. "We do have good kids. Now, if only one of them would get married." Here she gave Courtney The Look.

"Tell that to Angela," Courtney said. "She's the oldest."

"Angela can't seem to find a man who meets her high standards, and besides, she doesn't want children. You, my darling daughter, are my only hope. You know, I always thought Christmas weddings were nice."

Dad and Jonas had been talking about the pros and cons of chartering a fishing boat in Westhaven next time the parents came down to Moonlight Harbor, but the conversation had hit a lull just in time for them to hear.

"Mom," Courtney said, giving Mom The Look, the daughter version, back to her.

Mom held up both of her hands. "All right, all right. Just saying."

"I think you've said enough," Courtney growled.

"Come on, lovie, let's take a walk on the beach," Dad said.

"A moonlit walk on the beach, how romantic," Mom said. "That sounds like a very good idea. And now I'm thinking about that drink the waitress brought me at dinner. Sex on the Beach."

Dad shook his head at her. "You're a hussy."

"And I'm all yours," she said, batting her eyelashes at him.

He smiled indulgently at her and held out his hand.

He was balding and skinny (except for the pot belly), but she looked up at him like he was Henry Cavill or Brad Pitt. "Don't wait up for us," she said as she took his hand, and off they went.

Courtney rolled her eyes and shook her head. "My family is our own reality show."

Jonas chuckled. "Your folks are nice. And I like your mom."

"She has a good heart," Courtney said, remembering all the times her mother had slipped her twenty dollars when she was struggling, saying, "Don't tell your father. He thinks you should stand on your own two feet." This was often after her stepfather had slipped her a fifty, saying, "Don't tell your mother. She thinks you should stand on your own two feet."

She had stood on her own two feet, and for a while, those feet had been planted on her parents' shoulders, God bless them.

"I think I'm going to bed," Annie said, picking up a couple of empty glasses. "I have a food truck to run tomorrow."

"Thanks for taking time off to be at my grand opening," Courtney said to her. "You're the best."

"I'm happy it went so well. You deserve it," Annie replied.

"Yeah, you do," put in Jonas.

Annie left, and then it was just Courtney and Jonas. He moved to join her on the couch and she put her legs up on his lap, leaned an arm over the back of the couch and smiled at him.

"You're still here. My mom hasn't scared you away?"

"Nope. And your mom's right, you know."

"About sex on the beach? Ugh. Sand in your butt crack."

That was classy. Maybe she was more like her mother than she cared to admit. Well, there could be worse people to be like, that was for sure.

"No, about us getting engaged. What do you think?"

She thought it was a great idea.

"There's no one I'd rather be with. Not like this though," she said.

He looked at her, puzzled. "What do you mean not like this?"

She was going to look stupid, but, "I need more."

"More," he repeated. Now he looked completely confused.

"You know how my first husband proposed?"

"Uh, no. That subject has never come up."

"We were at Dick's Drive-In, getting hamburgers, and he said, 'Hey, babe, we should get hitched.'"

"Romantic."

"Yeah, well, dummy me. I said, 'Okay.' So we drank

our milkshakes, went back to my dorm room and had sex. The next weekend we ran off to Vegas, where we picked up cheap rings at a pawn shop, and went to a bargain wedding chapel called The Love Nest for a cheapo ceremony, and that was that. At twenty it sounded like a good idea. My parents liked him okay so why not?

"Of course, Mom was bummed that I didn't have a big wedding and Dad wished I'd waited until I was older. After a year and a half, so did I. Starter Marriage 101. I don't want to do that again. Getting married is a big deal and so is getting engaged."

"Okay, I get it," Jonas said, nodding.

"Not that it's all about the bells and whistles. It's about matching up with the right person. I know that. But I guess this time around I want a movie moment. I want everything special right from the start. And I don't want to get engaged just because my mom said something and now you feel like you need to say something."

He frowned. "You can't think that's why I asked you just now."

"No." He had a hand on her leg, the comfortable gesture of a man who loved his woman. They were good together. No, they were great. Kind of stupid to make him jump through hoops. "I know it sounds dumb, but I really want something romantic I can tell my kids…our kids about someday."

Courtney was not shy by nature, but now she felt shy, almost afraid to look him in the eye. She concentrated on that hand on her leg, a strong hand with long fingers, a hand that gave her goose bumps every time he touched her.

He gave her leg a little squeeze. "I get it now."

"Do you? Really?" She lifted her gaze and saw him

looking at her like a pirate would look at a chest of gold doubloons.

"Yeah. And you know what? You're right. I want a good story to tell our kids, too."

That willingness to look at life through her eyes, to see her point of view, was one of the many things she loved about him. "You're the best," she said happily.

"I know," he said, all cocky. Then he turned serious. "So here's the deal. I don't want to lose you, so figure that you're taken. Got it?"

Her heart gave a little squeeze. Oh, yes, she got it. And she wanted it. She nodded.

"We're together. For good. Sometime, before this year is over, I'm going to give you a proposal to remember. You won't know when it's coming. It'll be a surprise. You'll just have to wait and see what I come up with. Deal?"

"Deal," she said.

"And tell your mom she's gonna have to wait, too," he added, making Courtney snicker.

They sealed the bargain with a kiss. And then a few more, to make sure the agreement was fully cemented.

"I love you, Court," he murmured, "and I promise you we'll do this right."

As far as she was concerned, they already were.

Courtney was one happy woman when the gang met at Aunt Edie's the following Friday night. "Everything in my life is so perfect right now," she reported. "I'm almost afraid to enjoy it. You know?"

Jenna did know. She felt a little that way herself. She'd first come to Moonlight Harbor feeling like a one-woman disaster area. Now, here she was with a purpose in life, a great community of friends and a man who was committed to her. The future looked blindingly rosy. It was almost too perfect.

Maybe that was why, somewhere at the back of her mind, she kept waiting for that other shoe to drop. *Waiting for the other shoe to drop.* Ha! Had Cinderella felt that way?

"There comes a point in every woman's life when she gets to a season of perfection," Aunt Edie said. "It looks like your season is here."

"It is," Courtney agreed.

"The important thing is to recognize it," Aunt Edie continued, managing to look at both Jenna and her mom, who was back in town, all her furniture in a U-Haul truck in the parking lot, and had joined them in time for that bit of sage advice.

"I certainly do," Mel said, "and I'm so excited about moving into my new house tomorrow."

"Have you got enough help?" asked Nora. "I can send one of my boys over."

"No, I think we're good," Mel said. "Celeste and Henry are coming down."

"Plus we've got Sabrina and her boyfriend and Ellis, Brody and Seth," Jenna added.

"Brody *and* Seth?" Courtney raised an eyebrow at Jenna.

"They both offered," Jenna said. "Mom, why don't you tell everyone about your new digs?"

And that, thank God, turned the subject in a new direction. But later, when everyone was going back for seconds of Annie's shortbread, Courtney asked Jenna in an undertone, "Both Seth and Brody? Seriously? How's that going to work?"

"It'll work fine," Jenna replied. "We all know where we stand."

"Okay," Courtney said dubiously.

But even though they all knew, Jenna felt the undercurrent of dislike as the two men worked side by side the next day to move in her mom's furniture. They said little enough to each other except for when it came time to move in Mel's big sleeper sofa.

Then it was great teamwork, with encouraging words like, "Put some muscle into it," "Lift your end up more," "Watch what you're doing, man," "Hey, you're gonna push me on my ass," and, "Look out for that corner."

"They're having fun now," Celeste murmured to Jenna, who was trying to ignore the sniping.

Ellis West set down the armchair he'd carried in. "Need some help, fellas? Scott," he said to Sabrina's boyfriend, who had come in through the patio with a box, "run around to the front and get on that other end with Seth, will ya?"

"We've got it, Ellis," Brody snapped.

"Yeah, I can see that. Here, let me give you a hand."

With the addition of two more men, the big monster was finally settled by the front window.

"Teamwork, that's the spirit," said Aunt Edie, who'd been determined to come along and help.

She'd been put in charge of unwrapping dishes, something she could do while sitting at the kitchen table. Even seated, she was working at a snail's pace. She looked tired and Jenna wished they'd been able to convince her to stay home.

"We were doing fine," Brody muttered.

"Sure you were," Ellis scoffed. "Come on, help me guide that freezer into the garage."

Brody followed him back out the door, pouting like a twelve-year-old, and Seth was right after them. Another pouting twelve-year-old.

"It might not have been such a good idea to have both those men to help us," Mel said after they were out of earshot.

"What could I do? They both offered."

"You definitely have a hard choice to make," put in Celeste as she took baby Edie out of her portable playpen.

"Not really. Only one is truly interested."

"I've seen how Seth looks at you," Celeste said.

"You can't build a relationship on looking. Brody's the one who's in the game. Seth's on the sidelines."

Sabrina came in carrying a box of pictures, and that ended the conversation.

By eleven, both Scotty and Sabrina were gone, off to their summer jobs, her to work in the ice cream parlor and him to help the go-carts keep racing.

Meanwhile, the men kept bringing in boxes. Ellis had a good twenty years on the two younger men, but he was built like an ox and had the stamina of one as well. More than once Jenna caught her mother sneaking peeks at him.

"I can't believe how much I still have left after everything I got rid of," Mel said when Brody came in with yet another box.

"Hard to get rid of a lifetime of memories," Ellis said to her as he set one down marked Books. "I was lucky my girl took a lot of our stuff off my hands, all those things women love."

"You have a few things," said Jenna. She'd been to El-lis's house for more than one chamber of commerce party.

"Oh, yeah. A couple of glass floats I've found on the beach. Gotta have that, and some things the granddaughters made for me. But the good china and the fancy figurines and jewelry are all gone. My wife always said she'd have no problem with me finding someone else if she went first, but if her replacement got her things she'd haunt me. I think she was only half kidding."

"Guess she didn't have to worry about you replacing her," Brody said, setting down the box he'd brought in.

"Not yet," Ellis said. "But you never know," he added, and smiled at Mel, who blushed and got busy digging pots out of one of the kitchen boxes.

"This is the last of it," Brody said to Mel. "You're officially moved in." He came over and put an arm around Jenna. Seth, who'd come down the hall from depositing a box in one of the bedrooms, arrived in time to see, and his lips pressed together so tightly the skin around them turned white.

Jenna knew her skin was far from white. She probably looked as red as the nail polish on her hands. Although what the heck did she have to be embarrassed about? She and Brody were an item now.

"Okay, then, time for food," she said, stepping out from under his arm and grabbing her cell phone from the counter. "Drinks in the ice chest, men, and I'll order pizza."

Ellis helped himself to a can of Coke and settled at the kitchen table with Aunt Edie. Henry and Brody joined him, and Seth distanced himself, parking on one of the bar stools at the counter. Yep, buddies for life, those two.

Mom looked at Jenna as if to say, *I told you so*, and she shrugged.

Ellis, however, was relaxed and right at home. "I hope you're going to be happy here," he said to Mel.

"I'm sure I will be. I'm with my family and I'm making some wonderful new friends."

"We're a very friendly bunch," he said.

"Yes, we are," Brody agreed, and grinned at Jenna.

Seth said nothing. Mr. Green-Eyes.

If he was feeling jealous seeing her with Brody, it was nobody's fault but his own. Seth Waters had his chance and he blew it.

The pizza arrived, and the men wasted no time in digging in.

"Pepperoni, my favorite," Brody said to Jenna.

"Mine, too," said Seth. "Thanks for feeding us." Green-eyed but determined to be civil. And let her be with another man. Well, it was his loss.

"Thanks for helping," she said.

"Happy to," he replied.

"You bet," said Brody, injecting extra enthusiasm into his voice to make up for getting beaten to the politeness punch.

The heavy lifting was done, and once the pizza was finished there was no reason for the men to remain. Seth was the first to leave, offering to help Mel with any handiwork she needed.

Not to be outdone, Brody said, "I'm here if you need anything." Then, making sure everyone knew exactly who had the claim on Jenna, he gave her a kiss. "Give me a call when you're done. I'll take you to the Porthole." With that he left to go with Henry to turn in the rental truck.

Ellis was the last to leave. "Going out to eat sounds like a good idea," he said to Mel. "You're going to be pooped after all this. How about I take you out to dinner?"

All right. Things were moving along quite nicely for her mom.

But as soon as Jenna looked at her mother, she knew what the response would be.

Good Lord, what was with the Jones women? Why was it so darned hard for them to sort out their love lives?

Twelve

"I think I'd better pass," Mel said to Ellis. "I'm pretty tired."

She saw a flash of disappointment roll over his face, but he was a gentleman. "Another time, then," he said.

"Another time," she agreed, and wondered if she really wanted there to be another time.

Ellis was a kind man, good company and good-looking. And she did like the idea of being friends. But thinking beyond that made her uncomfortable, and it was plain to see he was interested in more than mere friendship. Really, wasn't dating at this age a little…silly? Not according to Aunt Edie, but then, she'd always marched to her own unique drum.

"Mom, you should have taken him up on his offer," Jenna scolded after Ellis had left.

"It's probably not a good idea," Mel said. "I think he wants more than friendship and I don't want to encourage him and give him false hope."

"How do you know it would be false hope?" Celeste argued.

"There was only one man for me. There will never be another," Mel replied.

"Isn't that like walking on the beach and saying, 'I'll never find another agate?'" Celeste argued. "There are lots of pretty stones on the beach and lots of really nice people here on earth."

"I'm not saying Ellis isn't nice," Mel said. "But your father was the love of my life. I wish you'd gotten a chance to know him. He was kind and funny and the most handsome man I'd ever seen."

He'd had one of those perfect symmetrical faces and had been built like a Greek statue. It had been more than his looks that attracted her though. He'd had charisma. There was something about his smile that drew people to him. The party started once John walked into the room. Even more important, he'd been a man people could count on—always there when a friend needed help with a move or a home improvement project. She'd given him her heart even before he asked for it.

Ellis was the kind of man who drew a woman's attention, too, with that strong chin of his and his easygoing personality. But she'd been alone so long she didn't think she could change from single to taken at this point in life. And she'd surely wind up comparing Ellis to John at every turn, which wouldn't be fair. John had had his faults, but over the years they'd turned to a soft blur, then vanished. Now he was a paragon of the ideal husband. How did a woman replace a paragon?

She, on the other hand…her flaws had come into sharp focus with age.

"I can't imagine being with a man," she confessed.

"You mean like hanging out?" Celeste persisted.

Mel was thinking in more intimate terms. She was no twenty-year-old. The idea of showing her aging body to a man was intimidating. It was one thing to grow old together, to have those imperfections make their appearance slowly and with stealth. You saw your mate through the fuzzy lens of memory and love, still seeing dewy, tight skin and a firm young body. There was no such lens when you came into a relationship at this point.

"It would feel awkward," she said, not wanting to talk about sex with her daughters.

Aunt Edie had no such reservations. "I hope you're not talking about sex, Melody," she said, making Mel blush. "You're still a beautiful woman, both inside and out. And let me tell you, even though we older women look different on the outside, the feelings are the same inside."

"I hope you're not going to tell us how you know that," Celeste said, making a face.

"You young ones," Aunt Edie said, her mouth dipping down. "You think you've got the market cornered on love. But we all need love, no matter what our age. Don't you forget that, Melody. You cherish those memories of your wonderful husband, but don't let them rob you of living in the here and now."

"I'm not," Mel insisted. There were many ways to live in the here and now, and not all of them included a man.

Aunt Edie didn't look convinced. "Are you sure, dear?"

"I'm very happy as I am."

"I never said you weren't. You've made a good life for yourself all these years. But that's not to say you couldn't be happier. Think about it."

Mel did, long after her family had left. She was content with her new house. It was charming with its bay window and its little front yard and flowerbeds overflowing with lavender and rosemary and those lovely rhododendrons. And right off the back porch was the beach. But now, with no one in it save her, it felt a little empty.

That, she concluded, was because she hadn't yet filled it with memories. She would.

She puttered around for a while, then opted for going to bed early. Ellis and Seth had set up the bed for her and she only had to make it up.

Ellis.

She put on her nightgown, one she'd had for twenty years—red satin with lace trim. She'd bought it on impulse, on sale after Valentine's Day. She remembered thinking how John would have loved it. Red had been his favorite color.

She studied her reflection in the bathroom mirror. Her breasts sagged and the skin around her neck was going slack. She had a tummy and that tummy had stretch marks. They hadn't bothered John, but that was because those marks were souvenirs of the children they'd made together. She leaned in closer to the mirror. She didn't have much gray in her hair, though, and other than some fine lines around her eyes, her face didn't look too bad. Alas, men never looked only at a woman's face.

What would it be like to be with someone again, to have a strong body to cuddle up to at night? If she was wondering this, maybe it meant that, on some level, she was open to having a love life again. Heaven knew she'd missed the intimacy and companionship of marriage.

She was attracted to Ellis, but could she ever love him as much as she'd loved John? Even half as much? She wasn't sure.

It kept boiling down to one simple question: How much was she willing to risk at this point in her life? Losing her job, selling her home, moving—those were all high on the stress chart, and they probably amounted to enough change to last her for quite some time. She didn't need to plunge into the murky waters of a new relationship on top of all of that.

She got into bed—the bed that Ellis had helped set up—and pulled up the covers. It was a queen. There was room for more than one.

"Oh, go to sleep," she muttered, and shut off her bedside lamp.

Unlike her mother, Jenna had no problem being taken out to dinner. She and Brody enjoyed crab cakes (for her) and steak and lobster (for him) at the Porthole, and, later, a sunset walk on the beach. The waves danced along the shore, their lacy froth making a gentle swoosh like a dancer's skirt, and the sun set the sky on fire, a final reminder of its power before leaving to let its quiet sister, the moon, take over.

"It's so beautiful," she said as they walked close together, his arm around her shoulder. "Funny how I thought my life was ruined before I came here. Turns out it was really just beginning."

"I'm glad you came," he said. He stopped them and switched from an arm around her shoulders to both arms around her waist. "My life sure began again when you hit town." He smiled down at her, then did what Brody did best. He kissed her.

Yes, this was happiness, being with someone who wanted to commit to you, knowing you'd have a safe and secure future together.

"Jenna," he said softly, "you know how I feel about you."

She did. Was he going to propose right then and there? Suddenly she felt...what did she feel? Surely not anxious. What was there to be anxious about?

She nodded. And pulled back. Oh, bad body language. What was she doing?

"I'm not going to let you get away," he said softly, and tucked her right up close again.

With the sun going down the temperature was dropping. The body heat felt good. Body heat. Feeling good. What was she waiting for? *Just say it, Brody. Ask me right now. Let's do this thing before I chicken out.*

But she'd pulled away. He'd gotten the message. He started them walking again.

"We need to make this official," she said, determined to move them in the right direction.

He studied her. "Are you sure?"

Brody was great. What was there not to be sure about? She smiled up at him. "Yes, I'm sure."

"Well, then, I'm thinking I should be looking around for some bling for your poor naked finger."

"I'm thinking that, too."

He grinned. "So, want to come over to my place and really make it official?"

"After my finger's not naked."

He chuckled. "I can hardly wait to see you in the ring. Just the ring."

"Come on back to the house. We can watch a movie."

"I'd rather watch you."

She shook her head at him. "You are so full of it."

"Is that what you think?" he demanded, pretending to be insulted. "Jenna Jones, I never get tired of looking at you."

Damien had never said anything like that to her. She was ready to be with someone who really appreciated her. That someone was Brody. What a perfect ending to her story.

No, she corrected herself, a perfect beginning. This was a new story, a much better one. Happily-ever-after at Moonlight Harbor. Beach walks at sunset, dinners out, having someone who was the polar opposite of her ex, willing to talk about something besides himself. Yes, it didn't get any better than this. Brody was a great guy and she was lucky to have him. She'd make him happy.

They went back to the house to find Aunt Edie on the couch, working on her afghan, finishing up watching *Casablanca*.

"We'll always have Paris," Rick said to his former lover, Ilsa.

"Not the same as having the woman," Brody said. "Anyway, I'll take Moonlight Harbor and walks on the beach over Paris any day."

He looked speculatively at Jenna. "But what about you? Would you rather have Paris?"

"I wouldn't mind visiting, but I wouldn't want to live there. Moonlight Harbor has my heart."

"Paris would be a wonderful place to honeymoon," Aunt Edie said slyly.

Jenna could feel herself blushing although she wasn't sure why. It was now obvious to everyone, including her, that she and Brody were a permanent item.

He chuckled. "It might be at that." The movie credits began to roll and he said, "Okay, ladies, time for a second feature. What have you got with guns and gore, Edie?"

"Nothing," she said. "Well, except for one of those Jack Reacher movies." She looked accusingly at Jenna. "Jenna bought it for me."

"You know you enjoyed it," Jenna said.

"Sounds good to me. Let's put it on," said Brody. He knelt in front of the wicker basket that held the DVD collection Jenna had made for Aunt Edie—streaming still wasn't her thing.

"It was exciting, I'll say that," Aunt Edie conceded. "And that Tom Cruise is such a cutie. Not as cute as James

Garner was, mind you. Nobody was as gorgeous as him when he was in his prime."

"Yeah, but Tom is a man of action," Brody said. "Gotta love that."

"He doesn't say a lot in this movie though," said Aunt Edie.

A man of action who didn't say a lot. Who did that remind Jenna of? Never mind Seth. He was history now, the road not taken. Brody was the future, a perfect future.

She made popcorn and he got the movie going and they all settled in to watch it. Cozy, homey, comfortable—this would be the rest of her life. Safe. She was more than ready for that after the drama and heartbreak Damien had dished out.

The movie came to a satisfying end, with the fictional Jack Reacher riding off into the sunset—on a bus instead of the proverbial horse—ready to continue righting wrongs.

Sabrina and Scotty arrived, hungry after a night of laser tag at Sabrina's friend Hudson's house.

"How was laser tag?" Jenna asked.

"It was wig," Scotty said.

Which Jenna knew meant awesome. Hey, she was on top of things.

"Do we have any cookies left?" Sabrina asked Aunt Edie as Scotty plopped on the floor and stretched out his legs.

"We do. I'll get you some."

"I can get them," Sabrina said easily and hurried off to the kitchen.

"What did you guys do tonight?" Scotty asked politely, taking in the three oldies.

Walked on the beach, kissed, the usual female fantasy

stuff. "We watched a movie with Aunt Edie," Jenna said. Yep. Nice, cozy and homey.

Scotty nodded politely. "Cool."

Probably pretty boring compared to laser tag.

Brody took the arrival of the kids as a signal to leave and stood. "Guess I'll get going," he said.

"I'll walk you to the door," Jenna offered.

Once there, he snugged her up against him for a final kiss. She could get used to this.

"I can't get enough of you," he whispered against her hair.

Oh, yeah. More good female fantasy stuff. Except this was real life now. Her life.

"You always know what to say," she told him.

He should have. He'd had enough practice. With several women in town, as a matter of fact.

But so what? She was the one he wanted.

Yes, her life was moving forward. She found herself too keyed up to sleep, even after she'd shooed Scotty off and Aunt Edie and Sabrina had gone to bed—one to sleep, the other to text with her friends. The beach was calling.

She crossed the dunes to find someone had a small fire going, a solitary man. She knew exactly who. She should turn back. Beach fires with Seth would hardly be appropriate now that she was moving forward with Brody.

She started to back up, but he had eyes like an owl and he'd seen her. "Join me," he called.

It would be rude not to. He was a big part of her life at the Driftwood. They were friends.

"Your mom all settled in?" he asked as she took a seat next to him on a log.

He pulled a can of root beer out of the mini-cooler at his feet and offered it to her. He knew she wasn't a beer drinker. Had he hoped she'd see his fire and join him and planned accordingly?

She took it and popped the top, took a drink. She suddenly felt a little hot, sitting there by the fire.

"Yep. I think she'll be happy down here."

"Pretty hard not to be. Nice house."

"She could have stayed with us, though," Jenna said. "We'd have made room for her."

"Parents like having their own digs. Both my brother and my sister have tried to talk our mom into living with them. She says the only way they'll get her out of her place is feetfirst."

"What's your mom like?"

"Good-hearted, strong. My dad wasn't in the picture for long. She pretty much raised us single-handed. She's a lot like your mom, only a little rougher around the edges."

"Will she ever come up here and visit?"

"She says she'll make the trek if I get married." He cleared his throat, took a drink from the beer can he was holding.

"Which will be in a parallel universe," Jenna said.

A little resentfully? No. She had no reason to be resentful. Her life was all sorted out. She moved them on to new conversational territory. "Thanks again for your help today."

"You didn't really need me. You had plenty of help."

"I'll always need you," she said. As a friend, of course.

"I don't think so. You've got the house peddler now. Looks like things are getting serious between you two."

"I need to get serious with someone," she said.

"Yeah, you do," he agreed, but didn't volunteer for the position. "I want to see you happy."

"With another man."

"The guy's got money, a fancy house, fancy car."

"As if that stuff's important to me? How shallow do you think I am?" she demanded.

"You're not, but there's nothing wrong with having a good life. He'll be good to you."

"I need somebody to be good to me." It was about time. Past time.

"You deserve that," he said.

All this nobility. Blech. "You don't have to be so agreeable, you know."

"How do you want me to be?" He sounded irritated.

Jealous. Angry. Willing to fight for her. "Why did you invite me to join you, anyway?"

"Heard you coming. I was being polite."

"Polite, huh? You know what? You're a tease."

He crumpled his beer can and tossed it in the minicooler. He shoved it shut, then stood and doused the fire with a nearby bucket of water.

"No, I just have a hard time letting go," he muttered.

"No one told you to let go," she snapped.

He kicked sand over the sizzling mess. "No one had to." He picked up his cooler and bucket. "Good night, Jenna."

It was suddenly very cold with the fire doused. She stood, shivering, and watched him walk away. Seth was damaged and there was no mending him because he wouldn't let anyone close enough to do that. She truly had made the right choice.

She went to bed and slept dreamlessly all night. That bothered her almost more than the crazy dreams she'd been having, though she wasn't sure why.

There was little enough time to think about it. Between family breakfast and church, Sunday was a busy morning. Right after lunch, Brody took Celeste and Henry house hunting. Henry had gotten money from his publisher and was finally open to looking. They'd decided to keep the houseboat as a rental and had set a budget for what they felt they could spend on a house and Celeste was now a woman on a mission. Sabrina and Aunt Edie stayed behind to play with the baby while Jenna went on the hunt with her sister and brother-in-law.

The house Celeste had lusted over hadn't lasted, but she'd found more on the internet and had finally convinced her long-suffering husband to come look with her. Henry balked at the price on the first house, and vetoed even going inside no matter how hard she begged.

"If we go in it we'll want it," he said.

"They always look at houses that are over budget on *House Hunters*," she argued.

"We're not on *House Hunters*," he argued back. "Don't do it to me, Brody."

"Henry's right," Jenna said, taking his side.

"How much is he paying you?" Celeste cracked, then said, "Okay, I can compromise. We'll pass on that one."

They saw a new build that had yet to be landscaped, and a two-bedroom house that didn't offer any office space, which Henry insisted on having if he was going to move. The next house was on the Bell Canal, so named because of its unique shape, and had a fenced-in front yard where Edie could play when she got older. Out back was more yard, also fenced, with a gate that led to the canal and a dock.

"We could all go kayaking," Celeste said.

"That would be cool," Henry admitted.

Jenna thought so, too. She'd gone a couple of times the summer before with Brody and had found it both relaxing and a good workout.

The house only had two bedrooms, but the owners had

taken up half the two-car garage with a room that served as a man cave. "You could have your office there," Celeste said to Henry.

He looked around, rubbed his chin thoughtfully. "Yeah, it could work. It's sure more room than I've got on the boat." To Brody he said, "It's eight thousand over our budget. Think the owners would take less?"

"Very possibly," Brody said.

Celeste groaned. "Henry, this is no time to be cheap. Someone will come in and offer full price and we'll lose out."

"Or the owners will take our offer and we'll make a deal," Henry said. "Didn't you say this has been on the market for a while?" he asked Brody.

Brody checked his printout. "Thirty-one days. They might be open to an offer. Want me to make the call?"

"Yes!" Celeste said eagerly and Henry nodded agreement, and Brody took them back to Aunt Edie's to await the answer.

"It's only eight thousand dollars less than they're asking," Celeste said hopefully to Jenna as they took Nemo for a beach walk. "That's not much."

"It might be to the sellers. You never know about people's finances." Eight thousand dollars was still a lot of money to her.

Celeste gnawed on a corner of her lip. "Henry probably won't budge on the price. If I could just get him to see what a good investment it is."

"It is a good investment, but if you wait you might find something you like just as well for the amount you can afford to pay."

"We can afford to pay that amount," Celeste insisted. "And prices will only keep going up here."

"I guess you two have a lot to talk about," Jenna said.

"Or fight about."

It took a while for the other real estate agent to track down the owners, who'd gone off somewhere for the day, and when he did the answer came back as a firm no.

"Sorry," Brody said. "It's not that much of a difference and I thought maybe they'd go for it."

"That's a shame," Aunt Edie said.

"That's a shame," repeated Jolly Roger from his cage.

Celeste looked pleadingly at Henry, who was sitting next to her on the couch. Poor Henry actually squirmed.

"I can get a job teaching down here," Celeste said.

"And then who will watch Edie?" he argued. "I've got a deadline."

"Okay, I can substitute, just work a couple days a week. Mom would love to help with the baby."

"She would," put in Jenna. "She's already offered to help me in the office at the Driftwood." Oh, no. Had she just helped her sister gang up on Henry? "Sorry," she muttered. "I'm Switzerland. I'm neutral."

Henry gave her a half smile. "Yeah, I can tell." To Celeste he said, "Let's take a walk and talk about this, okay? Give us a few," he said to Brody.

"Sure," Brody said easily.

"Henry, if you don't want to do this, there's no sense even talking," Celeste said, resigned to her fate.

"Come on. You can pretend we're filming an episode of *House Hunters*. The couple always goes somewhere and talks about the houses they saw, right?"

"But we already picked one," she pointed out. "If you won't go full price, there's nothing to talk about."

"Yes, there is," Henry said, and stood up.

Celeste frowned, but she stood, too, and followed him through the house and out the back door.

"Poor guy. Nothing like putting him on the spot in front of all of us," Jenna said. "He's actually a little shy," she explained to Brody.

"No man wants his in-laws watching while he hashes out something this big with his wife," Brody said.

"I don't think he's going to budge," Jenna said.

"You never know," put in Aunt Edie, who'd stuck around for the great house debate. "Your sister can be pretty persuasive."

It appeared she could, indeed, because half an hour later she and Henry were back. She was practically giddy and he was smiling. Not the biggest smile Jenna had ever seen. It looked more like the smile of a gracious loser.

"Are you sure you're okay with this?" she asked him as Brody stepped out on the porch to make the call.

Henry nodded. "I want Celeste to be happy. And she's right. It's not that much over our budget, and buying down here is a good investment. We can make it work."

"Keep murdering people for a living and we'll be great," Celeste said, and kissed him.

The full price offer was accepted, and later that evening, Brody took the whole family out to dinner again to celebrate.

"You didn't have to do that," Jenna said afterward when the two of them sat on his deck, watching the sun set.

"Sure I did. A smart real estate agent always goes the extra mile."

"Does that mean you'll be around for another moving day?" she teased.

"I'll be around for longer than that," he said.

Ah, yes, life was good at the beach.

It was even better on Monday, when she sat down at her computer in the motel office and discovered that they had gotten a booking through the website for the July Fourth holiday. No more vacancies at the Driftwood. Yay!

Then she saw the name.

Noooo.

Thirteen

Mel was working on putting her bedroom to rights when Jenna stopped by. "How's it coming?" she asked when Mel let her in.

"I'm making progress."

"Do you need help?"

"No, you all helped with the hard part."

Jenna pointed to the kitchen. "Looks like you've got the kitchen done." She walked over to the counter where Mel had set out her vintage cookie jar and gave the ceramic pig a pat on the head. "This makes it look like home."

"It'll be more like home when I have a chance to bake some cookies for it," Mel said. "Would you like something to drink? I have plenty of pop leftover from Saturday."

"No, I'm fine. I can't stay long anyway," Jenna said and settled on the couch.

Obviously her girl wanted to talk. Mel took a seat at the opposite end. "How's everything at the Driftwood Inn? You don't need me yet, do you?"

Of course, if she did Mel would drop what she was doing and go over. One of the lures of moving to the beach had been the opportunity to be useful.

"I can manage for now," Jenna said, "but I could use you on July third. We're going to be busy with people checking in, and I have three massages scheduled for that day."

"I'm happy to help," Mel said. "Are you all booked up now?"

"We just filled our last room." Jenna made a face.

Ah, here was the reason for the visit. "That's a good thing, isn't it?" Mel asked.

"In this case, not really. It's Winston."

"Oh."

Mel wasn't sure what else to say. Jenna hadn't exactly enjoyed her cousin's last visit to Moonlight Harbor. The fact that Aunt Edie didn't like him also affected Jenna's attitude.

It was a shame, really. He and Jenna and Celeste had happily played together as children when the families met up at the beach. But, sadly, where Jenna had grown up to become responsible and hardworking, Winston had turned into a mooch. His job history was spotty and his familial loyalty was suspect, especially when it came to Aunt Edie. Still, he was family. What could you do?

"He's only coming to suck up to Aunt Edie and tear me down. Last time he was here he told me I was in over my head."

"This time he'll see that you aren't," Mel said.

"Even if he does he'll never admit it. I'm sure he'll find something to complain about no matter what room I give him, and I know he's going to expect to get one for next to nothing if not for free since he's family." Jenna scowled. "But he's only family when he wants something. Of course he'll invite himself to our beach party if he gets wind of it."

"At least you'll be outdoors and little Win-Win won't be able to get in the house and terrorize Roger." Jenna rolled her eyes at the mention of Winston's son and Mel hurried on. "It's only for a couple of days, darling."

"I wish. He's booked for the whole long weekend. He'd better not think he's getting a free room at the height of tourist season." Jenna shook her head. "I know it's wrong to have such a bad attitude, but honestly, I can't stand him."

"Why do you think that is?" Mel asked.

She sounded like a counselor. But then, in a way, she was. It went with the territory when you were a mother. Her daughters still came to her for advice, the same as she'd gone to her own mother.

Sadly, she'd lost her mother the year before Jenna moved to Moonlight Harbor. At least she still had her mother-in-law. And dear Aunt Edie.

Jenna rubbed her forehead. "I think it started with that visit when I first moved down here. He's such a loser and a leech, but he acted so superior. Kind of reminds me of Damien. I guess that's the real reason he bugs me."

"That probably sums it up," Mel agreed. "But he's made a reservation in good faith, so you can hardly turn him away. Anyway, I'm sure you won't see much of him. He and his family will want to watch the parade and play on the beach, visit the booths and go on the rides down at the pier."

"You're right. And if I don't see him he won't find out about our annual beach fire."

"I wouldn't count on it," Mel said, but hurried to add, "Don't worry though. I certainly won't tell him." Unless he asked outright if they were doing anything. Then she'd be trapped. Lying wasn't in her repertoire.

"You'd better hope he doesn't find out you bought a house down here. He'll be wanting to stay with you. Last I heard he'd lost his latest job. He and Kelly could happily camp out in your second bedroom forever and stick Winston Junior on the sofa bed."

Mel wasn't particularly close with either Winston or his father, her brother, but she knew she'd feel honor bound to host her nephew and his family at her place if Winston ever asked.

The idea of having company when she was barely moved in was almost enough to make her shudder. Not that she didn't enjoy entertaining, but there was a time for everything, and this wasn't the time. Moving was exhausting and she knew she'd be setting things right for weeks. She couldn't imagine cooking for company on top of that.

Winston would certainly expect it. He took after his father, who was a little on the lazy side and not very good at taking responsibility for himself. Arthur had hit her up for several loans over the years when he was in between jobs. Other than exchanging Christmas and birthday cards (the ones from him always signed by his wife) and her calling him occasionally to check on him, those were about the only times she'd heard from him. He certainly hadn't been there to offer support when John died. Winston would have no problem considering her home his home—coming often and staying long.

"I hate how he's been trying to ingratiate himself with Aunt Edie for the last few years, and now he's coming back like a bad smell."

"You have to put up with family," Mel said. She wished John had come with brothers. She knew she'd have been close with them.

Of course, that was assuming they'd have turned out like him. Siblings could be as different as night and day. She and Arthur were proof of it.

"I'm sure it will all work out fine," she said to Jenna. "Things have a way of sorting themselves out."

"If I had my way I'd sort Winston completely out of our lives," Jenna said.

She was still grumbling when someone knocked at the screen door. It was Ellis West, bearing a bouquet of pink and white roses.

Mel's heart rate picked up at the sight of him.

"Did I interrupt you girls?" he asked as she let him in.

"No, I was just leaving," Jenna said, standing up.

"You don't have to rush off," Mel told her. It wasn't as if she and Ellis needed their privacy. In fact, since she was leery of getting too involved with him, she was glad to have her daughter there as a buffer.

Jenna had no intention of buffering, however. She gave Mel a quick kiss on the cheek and then was gone.

"I thought you might like some flowers for your new home," Ellis said, handing them over.

"Thank you. I do love roses."

She took them to the kitchen and pulled out a large cut glass vase from one of the cupboards. It had been her mother's and she treasured it.

"It was so thoughtful of you," she said.

Ellis was a thoughtful man. Good company, generous. Any woman in her right mind would be encouraging him.

She filled the vase with water, saying, "Sit down. May I offer you something to drink? I was just telling Jenna, I have pop leftover from moving day."

"Sure, I'll take a Coke when you're done," he said, and settled on the couch where Jenna had just been.

"Flowers make a room look so special," she said as she arranged them in the vase.

"My wife loved flowers."

She could picture him stopping off after work and picking up flowers. For John and her that sort of thing had been a luxury. Still, he'd always gotten her one long-stemmed rose for Valentine's Day.

Mel set the vase on the kitchen counter, then brought him his drink and sat in a chair. Smiled at him. He looked so at home on that couch. Almost as if he belonged.

"You getting settled in okay?" he asked.

"I've got the kitchen squared away," she said. Now would he expect her to invite him for dinner? "And I'm slowly getting the bedroom set to rights." Did that sound provocative? "I'm getting a lot done," she finished. And that sounded like an efficiency report. "I've already met the neighbors on one side. Two sisters, both retired schoolteachers. They brought me jam."

As if he cared what they brought her. Her conversation was about as sparkling as a dirty glass.

"But nobody's brought me flowers," she said. "That was kind of you."

"It's been a long time since I've brought a woman flowers."

He sounded wistful, and Mel was sure he was thinking of his wife. "What was your wife's name? You never told me."

"Camille."

"That's a very glamorous name."

"It fit her. She was a pretty woman. She'd have liked you."

"I think my John would have liked you, too," Mel said. The conversation suddenly felt a little too intimate. She switched gears. "I must say, you have excellent taste."

"I know how to spot an exceptional woman, that's for sure," he said.

She waved away the compliment. "I meant the flowers. I'm not exceptional."

"You don't think so, huh? I'd say anyone who could raise two such great daughters on her own qualifies for exceptional."

"You do what you have to do."

"Now you're here at the beach and you can do what you want to do. I thought maybe tonight you'd want to take me up on that offer of dinner," he said.

She'd been working hard trying to get things squared away, and the idea of cooking anything was far from appealing. And talk about appealing. There sat Ellis, smiling at her.

If Edie was there she'd say, *What are you waiting for?*

Mel was beginning to wonder. She still felt so conflicted. But here was Ellis, in her living room, on her couch, looking like he belonged. It was only dinner, for heaven's sake. And she did want to be friends.

"I'd like that," she said. "But nothing expensive."

"All right. How about Sandy's? It's casual dining but nice."

"It sounds perfect," she said.

"Great. I'll pick you up at six thirty." He finished his drink, then stood, saying, "I guess I'd better let you get back to work."

Another date. She felt suddenly giddy.

He'd barely left when Roberta, her friend from the old neighborhood, called. "How are you doing down there?"

"Fine," Mel said. "I love my new house."

"I'm glad. So this is all working out for you."

"It is," Mel said.

"Have you met many new people?"

"I have," Mel said, and thought of Ellis.

"Good. I hope you'll have me down when you're all settled in. I'm anxious to see your new digs."

"I will," Mel promised.

Roberta went on to fill her in on the goings-on in the old neighborhood. The young couple down the street were getting a divorce and their place was up for sale. Caroline fell down her daughter's stairs. Nothing broken, thankfully, but she was pretty sore and bruised.

"Other than that, nothing much," Roberta concluded. "I half envy you, getting a fresh start in a new place. I'm sure you're going to have lots of adventures."

Mel felt like she was perched on the edge of adventure. All she had to do was walk into it. She decided not to tell Roberta about Ellis. She already had enough people giving her advice.

She finished with her bedroom and then, after cleaning the tub, indulged in a bubble bath. She still had so much work to do, so much to unpack. But the kitchen and bedroom were taken care of, and that was enough for the moment. Life was all about balance. She'd rest for the remainder of the afternoon. The unpacking could wait.

The afternoon wasn't as restful as she'd hoped. She found it too hard to settle her thoughts. She kept jumping ahead to the evening, fretting over what she'd say, what she'd wear. Exceptional. Ellis thought she was exceptional. How did a woman live up to that?

She didn't, of course. Mel knew who she was—a simple woman who had raised a family. That was all. She didn't own a business, didn't have a college degree. She'd never had a chance to travel much. In short, she was nothing special.

But later, when Ellis picked her up, he managed to make

her feel special. He took in her skinny jeans and casual white V-neck top and said, "You sure know how to dress."

Well, yes, there was something she did well. It had been a little embarrassing getting caught in ancient yoga pants and a T-shirt earlier.

"I must admit, I do like pretty clothes."

"And I like seeing a well-dressed woman," he said. "A win-win for both of us."

Ellis West certainly was easy to please.

He didn't seem to find fault with her conversation as they dined. She told him about her book club and how she hoped to start one in Moonlight Harbor, talked about looking forward to helping Jenna at the Driftwood, asked how on earth he'd gotten that giant razor clam on top of the Seafood Shack.

"Let me tell you, it wasn't easy. I had to hire someone to come with a crane. Big excitement in town. For a day," he finished with a chuckle.

They moved on from there to the topic of travel. "Other than my honeymoon in Victoria, I've never been out of the country," Mel said. "Someday I would love to see Paris."

"It's a great city. Lots of history, good food. I could picture you walking along the Champs-Élysées," Ellis said.

"So you've been there, obviously."

"I took my wife for our twenty-fifth wedding anniversary," he said. "I wanted to take her there for our honeymoon but we were too broke."

"We were broke, too," Mel said. "I guess that's how most of us start out."

"It is," he agreed. "We didn't care. We were happy together. We ate a lot of franks and beans and mac and cheese though. It was nice when we could finally afford meat loaf. And Paris was worth waiting for. By our twenty-fifth we could actually pay for a meal in one of those fancy French restaurants."

"That's the beauty of waiting," Mel said. "If you wait long enough you eventually get where you want to be."

She was where she wanted to be, back full circle with both her daughters nearby. And maybe, someday, she'd get to Paris.

They finished dinner and wound up on the beach, seated side by side on a log, looking out at the water. "I never get tired of this view," Ellis said.

"I don't think I ever will," Mel said. After so many years alone it felt good to be with someone, sharing a lovely view. Sharing life. "I hadn't realized how much I missed this," she mused.

"What?"

"Just being with someone."

He nodded. "I'm with people a lot, but it's not the same when you're single."

"No, it's not," she agreed. "I'm glad you asked me to dinner."

"I hope we can do it again."

"I'd like that."

Sharing thoughts, sharing memories, talking with someone who'd been down that same dark path of losing a mate—it was like a tonic for her soul and she was glad she'd accepted his invitation.

"Only next time let me cook for you," she said.

"Home cooking. That's another thing I've missed. Not that I can't cook," he hurried to add.

"Oh? What do you make? Do you have a specialty?"

"Yeah. Fried eggs."

She chuckled.

"I eat out a lot," he confessed.

"That sounds good to me," she said.

"It gets old."

So did eating at home alone.

They stayed at the beach until the sun left the party and temperatures dropped. Then he took her home.

She toyed with the idea of asking him in but rejected it. Who knew what that would imply? Maybe he'd expect her to haul him off to her bedroom. It seemed like that was the norm in every TV show and movie she watched. Couples barely together for five minutes would wind up back at her place or his, ripping each other's clothes off. That wasn't her norm.

Again, at the door, he pointed to his cheek. "How about an encore?"

It was so sweet. She was happy to oblige. "And how about that dinner here with me tomorrow?"

"I could go for that," he said with a grin.

"What's your favorite food?"

"Pot roast. With spuds and carrots."

"I make a mean pot roast," she said. "Exceptional, in fact," she added, and was grinning, too.

"You've got my mouth watering already," he said. "Good night, Melody. Thanks for the companionship."

Companionship, a lovely word.

She watched him walk down the front walk to his car. "No, thank you," she murmured.

She shut the door and went to sit on her back porch and enjoy the night sky. She was happy. It felt almost disloyal to John.

That night she dreamed she was at a masked ball in some fancy ballroom in what looked like Venice, because beyond the ballroom doors she could see a canal with gondolas parked along it. Her fellow guests were dressed in fancy ball gowns and tuxedos.

She stood at the edge of the crowd wearing a red satin gown and ruby-red slippers like Dorothy had worn when she went to Oz. She was alone, searching the crowd for... who? She wasn't sure.

Suddenly a large man in a mask, wearing a dark cape over clothes from the nineteenth century, appeared. "Dance with me," he commanded, holding out a gloved hand.

That voice. She knew that voice. But from where?

"John, is that you?" she asked.

He didn't answer. Instead, he swept her onto the floor among the dancing throng. "It's time you lived a little," he said to her.

"I have been living," she informed him.

"No, you haven't. You've been waiting."

Next thing she knew he'd danced her out onto the veranda. The stars were shimmering and so were the dark waters of the canal. He drew her close and kissed her, and she felt it from the top of her head to the tips of her toes, which were curling inside those ruby slippers.

"Who are you?" she asked.

She awoke before she got an answer.

The day of Sabrina's graduation ceremony brought clear skies and sunshine. And a car for Sabrina that Seth had overhauled for Jenna. It was a bright blue 2014 Ford Focus hatchback that had needed some engine work and a ton of cosmetic repair, but it had turned out looking like new. They'd wrapped it in blue and gold ribbon, the school colors. Sabrina had been ecstatic, jumping all over the parking lot, hugging both Jenna and Seth, squealing loud enough to bring people poking their heads out of their rooms at the Driftwood.

She'd been almost as thrilled with the afghan Aunt Edie had made for her. "I'll treasure it forever," she'd said, hugging Aunt Edie.

Talk about treasuring forever. Jenna got all misty-eyed seeing her baby in her cap and gown. Senior pictures, prom picture, cap-and-gown pictures—Jenna would have enough to fill an entire photo album.

Happily, the ocean breezes kept the ceremony attendees cool as they sat in the Moonlight Harbor High stadium and cheered as the graduates walked forward to accept their diplomas.

"She looks so pretty," Aunt Edie said as Jenna snapped pictures with her phone. "And to think she graduated at the top of her class."

The top ten percent. Not quite high enough to be valedictorian, but high enough to make her family proud.

The whole family was there for the occasion, including Damien and the in-laws. It was one of many events they'd be attending together over the coming years. Aurora, the other woman, was history, but Jenna knew Damien had been seeing a new woman. Thank God he hadn't brought her along.

Of course, at some point, he would make it permanent with someone and both he and that someone would be present at Sabrina's wedding. The someone would probably get invited to bridal showers and baby showers and baby's first birthday parties.

Get used to it, Jenna told herself. Damien would always be on hand to pour salt on the wound he'd inflicted when he left her for another woman.

Except that wound was finally closing, so let him pour

away. Life in Moonlight Harbor was good and Jenna would soon have her own someone to be present at weddings and baby's first birthdays. She could let go of the old bitterness now. It was time. New beginnings all round. For Sabrina and her parents.

Both Seth and Brody had come to the graduation, and Jenna had taken a secret pleasure in the way Damien had looked them over. She especially loved how he'd frowned when Brody put an arm around her. Yes, living well was the best revenge.

With the ceremony over, everyone went back to the house, where Aunt Edie and Jenna and Mel and Celeste had worked together to prepare a feast. If a table really could groan, their dining table would have. It was loaded with platters of cold cuts and cheese, bread and condiments, fruit, veggies and dip, chips, and, of course, Aunt Edie's cookies. A punch bowl sat at one end, and on the other end was a basket with graduation cards that were probably stuffed with money and gift cards.

All their friends came and the living room was packed. Damien and his parents came, too. Jenna was polite to her former in-laws and civil to him. She was delighted that they didn't stay more than half an hour. That was hardly surprising, as Damien couldn't long endure being at a function where he wasn't the center of attention.

He'd gifted Sabrina with a work of art he'd made specially for her (and specially to show himself off). It was a sculpture of a woman created from nuts and bolts and silverware. Her hair had been formed from springs and her metal arms were lifted, reaching for the sky.

"I call it *Transition*," he'd said to Sabrina when he presented it to her.

"I call it tacky," Jenna had said to Celeste as he took his bow and departed.

"He probably will be famous someday," she'd replied.

"Maybe. For sure he'll never say, 'I owe my success to my ex-wife who footed the bill for years so I could play with garbage.'"

Oh, well. He was gone. Let the fun begin.

It did. Celeste had written a poem she titled "Ode to the Graduate," which listed all the important things Sabrina would miss such as homework and boring teachers. "And now she goes forth, her future sunny. I hope you all gave her lots of money," Celeste concluded, which made everyone laugh. "Seriously, I know my amazing niece will go on to do great things," she said. "Of course, that's what everyone says about graduates. But in Sabrina's case it's true. All the journaling you've been doing, I'm sure you're going to go on to become a famous writer."

"Maybe I'll write about you and Mom," Sabrina said to her.

"Oh, Lord, I hope not," Jenna said.

Nora produced a huge ice cream cake, her gift to the graduate, and put Sabrina to work cutting it. The attentive silence ended, and the guests began to chat.

"Good turnout," Seth said to Jenna as they stood watching Brody take a piece of cake to Aunt Edie, who was feeling tired and had settled on the couch. "Thanks for inviting me to the ceremony."

"Sabrina loves you. You're like one of the family," Jenna said.

"A distant cousin?"

She made a face. "Let's not use the word *cousin*. It only makes me think of my cousin, Winston."

"Who, I take it, was not invited."

"He wouldn't have come, anyway. There's nothing in it for him."

"Such a cynic," Seth teased.

"No, a realist."

He nodded to where Aunt Edie sat. "Your aunt looks pooped."

Jenna sighed. "She's really been slowing down this last year. She tires so easily. I wish I could get her to do less."

"Good luck with that."

"She was out of breath after climbing the stairs at the stadium," Jenna said.

"So was I."

"I wonder if I should take her to the doctor. She's not fond of getting checkups. But she really should go. In fact, I'm thinking we should talk to him together. I don't even know for sure what meds he's got her on, if any."

Jenna remembered the doctor asking Aunt Edie if she was taking her aspirin on the home visit he'd paid back when she'd given Jenna a scare. Was she still taking it? Should the doctor prescribe something stronger? For all Jenna knew, maybe he had.

Seth shook his head. "Like I said, good luck."

Good luck was right. When it came to her health, Aunt Edie was tight-lipped.

After the fun and frivolity was over and Sabrina was off partying with her friends, Jenna tippy-toed up to the subject.

"You look awfully tired, Auntie," she said.

"I am," Aunt Edie admitted, and heaved a sigh.

"You know, I was thinking. It's been a while since you've been to see Dr. Fielding."

"And it's going to be a while," Aunt Edie said firmly.

Jenna tried again. "It might be time for a checkup though. I could go with you."

Aunt Edie frowned at her. "Jenna, I'm not a child and I can certainly go to the doctor by myself."

"I just thought…" Hmm. How to phrase it so as not to alarm her aunt?

"I know what you thought. You're worried. But there's no need to be. I know I'm slowing down. I don't have the stamina I had when I was seventy, but that's to be expected. I'm fine, dear, really. Just wearing out, and that happens to all of us if we live long enough."

"I'd feel better if the doctor said you were fine."

"I tell you what, I'll go later this fall if it will make you happy."

"You could go now and get it checked off your to-do list. That would really make me happy."

"It's not on my to-do list. It's on yours."

Jenna frowned.

"Now, don't fuss. I'm fine. I'll go after tourist season is over. Right now I'm too busy."

Taking care of all of them, baking cookies for their guests at the Driftwood. "We could manage without cookies for a day," Jenna said.

"No we couldn't. It's a tradition now. Stop worrying, dear. Worry gives you wrinkles, and it doesn't accomplish anything."

It certainly wasn't getting Jenna anywhere with her aunt.

"I'll be fine. Let's talk instead about you. When are you and Brody going to get engaged? I've been ready to throw you an engagement party for the last year."

"Soon, I promise," Jenna said.

"I hope so," said Aunt Edie. "I don't want to have to keep worrying about you."

"You don't need to," Jenna assured her. "Anyway, worrying gives you wrinkles."

Aunt Edie wagged a finger at her. "You are a saucy thing."

Brody returned at that moment, bringing a movie he'd rented from Redbox that he thought Aunt Edie would enjoy.

"Oh, a movie about crooks. I do love those," Aunt Edie said happily.

"I figured you girls would be too tired to do much of anything," he said.

"You are the best, Brody," Aunt Edie told him.

Yes, he was. And they really did need to oblige Aunt Edie and hurry up and make what they had official.

Courtney turned the sign in the window of Beach Babes to Closed. Her first month in business had been great.

The old saying, be careful what you wish for, came to mind. She was paying the price for success. She was exhausted and, even though she'd rather have her toes cut off than admit it, a little overwhelmed. Dealing with suppliers and having no real day off was turning her into a zombie. Her designs were selling beyond her wildest dreams but keeping up with demand was a bit of a nightmare. Her seamstresses were sewing like mad and so was she, but it felt like trying to bail water from the *Titanic* with a teacup. When she wasn't in the shop she was sewing or working on the website and filling online orders.

"You'll have to hire more people," Jenna had told her. "Really, you should be home sewing and designing instead of being in the shop all the time. Anyone can ring up a sale. You're the only one who can design a dress. It's a little like running a motel. You get someone else to clean the rooms so you can manage the bookings."

Of course, Jenna was right. CEOs of big companies didn't man the phones. She was going to have to hire and delegate. She decided to drop by Brody's real estate office and tell him the new plan. She wanted to give him a progress report, anyway.

She found him in his office, visiting with Taylor Marsh, his star agent.

"Hi Courtney," Taylor greeted her. "Sorry I didn't make it to your grand opening. I had an open house that day. I'm going to get in though," she hurried on.

"No worries," Courtney said. Taylor had her own career to work plus a husband and daughter. Courtney wasn't keeping score.

She turned to Brody. "I came by to tell you that we've had an awesome first...whoa, what is that?" She pointed to the open ring box on the desk.

"I was just showing Taylor," he began.

"For Jenna?" As if she had to ask.

He nodded and grinned.

"I saw him come in with it and demanded to see it," Taylor said. "It's about time."

"Hey, it's not my fault it's taken so long," he said. His face was lit up like Times Square and he looked like a little boy on Christmas morning who'd gotten everything he'd asked for.

Courtney picked it up and examined it. The ring was white gold, with a princess cut diamond surrounded by twinkling round diamonds. It was dazzling.

"Where are my sunglasses?" she joked.

"Think she'll like it?" Brody asked.

"I already told him she would but he doesn't believe me," Taylor said.

"Oh, yeah," Courtney handed it back. "If she doesn't I'll marry you."

Brody chuckled, picked up the ring and looked at it. "I hope she'll like it."

"Does she know this is coming?" Courtney asked.

It would be horrible if he proposed and she turned him down. Although, really, why would she?

"Pretty much. I'm going to officially propose at the beach party on the Fourth."

"That should start some fireworks," Courtney predicted.

"One can only hope," he said.

So it was finally happening for Jenna. Courtney was glad for her friend. After everything she'd been through she deserved to be happy. And that ring, wow. Brody had to have paid a small fortune for it.

"Guess who's getting the most gorgeous diamond ring ever?" she said to Annie when she got home.

Annie didn't look up from the cupcakes she was frosting. "You."

"Me, at some point. But, no. Jenna. Brody just showed it to me." Courtney sat down at the kitchen table and dipped a finger in the frosting bowl. Chocolate. And… "What's in the frosting?"

"Lavender."

"Dibs on licking the bowl."

Annie smiled. "Too late. Emma beat you to it."

"Where is she?"

"Over at Addie's house." Annie piped a swirl of frosting on top of a vanilla cupcake, then handed it over to Courtney, who murmured her thanks and dove in.

"So they're finally going to take the next step," Annie said.

"It looks that way. Brody's pretty confident. He's going to make his big proposal on the Fourth at Edie and Jenna's beach party."

"I'm glad for her," Annie said. "She deserves a happy ending."

"She does," Courtney agreed. Then added, "So do we all. So do you."

Annie lifted a shoulder. "I'm good."

"I know, but don't you want to be better?"

"I don't know," Annie said, keeping her focus on decorating the next cupcake. "I don't think I'm a very good judge of men."

"Maybe you weren't in the past, but that's not to say you won't be in the future."

"Maybe not. But really, I'm so busy I don't have time for romance."

"Now, that's just sad." Courtney took another bite of her cupcake, then went to the fridge in search of milk to wash it down. "I can hardly wait to see Jenna's face when Brody whips out that chunk of bling."

"Speaking of bling, do you think Jonas might propose to you on the Fourth?"

"Well, he's got 'til the end of the year, so maybe. He doesn't have very many holidays between now and then."

"Christmas, New Year's Eve," Annie said.

"Yeah, I'm thinking New Year's Eve." She poured her milk, sat back down at the table and reached for another cupcake.

"Maybe he isn't planning on proposing on a holiday," Annie suggested. "Maybe he'll show up here one night dressed like Zorro or something."

"I'm not pumping him for info," Courtney said. "I might

succeed in prying vital information out of him and that would spoil the surprise."

"Who cares as long as it happens, right?"

"It will."

"He's perfect for you," Annie said.

Yes, he was. "I'm so happy these days I feel like I'm on a constant chocolate high."

"I'm glad," Annie said.

That was Annie, unselfish and happy for her friends. If only she could find someone.

At least Jenna was finally getting her happy ending. She was proof that if you waited long enough, all the tangles in your life worked their way out.

A Fourth of July proposal—Courtney's man presenting her a diamond ring with fireworks flashing in the background. Hmm. That idea sounded good to her. Did it appeal to Jonas?

Fourteen

This year the Fourth of July fell on a Sunday, which was great for the Driftwood Inn. All their reservations were for Friday through Sunday night and some clear through until Tuesday. Money in the bank.

People started arriving by one on Friday, hoping for an early check-in. Mel came over to help out at the check-in desk and Aunt Edie supplied them with butterscotch brownies and oatmeal cookies to offer the guests. The supply was already going fast by the time Jenna finished with her massage clients and got to the office.

Celeste's family were planning to come down and stay in Mel's new house, since the Driftwood was fully booked, and even though Mel fussed over not being settled in yet, Jenna knew she'd never turn her daughter away. The whole family together, the Driftwood at full capacity—it was going to be a great holiday.

Semigreat, Jenna amended as her cousin, Winston, lumbered into the office, his wife and son in tow. Winston had lost more hair and put on more pounds since Jenna last saw him, and he'd grown a beard, a guy-frizz mess dangling from the end of his chin. Maybe he thought it made him look more masculine. It only made him look scruffy. He wore a red tie-dyed shirt with a flag pattern on one shoulder and jeans. On a young buff guy that shirt would look good. Winston was not a young buff guy.

His wife, Kelly, had slimmed down and was wearing some very short shorts and a tank top to show off her new figure. She'd acquired some stylish new glasses as well. She'd put her hair in a sloppy bun but it still looked stringy. A visit to Waves would do wonders. Of course, Jenna was hardly one to talk. She needed to schedule a visit to Waves herself.

Winston Junior, known as Win-Win, had gone from an obnoxious three-year old to a pudgy little boy with a sullen frown.

"Well, cousin," Winston greeted Jenna. "Here we are, ready for a good time. Hey, Win-Win, look. Cookies." Winston gave his son an oatmeal cookie and grabbed two for himself. "You got our room ready? Can we check in early? We're anxious to get out and look around."

Interesting. No mention of being anxious to see Aunt Edie.

"Sure," Jenna said. The sooner she got him checked in the sooner he'd go away.

He leaned an arm on the counter and surveyed her domain. "The place looks better than the last time we were here."

"We've done a lot with it."

He nodded, taking that in. "How's Aunt Edie?" he asked, and stuffed half a cookie in his mouth.

"She's fine."

"Still going strong?" he asked without bothering to swallow first.

His question didn't sit well. What did he mean by that?

Was he hoping she wouldn't be? "She is," Jenna lied, what little warmth she'd been able to inject into her voice vanishing.

"Lucky for you," he said, his jealousy of her favored status ill-disguised.

"Lucky for all of us," Jenna retorted.

At that moment Mel came back into the office with a fresh supply of cookies.

"Hey, Aunt Melody. Remember me?" he said to her. "It's Winston."

How could she not? On his family's last visit when he was twelve he'd broken the Dresden figurine that Grandma Jones had given her mom and then hid the broken figurine under the sofa bed.

"How are you, Winston?" she replied.

She had a smile for him and a hug. All grace and kindness. Unlike her daughter, who wished he'd get swept away by a sneaker wave.

"Doing great," he said. "And Kelly's selling makeup now. She's a natural."

Right on cue, Kelly produced a booklet filled with bargains. "Let me know what you'd like."

Mel took it. "That sounds like a fun job," she said, not making any promises.

But Jenna knew her mom. Mel's middle name was Softie. And she did like her bath oils and lotions.

"So, what's the family rate?" Winston asked Jenna and started on another cookie.

"The rate you saw on the website." She was aware of her mother, Ms. Sweet and Proper, standing next to her and forced her lips up at the corners.

Winston's didn't mirror hers. "Jeez, you'd think you'd

give family a break. Thought maybe you'd have a free room for us."

"I'm sorry, Winston," she said. Maybe he'd go away.

"We are kind of on a budget. How about we stay at the house?"

Like that was going to happen. "There's no room. Honestly, Winston, you're already getting a bargain. We're not the most expensive place in town."

"Or the best," he sniped. "But we wanted to give you some business."

"I appreciate that," Jenna said. "And I'm sure Aunt Edie does, too."

Her last remark magically brought about an attitude adjustment. "Family is important," Winston said. (He must have been talking to her mom.) "And we did want to see Aunt Edie, didn't we, Kelly?"

Kelly nodded. "Sure."

"I want another cookie," Win-Win whined.

Winston gave him a couple. Then he took another two for himself. They were locusts.

"I guess we'll have to suck it up," he said and sneaked a look in Melody's direction.

Oh, no. Don't even think it. "Mom's got a houseful, too," Jenna said, wishing Mel had left Uncle Arthur off the list when she'd announced her new address. "Come on, Winston, it's not that much. You just said you were doing great. And you know we'll all buy cosmetics from Kelly." That much she could do.

"Okay, fine," he said, his voice a mixture of irritation and resignation.

Jenna gave him his room key and shooed him off before he could devour every last cookie on the plate.

"You're right. He is obnoxious," Mel said as she thumbed

through the catalog. "But that's family. Some are gold and some are brass."

"I'm not sure he even qualifies for brass," Jenna said. *More like wood. No, not even wood. Cow pies?*

"This bath oil looks lovely."

Jenna glanced at the picture. "It does. Oooh, lemon verbena."

"It comes in gardenia, too. I think I'll order some," Mel said. "And maybe I'll buy the face peel as well."

"Yeah, that face peel looks good," Jenna agreed. They were only on the first couple of pages. Yep, Winston wasn't going to lose money on this visit.

A few minutes later Jenna saw his car—a shiny new SUV—drive off, and it looked like her wish was going to be granted and they wouldn't see anything of Winston and company. But no, come dinner time, just as they were all about to sit down at the kitchen table, there was a knock at Aunt Edie's front door.

"That's probably Scotty," Sabrina said, and ran off to let him in.

Scotty. *Yes, it's probably Scotty*, Jenna told herself. Deep down she knew it wasn't.

Sure enough, she could hear Winston's voice booming from all the way down the hall. "Thought we'd drop in and say hi to everyone." Then there he was, in the doorway, his wife and son behind him.

"Hello, Winston," Aunt Edie said.

It wasn't the world's warmest welcome, but Winston soldiered on. "You're looking good, Aunt Edie."

Actually, she wasn't. She looked tired and pale. After baking cookies she'd actually spent the rest of the afternoon on the couch. Jenna and Sabrina had made dinner, which had consisted of fried chicken and potato salad from the grocery store deli, along with French bread and a tossed salad.

"That all looks good," Winston said, pointing to the feast on the table.

Not that there was room at the table. With Pete present there were already four of them seated around it.

The last thing Jenna wanted was to have to feed her moochy cousin. "There's no room here at the kitchen table," she pointed out.

"That's okay. We'll sit in the dining room," Winston said. "Plates still in the same place in the cupboard?" He walked over and helped himself. "Family don't need to stand on ceremony."

And, she supposed, family needed to be fed when they showed up. Even when they showed up uninvited.

Kelly reached across the table and helped herself to a chicken leg. "It's kind of you to feed us," she said to Jenna. "Thanks."

As if Jenna had any choice. But at least Kelly thanked her.

"That's what family's for," Winston said. Sabrina's eyes got big as he heaped a mountain of potato salad on his plate, practically emptying the container, and grabbed two pieces of French bread. "No breasts left?"

"We weren't expecting company," said Pete, glaring at him.

For once, Jenna and Pete were on the same page.

Winston's brows lowered and studied him. "And you're...?"

"Pete. I work around here."

Sometimes.

Winston nodded. "Ah. Well, nice to meet ya, Pete. Jenna can probably use the help. It's not easy running a place like this, especially when you haven't had any experience." He then turned his attention to his son, who'd picked the last piece of bread from the platter, and piled Winston Junior's plate almost as high as his.

"So that's the great-nephew, huh?" Pete said to Aunt Edie in disgust as Winston and family settled in the dining room. "What a mooch."

Ah, irony.

Winston finished up the last of the potato salad and then got back to the kitchen in time for ice cream. "The old inn's not looking too bad these days," he said to Aunt Edie.

She smiled at Jenna. "Jenna has done a wonderful job bringing it back to life. She's also on the city council now. Did she tell you?"

"Trying to be a mover and shaker, huh?" he said to Jenna.

"Doing my part," she replied.

Doing important business, like voting on whether or not to enact a leash law. She'd been one of the ones who voted in favor of it at the last meeting, thinking it would be safer for the town's dog population and make their owners more responsible. The people who loved to let their dogs run free on the beach hadn't been happy with her.

"I guess next you'll be running for mayor." How did Winston manage to make something that should be a compliment sound like an insult? "Did I tell you what I'm doing now, Aunt Edie?" he asked.

"No, Winston. I haven't heard from you since Christmas."

"Oh, well, yes. I've been busy, you know. Anyway, I'm in car sales. Working at a car dealership. I just started last month and I've already made four sales."

Which explained the new SUV. Four sales in a month. That didn't seem like much. But then, what did Jenna know?

"Car salesmen, they're all sleaze buckets," said Pete, at his usual diplomatic best.

Winston looked shocked, then irritated. But after that he managed a smile and a weak laugh.

"Not all of us," said. "Some of us are good guys."

Pete's only response was a grunt.

Winston cleared his throat. "Well, uh, I guess we should get on back to our room. Come on, family, let's depart. We'll see you all tomorrow."

"Are they coming over here every night?" Pete demanded.

It sure looked like it.

Aunt Edie frowned. "What does that boy want now?"

A free room, free meals.

As soon as they left, Jenna got on her cell phone and called her mother. "Heads up. We're coming to your place tomorrow for dinner. And if you run into Winston, for heaven's sake don't mention it."

There. That took care of Saturday night.

"Now, let's hope we can dodge him on the Fourth," she said to her sister later that evening as they sat together on the back steps of their mother's new home.

"Don't hold your breath," Celeste said. "Anyway, he's not really that bad."

"Yes, he is."

"He'll be gone after the Fourth and then you won't have to deal with him."

"Thank God," Jenna said. "I suppose, instead of letting him get under my skin, I should feel sorry for him. He's never found anything he's good at. That's got to be hard on his self-esteem. Maybe it's why he's always trying to make himself look so important and put down everyone else's success."

"There you go. Mom would be proud of you for having such an understanding attitude."

"I'll never be as good as Mom. She's amazing."

"Yes, she is," Celeste agreed. She put a friendly arm around her sister's shoulder. "But so are you. You're my hero."

Jenna gave a snort. "You need better heroes." She grinned at her sister. "But thanks."

"Anytime."

Venting with Celeste helped, and Jenna had to admit, Winston wasn't what was really bugging her. He was simply the cherry on a cupcake she was having a hard time digesting: worry.

She found Aunt Edie in her bed Saturday morning, too tired to get up and make breakfast, a sure sign that something was very wrong. Jenna fed Sabrina and Pete and then took a tray up to her aunt.

"You didn't have to do that," Aunt Edie said at the sight of the tray with the fried egg, toast and juice.

"I know. I wanted to. You do enough for the rest of us. It's time you enjoyed some pampering."

"I'm not very hungry, dear. Set the tray there on the bedside table and I'll eat a little later."

Jenna complied, then sat at the foot of the bed and studied her aunt. "Auntie, you don't look well."

"I'm not feeling myself, but it will pass."

"I'm going to call Dr. Fielding," Jenna decided.

"No, don't do that. I'm fine. I just need to rest a little," Aunt Edie said.

"I don't know," Jenna said dubiously. "Maybe you're coming down with something."

"Nothing more than old age. I'll take it easy this morning and be fine by lunch. You go ahead to the street fair and enjoy yourself."

"I don't need to go to the street fair," Jenna said.

"Of course you do," Aunt Edie insisted. "Go and have a good time with Brody."

"I'll see Brody tomorrow. How about I stay here and start on some of our food for the party?"

"Well, I must admit, I could use a little help."

"Okay, you relax today and I'll do the cooking."

Jenna could handle baking a cake and some chocolate chip cookies. She decided to make peanut butter as well since those were Brody's favorites. She'd pick up hot dogs and buns later, along with pop for the cooler, and they'd be good to go. Everyone always brought food and there'd be more than enough.

Sabrina was happy to help with the baking. "Aunt Edie's going to be okay, isn't she?" she asked as she assembled the ingredients for the cookies.

Jenna would have liked nothing better than to assure her daughter that the woman who meant so much to both of them would be fine, but she wasn't so sure herself and she didn't wanted to lie. To either of them.

"I hope so," she said. "I think from now on we're going to have to do a little more and find a way to get her to do a little less."

"Good luck with that," Sabrina said, sounding like Seth.

Jenna checked on her aunt a little before noon and saw that she'd left her egg and only eaten a little of the toast. She thought her great-aunt was asleep, but when she took the tray Aunt Edie murmured a thank-you.

"You didn't finish your breakfast," Jenna scolded.

"I'm not hungry," Aunt Edie said, and grimaced.

"Are you in pain? Where does it hurt?" asked Dr. Jenna.

"At my age, everywhere."

"How about a cup of chicken broth? We should get some more liquid into you."

"All right."

Aunt Edie's voice was lackluster. It was unnerving.

"Are you sure you don't want me to call the doctor?" Jenna asked when she returned with the broth.

"No. I'm tired. That's all. I'll be fine by tomorrow."

"I'm worried about her," Jenna said when she and Sabrina were at her mother's house that evening. It felt odd to be over there without Aunt Edie, but she'd opted to stay behind, claiming she wanted to read in bed. "She doesn't want me to call the doctor but I think I should."

"Wait and see how she is tomorrow," Mel advised. "Then, if she doesn't seem any better, you can call the doctor."

"I guess," Jenna said. She should call the doctor.

"Is she complaining of anything? Headache, dizziness, pain in her neck or jaw?" Henry asked.

Symptoms of a heart attack in women. "No," Jenna said, and the worry monster came back full force. "But then, she never complains about anything. I think I'd better get back."

"Pete's with her, isn't he?" Celeste said.

"That doesn't instill confidence. I'm going back to the house. Sabrina can stay though," Jenna added, looking at her daughter in the backyard, playing fetch with Nemo.

"It's not a bad idea to keep an eye on Edie," Mel said. "You'll feel better if you're with her."

Jenna knew she would. It seemed irresponsible to leave her great-aunt neglected while she had fun with the family.

Not that she was neglected. Pete had been more than

happy to keep her company. He had Jenna's cell phone and had promised to call her if Aunt Edie felt worse, but she still wasn't comfortable being away from home.

She said goodbye to everyone, then drove back to the house, knowing someone would make sure Sabrina, who'd ridden over with her, got back later.

She heard Pete talking as she went upstairs to her aunt's bedroom. Only Pete.

She poked her head in to see her aunt in bed, her eyes closed and a smile on her face, and Pete with a book, reading aloud. "'Her skin ached for his touch. She'd been waiting so long for him. He had to know that.'"

Pete reading a love scene with such feeling struck Jenna as comical and she couldn't help it. She giggled.

He looked up, his face lobster red, and scowled at her. "Your aunt wanted me to read to her."

"And who knew you were such a dramatic reader?" Jenna teased. "Do you need anything, Auntie?"

"No, I'm fine," Aunt Edie said.

She didn't look like she was in pain. She didn't look any worse than she had in the morning. She also didn't look like she wanted Jenna hanging around.

She waved Jenna away, saying, "Go relax, dear. Call Brody." Then she said to Pete, "Keep reading. It's just starting to get good."

Okay, Jenna could take a hint. She did call Brody. "I'm downstairs alone while Pete's up in Aunt Edie's bedroom reading a love scene to her. This is weird."

"Want me to come over and read to you?" he offered. "Or we could write our own."

"That sounds good," she said. "I've got cookies for you."

"I'll be right over."

Even with Brody's arms around her she couldn't stop

thinking about Aunt Edie. What if something was seriously wrong with her?

"Only one and a half of us is here," he finally said.

She sighed. "You're right. I'm sorry. I can't stop worrying. If she's not better tomorrow I'm calling the doctor."

"I'm sure she will be," Brody assured her, and kissed the top of her head. "She's a tough old girl."

"Yeah, but things happen even to tough old girls."

"Let's not borrow trouble," he said.

He was right, of course, but it was hard not to pull up at the drive-through of Trouble First National.

She didn't sleep well that night but she was relieved to wake up the next morning to the smell of bacon. Aunt Edie was better.

She arrived in the kitchen to find her aunt at the stove, frying bacon. Pete was by her side, taking toast out of the toaster. Pete helping in the kitchen? Jenna had to be seeing things.

"Aunt Edie, you're all better," she said, hurrying to give her aunt a hug.

"Of course I am," Edie said.

But after breakfast she decided to go back to bed. "So I'm rested up for tonight," she claimed.

"I still think I should call Dr. Fielding," Jenna said.

"I'll not have you calling the doctor," Aunt Edie told her. "His office certainly isn't going to be open on a holiday and heaven knows what he'd charge for a home visit."

"I don't care what he'd charge. I'll pay it happily," Jenna said.

"I know, dear. But I don't want you to." And that ended the conversation.

Jenna came out of the kitchen later to find Aunt Edie stretched out on the couch, Jolly Roger sitting on the back of it, keeping her company. She hadn't even made it up the stairs.

"I decided I'd rather stay here in the living room," she explained. "You know, I've been lying here, thinking about what a good life I've had. So many wonderful years with Ralph, watching you girls grow up. Having you and Sabrina down here with me has been a real joy."

Why was she talking like this now? Jenna felt suddenly cold, as if a dark shadow had passed over them.

"It's been a joy for us, too," she said, squeezing in at Aunt Edie's feet. "I want us to have many more happy years together."

"We can't complain if we don't," Aunt Edie said, and a fresh shiver crept over Jenna.

Okay, that was it. "I'm calling the doctor," she announced.

Aunt Edie frowned at her and shook a finger. "Don't you dare. There's nothing wrong with me other than old age, and no doctor can cure that. I'll be fine after I've had a nice rest. Now, go find something to do with yourself."

"Go find something to do with yourself," added Roger.

There wasn't much of anything left to do. Jenna wandered over to the office to check in on her mom, who'd offered to take the day shift.

"All is quiet," Mel reported. "Winston dropped in."

She suddenly looked like a woman who'd gotten caught cheating on her diet. Or saying something she shouldn't have.

Oh, no. Here it comes.

"He wants to join us tonight."

Yep, here it came. "Oh, Mom," Jenna groaned, "you didn't tell him about the beach party." Of course she had.

"What could I do? He asked me what we were doing."

Jenna sighed. "I guess we're stuck with him. Where is he now?"

"He and the family went to see the parade."

The parade. Normally the Driftwood Inn would have been participating, but Jenna had dropped the ball. With everything going on with Aunt Edie, she was glad she hadn't entered their float in it.

"Forgive me, dear. I couldn't lie to him," Mel said.

"No, you couldn't. Oh well. He'd have found us anyway, I'm sure. If you want to go home I can take over here," Jenna said. "Aunt Edie's resting and there's not much for me to do for the party at this point."

"All right. Celeste has been helping me at the house, but there are still a few things I want to get squared away. If you're sure you don't mind."

"No. I'm at loose ends right now, anyway, and manning the desk will give me something to do besides hover over Aunt Edie. I can tell she's not feeling good but she won't let me call the doctor."

"There's not much you can do, then."

"You're right," Jenna said, although it didn't make her happy. "She pretty much told me to scram. I wouldn't be surprised if Pete came in and kept her company. Do you know I walked in on him reading a romance novel to her last night?"

"That's so sweet," Mel said. "He truly cares about her. It just goes to show, you can find love at any age."

"Yes, you can," Jenna said, looking pointedly at her.

Mel ignored the look. "I'm happy to see you finding it with Brody."

"I am," Jenna said. "He's always there for me."

"Which is what we all need."

With that, Mel left before Jenna could make any observations about her love life. Jenna settled herself behind the registration desk and helped herself to a cookie…made by her daughter instead of Aunt Edie. Was her great-aunt really only tired or was she hiding something from Jenna? Or, worse, was she in denial?

Jenna was still fretting when Seth stopped in. "Wanted to see if there's anything you need," he said.

"A doctor for Aunt Edie."

His brows pulled together. "What's wrong with her?"

"She claims nothing and won't let me call Dr. Fielding." Jenna went on to relate her great-aunt's behavior over the last day and a half.

"Maybe she is just tired," he said when Jenna had finished.

She clawed her fingers through her hair, as if somehow she could also brush away her concern. "I don't know. It's so not like her. I'm worried."

"I get that," he said. "She's been the one constant in your life since you got here. Want me to go check on her?"

"Would you?"

"Sure."

"Then come tell me what you think."

He nodded and left. Watching him walk across the driveway, she thought, *She's not the only constant*. Seth had been there to help her, practically right from the beginning.

So had Brody. They needed to hurry up and get married. She was so done with keeping her love life stalled.

Seth was back ten minutes later. "She seems okay. Pete's with her. He's reading to her."

Jenna couldn't help but smile. "Another love scene?"

"Sounded more like a fight scene."

"I guess the plot has moved on," Jenna said. Then changed subjects. "Are you coming to the party tonight?"

"Maybe," he said. "The house peddler going to be there?"

"Everyone's going to be there," she said evasively. "You can't not come. It's a tradition now."

He smiled. Good Lord, that smile should be on the big screen.

"Guess I'll stop by," he said.

"Don't forget your guitar."

He nodded. "See you later." Then, after a goodbye tap on the counter, he was gone.

Now, where was she? Oh, yes, thinking that she and Brody needed to hurry up and get married.

The rest of the day sneaked past, and come five it was time to set up for fun at the beach. Seth was building the beach fire for Jenna when Cousin Winston and company arrived, bringing nothing but their smiles and their straw hats.

"Looks like you've got everything under control," he said, watching Seth work.

"Not everything. You can bring out the ice chest and the pop," Jenna told him. If he was going to crash the party he was at least going to earn the several hot dogs he'd consume.

"Sure," he said easily, and wandered off to the house.

"Who's that?" Seth asked.

"My cousin, Winston, the leech."

"I can see you're close."

"Ha ha."

"Every family needs a black sheep," Seth said.

Jenna knew he considered himself his family's. Perceptions could be so off.

Winston returned with an ice chest filled with a bag of ice. Behind him came Pete, carrying a couple of cartons of pop, a giant bag of potato chips stacked on top. Behind Pete, Jenna caught sight of Nora and her husband. She was bearing a large bowl. Jenna hoped it was her potato salad.

"Is this where the fun is?" Nora greeted her.

"You've come to the right beach," Jenna said, and they hugged. "Please tell me that's what I think it is."

"It is," Nora assured her. "We can't eat nothing but hot dogs and marshmallows."

"Sure we can," said Pete.

"You mean you're not going to eat my ranch potato salad?" Nora teased.

Pete not eating anything would be worthy of mention in *Beach Times*.

"Potato salad, that's different. Thought you were bringing that nasty one with broccoli and shit."

"Broccoli's good for you," Nora said.

"Bah. I'm with H.W.," Pete said, referring to the former president who'd also hated broccoli.

"And I'm with you, Pete," said Winston, giving Pete a slap on the back, which earned him a glare.

Sabrina came, bringing out cookies she'd baked as well as Scotty, who'd brought a bag of corn chips and a jar of salsa. "Thanks for inviting me, Ms. Jones," he said to Jenna.

"I'm glad you could join us." A nice, polite boy, who knew to bring something to a party. It was more than she could say for her cousin.

More guests soon arrived. The rest of Jenna's family came, Mel carrying a Crock-Pot of baked beans and Celeste holding a watermelon. Henry had his hands full with the baby and Nemo's leash. Courtney, whose boyfriend was manning the fire engine and parked farther up the beach in case of fires, showed up bearing wine and makings for the s'mores. Annie and her daughter brought a pan of brownies, and Tyrella had macaroni salad. Brody arrived with an ice bucket, holding three bottles of champagne and a box of small plastic champagne flutes under his arm.

"Champagne?" Jenna asked him.

"Sure," he said. "Why not?"

"Win-Win, no. Not before dinner," Kelly scolded as Winston Junior lifted the foil over Sabrina's cookies and helped himself to one.

"What the heck," Celeste said to her. "Life's uncertain. Eat dessert first. Right, Win-Win?"

The boy gifted her with a rare smile. "Right," he said with a nod of his head, then stuffed half the cookie in his mouth before his mother could disagree and take it from him.

Pete had gone to fetch Aunt Edie and now they returned, walking slowly across the dunes. "I think she looks better," Jenna said to Brody.

"Good. I'm glad she's here," he said.

The last guests to arrive were Brody's daughter and son, each with a boyfriend and girlfriend in tow, all bearing soda pop and chips, as well as a ton of fireworks and a Frisbee. Now the guest list was complete.

The party got going and everyone gathered around the bonfire to roast hot dogs. Seth pulled out his guitar and started playing. A perfect party, Jenna thought happily, looking around at all her friends and family.

Her gaze settled on Winston, who appeared determined to eat half the bowl of Tyrella's macaroni salad singlehandedly. Well, almost perfect. Every picnic had its ants.

Pete roasted a hot dog for Aunt Edie and sat next to her

on a log as she ate it. Her aunt looked so tired. Jenna didn't think she'd even last until sunset.

Sure enough, the sun was barely thinking about going down when she announced, "I'm going to go in now," in a thready voice.

She didn't look good. Her face was pale and she had a film of sweat on her forehead.

Jenna jumped up from her log and came to stand by her. "Are you okay?"

"I'm…tired," Aunt Edie said.

"You're sweating," Jenna said, thinking of the signs of a heart attack.

"It's warm by the fire," Aunt Edie said. "Now, don't fuss, dear. Stay and enjoy your guests."

"Our guests," Jenna corrected her.

"Yes, our guests. It's been a lovely party, one to re-member." Aunt Edie put a hand to Jenna's cheek. "You are a dear girl." Her eyebrows dipped and she pressed her lips together.

"Aunt Edie!" Jenna was panicked now. Something was definitely wrong.

"Stop fussing. I'm fine," Aunt Edie said, but her smile looked forced. "Pete, would you escort me back to the house?"

"Sure, Edie, old girl," he said, offering her his elbow.

Jenna watched them make their slow way across the dunes and gnawed on her lip.

She was aware of Celeste by her side. "Follow them, will you?" Jenna asked. "Something's not right. She's being stubborn, but I really think we need to take her to the emergency room."

"She probably doesn't want to make a scene in front of everybody," Celeste said.

"She doesn't want me to worry, I know. But I am worrying. If I follow her to the house she'll pretend she's fine. She won't suspect anything if you happen to come in. Tell her you came for more pop or something."

"Okay," Celeste said, and went after the pair.

They'd been gone several minutes when Brody came back from where he'd been playing Frisbee with his kids. "Where's Edie?"

"She wasn't feeling well," Jenna said. "She went back to the house."

"Well, darn. I should have broken out the champagne sooner." He reached behind the log where he'd stuck the ice bucket and pulled out a champagne bottle. Then he returned to Jenna's side. "Hey, everyone, I think it's time for some champagne."

He got no further than that. Celeste was approaching at a run, calling, "Jenna, come quick!"

The look on her sister's face said it all. Aunt Edie!

Fifteen

Jenna raced across the dunes with her sister, Brody right along with them.

"I called 911," Celeste panted. "I think she's having a heart attack."

No. Not that. Please.

They got into the house to find Pete in the living room with Aunt Edie. He had her stretched out on the couch. "She said she felt dizzy," he reported.

"Here, I think she needs to be sitting up a little," Brody said. He slipped an arm around Edie's shoulders, propped a pillow at her back, and helped her sit up.

"I'm causing so much trouble," she fretted. Her forehead was beaded with sweat, and her face was now white as a ghost.

"Where does it hurt, Auntie?" Jenna asked, kneeling in front of her.

"My shoulder, my back. I don't know. I don't feel myself. And I don't think that hot dog agreed with me."

This last statement had Pete, who'd roasted it for her, swearing under his breath.

"But I'm sure I'll be fine in the morning," she said. They

could hear sirens outside and that made her even more agitated. "Oh, dear. I don't need an ambulance."

"Now, Edie, old girl, don't you be worrying about that," Pete said. "They can get you to the hospital faster than any of us and have you feeling better right away."

Jenna was vaguely aware of Seth and her mother entering the room, of him asking Mel where the bathroom was, then racing up the stairs, taking them two at a time.

Sabrina had arrived, and at the sight of Aunt Edie, rushed to the couch. "Aunt Edie, are you okay?"

"She will be," Jenna said, trying to sound reassuring. Sabrina sat back on her heels and bit her lip. Jenna bit hers, too, trying not to cry.

Seth returned with a bottle of aspirin. He shook one out and handed it to Edie. "Chew this, Mrs. Patterson."

Winston had joined them now. "We should wait for the paramedics," he cautioned.

"No, we shouldn't," Seth snapped. "Go ahead. Chew it. It will help," he said to Aunt Edie, his voice softening.

"Does she have high blood pressure?" Winston asked Jenna. "Is she on some kind of medication?"

"I don't know," Jenna answered.

"What do you mean you don't know?" Winston scolded.

"It's nobody's business what I take," Aunt Edie said irritably.

Obviously. She'd always insisted on going alone to her doctor appointments. Now Jenna wished she'd insisted on going with her.

The ambulance siren was getting louder. "I'll let them in," Celeste said, and hurried to the front door.

Tyrella, Courtney and Nora had come in through the back. They hesitated in a little group at the edge of the living room, looking solemn and concerned.

"We'll be praying for you," Tyrella said to Edie as the paramedics came in.

They got to work immediately, asking Aunt Edie about her symptoms.

"He gave her an aspirin," Winston tattled, pointing to Seth.

"Good," said one of the paramedics, nodding his approval. They were already checking Aunt Edie's vital signs, taking her medical history.

"How long have you been feeling like this?" one asked.

"A couple of days," Aunt Edie replied, careful not to look at Jenna.

"Oh, Auntie," she said miserably. She knew she should have gotten Aunt Edie to the doctor.

"We'll take good care of her," the first medic said to Jenna. "We're going to get an EKG right away and send it on ahead to Gray's Harbor Community. You can follow."

Jenna nodded. She couldn't speak for the lump in her throat and she felt numb all over.

"I'll drive you," Brody said to her.

"I'm going, too," said Sabrina.

"So am I," said Pete.

"Me, too," said Winston.

"You can follow us," Brody said to him.

"We'll be right behind," Mel said to Jenna.

"Don't worry. We'll take care of everything here," Tyrella called as they left.

The drive to the hospital felt surreal. Jenna could see the ambulance ahead of them, its lights flashing. What was going through Aunt Edie's mind? She had to be scared. Jenna could hear her daughter in the back, crying, felt the tears racing down her own cheeks. They were all scared.

"Oh, God," she whimpered. *Please don't take Aunt Edie from me. Not yet.*

Brody reached over and put a hand on her thigh. "We'll get through this."

What choice did they have?

No one said anything as they waited in the hospital for news of Aunt Edie, Jenna on a chair next to her weeping daughter, holding her, Brody standing next to Jenna with a hand on her shoulder. Pete was pacing. Winston stood off to the side, an unnecessary and unwanted extra.

Mel and Celeste arrived, both red-eyed. "How's she doing?" Mel asked.

Jenna shrugged. "She's still with us. That's about all I can tell you. Oh, Mom," she added in a whimper, and Brody stepped aside so mother and daughter could hug.

The cardiologist came to talk with them. The news was depressing.

"The EKG indicates near or complete blockage, and an angioplasty is needed. We're getting ready to take her to the cath lab now. Once we're done we'll be able to tell you more."

So it was a waiting game. The medical team was efficient and moved fast, but time dragged in spite of their efficiency.

The doctor finally reappeared. The occlusion had been opened and a stent put in. There was the good news.

"When an attack like this happens, we want the affected artery opened within ninety minutes. We call this Door to Balloon Time," the doctor explained. "It appears your aunt exceeded this and has some cardiac muscle injury, which makes her outcome less than ideal." There was the not good news. "She's going to have to be very careful," the doctor concluded.

"Can we see her?" Jenna asked.

"Yes, but briefly. We're getting a room ready for her right now. She'll be spending some time with us here in the cardiac unit."

Which meant Jenna would be spending the night.

At last they were allowed to see Aunt Edie, and everyone trooped into the room. She was wearing a hospital gown and had electrodes all over her and was hooked up to a heart monitor. Some sort of IV drip was feeding into a vein in her arm. She looked so small, as if she'd collapsed in on herself.

She gave Jenna a weak smile. "I ruined your party."

"Our party," Jenna corrected her, "and you didn't ruin it."

"Everyone's praying for you," said Mel.

"That's sweet," Aunt Edie said.

"I guess you're going to be here for a while," Jenna told her, "but I'll stay with you."

"Me, too," said Pete, who'd claimed the spot by her head on the other side of the bed.

"I don't want you all to make a fuss," Aunt Edie said. Her voice was barely above a whisper, as if talking was a great effort.

"We're not," Jenna said. "We just want to be with you."

Aunt Edie looked to Sabrina, who was silently crying. "Now, dear, don't be crying."

"I don't want you to die," Sabrina blurted. Oh, great. The *D* word.

"We all die at some point. If it's my time, it's my time."

"It's not your time yet," Pete informed her.

She smiled up at him but said nothing to that.

"They've got you all fixed and you're good as new," he continued.

She shut her eyes. "At my age, there's no such thing."

"You're not that old," Jenna protested.

"I'm not that young, either. I'm edging toward ninety."

"You're not there yet," Jenna pointed out.

Aunt Edie didn't say anything to that, but her long sigh spoke volumes.

They all stood around, silent and watching, as if simply by looking at her they could make her instantly better.

Just when Jenna thought she'd fallen asleep, she patted Jenna's hand and said, "You're so sweet to be here with me."

"I'm here, too," put in Winston, who was having to content himself with standing at the foot of the bed.

"So you are," Aunt Edie said wearily. Her enthusiasm was underwhelming. She turned her attention back to Jenna. "You should all go home."

"I'm not leaving," Jenna said.

"Me, either," said Pete.

"Pete, you are a dear," Aunt Edie told him.

"Somebody's got to watch out for you," he said, as if he were the only one in the room.

But Jenna didn't take offense. Pete probably felt as helpless as she did, and she didn't begrudge him a place by her great-aunt's side.

The nurse came in to shoo them all out. There was a small couch by the window that she told Jenna could be made into a bed if someone wanted to stay the night. For everyone else, it was time to leave.

Jenna thanked her. "I'll spend the night. Can you take Sabrina and Pete home?" she asked Brody.

"I'm spending the night, too," Pete insisted.

"I doubt both of us will be able to stay in her room."

"Then I'll sleep on a chair in the waiting room," he said stubbornly.

"I'm sorry, sir. You can't do that," the nurse told him. "It's against hospital rules."

"Hospital rules be damned," Pete growled.

"She's in good hands, Pete," Brody said. "Let's go home and get a good night's rest. We can all come back in the morning. Want me to bring you some things tomorrow?" he asked Jenna.

She nodded. "Sabrina can pack me a bag." She gave her daughter a hug. "Try to get some sleep."

Sabrina sniffed and nodded, then let Brody lead her out of the room.

"I guess I'll go, too," said Winston.

Jenna just nodded. Good idea. She was ready for him to go. Home. Of course, now with this he'd plant himself in Moonlight Harbor like the dutiful relative he hadn't been.

With everyone gone, the beeps and sounds of the medical technology felt unnaturally loud. Disembodied voices from the nearby nurses' station, respectfully soft, invaded the room. A nurse came in and checked Aunt Edie's heart rate on the screen. Jenna had never felt so alone.

She sat in the chair next to the hospital bed and studied the woman who had given her a new start and been her rock. "Don't leave, not yet," she whispered. "Please, God, don't let her die. Just give us a couple more years."

Aunt Edie was coming up on her eighty-sixth birthday. Was it wrong to beg for more time with her? Right or wrong, Jenna kept begging.

She slept fitfully on her makeshift sofa bed that night, waking every time a nurse came in to check Aunt Edie. Whenever Aunt Edie stirred, Jenna bolted to her bedside to see if she was all right. By morning she felt like she'd been camping in a war zone, but she was relieved to see that her great-aunt was still alive.

The Jones women and Brody were the first to return the next morning, bringing Jenna fresh clothes and toiletries, as well as coffee and cinnamon rolls from Sunbaked, the town's bakery.

Winston arrived right on their heels, along with his wife and son. "How's the patient doing?" he asked cheerfully, setting a small vase of flowers on her bedside table. "I brought you some flowers, Aunt Edie."

"So I see," she said, and left it at that.

For years he'd been MIA, never even bothering to send cards or gifts on her birthday. Even when Jenna had been caught up in trying to keep her head above water financially and then coping with her divorce, she'd always tried to remember Aunt Edie on special occasions. She'd never wanted anything from her aunt, never stopped to think what she could get out of her. She'd simply loved the old woman and cherished the memories of happy times with her when she and Celeste were kids. Winston's fake love offended her.

"I think you're looking better today, Aunt Edie," he said.

Jenna didn't think so.

"Thank you, Winston," said Aunt Edie. "Now, if you all don't mind, I'd like to see Brody alone for a few minutes."

"Brody? Why him?" Winston demanded.

"Never mind why him. Let's just do what she asks," Jenna said, moving her irritating cousin out of the room.

Why Brody?

"Can we go home now?" Win-Win asked as they all stood around in the hallway.

A good idea, thought Jenna.

"No, we need to be here for our family," Winston told him.

"We don't all have to be here," Jenna said. "Go back to the motel. We'll call you if there's any change."

"No. I'll stay," Winston said.

"Daddy," Winston Junior whined.

Winston fished car keys from his pocket and handed them over to Kelly. "You two go back. I can catch a ride home later with someone."

It wouldn't be Jenna. She wasn't leaving.

Brody wasn't in with Aunt Edie long, and after he came out he said he had to make a call and excused himself. A call? For Aunt Edie?

Jenna was even more curious when Aunt Edie's lawyer showed up right before lunch.

"What's going on?" she asked Brody when, once again, they were all shooed out of the room.

"Updating the will, eh?" said Winston, shoving his hands in his pockets and rocking back on his heels. With that disgusting grin on his face he was the very picture of avarice.

"Is she?" Jenna asked Brody.

He pressed his lips together and nodded.

"But why?" Aunt Edie had already updated her will.

"She had a few things she needed to fix," he said. Jenna looked at him in confusion, but he shook his head and said, "It's not my place to tell you your aunt's business."

"I'm sure she knows what she's doing," put in Winston, and she wanted to kick him. It was horrible talking about things like wills at a time like this, anyway.

Pete arrived, bearing flowers and ready to go in and see Edie. "You can't right now," Brody told him. "She's with her lawyer."

"Oh, God," he said weakly. "She *is* dying."

Jenna laid a hand on his arm. "She's okay, Pete. Really."

He bit his lip and nodded, then stared down at his beat-up, dirty sneakers.

Poor Pete. He looked like the ancient mariner with his scruffy chin and his bloodshot eyes. The skin under them was sunken and had turned lavender. He obviously hadn't slept any better than Jenna.

"Come on," Brody said, "let's all get some lunch."

Pete refused to budge. The rest of them trooped down to the cafeteria. Jenna got coffee and left it at that. Winston went through the lunch line and loaded up his plate.

"There's no sense starving yourself," he said to Jenna as he joined her and Brody at a table. "That won't help her."

"He's right, you know," Brody said. "How about some salad? Or soup?"

She shook her head. "I'm not hungry."

Neither was Sabrina. Jenna didn't urge her daughter to eat. Mel nibbled on a roll and drank a cup of tea, patted Jenna's hand a lot.

By the time they returned from the cafeteria, the lawyer was gone and Pete was no longer standing outside in the hall. Once again, they all crowded into the room to find him sitting next to the bed, his flowers on the bedside stand, dwarfing Winston's offering.

"I'm feeling better," Aunt Edie said. "Really, you don't all have to be here."

"What else are we going to do?" Pete said. He held up a paperback with a bookmark stuck halfway through it. "Anyway, we have to finish this book."

"I'd like that," said Aunt Edie.

The day trudged on, with visitors coming and going, Pete reading to Aunt Edie until her eyes drifted shut. Late in the afternoon, her lawyer was back, along with Sherwood Stern, Patricia Whiteside, who Jenna knew Aunt

Edie had as her executrix, and another man Jenna had seen at the bank, who she was sure was a notary public. Once again, the visitors were shuffled out and the door was shut. Jenna didn't really care what Aunt Edie was doing to her will. She only hoped it would be a long time before they had to read it.

The lawyer and his team finally left, all stopping to say an encouraging word to Jenna.

Patricia hugged her. "Stay strong, darling."

"I'm sure she'll pull out of this," Sherwood said and gave Jenna's shoulder a wimpy pat.

She murmured her thanks and then went with the others back into the room. She had no idea what to say, so she simply stood by Aunt Edie's bed and took her hand.

Winston, however, had an observation to share. "Always a good idea to make sure things are taken care of, 'cause you never know."

Jenna gaped at him. Seriously?

He saw her horrified look and cleared his throat. "Not that we don't want you to live to be a hundred," he added.

"Oh, Winston, do go home. You're wearing me out," Aunt Edie said.

He blinked in surprise, then flushed red. "Well, uh, yeah. We don't want to wear you out. We should all go."

"I'm so tired," Aunt Edie said with a long sigh.

"She needs to rest," Mel said. "Come on, sweetie," she said to Sabrina.

"I want to stay," Sabrina protested.

"Someone's got to bake cookies for the reception desk," Mel told her.

That worked. Sabrina bit her lip and nodded.

"I want Jenna to stay," Aunt Edie said. "And Pete."

"I'll keep an eye on things for you at the Driftwood,"

Mel said to Jenna. Then she and Sabrina followed Winston and Celeste out of the room.

Brody was the last to leave. "I'll check on you later," he promised, and gave Jenna a quick kiss.

"Thanks for being there for all of us," she said.

He gave a quick nod and ducked out the door.

Pete read some more to Aunt Edie for a while and then fell asleep in his chair and started snoring.

Aunt Edie's eyes were shut and Jenna had assumed she, too, was asleep until she spoke. "You are such a treasure."

Was she speaking to Jenna or Pete?

"You gave the old Driftwood a new life and me, too," Aunt Edie continued. "So many lovely memories," she said with a sigh.

"We've loved being with you," Jenna said. Here came the tears. She wiped at an eye. "We'll make more."

"Maybe not. I think it might be my time."

"You don't know that," Jenna argued.

"No. But if I go, I go. Anyway, I'm ready to see my Ralph again. But don't you worry, dear. You'll be taken care of."

"That's the last thing on my mind," Jenna said.

"It's the first on mine."

"Don't worry about me. You helped me find myself again, and I'll be fine."

"I know you will," Aunt Edie said, and then fell quiet. Soon she was lightly snoring, a faint echo to what was coming from Pete.

They were both still asleep when Seth stopped by to see her. "How's she doing?" he asked Jenna in a low voice.

"About the same. I feel like she's losing her will to live."

He pulled up a chair next to Jenna. "Maybe she's ready to go."

"But if she's careful she could have several more years."

"Her body's wearing out. If she's ready to leave it, it's her choice. Let her be the captain of her own ship."

What he was saying made logical sense, but Jenna had no desire to be logical. And she didn't want Aunt Edie to be logical, either.

"I just want her for a little longer," she whispered and swiped away a fresh batch of tears. "Selfish of me, huh?"

"More like human," he said, and put an arm around her. "None of us like to lose people we love."

She laid her head on his shoulder. The tears were coming fast and hard now.

"It'll be okay," he murmured.

Just as Brody walked in, bearing an iced coffee from Beans and Books.

"Waters," he greeted Seth, his voice as cold as the drink he handed Jenna.

"Green," Seth said with a nod as Jenna pulled away and grabbed a tissue from the bedside table.

"How's she doing?" Brody asked.

"She's the same," Jenna reported. Which, she told herself, was better than being worse.

Meanwhile, Seth had left his seat. "I guess I'll get going. Let me know if you need anything," he said to Jenna.

She nodded and he left. Thankfully, Brody didn't comment on what he'd seen. This was hardly the time for petty rivalry.

Instead, he settled in to help with the vigil, taking Jenna's hand. "We'll get through this," he assured her.

She nodded. They would. They had to. There was never any way to go but forward.

Aunt Edie seemed to rally a little right before dinner.

"You're awake again," said Pete, who'd finally returned from slumber land himself.

"I'm so tired," she said.

"That's to be expected," Jenna said. "You've been through a lot."

Pete gave Aunt Edie's hand a pat. "You just rest. The docs will have you better in no time."

She shook her head. "I don't think so."

"Now, don't talk like that, Edie, old girl. You've got lots of life left in you."

"I have a life waiting on the other side, too," she said, and he frowned.

The nurse brought food for which her aunt had no appetite, and Pete wound up eating most of her dinner. Jenna found a rerun on the TV of *Charlie's Angels*, an old series Aunt Edie had loved.

"Dumb show," Pete said. "It never had no basis in reality."

"Kind of like the James Bond movies," Jenna retorted.

"Hey, those were good. Still are."

"I'm trying to listen, you two," Aunt Edie said, and they both shut up.

Visiting hours ended, giving Jenna and Pete something new to squabble about. "I'm staying with her tonight," he informed her.

"I've already got my things here," she insisted.

"You stayed last night," he said. "Anyway, you look like shit. You should go home and get a good night's sleep."

As if he didn't look like shit.

"Please," he added softly. "I just need some time with her."

Poor Pete. He was hurting as much as Jenna.

"All right," she said. "I'll have my cell on. Call me if anything happens."

"I will," he promised.

She kissed Aunt Edie's forehead and left.

And went back to the house to toss and turn all night.

The next morning when she returned to the hospital, she learned that her great-aunt was insisting on going home.

"I want to be in my own house," Aunt Edie said.

"But I don't know if the doctor's ready to release you yet," Jenna protested.

"I don't care what he is or isn't ready to do. They can't legally keep me here and I'm going."

And that was that. By one in the afternoon, Aunt Edie was back at the house, settled on the hospital bed Jenna had rented. Exhausted from the trip home, she fell asleep instantly.

"Keep an eye on her," Jenna said to Pete. "I'm going to pick up her prescriptions."

The doctor hadn't been happy to release Aunt Edie, and he'd prescribed all kinds of medicines, including a blood thinner. Jenna only hoped she'd be able to convince Aunt Edie to take them.

"If she's out of the hospital, it's a good thing, right?" Celeste asked when she checked in with Jenna.

She and Henry had gone home to start packing for their upcoming move, but she was checking in twice a day by phone.

"I don't know. I wish she'd stayed there. I don't make a very good nurse. I have a hard time bossing her around."

"There's a switch. You never had trouble bossing me around."

"Ha ha."

"Now that Aunt Edie's home again, is Winston talking about leaving?"

"Tomorrow, thank God. I've got my hands full with Aunt Edie. Having him here, hovering like a buzzard, is getting on my nerves. I'll be glad when life can return to normal."

"The new normal."

Which Jenna didn't like at all. Her patient hated using the portable commode, and had begun talking about sleeping in her own bed. By the following day she was insistent.

"I don't think you should tackle those stairs yet," Jenna said. "You're supposed to be taking it easy."

"I've had enough of taking it easy," Aunt Edie said. "Tonight I'm sleeping in my own bed."

"Let's talk about it tonight," Jenna said, hoping by evening she'd have found a way to discourage Aunt Edie from the trek to the second story.

Staying put wasn't the only thing Aunt Edie didn't like. She was balking at taking the prescribed medications.

"I've never had to take all those old people pills," she complained when Jenna produced her evening blood thinner medication along with her dinner. "I've always been healthy as an ox."

"Even oxen get sick," Jenna said, shaking out a pill. "And younger people take these, too."

"Just leave it on the TV tray. I'll take it later."

"When?"

"Later."

Short of forcing the pill down Aunt Edie's throat, there was little Jenna could do. Except coax.

"Won't you please take this? For me?"

"Won't you please stop nagging me?"

Jenna blinked in surprise. Aunt Edie never got snippy with her.

"I'm sorry," she said, "but I'm tired of being fussed over like I'm an invalid. I want to bake some cookies."

"Bake cookies?" This was really not a good idea.

"Yes, bake cookies," Aunt Edie said, and threw off the blanket Jenna had draped over her.

"It's getting a little late in the day. How about waiting until tomorrow?" Jenna suggested.

"I don't want to wait."

Pete came in just then, bearing ice cream from Good Times Ice Cream Parlor. "Brought you some deer poop," he said.

It was Aunt Edie's favorite flavor—chocolate ice cream, loaded with chocolate-covered raisins. But even the offer of ice cream couldn't distract her from her mission.

"Maybe later," she said. "I'm going to bake some oatmeal cookies."

"Edie, old girl, you're supposed to be taking it easy."

"Bah," she said. "I've had enough of that. If all I'm going to do is take up space, then I don't want to be here. Now, stop fussing, both of you. I'm fine."

They stopped fussing, but they both stayed in the kitchen while she worked.

By the time the first batch was out of the oven, she looked far from fine. Her face was ashen and she was shaky.

"I think I'll lie down now," she said. "Jenna, will you help me upstairs to my room?"

"Oh, Auntie, please stay down here," Jenna begged. Those stairs were going to be too much for her.

"I want to be in my own bed," Aunt Edie said firmly.

Jenna and Pete exchanged concerned looks.

"Okay, if that's what you want," he said. "Let me help you girls."

And so, with one of them on each side, they helped her up the stairs. She had to stop twice to rest and take a deep breath.

"Are you okay?" Jenna asked after the second pause.

"I'm fine, dear," she said. "Just a little winded. With all that lying around I've been doing, I got out of shape."

"You still look good," Pete said.

"Thank you, Pete. What would I do without you?"

"You don't want to find out," he joked.

At the top of the stairs, Aunt Edie put a hand to his cheek and said, "Goodbye, dear friend."

The smile he had for her vanished. "You mean good night."

"Good night, then," she said, and started moving down the hall.

"Did she take her medicine today?" Pete asked Jenna in an under voice.

Jenna shook her head. "She promised she would, but no. I've been fighting with her over it ever since she got home."

"Ornery old girl," he muttered, and before he turned away Jenna spotted tears in his eyes.

"That she is," Jenna agreed, and hurried down the hall after her great-aunt.

She helped Aunt Edie don a nightgown, assisted her in the bathroom, and then got her into bed.

Aunt Edie caught her hand. "Thank you, dear. For everything."

"No, thank *you*," Jenna said. Oh, Lord, she was going to start crying.

"A wonderful family, loyal friends, some good times—I've had a good life."

"You've made it good for a lot of us," Jenna told her.

"I hope so. One likes to think one's life has mattered."

"Yours has," Jenna assured her.

It was the last conversation they had. In the middle of the night, Aunt Edie suffered another heart attack and this time, in spite of the doctors' best efforts, she died.

Sixteen

If it hadn't been for her mother, Jenna didn't know how she'd have gotten through the first forty-eight hours after losing Aunt Edie. Jenna wanted nothing more than to crawl in bed and stay there, but the business of death was a demanding one and not something to be put off. Arrangements had to be made for Aunt Edie's cremation and interment in the Fern Hill Cemetery, not far from the town of Moonlight Harbor, and people had to be notified that Edie Patterson was gone. Copies of the death certificate had to obtained. The obituary had to be written for the newspaper, which Mel undertook. In the end, Piper Lee from *Beach Times* wound up doing a big write-up about Aunt Edie and the part she'd played in helping the town put itself on the map. Aunt Edie would have been pleased.

Celeste came back down to help with planning the memorial service, which was going to be held the following week at Jenna's church, contacting Pastor Paul, picking music, ordering funeral cards.

"I wish I was planning her birthday party instead," she said to Jenna.

Didn't they both?

Winston texted Jenna, wanting to know when the memorial was. How had he gotten her phone number? She sure hadn't given it to him.

Don't want to miss Aunt Edie's celebration of life. She could almost hear him, all chipper and friendly and...fake.

Memorial, she texted back. She couldn't bring herself to use the word *celebration.* Aunt Edie was gone and she wasn't in a celebrating mood.

Okay, Memorial.

She sighed and texted him the day and time.

Kelly and I will be there. Save us a room at the Driftwood.

In his dreams. We're booked solid. Most of Moonlight Harbor Is. It's tourist season.

We can stay with you then. We don't mind taking Aunt Edie's room.

Winston the leech stay in Aunt Edie's room? No way. No! "There," she said as she hit Send. "Hope I wasn't unclear."

Pretty selfish.

Jenna ground her teeth. Yes, you are.

Fine, he texted back, and she knew he didn't mean it in a conciliatory way. I'll work something out. Dad's probably going to want to come too. We'll find someplace.

She sincerely hoped he wouldn't.

But he did. He suckered her mom into putting him

and his wife up. Barely into her new home and her first houseguests other than her daughter had to be Winston and Kelly. And her aunt and uncle, as well, who'd invited themselves along. Jenna knew her mother had wanted some time simply to enjoy her new digs before opening the place up to houseguests. And now, of all people, she had Winston.

"Oh, Mom. What were you thinking?" Jenna groaned when she heard.

"That this is my brother and nephew and it would be wrong to refuse them," Mel replied.

Her mother was a saint.

"By the way, I'm sorry about giving Winston your phone number. I couldn't find a polite way to turn him down."

"Oh, well. After this I'll probably never hear from him again."

"Rather sad," Mel said. "You two spent a lot of time playing together on the beach when you were children."

"I guess one of us grew up," Jenna said.

"I feel a little sorry for him," said Mel.

"Sorry? For Winston?" She herself had said that not long ago, but she was now long past sorry.

"Yes. He's halfway through his life and he hasn't accomplished anything or been able to keep a job. I think he's jealous of you."

"Yeah, I've really set the world on fire," Jenna said, thinking of her failed marriage and the thin financial ice she'd been skating on ever since it ended.

"You have your corner of it. You restored the Driftwood and you've carved out a good life for yourself. And now you're on the city council."

"It doesn't seem that important now. Nothing does."

Jenna hadn't been able to bring herself to attend the July meeting. Who cared about deer and dog leash ordinances, sidewalks and fire hydrants? Who cared about convention centers and tourists? Why were people smiling? What was there to smile about? She felt like her heart was packed in ice.

Parker had given her a pass.

"You'll find your feet again," Mel said. "Aunt Edie would want you to. Meanwhile, though, it's okay to allow yourself time to grieve."

"There isn't enough time in the world," Jenna said miserably.

So far she'd lost a grandma and two grandpas and that had been hard. But this was worse. Aunt Edie had been part of her day every day since she'd come to Moonlight Harbor.

"I feel like I've lost an arm or a leg," she said. Or her heart.

"I know," Mel said. "But people learn to live without a limb. You will, too. And you'll live well. If you do that you'll be honoring her memory."

Jenna sighed. "Don't have much choice, do I?"

"No, you don't," her mother agreed.

And so she forced herself to take reservations, greet guests, cut checks, and do the necessary social media posts. The cookie baking she delegated to Sabrina. Seeing that plate of cookies on the reception desk every day made her cry, but she left it there. Aunt Edie would have wanted them to keep up the tradition.

Pete avoided the kitchen even though Jenna started leaving the door unlocked for him, and she didn't see him anywhere around the place. But one morning she stepped out the front door on her way to the motel office and found him on the porch, cleaning the railing. She couldn't help but blink in surprise. Had his body been taken over by aliens?

"Pete?"

"We'll probably have company after the service," he said. "You'll want everything looking shipshape."

"I do. Good idea," she said, and started down the steps.

"Jenna."

She turned, looked at him questioningly.

"I guess you'll want me to be moving on now," he said, focusing on his cleaning rag.

How many times had she wished he'd do exactly that? But now she couldn't kick the old guy out. The Driftwood was his home and Aunt Edie would haunt her if she made him leave it. And oh, Lord, she hated to admit it, but he'd become part of the family.

"No, Pete, I need you here."

"Well, then, uh, good," he said, still not looking at her, and got back to work. "Anything you need done, let me know."

Okay, now she was sure of it. He had been taken over by aliens.

Annie offered to cater the gathering after the service at the church, and Jenna gladly accepted. Courtney offered to help out at the office when she stopped by with a pasta salad Annie had made, but Jenna turned her down.

"You have the shop now."

"There must be something I can do," Courtney said.

"We've got it covered," Jenna said. "Mom's helping me and Celeste is here. And Seth's going to take some evening shifts behind the desk. Brody went with me to the cemetery."

Delivering Aunt Edie's urn to rest next to Uncle Ralph's would go down as one of the most awful moments of her life, even more horrible than the day she'd found out Damien had been cheating on her. Ashes to ashes, dust to dust—how blithely that got repeated at funerals. The reality of seeing her adorable great-aunt reduced to a small enough pile of ashes to fit in an urn... She shied away from the image.

"What a horrible Fourth," Courtney said, shaking her head. "I'm so sorry for you. Both of you. It sure didn't play out the way he expected."

"What do you mean?" Jenna asked.

Courtney looked first surprised, and then guilty, as if she'd been caught committing industrial espionage. "Uh, nothing."

"I can tell by your face it's not nothing. What?"

"Nothing, really. Hey, I have to get to the shop."

Jenna caught her by the hem of her linen jacket. "Oh, no you don't. What was Brody planning?"

"He'll kill me if I tell," Courtney said, and then, realizing the inappropriateness of that remark, blushed.

Jenna was sure she knew now, but she pressed her pal anyway.

Courtney caved. "He bought a ring. He was going to make a big proposal and give it to you at the party. Then... well, you know what happened."

Jenna nodded. Everything had slid south. She wanted to cry. Yet again.

"I shouldn't have said anything. I thought you knew."

"We were getting serious and he'd talked about getting a ring, but there hasn't exactly been time to work out details," Jenna said.

How sad. Aunt Edie would have been so excited. Jenna could feel the tears damming up in her eyes, ready to overflow and flood down her face. Would she ever stop crying?

Brody came by later that evening. Sabrina was out with Scotty, and Pete, Jenna supposed, was at The Drunken Sailor, drowning his sorrows. It was only her and Jolly

Roger, in his cage and tucked in for the night. The poor bird hadn't been himself. He'd hardly talked at all.

Seeing Brody walk through the front door was like seeing the fire department arrive to put out a house fire. More and more, she was coming to depend on him for her emotional stability.

"I heard a rumor," she said as they settled on the couch with glasses of lemonade. What was that look that crossed his face? It almost smacked of fear.

"What?" he asked. He sounded cautious.

"About you and me?"

"You and me."

"And a ring."

He looked relieved. What had he thought she was talking about?

"And an announcement on the Fourth?" she prompted.

He let out a half laugh. "Courtney has a big mouth."

"She didn't spill the beans on purpose. But never mind her. Is it true?"

He nodded. "Had the ring in my shirt pocket. I was about to make my big speech when all hell broke loose."

She leaned an elbow on the back of the couch. "How about making it now?"

"Seriously?"

"Yeah." She desperately needed something good in her life.

"Okay, I'll be right back," he said.

"Wait. Where are you going?"

"I'm missing a valuable prop," he said, and left.

She heard his car roar off and knew where he was going. So, it was finally happening. She'd made a decision and was moving on with her life. This was good. She was happy.

And her heart was going into A-fib. She got up and paced the living room. So much happening at once, she couldn't take it all in, let alone sit still.

She jumped when the front door opened and he let himself back in.

"What are you doing?" he asked.

"Dancing for joy. By the way, you are going to dance with me on our wedding day, aren't you?"

He sat back down on the couch and patted the sofa cushion. "Speech first."

She came over and snuggled up next to him. "Okay, I'm ready."

"I've been ready for the last four years."

"That's your speech?"

"No, here it is." He cleared his throat. "Okay, here goes. So, everyone, I know you all came to celebrate our independence, but I want to celebrate losing mine. I'm trading in my bachelor life for something much better. And here's the part where I take out the ring," he said to Jenna, pulling that small jewelry box from his shirt pocket. He opened the box and she blinked at the gorgeous diamond winking at her. "Jenna Jones, will you be my wife and make me the happiest, luckiest man in the world?"

Beautiful, romantic—those were the words every woman wanted to hear. "That's a beautiful speech," she said.

"You missed your cue," he teased. "You're supposed to say yes."

"You know the answer's yes," she said, and slipped her arms around his neck and kissed him. "Thank you for being so patient, and for always being there for me."

"I'm glad it's finally paying off," he said with a smile.

He took the ring out and slipped it on her finger. It fit

perfectly, and if that wasn't a sign that she'd made a smart choice, she didn't know what was.

Jenna showed Mel and Celeste her ring the next day when the three women gathered in Jenna's kitchen for lunch.

"It's beautiful," said Mel.

"It's about time," Celeste said, spooning baby food into Edie's mouth.

Yes, it was. And seeing that ring on her finger comforted Jenna. She'd lost Aunt Edie, but she'd gained a lifelong companion, someone she could trust and lean on.

"I see he finally proposed," Seth said when he stopped by the motel office to check on her. He lifted her hand and examined the new bling.

Seth holding her hand. She'd wanted that for so long. Just being near him always gave her a jolt. But love between them was a closed chapter now. Actually, it was a chapter that had never really been opened.

"He did," she said. "He'd wanted to at the party and then…" She couldn't finish the sentence.

"Edie would be happy," Seth said, and let go of her hand. "Anything you need done around here before the memorial?"

She shook her head. "No."

"Okay. Let me know if you think of anything," he said, and left the office.

She watched as he walked to his room. He was only going across the parking lot, but it felt like he was going much further.

No time to think about that, she told herself. She had a future to plan.

And a memorial service to get through.

It was held on a Sunday afternoon and the church was

packed. Even the mayor came to do homage to one of the town's Grandes Dames.

Winston and company showed up and joined the family as they gathered in a small room off the sanctuary before the service. "Jenna, it's been a long time," Uncle Arthur said to Celeste.

"I'm Celeste," she replied. "That's Jenna."

Uncle Arthur, like his son, was good at glossing over his missteps. He turned to Jenna. "And what a beautiful woman you've grown into. I wouldn't have recognized you."

Obviously.

"Thank you," she said, and left it at that. She couldn't bring herself to tell him she was glad he'd come. He was nothing more than a dusty figure from the past who'd set an example of irresponsibility for his son. She'd have been perfectly happy if the whole tribe had stayed home.

Aunt Grace, who had some class, looked embarrassed. "I'm sorry it's been so long and doubly sorry we're meeting again under such sad circumstances."

Instead of a hug, she patted Jenna on the shoulder, and Jenna thanked her. *And thanks for not being such a phony.*

The time to begin arrived and the family entered the sanctuary and sat in the seats allocated for them. The whole front of the church was filled with flowers, and a basket held envelopes with cards. Donations in Edie's name had already poured into the Moonlight Harbor Blue Moon Fund. In the future, many struggling businesses would be helped in the name of Edie Patterson.

Brody, as Jenna's fiancé, earned family status, and sat next to her. He put an arm around her, and she leaned against him, grateful for his support. Pete was with them also, stoic and staring straight ahead. Win-Win was already squirming in his seat.

Aunt Edie had never made any requests about what songs she wanted sung, so Celeste had made the selection, and recruited Seth to play his guitar and sing "When I Get Where I'm Going," a song that had been performed by Dolly Parton and Brad Paisley. Jenna wept all the way through.

She's with Uncle Ralph again and happy, she reminded herself. It wasn't enough to stop the flow of tears.

Pastor Paul kept his talk short and sweet. "When a loved one dies, people often tell us that person is in a better place. And it's true, they are. But that doesn't mean we're in a good place. Losing someone you love hurts, and I know Edie's family is hurting right now. As are many of us. Edie Patterson was a beloved member of our community, and she will be missed. But we can treasure our memories of the good times we had with her and take comfort from those. Let me read an excerpt from the Bible that I hope will bring comfort to Edie's family. This is from the book of Revelation. 'Blessed are the dead who die in the Lord from now on. Yes, says the Spirit, they will rest from their labor, for their deeds will follow them.' Edie Patterson had plenty of deeds to follow her. She had much to do with the success of this town. She worked hard all her life and she spent her later years making those around her happy. She can rest now. She's earned it." Here he smiled down at Jenna and she managed a smile back.

Pastor Paul then offered those who wanted to share memories of Aunt Edie the opportunity to do so. The testimonials lasted for an hour.

"When I lost my job she left a bag of groceries on our doorstep every week until I found a new job," one man shared. "She tried to do it secretly, coming early in the morning, but one day I spotted her tiptoeing down the driveway."

"She and Ralph loaned me the money to open up Good Times," said Nora.

"She was a dear friend," said Patricia Whiteside. "We actually referred people to each other's places."

"Her cookies were the best," said another man. "She baked me a batch every year for my birthday."

"She had the gift of hospitality," said Tyrella. "That woman never thought of herself."

How true. Jenna wanted to stand up and say something as well. *She saved me. When I was at my lowest she rescued me.* She couldn't. Her throat was too jammed up with tears. She grabbed another tissue from the box she and Sabrina were sharing and wiped at her streaming eyes.

Finally the service ended with everyone singing "Amazing Grace," and the mourners drifted out into the foyer, where Annie had set up a refreshment table with finger sandwiches and cookies. People hugged Jenna, offered condolences, then stood around in groups, eating and drinking coffee. Finally, the long day ended, and the family returned to the house for their own private sharing and reminiscences.

Jenna had hoped Brody would come, but he said, "You need time with your family."

"I need you, too," she said.

It was all she had to say. "Okay."

Even though Jenna's family was with her, the house felt empty.

"I hate this," Sabrina said bitterly.

"I hate this," echoed Jolly Roger.

You picked a fine time to start speaking, you stupid bird, Jenna thought.

Mel put an arm around her granddaughter. "I know. It's not easy having to say goodbye to people we love, but we have to. The old have to make way for the young."

"I wanted her to live long enough to see me get married," Sabrina said, her lower lip wobbling. "She promised to make my wedding garter."

"I know," Mel said, and hugged her.

Ugh. Would this day never end?

It did finally, and everyone went home. Sabrina shut herself in her bedroom with her cell phone. Even Brody finally departed.

Jenna sat on the couch, the emptiness of the room closing in on her. "What do we do now, Roger?"

"Give me whiskey," the parrot suggested.

"Good idea," Jenna said, and went to pour herself some wine.

She saw the beach fire from the kitchen window. Company. Comfort. She took her glass and hit the beach. She could smell the smoke from the fire and it made her think of beach parties and roasting hot dogs.

And then the memory of the last beach party they'd had hit her full force and she wanted to start crying all over again.

"I don't like to drink alone," she said as she settled next to Seth on their usual log.

"You've been around people all day. I'd think you'd want a minute to yourself."

She shook her head and took a sip of wine. "I don't want to be by myself." The fire was a spot of light in the darkness and she needed it.

"Where's the house...where's Green?"

"He left."

"Why didn't you ask him to spend the night?"

"I don't know," she said honestly. She took another sip. "I feel like a shipwreck victim."

"I'm not surprised." He threw another log on the fire, and sparks flew up like fireflies.

They sat for a moment, saying nothing, the only sound the crackling of the burning logs and the whoosh of waves kissing the shore.

Jenna finally spoke. "Thanks for singing today."

"I was happy to. I liked your aunt."

"Everybody liked her."

"So, a life well-lived."

"It was."

"Not sure you can ask for more than that."

"You're right. I just hate..." She stumbled over a sob. "I know it's stupid, but I feel so alone in that house."

He held up her left hand so she could see the ring as a reminder. "Not for long. You've got a new beginning ahead of you, got your family and friends. You have a good life, Jenna. You're on solid ground."

She took a shaky breath and nodded. "Why do I feel like I'm on sand?"

"Well, you are at the beach." The firelight played over his face and she could see the shadow of a smile. He gave her hand a squeeze. "You'll be okay."

She nodded. "I will. Thanks for reminding me."

They didn't say any more. Instead, they sat side by side and watched the fire burn itself out.

When she finally went to bed, she slept soundly. She woke up thinking she'd dreamed about Aunt Edie, but she couldn't remember what the dream was about. She could only remember her aunt saying, "I love you." It was enough.

* * *

The day the will was to be read, Jenna came down to the kitchen to find Sabrina making breakfast. "Aunt Edie's pancake recipe," she said to Jenna.

Jenna gave her a kiss and a one-armed hug. "Wouldn't Aunt Edie love to see you now. She'd be so proud."

Sabrina got teary-eyed, but she smiled. It was a relief to see her daughter smiling. "I figured you'd need a good breakfast today since you're going to the lawyer's."

Oh, yeah, that. Jenna sighed inwardly. The last grim piece of death business. Thinking about hearing the reading of the will made her feel like a vulture.

Winston, who was back in town and staying once more with her long-suffering, generous mother, had also been summoned to the law offices of Williams and Weaver, along with Jenna, Celeste, and Pete, and appeared perfectly happy to be a vulture.

But not necessarily happy for Jenna. "I suppose she'll leave you the Driftwood," he greeted her as she walked in with Celeste and Pete, making it sound like a crime to do so.

"I suppose so, since she promised to," Jenna said.

"You always were her favorite. I don't think she liked boys that much."

At least not one in particular. Jenna said nothing to that.

Edward Weaver's secretary offered them coffee, which Winston was more than happy to accept, and then settled them in a conference room with a big table surrounded by rolling leather chairs.

Next in was Patricia Whiteside, Aunt Edie's executrix. She hugged Celeste and Pete and Jenna. "I want you to know all I'm doing is carrying out Edie's wishes," she said to Jenna.

"Of course," Jenna said. What did that mean?

"A sad gathering," Winston said somberly after introducing himself to Patricia. "But at least we'll have something to remember Aunt Edie by."

"Not immediately," she told him. "It can take up to six months or even a year for a will to clear probate."

"A year," Winston repeated, shocked.

"Mr. Weaver is sure in this case it won't take that long, but you should plan on at least three months," she said.

"Oh. Well, it's not about things, anyway," Winston said.

Liar, Jenna thought in disgust.

Next came Edward himself. He was a short man with a wide girth, a balding head and glasses.

"I see we're almost all here," he said.

"Who are we missing?" Jena asked. "Was my mom supposed to be here?"

"No, I think your aunt already shared some jewelry with her. We're only waiting for…ah, here he is."

Jenna turned to see Brody being ushered into the conference room by the secretary and blinked in surprise. Aunt Edie and Brody had been pals, and he'd helped her now and then before Jenna arrived. Still, his presence seemed odd, especially since he hadn't said anything to her about being in the will.

He came up and gave her a kiss on the cheek.

"What are you doing here?" she asked.

Brody stumbled over his words. "This is, well, you know I always was a good friend to your aunt. Keep that in mind."

What the heck did that mean?

"All right. We can begin now," said Edward. "Gathering people for the reading of a will is an outdated practice and really isn't done anymore, but this was Mrs. Patterson's request."

"We want to honor her request," Winston said, sounding properly respectful.

Jenna wanted to kick him.

Edward cleared his throat and began. "As I'm sure you're all aware, everyone present is here because Edie Patterson has left you something."

Winston practically squirmed with excitement. So Aunt Edie had taken pity on him and left him something after all.

There were a couple of surprises. Aunt Edie had left five thousand dollars of Starbucks stock to Celeste. When had she gotten that? And why had Jenna never heard about it back when they were struggling to come up with money to fix up the Driftwood? Had Aunt Edie forgotten about it? Or just hidden it?

Her old boat of a car went to Pete, along with her husband's wedding ring. Both gifts were a surprise, especially the wedding ring, but, somehow, it seemed right. Pete pulled out a tattered old handkerchief and blew his nose.

The third surprise came in Aunt Edie's gift to Winston, and he was not pleasantly surprised. She'd left him a seascape painting that hung in the little dining room. "To remind him of the good times he's had at the beach," read Edward.

"That's it?" Winston demanded.

It was a textured seascape by an up-and-coming artist and worth around five hundred dollars. What a waste giving it to someone who didn't appreciate its beauty or know its value.

"It's more than you deserve," Jenna snapped. "The only time you've ever gotten in touch with Aunt Edie was when you wanted something."

"You're a fine one to talk," he snapped back.

"We're not done here," Edward said sternly. "Let me continue."

He did, which only made Winston angrier. "The house to Jenna?"

"Will you stop?" she demanded, and he crossed his arms across his ample middle and scowled.

What had her aunt been thinking to gather them together like this? Jenna felt like a character in an Agatha Christie novel.

In addition to the house, she also inherited Jolly Roger. And the Driftwood Inn went to...

Brody!

Seventeen

Jenna gaped in shock at Brody, who looked back at her as if he was the sorriest man in the world that she was getting this news. He was the sorriest man in the world all right.

She could barely concentrate as the lawyer finished. As agreed to by Brody, Jenna would remain on as manager of the Driftwood and be given a salary.

She was now nothing more than a paid employee.

Aunt Edie had always said the inn would come to her one day. She'd promised. It was why Jenna had come to Moonlight Harbor in the first place. It offered financial security for her and her daughter. She'd poured her heart and soul into revamping it. And now, just like that, it was gone, given to someone else. No knife could cut as deeply as this betrayal.

She reminded herself that the vintage motel had belonged to her aunt and she had every right to leave it to whomever she wanted. But Brody! And why hadn't he told her? He should have. Not saying anything, it was…sneaky.

"Guess all that sucking up didn't do you as much good as you thought it would, did it?" Winston gloated as they left the office.

"You shut your yap," Pete snarled.

"You need to leave," Brody said firmly.

"Fine. I've had enough of this place anyway," Winston said. "Don't bother sending that stupid painting. I don't want it." He shoved his hands in his pockets and slouched off.

"Good riddance," Pete said.

"At least she left you the house," Celeste pointed out.

Yes, that was something to be thankful for. But the Driftwood Inn. Aunt Edie had known how much Jenna loved the old place, had seen how hard she'd worked to make it a success. What had she done to make Aunt Edie decide she couldn't trust Jenna enough to leave it to her?

Jenna nodded, unable to speak. She started toward the car.

"You and Pete go on ahead," Brody said to Celeste. "I'll bring Jenna back."

Jenna found her voice at that. "No, I'm coming with you," she said to her sister. To Brody she said, "I have nothing to say to you." She turned to walk away but he caught her arm.

"I know how this looks," he said.

"And I see how it is," she retorted.

"You've got to believe me, Jenna. This was not my idea. Your aunt had her reasons."

"Reasons put in her mind by you," Jenna accused. "When I first came here you were trying to talk her into selling the Driftwood, offering to be the listing agent, of course. Now you've done even better for yourself. Instead of selling it and getting a commission, you can sell it and keep all the money."

This was the second man she'd wasted her trust on. She pulled off her engagement ring and held it out.

His eyes grew wide and his tanned face flushed. He shook his head. "No, you can't mean this."

"Oh, yes I can. You knew Aunt Edie wanted me to have the Driftwood and you…betrayed me."

He made no move to take it so she reached over and shoved the ring in his shirt pocket.

"Jenna, please. Let's talk."

She shook her head. "From now on all we'll have to talk about is the running of the Driftwood. Let's get out of here," she said to Celeste, and marched to her sister's car.

It was a silent ride home. For once, Pete was smart enough to keep his mouth shut.

After the sisters were in the house, Celeste was the first to speak. "Maybe there's some explanation."

"There's an explanation all right. He talked Aunt Edie into leaving him the Driftwood, probably when they were alone in her hospital room. Which makes him the lowest of the low." She could hardly get out the next words. "He's been using me all this time." Talk about a long con.

"He can't have been," Celeste said. "I know he loves you."

"He loved what came with me. Which he'd have inherited anyway once we were married. But then Aunt Edie had her heart attack before he could officially propose, so he had to go to plan B and hope that I wouldn't notice." The tears were flowing again, and Jenna rubbed her forehead as if she could scrub away all the horrible thoughts bouncing around in her brain. "All this time he hung around, acting like Mr. Wonderful. He's no better than Winston! And what does he need with an old motel? He's got property all over town."

"Property all over town," agreed Jolly Roger.

Jenna ignored him. She fell onto the couch, staring

straight ahead, wiping at her streaming eyes and seeing nothing but an empty future. Celeste sat down next to her and put an arm around her shoulder.

Sabrina came into the room. "Mom, what's going on?"

"Aunt Edie left the Driftwood to Brody," Celeste explained as Jenna struggled to pull herself together.

"To Brody? That's weird."

"No, that's Machiavellian," Jenna said, blinking back fresh tears.

She would not cry over this in front of her daughter. Would not. A mutinous tear escaped in spite of her determination.

"Does it matter? Aren't you guys getting married?" Sabrina asked.

"No!"

Sabrina sat down on the little chair with the seashell fabric and gaped at Jenna, who was now reaching for a tissue from the box on the floor by the couch. She'd lost track of how many boxes she'd bought since Aunt Edie died.

At last Sabrina ventured, "What about the house? Do we still have a place to live?"

"She left the house to your mom," Celeste said.

"That's good, right? At least we'll still be here in Moonlight Harbor."

Where Jenna had planned to live the rest of her life. Now the last thing she wanted was to stay in Moonlight Harbor, working for Brody Green, the user. The same man who'd made such a pretty speech right on this very same couch and given her a ring. She reached for more tissue.

Sabrina knelt at her feet and laid her head in Jenna's lap. "I'm sorry, Mommy."

After that she said nothing. Neither did Celeste. They simply sat there with her.

They were still there when her mother came in. "Winston told me," she said. She squeezed in on the other side of Jenna and laid a hand on her arm. "Sweetheart, I'm really sorry."

"How could Aunt Edie could do this?" Jenna swiped at her wet cheeks and blew her nose. "I love the Driftwood. I've done a good job running it. I...don't understand."

"I don't either," Mel admitted.

"And it's not just about the inn. It's... I feel..." Unappreciated, betrayed. She couldn't bring herself to say it, but there it was.

"I'm sure she had a reason," Mel said.

"That's what Brody said. I did it again, didn't I? I chose the wrong man." *Great thing to say in front of your daughter.* Jenna rubbed her throbbing head.

"Sabrina, dear, how about making your mother a cup of tea," Mel suggested. "And see if you can find some aspirin."

"I thought he was such a good guy," Jenna lamented as her daughter disappeared to make tea.

"He is. You know he is," Mel said.

"He's always been there for you," put in Celeste.

"Then why did he do this?"

"I don't know," Celeste admitted. "It doesn't make sense."

"And why blame Brody? It was Aunt Edie who changed the will," pointed out her mother.

Because it was easier to blame Brody. Jenna simply couldn't face the idea of Aunt Edie pulling the rug out from under her.

She shook her head. "I'm sure he influenced her."

"At least he showed his true colors before you married him," Celeste said.

How could she have been so wrong about someone? What kind of psychopath was Brody that he'd been able to fool her?

And yet he'd helped Courtney get Beach Babes. That wasn't the behavior of some heartless villain.

Wait a minute, though. Courtney didn't own it outright yet. Brody could just as easily screw her over, too. Whatever contracts she'd signed with him, Jenna hoped Courtney had taken them to Edward Weaver or his partner to look over.

Listen to yourself, she thought. *A day ago you were in love with this man and ready to marry him and now he's your arch enemy.*

Yeah, well. That was how life went sometimes. One minute you were a sucker, and the next you wised up.

She blew her nose one last time. "I can't do this. I can't stay here and work for him. I'm done."

"What do you mean?" Celeste asked, sounding alarmed.

"Someone else can run the Driftwood. I'm not staying to help the man who brainwashed my aunt and cheated me out of it. I'll sell the house and move. Let someone else be on the Moonlight Harbor city council."

Sabrina was back with a steaming mug and a bottle of aspirin. "Move? We can't move. All our friends are here."

"Nothing's decided, darling," Mel said, taking the mug and bottle from her.

"And I'm starting college," Sabrina continued. "And Grammy just moved down and Aunt Celeste just bought a house."

And Jenna was ruining everything. She opened her mouth to speak but nothing came out. Her right eye began to twitch.

Sabrina looked at her as if she was the world's worst parent. "I can't believe you'd do this to me. Again!"

"I just…." Jenna began. *Just what? Just don't want to stay? Want to curl up in a fetal ball? Want to drown Brody? Want to start my whole life over on some remote island in the Caribbean?*

Sabrina didn't wait for her to finish her sentence. She stormed out of the room and up the stairs. The slamming of her bedroom door reverberated through the whole house.

Jenna covered her face with her hands. "I hate my life."

"Give the dust time to settle," Mel advised. "Things will work out. Remember, every storm brings—"

Jenna cut her off. "Don't. Say it. Please." If there was one thing she didn't want to think of right then it was rainbows and pots of gold and other stupid happy endings.

Her cell phone pinged. Celeste pulled it out of Jenna's purse and handed it over. "It's Brody."

Jenna tossed it aside. As if she ever wanted to talk to him again.

They heard angry footsteps stamping down the stairs. The front door opened and then slammed shut.

"It looks like Sabrina's going out," Mel said diplomatically. "Why don't you girls come over to the house and have a bite to eat? Winston is gone now."

Jenna shook her head. "I don't feel like eating."

"I should get back home," said Celeste. "I promised Henry I'd be back by dinner and take over baby patrol. Are you going to be okay?" she asked Jenna.

"Of course. I'm a big girl." Also a big fool. "You guys go on. I'll be fine."

Who was she kidding? She wasn't sure she'd ever be fine again.

Her mother and Celeste left, and Jenna found a bag of

Cheetos in the pantry and devoured the entire thing. There. That helped. Not.

The day wore on. She didn't hear a peep from her daughter, who was probably never going to speak to her again.

Finally she texted Sabrina. I was just venting. We won't move.

At least not until Sabrina finished college. By then she'd probably be off to start her own life and Jenna would be free to go wherever she wanted.

The only problem was that there was no place she wanted to be but Moonlight Harbor. Correction: the only place she'd once wanted to be. She could relocate to another town farther up the beach and still be close to her family. At least if she got out of town she'd never have to see Brody again.

Brody. She felt the tears starting.

No time for tears. She had a motel to run.

For someone else. Aunt Edie had offered Jenna a sop by keeping her on as manager. But how could she stay on and manage a place she loved so much, a place that was supposed to have been hers?

She gave her teeth a good grinding, then blew her nose one last time and walked over to the motel office. She had work to do.

She kept herself busy all afternoon. She also resisted the temptation to answer Brody's many texts and calls.

At last she caved. Stop harassing me!

I need you to understand, he texted back. This isn't how it looks. Don't give up on us.

Too late. I'll stay on and manage the Driftwood until you take possession. Then I'm done.

Done. She didn't want to be but she sure didn't want to stay. How could she?

Maybe she needed a little distance. Maybe by the next day the wound wouldn't feel so raw.

Who was she kidding? It was just as raw the next morning.

"At least she left us the house," Sabrina said as she dished up oatmeal for her mom.

Sabrina was becoming quite the queen of the kitchen. Aunt Edie would have been proud to see her stepping in and taking over.

Aunt Edie. *Why did you do this to me?*

"Yes, that's a blessing," Jenna said, trying to stay positive for her daughter.

And herself. Inheriting a house was nothing to sneeze at. What an ingrate she was!

Sabrina joined her at the kitchen table. It felt so weird not to have Aunt Edie there with them.

"Do you hate Brody?" she asked.

"Temporarily," Jenna said. "We both know it's wrong not to forgive people, but sometimes it takes a while."

Sabrina nodded and took that in. "I think he should give the Driftwood to you."

Funny, she thought the same thing herself. "That would be a pretty big gift."

"Not really, not if he wanted to marry you."

Jenna shoved away her bowl of oatmeal. "It's all water under the bridge now." And the riverbed was dry.

"I never liked him that much anyway," Sabrina said. "I'm glad you guys broke up."

So was Jenna. Glad. And sad. And disappointed and angry.

Pete knocked on the back door, then stepped into the kitchen. "Thought I'd see if you need anything done."

Who was this new and improved Pete? Jenna couldn't get used to him.

"Not today," she said. "Want some oatmeal?"

"Pablum," Pete said in disgust. "No, thanks." He started to leave.

"Wait a minute," Jenna said. "I need to give you what Aunt Edie left."

"You gotta wait for the will to clear probate," he said.

"Not for this. Pour yourself a cup of coffee. I'll be right back."

Jenna ran up the stairs to Aunt Edie's room. She had to take a deep breath before going in. Seeing that empty bed was a nightmare. She averted her eyes and hurried over to the antique dresser where Aunt Edie kept her jewelry box and opened it. It didn't take long to find Uncle Ralph's wedding ring, a simple gold band. It would look good on Pete.

Back in the kitchen, she gave it to him and he put it on. It was a little big on him.

"You might have to get it sized," Jenna said.

He looked at it and nodded. Sniffed, cleared his throat to swallow a sob and said, "Thanks." Then he left.

Jenna watched him walk down the back stairs. He looked like he was carrying the weight of the world on those scrawny old shoulders.

Damien called the next day to complain about not seeing Sabrina. No reason she couldn't drive up for a visit now that she had a car.

Other than having a job and a life.

It was the first she'd heard from him since Sabrina's graduation. "Sorry about your aunt," he said. "Sabrina told me she died. I guess you own the Driftwood now."

Cousin Winston wasn't the only buzzard in her life. Of course Damien would be snooping around, hoping to sic his lawyer on her for more money before the clock ran out on his spousal support.

"Sabrina didn't tell you about the motel?"

"Tell me what?"

"I didn't inherit it. Aunt Edie left it to someone else."

"You're kidding."

"I wish I was."

"So you moved down there for nothing."

"I moved from nothing, so it doesn't matter," she said, thinking of the wreck her life had been when she left for the beach. For a while, she thought she'd found everything she'd ever want.

"Cute," he said irritably. Then he switched conversational gears. "I'm not getting a straight answer from Sabrina. She can't be working every weekend this month."

"Yeah, she can. She's saving money for school."

"My folks want to see her."

Always it was the folks. "You know, Damien, it's odd. How come I never hear you say that you want to see her?"

"That goes without saying. What the hell are you implying?"

Okay, time to shut that can of worms. She was too emotionally exhausted to fight.

"Nothing. Look, if you want to see her you'll have to come down here. And you'll have to find some other place to stay. We're all booked at the Driftwood so I can't comp you a room. Your parents would probably love the Oyster Inn."

"That's a pricey place."

"It's worth it." And his parents could manage it just fine. "You decide and work it out with Sabrina. Other than her working we don't have any big plans for the rest of the summer."

Not that there was much left of it.

Just as well. Jenna had no interest in doing anything. She let calls from her friends go to voice mail and, when her mother called to check on her, turned down Mel's offer to come over for lunch. Food. Meh.

Sabrina, dutiful daughter that she was, made sure she was around to have dinner with Jenna that evening, not that Jenna ate much of the frozen pizza they'd heated. But then Scotty called and Jenna shooed her off. Someone needed a life.

With her daughter gone the house felt vacant and she found herself wandering around it. Into the dining room, to stare at the painting Winston had passed on. *Life's good at the beach. Yeah. Well, not so much these days*. Upstairs to stand in front of the closed door to Aunt Edie's bedroom. Someday she would have to go in there and clear out her great-aunt's things. There was a depressing thought. She went back downstairs and into the kitchen. What was she doing in there? She wasn't hungry. She'd just had dinner. She wound up in the living room, staring at the TV.

Maybe she'd stream some reruns of *Downton Abbey*. By herself.

Maybe her mom would like to join her. Or they could play some gin rummy. Or Mom could listen to her mopey daughter complain about her life.

She put in an SOS to Mel, disguised as a casual phone call. *Long time no talk. Ha ha*. "What are you up to tonight?"

"You caught me going out the door."

"Oh. You're going out?" She sounded like a disappointed little kid. Good grief, she was pathetic.

"Ellis is taking me to the Porthole. Did you need something, darling?" Mel asked.

Other than a shoulder to cry on? "No, no. I thought if you weren't doing anything..." *I want my mommy.*

"I can cancel my plans," Mel hurried to say. "I know Ellis wouldn't mind."

Of course he would. "Don't do that. I'm glad you two are going out. It looks like things are moving right along between you."

"We're friends, that's all," Mel said.

"Yeah, right. That's how it started with Bro..." Jenna cut herself off. She and Brody were no longer an item. They weren't even friends. "You have a good time. I'll catch you later."

"Why don't you come over after we get back?" Mom suggested. "We can all play cards."

Just how every man wanted to end a date. "No, that's okay. I'll talk to you tomorrow."

She decided to give her sister a call. Celeste picked up on the fourth ring.

"What are you doing?" Jenna asked.

"Going crazy trying to finish packing everything. Henry's got somebody who wants to rent the houseboat coming over in, heaven help me, twenty minutes and it looks like a bomb went off in here."

Okay, Celeste had no time to chat. "I'd better let you go."

"No, I can multitask. What's up?"

"Nothing. I was only calling to yak." *And feel sorry for myself.*

"Are you okay?" Before Jenna could answer, her sister's attention was diverted. "I know the baby's crying, Henry. Can you get her? I'm on the phone here."

"You'd better go. I'll talk to you later," Jenna said, and pushed End.

"I hate my life," she told Jolly Roger.

Roger had nothing to say. He cocked his birdy head and looked at her.

"Yeah, that's not a phrase you want to learn."

The beach was calling. Jenna grabbed a half-full bottle of wine, a blanket and a plastic glass along with some matches and old newspaper for starting a fire, then made her way across the sand dunes. By sunset she'd gathered plenty of driftwood and had a nice fire going. She saw a lone figure in shorts and a T-shirt jogging along the beach. The setting sun cast him in shadow, but she'd know that muscled body anywhere.

He slowed down and walked up to her. "What are you doing here by yourself?"

She held up her plastic cup. "Drinking."

"Alone?"

Not a good habit to start. She was going to have to switch to chocolate.

"Yep. I'd offer to share but I only brought half a bottle and I intend to drink all of it."

He dropped onto the log next to her. "Where's the house peddler?"

"I don't know and I don't care," she said, and took a big gulp.

"First fight, huh?"

"And last. I gave back the ring."

Seth sat perfectly still, saying nothing. It was as if his lips had suddenly been glued shut.

"Aren't you going to say anything?" she prompted.

"What do you want me to say, that I knew all along he was a shit?"

"Something like that would be nice."

"Sorry. I don't think he is."

"Oh, yeah? Well, I know he is," Jenna said, and proceeded to fill him in on Brody's betrayal.

When she was finished, he shook his head and said, "Weird. I thought Edie was going to leave you the Driftwood."

"That's all you've got to say?" Jenna demanded.

"What are you gonna do now?"

That wasn't what she'd wanted him to say either. Although she wasn't sure exactly what she wanted.

"I'll stay on and run the Driftwood until it passes to Brody. Then after that, I don't know. Once Sabrina graduates from college I'll probably sell the house and move."

"Where?"

He smelled musky from his run. Why did that make her think of sex?

"What do you care?" she muttered.

"You shouldn't leave," he said. "You belong here."

She finished off her drink, ignored the bottle at her feet. Wine was for celebrations and pity parties didn't count.

"I don't know where I belong. Nothing has worked out and I'm hollow inside."

"What about all the friends you've made, the fact that you've got family within spitting distance?"

She bit her lip. She was going to cry. Again. Lately it was what she did best.

"I don't need a pep talk right now." What she needed was for him to lay her down right there in the sand and kiss her stupid. Nothing wrong with a rebound relationship. The other kind hadn't worked.

"Guess not," he said, and put an arm around her shoulder. She leaned against him and he kissed the top of her head. "Things have a way of working out."

They sure did, and there was nothing good about the way they were working out for her.

"I don't want to be alone," she whimpered.

"You're not."

"I'm not talking about my family. I'm talking about... love. Why can't I make it work with anyone? What's wrong with me?"

"Other than poor taste in men, nothing."

She looked up at him. "Yeah?"

"Yeah," he said softly.

Kissing close, just a breath away. Those gorgeous lips made a great target. She moved toward them.

He took his arm back and moved the target. "Let's not go there."

"No, let's."

"You're lonely and you're not thinking clearly," he informed her.

"You want to be with me. I know you do."

"A week ago you were engaged," he said as if she'd slipped a cog.

"That was a mistake."

"So is this. I'm not saddling you with my past."

"Go ahead, saddle up, cowboy."

He stood. "You'll thank me in the morning."

"No I won't, and I'm not thanking you now."

"Good night, Jenna."

He said it as if she were a little child who didn't want to go to bed. Well, she wasn't a child and she did want to go to bed.

"There is nothing good about this night," she grumbled as he walked off toward the motel.

Then, since there was no one to watch her make a fool of herself, she indulged in a good, long, howling crying jag. Yep, life was good at the beach.

Eighteen

"I can't seem to stop crying," Jenna told her mother when Mel came to help her at the reception desk on Friday, always her busiest day. "It's like this well that won't run dry. I think about Aunt Edie and how much I miss her and I cry. I think about Brody and how close we came to having a life together and I cry. And then I think about not having the Driftwood and I cry."

"You wouldn't be human if you didn't," Mel said, wrapping a comforting arm around her. "Life brings its share of tears."

"I'm tired of them, Mom. I thought I was past that when I came down here. Thought I was finally getting my life together."

"You have," Mel said, giving her a squeeze.

"I don't feel like it. I feel like for every step I take forward I get knocked back two. Everything that's happened, it doesn't seem right. And I know it's immature to say it, but it doesn't seem fair. I'm grateful for the house but I'm mad about the Driftwood. I wouldn't be if Aunt Edie hadn't promised it to me. I don't know what I did to disappoint her."

"Nothing, darling. She loved you and she was so proud of you."

In the end, she wasn't proud enough to trust Jenna with the future of the family business. Somehow, during her last visit with Brody, he'd convinced her not to. Brody, who was unrelated and who'd had nothing to do with the success of the vintage motel.

Except Aunt Edie had asked to talk with him. Had she wanted advice? Maybe she'd asked him to promise to watch out for Jenna and he'd convinced her the best way to make sure of that would be to put the Driftwood in his hands. It was wrong, all wrong.

"Sometimes I just…want to scream at God, 'Why?'"

"I've felt that way myself. I still do."

So many years after losing Dad? Here was a shock.

"Only recently I was asking God, 'Why have you been so good to me to give me two beautiful girls and so many new friends?'"

Okay, that made it official. Jenna was an ingrate.

"Mom, you're too perfect," she said miserably.

"No, I'm not. Believe me, when your father died my thoughts were far from perfect. But each day the sun rose and it was time to get up and put one foot in front of the other. And each day living got a little easier. It will for you, too. Somehow, some way, God will help you sort things out. Eventually those dark clouds will part. Wait for it, Jenna. Don't give up."

She had a daughter. She didn't have any choice but to put one foot in front of the other. Only problem was, these days her feet weren't taking her very far. How had she managed to mess things up so much?

* * *

Courtney got busy in the kitchen as soon as she finished working on Friday, baking her one specialty, brownies. From a mix.

Annie walked in with groceries as she was loading the dishwasher. "Do I smell chocolate?"

"One of the world's greatest fragrances," said Courtney.

"Actually, it's an aroma." Annie dug out a jar of peanut butter and stuck it in the cupboard.

"Well, it should be a fragrance. You can get chocolate-scented candles. Does anybody make chocolate perfume?"

"I hope not. If I wore that I'd be hungry all the time. Are you taking those over to the station for Jonas and the guys?"

"No, I'm taking them to Jenna's tonight."

Annie paused in front of the fridge, a package of butter in her hand. "Jenna's? It hasn't been that long since her aunt died. I can't imagine she wants us all over there. In fact, maybe she doesn't want to keep doing this at all."

"She needs this. She needs us."

"Some people need time alone," Annie pointed out.

"I don't think Jenna's one of them."

"If it was Celeste I could see it."

"Yes, she's the party animal, but Jenna isn't wired for being a hermit, either. She may not blab about her hurts to everyone, but she's never been like this. She's like the Sphinx on death row. She needs hugs and chocolate. So, are you coming with?"

"Okay," Annie said, still sounding dubious. "Emma's at Addie's. I'll see if she can spend the night. I still think this is a mistake though."

Hmm. Maybe Annie was right. Courtney put in a call to

Nora. "What do you think?" she asked after she'd shared her plan.

"I think it's a good idea," Nora said. "Nobody's seen anything of her since the memorial service. She could probably use some cheering up. I'll call Tyrella and Patricia and Cindy."

There, Courtney thought as she pushed End on her phone. She knew she was right.

But that evening when she and Annie and Nora and Tyrella all showed up on Jenna's porch, she wasn't so sure. Jenna was dressed in a long sleep tee and holding a huge bag of Hershey's Kisses. She blinked at the sight of them and took a step back. She looked more like she was in shock than wanting to let them in.

Courtney brazened it out. "You need more chocolate," she said, holding out her plate of brownies.

With that Jenna burst into tears.

It wasn't the first time Jenna had made a public spectacle of herself. Only that afternoon she'd checked in an older couple and the woman, who looked a lot like Aunt Edie, had been disappointed with the room.

"You have all those pictures of the beach on your website. I thought this came with a view," she'd complained.

"The beach is right out your back door," Jenna had said.

"But no view."

Jenna had been in no mood for complaints. "Then you'll probably want to find some big, fancy motel with two stories that will give you a view," she'd said, barely able to remain polite. "But you won't find one with more heart than this one. My great-aunt built this place back in the sixties and we poured ourselves into fixing it up. She always baked cookies for our guests and we treated everyone who came here like they were special. And she just died and it's not the same without her and..." She hadn't been able to finish the sentence. She'd topped off her unprofessional behavior by blubbering like a baby.

The woman had wound up consoling her and assuring her that she and her husband would love the room. After they'd left Jenna had chided herself for her lack of control. This wasn't her. She wasn't rude to paying guests. She didn't tell strangers her troubles and boo-hoo in front of them.

Except maybe this was the new her, the new, unimproved Jenna Jones who'd finally been cosmically kicked one too many times and didn't want to get up again. Pathetic.

She'd managed to go through the rest of the day tearfree and had finally come back to the house ready to hole up with a bag of Hershey's Kisses.

She'd just gotten comfy and now here was company on the doorstep. What the heck?

Friday night, of course. It was time for the weekly gathering her great-aunt had presided over for years. Except they hadn't gathered since she died. Aunt Edie had left the building. Forever.

"We should leave," Annie said.

"No, it's okay. Come on in," Jenna said, sniffing back a sob.

They came in and Courtney installed her on the sofa, sat next to her, and set the plate of brownies in her lap. "Somebody get this girl a glass of wine," she commanded.

"I'm on it," said Nora, who'd come bearing a bottle of white wine along with a carton of chocolate peanut butter ice cream.

Jenna watched as her friends got busy setting out plates and wineglasses. "I should go get dressed."

"Nah. This is a come as you are party," Courtney assured her.

"I wasn't expecting anyone."

She hadn't had the heart for entertaining, especially the Friday night group. Without Aunt Edie it didn't seem right.

"You know your aunt would want us to keep doing this," Courtney said as if reading her mind.

Jenna bit her lip and nodded. "It's just that…"

She didn't even know how to finish the sentence. She hadn't confided her feelings to anybody other than her mother and sister.

"Too soon? Want us to go?" Now Courtney looked uncertain.

Her friends were reaching out to her, anxious to help. Jenna didn't want to be an ingrate.

She shook her head. "No, stay."

"I know it's got to be hard without her," Courtney began.

"It's not just that. It's…" *Everything.*

Nora appeared with a glass along with a small bowl of ice cream. "Wine and ice cream to go with your brownies. Now you're set."

"Except for my shortbread," Annie said. "I just took it out of the oven half an hour ago. I'll get you a piece."

Jenna nodded and stared at the goodies her friends were piling onto her.

"Jenna, if you're rather be alone…" Nora began.

In the house all by herself, feeling sad and pitiful. "No. I need the love."

"There's nothing like girlfriends for that," Courtney said. "Well, and boyfriends."

"I don't have a boyfriend. Brody and I are no longer together," Jenna said and shoved half a brownie in her mouth. She was aware of Courtney and Nora exchanging looks.

Tyrella, who'd been finishing setting goodies on the table, joined them now, a small plate of cheese and crackers in her hand. "No longer together?"

"Wait a minute. What happened?" Courtney asked.

"We're not a fit," Jenna said, resisting the temptation to bad-mouth him.

"You could have fooled me," Courtney said.

Brody had fooled a lot of people, including Jenna. She inhaled the second half of her brownie. Annie returned with some shortbread and she took that, too. Bring it on. So what if she was turning into a carboholic?

"At least you still have your friends. And the Driftwood," Courtney said.

That did it. Round three for Blubber Baby.

"What on earth? Talk to us," Tyrella said, taking her position on Jenna's other side.

There was a knock on the door and Annie went to open it.

"I don't have the Driftwood," Jenna said between sobs. "Aunt Edie left it to Brody."

"Brody!" echoed Nora just as Cindy Redmond walked in.

"What about Brody?" she asked, taking a nearby chair.

"Edie left him the Driftwood," Nora explained.

"I always thought it was to go to you," Courtney said.

"So did I," Jenna said, looking around. Where had that stupid box of tissues gone? She gave up the search and grabbed the napkin Courtney had provided and blew her nose.

"There's got to be some explanation," Nora said.

"There isn't," Jenna said, her voice wobbly. "I'm managing it for him. I inherited the house," she added, not wanting her friends to think her great-aunt had left her destitute. "But…" She couldn't finish the sentence. How to explain how very much the old motel meant to her and what a blow it had been to lose it?

Voices in the front hall announced another visitor and Annie ushered Patricia in. The older woman looked warily at Jenna as if unsure of her welcome. Jenna didn't have anything against her. As executrix of Aunt Edie's will, she'd only been doing her job. It was hard to face her, but Jenna managed a small smile.

"We get it," Cindy said. "I can't imagine how I'd feel if I had to close the candy shop."

"I know how we'd all feel if you did," Courtney joked, then frowned at her lapse in taste.

"We understand," Nora said. "We're all businesswomen. But it's odd. Edie wanted you to have the Driftwood."

"Jenna, you have to know how bad I feel that things turned out the way they did," Patricia said. "I have no idea what she was thinking, but I'm sure she had her reasons for changing the will."

"Obviously, she changed her mind. And it's not hard to guess who helped her change it," Jenna added bitterly.

"It's so out of character for Brody," Nora mused.

"People get greedy," said Annie.

"It's hard, but you have to forgive him," Tyrella told Jenna, getting to the heart of the matter.

"I know," she said. "I will." Eventually.

Eventually was a long way off, and in the meantime, it was impossible for Jenna to find the warm feelings she'd once had for Brody. She kept their chance encounters polite and chilly. He always had the gall to look hurt.

What was that old movie line? *This town isn't big enough for the two of us.* She wished she hadn't promised her daughter she'd stay. She wanted out. Out of the house she'd been left, out of Moonlight Harbor, out of her misery.

After seeing Brody at the bank she found herself knocking on the door of the room Seth rented. His workday was barely over and he answered wearing his work jeans, boots and a dirty T-shirt. His dark hair was tousled and his chin was working on a heavy five o'clock shadow. Messy couldn't disguise gorgeous.

He stepped aside to let her in. "What's up? Do you need something done?"

Nothing was up and it made no sense for her to be there, bugging him. "No. I guess I just needed someone to talk to." Okay, how stupid did that sound? Her mom was a five-minute drive away. Jenna could have gone over to her place.

"Everything okay with Sabrina?"

"Yes, she's great."

"Pete giving you grief?"

"No."

"Then what?"

"I hate my life," she blurted. "I hate that Brody will own this place once the will clears probate and I'll be working for him."

Seth nodded, taking that in. "Well, then, leave. Quit. Run away."

She glared at him.

"Kind of pathetic considering how hard you worked to restore it, but hey, if that's what you want to do."

She'd come for some sympathy and comfort and instead had just been made to feel smaller than a sand flea. Her cheeks sizzled with a mixture of anger and embarrassment.

"Don't you judge me. You have no idea what this is like for me."

"You think you're the only one who's ever gone through something hard?" His face was like granite.

"So I'm supposed to suck it up and be miserable?" she demanded.

"Yeah, you've got a lot to be miserable about, inheriting that nice house."

"You are a heartless bastard," she snarled.

He shrugged. "I guess I am."

She stormed out of the room and off down the beach. She probably had enough steam coming out of her ears to propel her all the way back to Seattle.

As it turned out she didn't have as much steam as she thought. She didn't get far before she remembered what he'd gone through before he came to Moonlight Harbor. Then she remembered all the times he'd been there for her, all the ways he'd helped her, the latest being restoring that car for Sabrina.

She went back and knocked on his door again. A timid knock from a woman about to serve herself a big slice of humble pie.

He opened it and regarded her—not angrily but somberly.

"I'm sorry. You're not a heartless bastard."

"Yeah, I am. Come here," he said, and folded her into his arms.

She laid her head on his shoulder, feeling like a damaged ship limping into harbor.

"I should have been more sympathetic," he said.

"No, you're right. I'm being a whiner."

He gave a soft chuckle. "Maybe a little, but we all should be able to whine once in a while. With everything that's happened, you earned the right. Look at the big picture though. You got the house, you've got your family down here now, you've got a good kid. You've got a paycheck and you've got your massage business to fall back on. It could be worse."

"You're right," she said with a sigh. "I guess I'm having a hard time dealing with feeling betrayed."

"Not easy, but you can deal with it." He took her by the arms and moved her a foot away so she could look at him. "Suck it up, Jenna, and be the heroine of your own story. You can get through this. I know you've got it in you."

She bit her lip and nodded.

"Now scram," he said gently. "I've got things to do. And so have you."

She wished he had things to do with her.

Just as well, she told herself. When it came to men she was the world's worst judge of character.

Back at the house, she opened the door to Jolly Roger's cage so he could have some freedom. But the bird stayed on his perch, muttering to himself.

"I'm sorry, Roger. I've been ignoring you a lot."

"Roger's a pretty bird," he reminded her.

"Do you miss her?"

"Give me whiskey," Roger demanded.

"I know how you feel," Jenna told him.

She was about to start dinner when Pete showed up at the kitchen door, bearing a pizza box. "Thought you might not want to cook," he said.

She didn't. Sabrina was meeting Scotty at the Seafood Shack and Jenna had no desire to bother with dinner for one.

Pete's kindness was an unexpected surprise, and one

that needed to be rewarded with appreciation. "Good idea," she said. "Come on in."

"The kid home?" he asked, setting the box down on the kitchen table.

Jenna pulled two plates from the cupboard. "No, she's out with her boyfriend."

Pete grunted. "Not around much these days," he observed, pulling a couple of cans of root beer from the refrigerator.

"It happens when kids get older."

"Pretty soon you'll be all alone."

Jenna sat down at the table and frowned at him. "Gee, thanks, Pete. That cheers me up."

Except she'd probably always have Pete. Brody had said he could keep his room at the Driftwood for as long as he wanted it.

"Sorry," he muttered. "You're still a fine-looking woman. You oughta find some man and get married."

"I'm through with men," she said.

"What, you're into women now?"

"I'm done with relationships, period. I'm obviously a rotten judge of character."

He shook his head and helped himself to a slice of pizza. "Brody ain't so bad."

"He ain't so good, either," she said.

"Get back together with him and you can have the Driftwood."

Get back together with him? She couldn't even stand the thought of him.

"I don't believe in using people," she said, and that ended the conversation. They ate the rest of the meal in silence.

After three huge slices he was done. "Guess I'll be shoving off," he said.

"Thanks for the pizza," she said.

"You've lost weight. You need fattening up."

Pete's new role, mothering Jenna. She couldn't help smiling.

He started for the door.

"Pete," she said, and he stopped and turned.

She pointed to his left-hand ring finger where Uncle Ralph's old wedding ring now sat. "The ring looks good on you."

He pressed his lips together tightly, nodded, then ducked out the door.

Who knew Pete would turn out to have such a heart of gold? Certainly not her when she first met him.

Yes, indeed, she was a terrible judge of character when it came to men.

Much to Mel's delight, Celeste and Henry finally moved into their new house in Moonlight Harbor. Sabrina and Scotty were on hand to help when they all met the U-Haul truck with Henry at the wheel early that morning. Celeste was right behind him in the car, with baby Edie in her infant seat in the back.

She jumped out and exclaimed, "We're finally here, all of us!"

Both her daughters nearby and the grandbaby within easy reach. Life didn't get any better than that.

Maybe it did, she thought as Ellis pulled up in his classic convertible.

Seth came as well to help with the heavy lifting. No Brody this time.

Mel was still trying to figure out what her aunt had been

thinking when she left the Driftwood Inn to him. Sometimes, she felt almost as cheated as her daughter. Such a wrong turn. And so wrong of him to accept when he could have promised to deed it over to Jenna. He'd claimed to love her, but if this was how he showed love Jenna was well rid of him.

With so many people helping the work went fast. By the time Scotty and Sabrina left for their jobs, the furniture had been unloaded as well as most of the boxes.

"He's such a nice boy," Mel said to Jenna.

"Yes, he is," Jenna agreed. "At least my daughter has figured out how to pick well."

"Brody's not the only fish in the sea," Mel said.

"I'm done fishing."

"Don't give up on love. Love hasn't given up on you."

"I seem to remember you saying that to me a few years ago," Jenna said, unimpressed.

"It's still true."

"Between you and Celeste and my friends I have plenty of love," Jenna assured her.

"There's love and then there's love," Mel said.

Jenna cocked an eyebrow at her. "You do realize I could say the same thing to you, right?"

Mel got busy unpacking towels.

But her daughter's words stuck with her, and later when Ellis asked her if she'd like to get in some beach time, she said yes. They stopped at the Seafood Shack and got to-go bowls of clam chowder, then settled on a log and enjoyed the view—blue sky over an endless stretch of water making its way to the beach. Gulls circled overhead, riding the wind currents, calling to each other.

She took in a deep breath of fresh, ocean air. "I'm so glad I moved down here."

"Me, too," Ellis said. "I'm glad your daughter finally talked you into making the move. I owe Edie a debt of gratitude for bringing her down."

"It was the best thing that could have happened to her," Mel said. "Except now." She shook her head. "I don't understand why Aunt Edie left the Driftwood to Brody when she'd promised it to Jenna. It's rather tarnished her life here."

"It's not like Edie to go back on her word. Somehow, she must have thought doing things the way she did would be best for Jenna."

"Jenna is perfectly capable of running that motel."

"She still is running it," Ellis pointed out.

"It's quite a step backward from being the future owner to the being the manager," Mel said. "I don't think she'll ever trust another man again."

"It wasn't a man who left Brody the Driftwood."

"No, but Jenna's convinced Brody influenced Aunt Edie's decision. I feel so bad for my daughter. It about broke her heart."

"She's young. And she's smart. She'll bounce back. You can't give up on life just because of a few disappointments. None of us can."

Mel studied him. "Why do I get the impression we're no longer talking about my daughter?"

He turned from watching the gulls to look at her. "Because she's not the only one with a lot of life ahead of her." He softened his voice. "I think you and I have got some good years ahead of us. What do you think?"

That he had a wonderful, manly face with that strong chin. She found the little cleft in it fascinating. Almost as fascinating as his deep voice that rumbled like thunder. A part of her that had been asleep appeared to be awakening, and it wanted more than friendship, yearned for a man's touch. Could she love another man after so many years of carrying the torch for her husband?

"I don't know," she said.

"I do." He took the nearly empty chowder container out of her hand and set it next to him on the log. Then he put both arms around her and drew her up against him.

Her heart began to flutter. Nerves? Excitement? Fear? Maybe all of the above.

"Ellis, what are you doing?" she protested. A mere formality and they both knew it.

"Something I should have done long before this," he said, and kissed her.

Kissing was like riding a bike. You never forgot how.

And like getting back on a bike, it felt great.

Nineteen

The days began to bleed together as the last of summer slipped away. Sun, beach, waves…just another day in Paradise.

Jenna remembered her mother's words, and kept doing her best to put one foot in front of the other, keeping the house clean, taking her turn baking cookies for the Driftwood's reception desk, working hard to ensure things ran smoothly and their guests were happy. Keeping her massage business going and working the kinks out of her clients' muscles. If only she could work out the kinks in her attitude as easily.

Celeste and Henry settled into their house and, come Labor Day, the family gathered there for dinner. Mel brought over potato salad to go with the burgers Henry was grilling on the back porch, and Jenna brought ice cream from Good Times Ice Cream Parlor.

"It's so great to all be together," Celeste said as the three women sat at the patio table, watching Henry slave over a hot grill. "You should have invited Ellis, Mom."

"Sometimes it's nice to just have family," Mel said.

"Isn't that right?" she cooed to baby Edie, who was in her lap.

Edie gave her grandma a big smile and a laugh to say she agreed.

"He could end up being family," Celeste said with a sly grin.

Mel's cheeks took on a rosy hue. "He's an awfully sweet man."

"He's a hottie. Better than Sam Elliot, right?" Celeste said. "Is he a good kisser?"

The roses on Mel's cheeks went from pink to crimson. "That will be enough questions, Miss Snoopy."

Celeste giggled and Jenna smiled. There were still things in life to be happy about. She needed to remember that.

But it was hard to stay happy when you hurt. Happiness was such an energy-sapping emotion.

So was sorrow, and she alternated between the two. Even though Sabrina was at home (sort of) and Jenna and Pete often shared a meal together, the house felt empty, like something precious had been lost. It was hard to walk into the kitchen and not cry. Aunt Edie should have been at the stove, baking cookies.

Jenna was determined to be a faithful guardian of the Driftwood, but she often felt like a deserted lover, hanging around where she was no longer welcome. *I'm only going through the motions*, she thought. At home, at the motel, especially when she went to her city council meetings. Who cared about beautifying the town or building a new dog park? Who cared about a convention center?

Parker Thorne, that was who. "How are you doing?" she asked when she came to Jenna for a massage.

"I'm all right," Jenna said as she worked on the mayor's shoulders. "Your shoulders are really tight, Mayor."

"I do carry all my stress in my neck and shoulders. But I know you'll get the kinks worked out. Let's not talk about me though. I'm concerned about you," Parker said. "You've been such a great addition to our city council, but you seem to have lost your steam."

"I've lost more than steam. I lost my aunt," Jenna reminded her. Not to mention the future she'd looked forward to.

"I know. And we all miss her. But don't you think she'd want you to carry on in her absence? She was one of Moonlight Harbor's early visionaries."

Jenna concentrated on putting more massage oil on her hands. "I'm aware of that."

"Your constituents are depending on you."

"I'm doing my job," Jenna insisted. Even if only half-heartedly.

"You are. But I know you had big dreams for this town. I'd hate to see you lose sight of them. The council needs that young blood."

She was the youngest one on the council. Funny, she felt old and tired.

She thanked the mayor for her concern and promised to do her best to serve her constituents.

"You could start by presenting your research on that convention center you've been so fired up about," Parker suggested.

"I'm not ready," Jenna said, then added, "Maybe someone else could look into that."

"Jenna, this was your idea."

"Frankly, I can't get fired up about it right now. I can't get fired up about much of anything these days. I'm sorry."

"I understand," said Parker. "But life goes on."

Yes, it did. Jenna just had to figure out a way to get it to go smoothly again.

She finished up with the mayor, then walked over to the motel office, entertaining thoughts of resigning her position on the council.

That wouldn't be right. She'd signed on to do a job. Campaigned for it, even. Hopefully, at some point, she could regenerate her enthusiasm for it.

She'd finished checking in two women who'd come down to the beach for a girls' getaway when Seth stopped by the office.

"Wanted to let you know I'm moving," he said.

Her heart went cold. "Moving?" she repeated. "Where?" *Not away from Moonlight Harbor, please.*

Although maybe it was for the best if he was. Nothing had happened between them and nothing ever would. First Brody, now Seth. This confirmed it. She was meant to be alone.

"Up the beach a mile. I'm buying the Morgans' old place. Not from the house peddler," he hurried to add. "It's a private deal. They don't want to come down here anymore and their kids don't want it."

She knew the house. It was a two-story fixer-upper in need of a new roof, a new deck and a fresh paint job at the very least. But, like Aunt Edie's house, it had a great view.

"It needs a lot of work," he said, "but the price is right, and they'll carry a contract."

"A good deal for you," she said. "When?"

"End of October."

"We'll miss you around here."

"Looks like Pete's stepping up to the plate finally. You'll

be fine. If you need something major done you'll know where to find me."

"I'm happy for you. It will sure beat living in a room in an old motel," she said.

"Not necessarily, but it's time to move on."

Time to move on. What was he trying to tell her?

She nodded. He nodded. There really wasn't anything left to say.

She watched him walk off across the parking lot. "Life goes on," she told herself. Ugh.

Ugh was how she felt about going to the September city council meeting, but she went (after asking the mayor not to bring up the subject of the convention center). She had done some research before her life got turned upside down, but she was in no mental state to do more at the moment.

"Very well, it can wait," Parker had assured her. "But I do want you at this meeting, Jenna. I have a special piece of new business to introduce."

Jenna had been afraid to ask. With Parker, one thing was for sure. It would be self-serving. Parker loved taking credit for things and she adored the limelight.

As it turned out, the mayor's new business item was only mildly self-serving in that Parker made it clear the suggestion was her idea. And what an idea it was. Jenna blinked in surprise when she saw it listed on the agenda. Seriously?

"Under new business, we have my proposal that we honor one of our influential and beloved citizens who has gone to her great reward," Parker said. "I hope the council will vote unanimously to name our new dog park after Edie Patterson, calling it the Edie Patterson Memorial Park."

A dog park. Aunt Edie was not a dog lover. She'd barely tolerated Nemo. And now they wanted to name a dog park after her? If she was up in heaven looking down, her eyes were rolling.

Jenna couldn't help it. She laughed. Parker glared at her and that made her laugh even harder.

Meanwhile, all the Moonlight Harbor residents who regularly came to watch the council in action gave the idea a standing O.

Everyone settled down and Jenna turned off the laugh machine and wiped her eyes. As Aunt Edie's relative she was obliged to say something properly grateful.

"I'm overcome with joy," she said, and coughed down a giggle. "I know my great-aunt would appreciate the honor our mayor is proposing we bestow on her." Snort.

Really, having a park named after you was an honor, right? And since there was no such thing as a parrot park, this would have to do.

The motion carried unanimously and, shortly after, the meeting adjourned.

Aaron Baumgarten, star reporter for the *Beach Times*, who covered the council meetings, came up to Jenna to offer his congratulations.

"If you report that I laughed, I'll cancel my subscription," she said.

"I won't," he promised. "I'm simply going to say you were overcome with joy. Off the record, I take it Edie wasn't a dog lover."

"Aunt Edie loved everyone and everything."

Aaron snickered. "Jenna, you're turning into a politician."

"It was a nice thought and it's the thought that counts," Jenna insisted. And no, she was not turning into a politician. She was simply learning how to be diplomatic.

"Aunt Edie would have laughed, too," Celeste said when

Jenna called to tell her. "Oh, my gosh, I can see all the dogs marking their territory at the foot of the sign. I'll make sure Nemo leaves a calling card."

That made them both giggle. Then, as Jenna described how pissed Parker had looked at her inappropriate response, the giggling escalated to laughter.

"This is the first time I've heard you laugh since…in a long time," Celeste amended. "Maybe you should start making a habit of it."

"Maybe," Jenna said, but she wasn't making any promises.

Plans went forward for the dog park and September moved on. Tourist season began to wind down and both the town and the Driftwood Inn grew less busy. Seth still stopped by the office a couple of times a week to see if Jenna needed anything and she told herself that nothing would really change once he moved. Nothing was happening with him living in close proximity, and nothing would happen once he relocated to a place farther down the beach.

Come the end of the month, Sabrina started school at the nearby community college.

"I love my Women's Studies professor," she gushed as she and Jenna and Pete sat at the kitchen table, eating fried chicken and coleslaw from the deli at Beachside Grocery.

"What do women need to study that the rest of us don't?" Pete demanded as he helped himself to a second chicken leg.

"A new view of literature, history, politics and sociology is required for us to have equal representation," Sabrina informed him.

"You've been equal for years," he scoffed.

"It's attitudes like that that hold us back," Sabrina retorted hotly.

"Bah," Pete said in disgust. "They're filling your head with all kinds of nonsense at that school."

"No, they're going to expand my worldview." Sabrina turned to Jenna. "Remember Aunt Celeste's toast at my graduation party? I think I do want to become a writer. Did you know that women's stories don't get the same respect as men's even though we have a bigger share of the market?"

"You can't make a living as a writer," Pete said.

"Tell that to Nora Roberts," Jenna said, jumping into the fray. "I think you'll be a great writer," she said to Sabrina. "What would you write about?"

"Write about sex," Pete advised. "Sex sells."

"Maybe I'll write about my amazing mom," Sabrina said.

"Now, that's a good idea," Pete said, surprising Jenna. She looked at him in shock, and he shrugged and said, "Why not? You can become a celebrity and then you'll double the number of guests who want to come here."

And stay in the sweet little vintage motel she'd brought back to life only to lose. She was dreading the day the will cleared probate.

"I'm glad we didn't move," Sabrina said.

At least someone was.

"Time is a great healer," Mel reminded Jenna when she came to take her shift at the Driftwood.

Mel hadn't wanted to accept money when they first talked about her helping out, but Jenna had insisted on putting her on the payroll. Now she was glad she had. The least Brody could do would be to pay her mother.

Jenna took one of the cookies her daughter had made off the plate on the reception desk counter. Chocolate chip, Aunt Edie's recipe. Why didn't they taste as good?

"I know you're right. I wish I'd heal faster," she said.

She still found herself lying awake at night, missing the good times she'd had with Brody, wondering where things went wrong. For a moment there, she'd thought she'd found the perfect life.

"Deep wounds take time," Mel said. "You'll get there."

"I just wish I had an ETA," Jenna said. If only life was that simple.

September leaves caught fire, died and fell, and the air took on a nip as October muscled its way into their lives, and still Jenna's healing process dragged slowly. Other than seeing her family and hosting the weekly Friday night gatherings, she kept her social life to a minimum, preferring to hole up in the house, numbing her brain with TV movies.

Courtney stopped by on a Sunday to try to convince her to come out line dancing, something she hadn't done since losing Aunt Edie. She hadn't had the heart for it. It seemed so…frivolous. Besides, Brody would most likely be at The Drunken Sailor, hanging out at the bar, chatting up the waitresses.

"No, thanks," she said. "I've got things to do."

Courtney pointed to the television. An old episode of *Downton Abbey* was playing. "What? Watch TV? Come on. Your mom's manning the reception desk. There's no reason why you can't get out and have some fun."

"I have Friday nights with you guys. I don't need to have fun," Jenna said stubbornly. Okay, that hadn't come out right.

"What would Aunt Edie say?" Jenna scowled and Courtney tried a different approach. "You've got to get some exercise."

"I walk on the beach. That's enough exercise. Go have fun without me."

"Don't worry, I will," Courtney said. "But I'd have more with you."

Not in Jenna's current state of mind.

"I suppose you're not going to go to the chamber Halloween party, either," Courtney ventured.

"Where's it being held?" Jenna had no idea as she hadn't been to a chamber of commerce meeting in months.

"Not at Brody's, if that's what you're worried about," Courtney said. "It's at Kiki's house."

"But he'll be there. That would be too awkward for words, so no thanks."

"No thanks," repeated Jolly Roger, not wanting to be left out of the conversation.

"It's a small town. You're going to run into him."

"I don't have to do it on purpose."

"I sure hate to see you moping around here, not having a life," Courtney said.

"It's okay. I'll live through you. By the way, when is Jonas going to get around to giving you that ring? It's supposed to be this year, right?"

"The year's not over," Courtney said. "Although now I'm kind of regretting demanding he do something special. It feels like it's taking forever. And I'm not looking forward to Thanksgiving with my parents if I don't have a ring."

Thanksgiving. Sigh. It would be their first one without Aunt Edie. At least Jenna had the rest of her family living at the beach with her. That was something for which to be thankful.

So was taking baby Edie trick-or-treating for the first time. Not that she knew what was going on, but she looked adorable dressed as a goldfish in an orange fleece costume with padded fins. Henry had already volunteered to eat the candy she collected.

Seeing all the children dressed in their costumes, eagerly running from house to house, put a smile on Jenna's face. It brought back happy memories of the fun she and Celeste had experienced as kids as well as the delight she'd taken in putting together costumes for her daughter and taking her out on the big night.

Once they got back to Celeste's place, the sisters skimmed all the good chocolates off the top of the haul and streamed *Beetlejuice*. Jenna actually enjoyed herself, and drove away from her sister's feeling happy for the first time in months.

Until she drove down Kiki Strom's street and saw it lined with cars. The chamber of commerce party was in full swing. Jenna recognized Brody's snazzy convertible. He'd be in his element, probably dressed in his devil costume. Very appropriate.

"You should be glad I'm not a witch," she muttered as she drove by. "I'd turn you into a toad."

Except he already was one. Yep, workin' on that forgiveness thing.

Mel went with Ellis to the chamber of commerce Halloween party. She hadn't been to a costume party since she was with John and she'd been at a loss for ideas. Ellis had suggested they go as pirates. Appropriate for living at the beach, she thought, and agreed, although she felt a little silly wearing the boots and leggings and fancy jacket. She loved the hat Ellis had found for her—a fabulous tricorne with a big gray feather. But still, this was an outfit meant for a woman her daughters' age.

Ellis, on the other hand, looked perfect in his long coat

and breeches and boots. He, too, had a hat any pirate would envy. He'd completed the look with an eye patch, which made him look charmingly dangerous.

"Look at you two. You look wonderful," Kiki greeted them. She was dressed like Minnie Mouse, wearing big ears, a tail sticking out from under her ruffled red skirt. Her husband was a Mickey to her Minnie, and he, too, had big ears. His tail stuck through a slit in the back of his red Bermuda shorts.

"Don't make me walk the plank," Kiki's husband joked.

"Don't try to steal my treasure, then," Ellis replied, putting an arm around Mel's shoulders and making her cheeks heat with embarrassment.

She knew several people at the party. Nora and her husband were there, dressed as bags of M&M's. Tyrella Lamb had come as a cat. And there was Brody, wearing a red cape and devil horns. How appropriate.

Mel reminded herself that she'd forgiven this man who'd hurt her daughter. She still wanted to whack him with the fake sword she had in her belt.

When she'd accepted Ellis's invitation, she hadn't stopped to consider that Brody would be there, and it felt disloyal to Jenna to be at a party with him. She saw him looking her direction and pretended not to. She hoped he'd understand where her loyalties lay and not approach her.

"How about something to drink?" Kiki was saying. "I have a great fruit punch. Or wine, if you'd prefer."

"Punch sounds wonderful," Mel said, and drifted over to the punch bowl—a large pumpkin with an eerie fog floating up from it thanks to dry ice in one of the metal bowls inside it. "Isn't this clever," she said, turning to smile at Ellis.

But it wasn't Ellis behind her. He'd been waylaid by someone.

"Brody," she said and gave him a weak smile.

"Hi, Mrs. Jones," he said. His expression told her he felt as uncomfortable as she did. "How are you enjoying your house?"

"Very much," she replied. Her voice probably was almost as cold as the dry ice creating the spooky fog around the pumpkin punch bowl.

He nodded, his gaze not quite meeting hers. "How's Jenna?"

"She's heartbroken."

The pain on his face looked convincingly real. "I wish I could explain," he began.

She held up a hand to stop him. "It's past time for explanations, wouldn't you say?"

His jaw clenched.

Ellis joined them. He and Brody shook hands and said stiff hellos.

The Hatfields and the McCoys, Mel thought. Everyone had to choose sides.

"I'm sorry things turned out the way they did," she said and Brody nodded, looking miserable.

It was a shame. She'd thought so highly of him. Avarice was an ugly flaw.

"All right, everyone," Kiki called. "Who's going to join me in the basement and bob for apples?"

Brody took advantage of the distraction to slink away.

"I guess I should have thought it through more carefully before asking you," Ellis said. "My only excuse is I've never been in a situation like this before. We all used to get along down here."

She should have thought it through more carefully before accepting. But she said, "It's okay. And really, this is between Jenna and Brody."

"That's what I thought," he said. "I figured I'd be like Switzerland. Neutral. Not so easy being Switzerland. We can leave."

"We just got here. How would that look?"

"At our age we don't need to care how we look. They'll be having a costume contest over at The Drunken Sailor. Let's go see if we can win."

She nodded. She remembered telling Jenna that it took time for wounds to heal. It looked like it also took time for mothers to be able to face the one who'd caused those wounds to their daughters.

Twenty

Come the beginning of November, the Driftwood Inn officially became Brody's, and Jenna tendered her resignation. She frowned at the sight of him when he walked into the office. Had he come to gloat?

"I'm coming to ask you not to resign."

"I'm sure you can find someone more capable," she said stiffly.

"I don't want someone more capable. I want you. Wait, that didn't come out right."

"Maybe it came out exactly as you thought. Is that what you said to Aunt Edie, that she needed someone more capable in charge, like you?" Darn it all, here came the anger again. She hated the sour feeling it left in her stomach.

Brody showed a flash of anger, himself. "You forget, she was the one who wanted to talk to me."

"What had she wanted to talk to you about?" Jenna demanded.

"You." He let out a frustrated exhale. "She had your best interests at heart. You've got to believe me, this isn't how it looks."

"Well, however it looks, I'll be done here in two weeks."

"Stay on a while longer. I'll pay whatever salary you name."

"Stay here and run what should have been mine for you? Do I look like a masochist?" Maybe she was.

"Can you stay until May? Please? Charge me whatever you want. I promise you, this will all work out."

"It already has. For you."

He had the nerve to look as if she'd stabbed him in the heart. It was more straightforward than what he'd done to her. He'd stabbed her in the back.

Okay, enough. She had to lose the bitterness.

She took a deep breath. "All right, let's leave the past in the past."

"Then you'll stay?"

"What will you pay me?"

The price he named was ridiculously high.

"That's too much. You'll lose money."

"I don't care," he said.

"Since when don't you care about money?" she taunted. He made enough of it.

"I'm trying to do what's right here."

"If you want to do what's right, let me buy the Driftwood from you. Work out a deal with me like you did with Courtney." Surely he didn't really want to keep the place. "I'll pay whatever price you ask."

"Give me until the end of May and then we'll talk," was all he said.

She sighed inwardly. He was stalling her. Why? What devious plan did he have up his sleeve?

For one irrational moment she had a strong desire to tell him what he could do with his offer, but she had to be practical. If Brody was willing to pay her a ridiculous sum to manage the place then she needed to take it. She had a kid in college and she had to build up her massage business some more. It wouldn't hurt to have some extra money to salt away. What difference would a few more months make?

"All right," she said. "Until the end of May. Then maybe we can talk about a deal."

Surely if he was planning to sell the place come spring he'd give her the first chance to buy it, if not for the sake of what they once had then simply to be ethical and do right as he insisted he was trying to do.

"Good," he said, making no promises.

That was the end of the conversation between two people who had, only a few months earlier, been contemplating marriage. He left and she cried.

Courtney was thrilled with how well Beach Babes had done over the summer. Sales had continued strong clear through Labor Day. They'd fallen off in October, and come November the store had a lot of quiet days.

That was fine with her. She needed to design and create and restock for Black Friday sales as well as Seaside with Santa, the last tourist hurrah before the town went to sleep until spring. She opted to close the shop Mondays through Wednesdays and open up for a long weekend starting Thursdays. Brody, her silent partner, had agreed with her decision.

Brody. It was hard to believe he'd purposely muscled Jenna out of inheriting the Driftwood when he'd been so good to her.

Courtney had actually pressed him about it and had gotten a very cryptic answer. "I know how it looks."

"Yeah?" she'd prompted.

"I don't want to talk about it," he'd said, wiping the usual Brody smile off his face.

And that was that.

"I don't get it," she said to Jonas as they looked around Collective Creations Art Gallery for a hostess gift for Jonas to bring to her parents on Thanksgiving. "Why would Mrs. Patterson leave the Driftwood to him and not Jenna?"

"Don't know," Jonas said. He picked up a clear glass pelican with a small fish in its belly. "What about this?" he asked.

"Mom will love it. How much is it?"

"Who cares? It's cool. And it'll score me points."

"The only thing that's going to score points is if I have a ring on my finger," Courtney said.

"Your mom's gonna have to be patient, 'cause I'm doing this right."

Patience wasn't her mother's best virtue. She raved over the glass pelican when Jonas gave it to her Thanksgiving Day but was quick to add, "Of course, what I'd really like is to see my girl settled."

"She's settled," Jonas assured her.

Poor man. It seemed he got grilled by everyone. Her grandpa wanted to know what he did to keep busy when he wasn't at the fire station, as if that wasn't enough. Did he have a second job?

Not really. He spent a lot of time helping some of the older women in town when they needed household repairs and he liked to putter around on cars.

"Can't do that much on the newer models," said Gramps.

"Not on the engines, but I can fix brakes, change spark plugs and oil, that kind of thing. Got a house that I'm fixing up."

"For anyone special?" asked Mom. Just a little nudge, subtle as a bulldozer.

"For someone very special," he said.

Next Gramps wanted to know how Courtney's business was doing.

"It's going great," she said. "I've still got tomorrow and our Seaside with Santa festival coming up, and that will bring in customers. During the off season I'll work on designing more clothes and building my inventory back up. Actually, it was a little slow the last few weeks, so I've already started."

"We're so proud of you," Mom said to her. "You've come a long way since…"

"Your starter marriage," her older sister Angela supplied.

"Everyone makes mistakes," Mom said.

"Yes, look at me," joked Courtney's Aunt Marlys, eyeballing Uncle Jed.

"Best mistake you ever made," he said, not at all ruffled.

"It's all about landing on your feet," added Dad.

Courtney had definitely landed on her feet.

"When is that boy going to give you a ring?" Mom demanded as the women gathered in the kitchen and began cutting the pumpkin and pecan pies.

"He's waiting for the perfect moment," Courtney said.

"Every day has twenty-four hours' worth of perfect moments," Mom informed her. "You need to hurry up. The longer you wait the harder it is to get pregnant. Your eggs are getting old."

"My eggs are fine," Courtney replied, irritated.

"Mom, give her a break," said Angela, coming to her rescue.

"Don't listen to your mother. She's always been a bossy

thing," Aunt Marlys said to Courtney, patting her shoulder on her way out to the dining room with the first two plates of pie.

"I'm not being bossy," Mom insisted. "I'm being encouraging."

Was that what you called it?

"I'm so done seeing parents until the new year," Courtney said as she and Jonas started the drive home. "Mom is making me nuts."

"I like your mom," he said, flipping on the windshield wipers.

"You would. She gave you half a pie to take home."

"You're jealous 'cause she likes me better," he teased.

"I almost think she does. And who could blame her? You're as close to perfect as a man can get."

"I'll remember that when you give me a hard time about leaving my clothes lying on the floor."

"I bet you don't do that at the station."

"That's different. Gotta keep things neat there."

"Gotta keep things neat once we're official and living together," she said.

"We're already official. Don't doubt it."

She didn't. But maybe there was more of her mother in her than she cared to admit. Like Mom, she was starting to get impatient.

It was the first Thanksgiving Jenna's mother wasn't with them. Mel had gone to Bellevue to celebrate Thanksgiving with some of Ellis's family, proof that they were easing into something more serious than friendship. It seemed odd not to have her at the dining table, sharing their feast.

And it felt all wrong not to have Aunt Edie with them. Even though Sabrina was in the kitchen, helping Jenna get the meal ready, it wasn't the same without Aunt Edie there, fussing over the dressing and baking the pumpkin pies.

Pete had examined them as they sat cooling on a rack and gave them his seal of approval. "They look good, kid," he said to Jenna.

Kid. This was a new nickname. At least he wasn't calling her old girl.

"They look good, kid," Jolly Roger agreed from his kitchen perch.

"Thank you, both of you," Jenna had said.

Aunt Edie would have been happy to see Roger being allowed in the kitchen to watch the goings-on. And she'd have been delighted to see Jenna and Pete actually getting along. Who knew how long that would last? Probably until spring, at least, when they'd be busy sprucing up the Driftwood. By then, Jenna suspected Pete's back would start acting up and they'd slip into the old familiar patterns once more.

Spring. She had until the end of May to convince Brody to sell her the Driftwood.

She pushed the thought out of her mind. She was going to concentrate on today and today only, and think about the things in her life that were good.

Even with Mel and Aunt Edie missing, the table was full. Celeste and Henry and the baby were there, eating the first of two Thanksgiving dinners, the second to happen when they spent Saturday with Henry's family. Seth was at the table, also.

Jenna had been surprised he'd accepted when she'd stopped by his new house and invited him, sure that he'd be making the trek to Tacoma to see his brother.

"Not this year," he'd said. "They're doing Thanksgiving with the in-laws."

"Well, then, good," she'd said. "We need somebody to eat the drumsticks."

"It'll be a tough job but I'll manage," he'd said.

Friendly banter. That was all there would ever be between them. She told herself she was fine with that. Yes, she was.

Normally, Mel would have said the Thanksgiving prayer, but with her missing it fell to Jenna. There were a lot of things she was not happy about, but she focused on giving thanks for the food on the table, a new baby in the family, and the fact that they all could be together. And really, weren't those the important things in life?

"Amen," Celeste said enthusiastically when she finished.

Seth smiled at Jenna and her heart gave a little squeeze. At least she still had one man in her life she could count on.

"Amen and all that," said Pete. "Pass the spuds."

"It looks great," Henry said to Jenna. "You ladies did a good job."

"Edie couldn't have done better herself," Pete added. High praise, indeed.

Conversation at the table ranged from how Sabrina was doing in her college environment to Henry's new book.

"What's it about?" Sabrina asked.

"It's about a man who, uh, takes advantage of women," Henry said. He shot a nervous glance in Jenna's direction and his face flushed. "But not…" The flush got deeper. "Not like…" He cleared his throat. "He's a serial killer who marries women and murders them for the insurance money."

"Doesn't sound very original," observed Pete the diplomat.

Henry didn't take offense. He helped himself to more

dressing. "The twist is that the last woman he marries does the same thing."

"Now, there's a cool twist," Jenna said. "Does he get what he deserves in the end?"

"Oh, yeah," Henry said.

She saluted him with her wineglass. "I'll drink to that."

Once the meal was finished and most of the mess cleaned up, everyone moved into the living room for fun and games, the grown-ups taking chairs and baby Edie set up on a blanket on the floor with her toys, Nemo lying nearby.

"Charades," Celeste said gleefully, handing out pencils and slips of paper. "Everyone write down the name of a book, movie or song you think will be hard to act out. We'll do boys against the girls."

"Oh, no. Not me," Pete said, waving away the paper and pencil. "I ain't making a fool out of myself."

"I ain't making a fool of myself," Jolly Roger agreed from his cage. "Call the cops!"

"Oh, come on, Pete, you have to," Celeste wheedled. "Otherwise the teams will be uneven."

He crossed his arms over his chest and shook his head. "Hu-uh. That's a girl game."

"I'm with Pete," said Seth. Edie crawled over to him, and he picked her up and started bouncing her on his knee. "Anyway, I can't. I've got the baby."

"You guys are such wusses," Henry taunted.

"I think the least you can do is cooperate, considering how hard we worked making dinner," Celeste said to Seth. "And you did have two helpings of my broccoli casserole."

"I didn't know it was going to cost me," he said, but he took a pencil and piece of paper, which Edie immediately tried to grab.

With Seth whipped into shape, Celeste turned to Pete. "Aunt Edie would have wanted you to play."

If looks could kill, Jenna thought, seeing his response. "You know she's right."

"I'll be permanent guesser," he conceded, and took a slip of paper.

"Now our numbers are off," Celeste complained.

Sabrina's phone signaled a text and she eagerly checked the screen. "Yes! Scotty's on his way over. He'll play."

"Good. He can make a fool out of himself," Pete said.

Scotty arrived within minutes and so the game began, girls against boys, with Pete securely anchored in his chair as permanent guesser for both sides. The boy was cheerful and a good sport and was more than happy to act out what was on the paper he'd drawn from the bowl Celeste presented him.

It turned out to be a song, "Dance Monkey" by Tones and I, and had him gyrating and hopping about like a monkey. To the women's surprise, the men got it right away.

"I thought that would stump you," Celeste grumbled.

The women didn't fare so well. Sabrina failed to get them to guess the title of the book *Nothing to Lose*.

"By Lee Child," Seth said.

"Oh, yeah, he's great," Henry said. "I've read all of his books."

The women didn't do well on their next turn, either. Celeste had drawn a song, and got right into it, falling on her back, doing a fairly good imitation of something in the stages of rigor mortis, her legs drawn up and her hands cupped like paws.

"Dead," Sabrina guessed, and that started it.

Although she and Jenna were able to manage *dead* and *the*, the rest of the words eluded them, no matter what crazy gestures Celeste tried. And she tried all kinds, shaking her bottom and plugging her nose, making a face. It only generated guesses like *stinky* and *fart*.

"That was impossible," she said when time ran out.

"What was it?" Sabrina asked.

"'Dead Skunk in the Middle of the Road,'" Celeste told her.

"What? There's no such song," Jenna protested.

"There sure is," said Pete, who'd obviously contributed it.

"Who sang it?" Celeste challenged.

"Loudon Wainwright." Pete crossed his arms over his chest again and looked around, daring everyone to contradict him.

Sabrina's fingers flew over her cell phone. Her eyes got big. "There is such a song. 'Dead Skunk.'"

"Told you," Pete said.

"Oh, brother," Jenna said in disgust. "Leave it to you to come up with a title like that."

Seth was next, looking resigned to his fate as he gave up the baby and drew a slip of paper from the bowl Celeste presented him. "Another song," he said with a frown.

Celeste pointed a finger at him. "Hey, no talking."

He started acting out clues. Much to Jenna's amusement, Pete got into it. "You," he called.

Seth motioned for him to keep trying. *You're on the right track.*

"Me."

Seth shook his head and made a motion with his hands that might have meant either that he wanted to hitch a ride or that Pete should go back to his earlier guess.

"You," Pete said again, then corrected himself. "You're."

Seth nodded and held up a finger.

"You're a finger," Pete guessed. "Giving you the finger."

Seth shook his head in disgust.

"One," guessed Scotty, and Seth nodded eagerly.

Funny that Seth was getting into this considering how reluctant he'd been at first, Jenna thought, and couldn't help smiling.

The clues went on and so did the guesses.

"Little word," said Scotty. "A, the."

Seth nodded.

"The?" Scotty concluded.

"'You're the One That I Want,'" crowed Pete. "John Travolta and Olivia Newton-John. What a hottie she was in that black leather."

Seth smiled. Gloating, since the guys were ahead.

Except for a moment there, Jenna thought he was smiling just at her. Was he?

No, the moment was gone and she'd imagined it.

Twenty-One

Once Thanksgiving and Black Friday ended, the holiday frenzy began. Local businesses decorated to the hilt with wreaths in their windows and trees dressed up with starfish and seashell ornaments. Shelves were stocked with tempting goodies in anticipation of the final tourist invasion of the year—the Seaside with Santa festival—everyone praying and crossing fingers and toes that the weather would cooperate. Holiday party invitations got sent out, and Beach Lumber and Hardware sold out of holiday lights.

Courtney and her team of seamstresses had worked like mad to keep Beach Babes stocked, and she'd had the satisfaction of seeing the latest batch of vests and jeans she'd designed fly off the racks on Black Friday. Those hardworking women would all be getting a Christmas bonus. Now the mannequins in her shop window sported holiday wear and Santa hats (decorated with machine embroidered seashells, of course). In addition to the clothes, people were also buying jewelry and scarves to give away as presents.

"My mom will love this," Jenna said to her as Courtney rang up a taupe-colored fringed scarf with a starfish print.

"Those have been selling like crazy," Courtney said.

"It looks like a lot of things have been selling like crazy," Jenna said, glancing around. Some of the racks were already becoming sparsely populated.

"They have. I've got more inventory coming this week. Hopefully it will get me through the holiday shopping season. I've got to admit, this shop owner thing has turned out to be a bigger bite than I thought it would be. Sometimes I feel like I've been swallowed by a whale."

"Jonah survived it. You will, too. Success, the struggle is real."

Courtney grinned. "I know, right?"

"Are you going to do anything for the parade?" Jenna asked.

"For sure."

Jonas had offered the use of his truck, and she'd ordered a banner for it. She'd considered putting mannequins in the back to keep her company and model her fashions, but decided to use live models instead. If the wind whipped up, at least they wouldn't get blown over. She'd already convinced Moira to be a model. Annie had refused, claiming too many holiday parties to cater, but Courtney knew she was really balking at the idea of having so many eyes on her.

"Is Celeste going to be on your float this year?" If not, maybe Courtney could snag her.

"I don't think Celeste is ever going to be on a float again after her first Seaside with Santa parade. She still complains about how she almost froze her tail off."

Courtney snickered. "Not easy being a mermaid in a storm." Okay, she'd have to find another sucker to keep Moira and her company back there.

Jenna left, and two more customers slipped in before

closing time. One bought another of the starfish scarves, and her friend purchased a stylish red rain slicker.

After that it was closing time. Courtney locked up and went home, ready to devour the dinner Annie was making.

The aroma of spices and something chocolate baking greeted her as she walked in the door. "Smells like heaven in here," she called.

She entered the kitchen to find Emma parked at the kitchen table, doing homework, and Annie taking a batch of brownies out of the oven. A giant pot on the stove said, *Chili, it's what's for dinner.* A pan of cornbread sat cooling on a rack on the counter.

"You are amazing," she said to Annie.

"I try," Annie said modestly.

"Hey, Chickadee-dee," Courtney said to Emma. She walked over to where Emma sat huddled over her math book and gave her a hug. "How's the schoolwork coming?"

"I hate math," Emma grumbled.

"Yes, but it comes in handy when you're baking and have to double a recipe or when you're running a business."

"I don't want to run a business," Emma said. "I want to be a hairstylist like Moira. Remember, Aunt Courtney?"

"Hairstylists have to do all kinds of math when they're mixing those colors," Courtney said. Or not. Who knew? "Plus you'll be so successful, you'll have to be good at math to keep track of all that money you're going to make."

"I'll hire somebody to do that," Emma said.

Kids today. They were too smart.

Courtney shed her coat and went to her worktable to finish a final design for her spring line. She was almost done when Annie announced that dinner was ready.

Emma had finished her homework and set the table, and

the three sat down for a cozy winter dinner. Well, it was cozy until discussion of Christmas plans came up.

"Can I spend Christmas Day with Daddy?" Emma asked.

Annie and Courtney exchanged looks. Daddy still didn't have his act together and was living in a dumpy apartment one town over, where he hadn't yet worn out his welcome. He had visitation rights, which he rarely used, and the last time he'd used them, Annie told Courtney she'd smelled the booze on his breath from a foot away. He'd been buzzed and obnoxious and she'd been glad they'd been meeting in a public place.

"We'll see," Annie said.

Emma's mouth fell down at the corners. "I know what that means."

"It means we'll see."

"If I can't go to Daddy's, can he come here?"

Annie's expression asked Courtney, *What should I do?*

The rental agreement was in Courtney's name. She could refuse. But girls needed to see their daddies, even if that daddy was a loser. And maybe, for one day, Greg could behave.

"I'm okay with it," she said to Annie.

"Yay!" Emma crowed.

"Let's see what your mom and dad can work out though," Courtney quickly added, helping Annie keep her options open.

"Thanks," Annie said to her after the dishes were cleared and Emma had gone to brush her teeth.

"We can handle it," Courtney said, and poured herself a cup of mint tea. "He can come in the afternoon after Jonas and I are back from seeing our families. That way we'll be here to make sure he keeps his shit together. But tell him if he comes he has to come sober or we won't let him in."

"Hopefully he can manage that," Annie said glumly. "Sometimes I wish I'd never met him."

"But if you hadn't, you wouldn't have Emma," Courtney pointed out.

"I know. And she's worth all the misery he brings into my life. If only he'd stop drinking."

"That would be the best Christmas present he could give his daughter."

"It would be a nice present for his ex-wife, too. Emma still blames me every time he creates a problem or messes up and things don't go right."

"She will for a few more years," Courtney said. "Then her eyes will be opened and you'll be her new best friend."

"I sure hope you're right," Annie said.

"I am. Trust me. Come on, grab something to drink and let's go see what we can stream on Netflix."

They made their way into the living room just as the sound of music drifted in from outside.

Emma came bounding down the stairs. "The fire truck is here!"

Sure enough, the Moonlight Harbor Fire Department had sent out one of its two trucks, all decked out for Christmas with multicolored lights and a big wreath, to serenade the neighborhood. Emma rushed to the front door and threw it open to the strains of "Santa Claus Is Coming to Town." Other residents on their street were also opening their doors to listen and wave.

The truck stopped, and out hopped Santa, carrying a black velveteen sack over his shoulder.

"He's coming to our house!" Emma cried as he started up their front walk and threw open the door.

"Hello, ladies, merry Christmas," he said once he reached the porch.

Courtney knew that voice. "Santa, aren't you a little early?"

"Not according to your mommy, little girl," he said with a wink. "I know you've been naughty this year, but Santa likes naughty girls."

"He doesn't," Emma scoffed. Even though she was no longer a believer she still knew the Santa rules.

"Uh, no, you're right. So be good and mind your mommy." He turned back to Courtney. "As for you, young lady, Santa has something special for you." He whipped the bag around from his shoulder and reached down deep. He pulled out a small black box with a gold lid and a red ribbon and handed it to Courtney. "You can open it early."

This was it. With trembling hands, she pulled off the ribbon and the lid. And yep, there was the ring box. She opened it and discovered the most beautiful diamond she'd ever seen—a big fat solitaire set in a white gold band.

"Wow," she breathed.

"Sorry I forgot the fries," joked Santa, referring to Courtney's long-ago starter marriage proposal. "So, what do you say, Court? Will you make my life perfect and marry me? Santa needs a Mrs. Claus."

"Oh, Jonas, yes!" she cried, and threw her arms around him and kissed him.

The driver behind the wheel of the fire truck gave a celebratory honk while the neighbors, catching on quickly, applauded.

"How'd I do?" Jonas asked her. "Is this memorable enough to share with our kids?"

"You bet. Thank you. You are amazing," she said, and kissed him again.

"Come on, Santa," called the fireman from behind the wheel. "We got other neighborhoods to hit. Good luck, Courtney," he added. "You're stuck with him now."

"Fine with me," she called back.

She gave Jonas one final kiss, then shut the door as the truck rolled away, switching from "Santa Claus Is Coming to Town" to "Joy to the World."

"Put it on," Annie said.

Courtney did and the diamond sparkled and winked at her.

"Wow," said Emma.

"This is the best Christmas ever!" Courtney cried, hugging herself. She took both Annie and Emma by the hand and started them all dancing in a circle, Annie smiling and Emma giggling.

"We have to celebrate," Annie said. "I'm making hot chocolate."

"And I'm calling Moira and Jenna and Celeste. Let's party!"

Jenna was delighted for Courtney. She'd finally found her happy ending.

At least someone had, she thought wistfully as she drove back home after consuming enough chocolate at her friend's impromptu celebration to keep her up all night. It was late and Sabrina was in bed, conked out. The place was quiet as a tomb.

Tomb. Don't go there.

Jenna locked the door and climbed the stairs to her room. Her lonely room.

Alone. Only a few months ago she'd thought she was going to be sharing a bed with someone. And a life.

"You still have a life," she lectured herself. So what if

it wasn't the one she'd wanted? It wasn't all that bad. She had her family and her friends, the beach, a lovely house. Life was what you made it and she'd continue to make hers as good as she could.

Which meant celebrating the season. She took her daughter to Crafty Just Cuz to make miniature Christmas trees from sea glass and did a mother-daughter outing to Waves to get their hair cut and colored. She also finally persuaded Celeste to ride in the Seaside with Santa parade on their float, made to look like a miniature Driftwood Inn. This year the weather was kind to them. No storms, no power outages.

No Brody to pitch in and help.

Never mind him, she'd told herself. He was the past and from now on she was all about the future.

She'd made sure both she and her sister were dressed warmly in matching black leggings, red coats with faux-fur-trimmed hoods, and white mittens. She'd enjoyed throwing saltwater taffy to the kids in the crowd, and after the parade they'd gone to Mel's house for chowder. A lovely day. See how good life could be without the man you'd planned to marry?

Christmas Eve was lovely, too, with the whole family attending service at church. *You have so much to be thankful for*, Jenna reminded herself as the musicians played "Silent Night."

She told herself the same thing the next day when they were at her mother's place, opening presents. Henry's family came down to join them and Mel's new house was filled with people and laughter. *How Aunt Edie would have loved this*, Jenna thought wistfully.

Mel gave Celeste a gift card to Beachcomber so she could buy some beachy decor for her new house. She thrilled Sabrina with a Beach Babes gift card, and also gave one to Jenna, saying, "I know you won't splurge on clothes for yourself, and I think you deserve a little spoiling."

Ellis West joined the crowd for Christmas dinner, bringing a gigantic box of chocolates for everyone to enjoy and a bottle of expensive perfume for Mel. Those two were great together and Jenna was glad to see her mother so happy. Mom deserved it.

So did she, she thought. She chased away the frown that was threatening to invade with the reminder that she was happy. Happy, darn it, happy!

Pete, who had also been invited, arrived bearing red velvet whoopie pies he'd picked up at the bakery. The only person missing was Seth, who'd gone to celebrate Christmas with his brother. Who cared that he wasn't there? Not her.

As for Brody, she really didn't care where he was or what he was doing. Except she couldn't help wondering. They should have been together, celebrating, looking forward to a wedding in the new year.

Aunt Edie should have been there, too. Jenna had baked her famous sugar cookies and shed some tears in the process.

When they got to dessert, Pete took a bite of one, and said, "These are as good as Edie's."

A bittersweet moment, for sure. Aunt Edie would have been happy to see everyone still enjoying her cookies. How sad it was not to have her there with them. *Oh, Aunt Edie, why did you have to die on me?*

After Christmas dinner, Sabrina left to spend time with Scotty and his family, and Jenna returned home to Jolly Roger. She went to the fridge, dug out a fresh carton of eggnog and poured herself a ginormous glass. Calories be damned. It was Christmas. Ho, ho, ho.

Ho, ho, ho, changed into happy new year. For Celeste and Henry, who were going to be at the New Year's Eve bash at Sandy's. For Pete, who was off to ring in the new year at The Drunken Sailor. For Sabrina, who was partying with her friends. For Courtney and Jonas, who planned a candlelight dinner for two at his place. For Annie, who was catering a New Year's Eve party. For Mom and Ellis, who were headed for a chamber of commerce party with all the rest of Jenna's friends. And...him. For Seth...who knew what he was doing? She'd fished around subtly. ("What are you doing for New Year's Eve?") He'd been evasive. ("Nothing." Ha! Like she believed that.)

So it was her and Jolly Roger and baby Edie, who was spending the night at Aunt Jenna's house. "Happy new year, guys," she said as she changed Edie's diaper. "What do you want to do tonight?"

"Give me whiskey," said Roger.

"We can't drink. We're babysitting," she informed him. "I think I'll have some sparkling cider. Milk for you," she informed Edie, who laughed and kicked her legs.

"Yeah, enjoy that happiness while it lasts," Jenna said to her, standing her up. "It gets harder as you get older. Oh, brother, listen to me. I'm like that old woman in the Dickens novel. Who was that, Roger? Miss...something. Miss...Hag. Miss Hammer... Miss...oh, who cares? At least I don't have a bunch of cobwebs hanging around. And I'm not a total man hater. I'm selective."

No, no. No hating Brody. That was wrong and she was so over that. Well, sort of. Almost. Sometimes.

It was New Year's Eve, the perfect time to make a resolution. "Okay, everyone, I'm resolving to quit being mad at Brody."

Edie blinked in surprise and Jolly Roger made another demand for whiskey.

"I know, it's a big hurdle to get over but I can do it. I'm going to be a better me in the new year. I'm going to... well, I'm going to be better, that's all. This next year will be a good one. I'm going to make sure of it."

It had to be better. Her life had nowhere to go but up.

One great thing was going to happen to her in the next year. Come spring, she would be finished with spousal support. No more checks to Damien. Now, there was something to look forward to.

She kissed Edie's fat little neck. "We are going to have a great year."

Twenty-Two

Mel and Ellis finished ringing in the new year parked at the beach, watching moonlit waters roll in to kiss the shore. Linda Ronstadt softly serenaded them on the radio.

"This is a lovely way to end our night," she said to him as he uncorked her baby bottle of champagne.

He poured it into the plastic glass she held out. "I wanted to ring it in, just the two of us. I probably don't have to tell you how great these last few months with you have been," he said and poured champagne into his own glass.

"I feel the same way." Finding a wonderful man at this point in her life—who'd have thought it? "It's been a gift."

"I'd like to keep the gift going."

"Me, too," she said.

"I think you're an amazing woman and I don't want to let you get away. Would you be willing to spend the rest of your life with me?"

"Are you asking me to marry you?" Maybe he simply wanted to move in together.

"If you don't want to…" he began.

"I didn't say that. I know by this time of life a lot of people like to avoid that kind of commitment so they can keep their assets separate. We both have children to consider..."

"But I think our children would love to see us tie the knot. I know I would," he added, smiling at her. "What do you say, beautiful? A wedding with both our families there, then a future of shared sunsets and sunrises?"

Mel felt as bubbly as the champagne in her glass. "I say that sounds like a wonderful idea."

"All right," he said. "Is this a happy new year or what?" He set the champagne glasses on the dash.

The happiest one she'd had in a very long time, she thought as he kissed her. Who needed champagne, anyway?

It was well after one in the morning when she got home. Home. They'd have to discuss what to do about the fact that they both owned houses. Would Ellis want to live with her in this house? His was much bigger. She loved this little place, but his would accommodate large family gatherings—a very good thing considering the fact that with one little yes they'd both doubled their family size. She could hardly wait to introduce her daughters to his children, could already envision summer gatherings, with grandchildren playing on the beach.

Maybe they could keep her place and rent it out. That way she'd still have something to pass on to her girls, and his children wouldn't see her as an interloper. Not that they'd appeared to when she met them. His family seemed genuinely glad that he'd found someone.

She knew her girls were equally happy for her. Who'd have thought it? She'd never dreamed she'd find love at this point in her life.

"I'm happy, John," she murmured as she snuggled into

bed. "I'll always love you, but you're gone and I'm still here and I don't want to be here alone anymore."

That night she dreamed again that she was back at the masked ball. When it came time to unmask, the man with whom she'd been dancing turned out to be Ellis.

She felt a presence standing behind her and heard a voice whisper, "It's all right, Mel. I want you to be happy."

She couldn't see the source of that voice, but she knew who it belonged to. "Thank you," she said, and let Ellis lead her out onto the floor for a new dance.

She awoke the next morning wondering if she'd not only dreamed the ball but dreamed about a marriage proposal as well. But no, Ellis called her later and his first words to her were, "Good morning, future Mrs. West." It hadn't been a dream.

He invited her over to his place to watch the Rose Bowl game. She couldn't remember the last time she'd done something with someone on New Year's Day. None of her girlfriends watched football and she usually spent the day cleaning her closets and putting together donations for Goodwill. Now she had someplace to go, something to do, and a wonderful man to do it with.

"I haven't watched football in years," she confessed as they settled on his couch with chips and salsa and soft drinks.

"Not into football?" He looked almost wary.

"Would that be a deal breaker?" she asked.

"Not at all. I happen to like the game. Was hoping maybe you do, too."

"I used to watch with my husband. He graduated from the University of Washington and was a big fan of the Huskies, so we watched a lot of college football. After he died I guess my interest in the game died right along with him."

"Think we can revive it today?" Ellis asked.

"I think so," she said. "I'll be happy to host Super Bowl parties."

"All right," he said eagerly. "Your place or mine?"

"I guess that depends on how many people we invite."

"Speaking of houses, do you want to keep yours?"

"I was just thinking about that last night. I love my house," she admitted. "It felt like home the minute I walked in the door. But your place feels like home, too, and now that we have two families to blend maybe we should be in a bigger house."

"More house to take care of," he said.

"I don't mind. I enjoy taking care of houses. And people."

"I like the sound of that," Ellis said.

So did she.

He didn't waste any time getting her a ring. Come January second, they were at the jeweler's.

"That diamond's not big enough," he said when she pointed to the one in her ring size that she liked, an oval halo pavé in yellow gold.

"It's plenty big enough," she assured him. "May I try it on?" she asked the clerk.

"Of course," he murmured, taking it out of the case.

She slipped it on her finger and held up her hand, admiring it. "I love it. It's beautiful."

"Just like the woman wearing it," said Ellis. "Okay, I guess we'll take it."

They left the store hand in hand. She felt sixteen again.

"Think your girls are going to be happy?" he asked.

"I know they will. They've been nudging me in your direction ever since we met. How about your kids?" His daughter had certainly been welcoming when Mel met her at Thanksgiving.

"Oh, yeah. Now my daughter can stop worrying about old Dad bumbling around the house with no one to watch over him."

"Bumbling?"

He shook his head. "My kids think I'm old."

He wasn't as old as her. A sudden moment of panic hit her. She'd never told him her age.

Her concern must have shown on her face because his brows pulled together. "What?"

"You're not even sixty yet," she said.

"I keep telling my kids that. I'm still in my prime."

"I'm not," she said softly. "Ellis, I'm older than you. By several years, I think."

"Is that what's bothering you?" He smiled and shook his head. "At this point in life, who cares? I'm bigger than you so it all balances out."

"Are you sure?" She was into her sixties and he hadn't yet hit the big 6-0. She confessed her age and waited for him to tell her the deal was off.

"That's not much difference at all. Besides, I always wanted to be a boy toy."

She frowned. "I'm not *that* much older."

He chuckled, raised her hand to his mouth and kissed it. "You're right, you're not. You're beautiful and I love you. Come on, let's get something at Good Times."

Nora was happy for them and offered them free hot chocolate on the house. "What do your girls think?" she asked Mel.

"They don't know yet," Mel said.

"I bet they won't be surprised once they hear," Nora predicted.

Mel decided that, rather than call her daughters and tell them, she'd invite them over for dinner and see how long it took them to notice her new jewelry.

Celeste had been too busy getting Edie's snowsuit off and then settling her in the highchair Mel kept at the house to notice anything, and Jenna had been only half-present. She'd made an effort to enter in, but Mel knew she been struggling to find the happy in the holidays.

Suddenly she felt guilty over being so happy when her daughter was so miserable. If only Jenna could find a true and lasting love.

Henry was the first to notice Mel's ring when she passed him the plate of French bread.

His eyes got big and he looked at her questioningly. *Something new?*

Celeste was next to catch on. "Oh, my gosh! Mom!"

Jenna rejoined them mentally. "What?" She looked at Mel, confused, and Mel held up her left hand.

Her daughter may not have been happy with her own life, but she was delighted for her mother. "Mom, this is wonderful," she said, jumping up to hug Mel.

"Guess we don't have to ask who the man is," Henry said.

"I guess not," Mel agreed.

Celeste grabbed her hand and lifted it for a closer look. "Wow! This is gorgeous."

"You so deserve to be happy," Jenna said.

So did Jenna. Even as they all celebrated the big change in Mel's life, she sent up a silent prayer. *Please, God, give my girl someone wonderful to love her.*

Love. Bah, humbug, Jenna thought when she woke up on the worst day in the world for people who were alone.

Oh, yeah. Bah, humbug was Christmas. Well, it worked fine for Valentine's Day, too.

"Valentine's Day sucks," she coached Jolly Roger as she took the cover off his cage and woke him up for the day. "Valentine's Day sucks, Valentine's Day sucks."

Roger bobbed his head.

"You've got to agree. You don't have anyone, either," she said. "Come on, repeat after me. Valentine's Day sucks."

"Valentine's Day sucks," he said in his birdy voice.

"You're darned right it does."

She'd approached the day determined to be positive. She'd have a Valentine's orphans party and invite Annie and Tyrella over for dinner.

But Annie was catering a private party and Tyrella had a man she'd been getting to know online coming down from Seattle to take her to dinner. As a matter of fact, he'd booked a room for the night at the Driftwood, and Tyrella wanted Jenna to keep watch and let her know when he arrived.

Darrell Banks—Jenna remembered a reservation coming through in that name via the website—was over six feet tall. Tyrella had told her all about him. He was a minister at an apostolic church, loved animals, and was sooo wonderful. Jenna was seeing the writing on the wall there. Tyrella wasn't long for Moonlight Harbor.

So much for Jenna's orphan party. She was the only person with nothing to do. Her mom and Ellis were off to meet her friends from the old neighborhood, Celeste and Henry were planning a cozy celebration for two at home. Jenna was...going to get some chocolate.

After she'd checked in Tyrella's new man and finished her work for the day, she went in search of that chocolate she'd promised herself.

She found a five-pound box of it at Beachside Grocery. Perfect.

"You planning to eat all that single-handed?" asked a deep voice.

She turned to see Seth Waters looking at her with an eyebrow raised. She hadn't seen much of him since he'd joined her family for Thanksgiving. It had felt so strange not having him around. At the sight of him her heart gave a little stutter.

"I am." If she wasn't going to have sex she could at least have chocolate.

He studied her, a concerned look on his face. "You doing okay?"

"No, but thanks for asking."

"Things will get better. You know they will."

She hugged the huge heart-shaped box of fat bombs to her chest. "How do you know? Are you psychic now?"

"It doesn't take a psychic to know that you won't stay single forever." He reached over and started to take the box from her.

She held on tight. "We can't be parted."

"You'll be reunited, I promise," he said. "Now, let go. I'm getting this for you."

She was so shocked she loosened her hold. "You are? Why?"

"Because it's Valentine's Day and a pretty woman shouldn't have to buy her own chocolate."

It sounded like something Brody would say. The thought came loaded with a good dose of melancholy.

"Thanks," she said.

"Glad to help out. Is there anything else you need to get through the night?"

There was no point telling him about the sex thing. He

wasn't going to volunteer for the job, the big chicken. She shook her head.

"Okay, come on," he said, and started them toward the checkout register.

"Is that why you came in here, looking to buy chocolate for some love charity case?" she asked, falling in step with him. "I don't see any groceries in your basket."

"I'll get them when we're done."

"You can get your chocolate, too. I won't laugh."

He half smiled at that. "I'm just here to stock up on beer."

"Are you going to sit at home and drink all by yourself?"

"Nope," he said, and left it at that.

What was he going to do? Probably head over to The Drunken Sailor and play pool. Valentine's Day wasn't half as hard on men as it was on women.

"I like to play pool," she volunteered.

"Be sure to include that in your profile when you're on Match.com."

"Sheesh," she muttered. "I just wanted to have a little fun."

"You're getting chocolate. It lasts longer."

"Not the way I plan to go through it." If he hadn't been buying a big box for her, she'd have kicked him in the that gorgeous butt. "Kind of inconsistent, don't you think? Being all noble about not wanting to get together and yet buying me chocolate."

They were at the check stand now. He set the box down on the belt and turned to her. "I'm buying you chocolate because I don't want you to be sad. I'm not getting together with you for the same reason. Plus, it wasn't that long ago that you were serious with the house peddler."

"I was wrong about him, okay? I should never have been with him."

She was suddenly aware of the person in line in front of her turning to gawk and she realized she was half shouting. She could feel her ears burning. And her cheeks. Okay, her whole head was on fire. The fire got worse when she saw who was one check stand over, buying steak and lettuce and tomatoes. Brody didn't turn to look at her but she knew he'd heard by the way his body stiffened.

"Oh, boy," she muttered.

Seth paid for the box of chocolates, then handed it over. He took her by the arm and escorted her out of the store, neither of them speaking.

She was the first to break the silence. "I hate my life."

"I know."

"But I love chocolate."

"I know that, too."

"Thanks. It was really sweet of you."

"Hang in there, Jenna. Things really will get better."

She stood hugging her Valentine's gift and watched as he walked back into the grocery store. How could things get better when nothing had worked out with either of the two most important men in her life?

She went home and made herself a sandwich for dinner. Turkey, this year's Valentine's special.

She'd taken her first bite when Pete poked his head in the kitchen door. "Gotcha something," he said, and held out the baby version of the big box Seth had bought her.

Another facet of the new and improved Pete. "Candy? Who are you?"

He scowled. "Don't get smart or I'll take it back."

"Sorry. Come on in. Have you eaten yet?"

He shook his head and plopped down at the table. "Not hungry."

A look of dejection stole over his face. Poor Pete. He was alone on Valentine's Day, too.

"Have you got plans?" she asked.

He shook his head. "It's not the same as last year."

Jenna sat down across the table from him and he looked at her, his mouth working like he was going to cry. He twisted the gold ring on his left hand.

"Wish we had some of Edie's cookies," he finally said.

"Me, too," said Jenna. "Maybe I should make some."

For a moment he perked up. Then he shook his head. "Nah, I got stuff to do."

Like go to his room and watch TV.

Jenna came to a sudden decision. "Are you sure? I was going to watch a movie. Why don't you join me?"

"What are you gonna watch?" he asked suspiciously.

"I haven't decided."

She'd bought her great-aunt all manner of chick flick DVDs. There had to be something in there for a couple of Valentine's Day losers.

"I guess," Pete said, and ambled out to the living room. "Maybe I'll take a sandwich after all," he said over his shoulder.

She made him a sandwich and pulled a can of pop from the fridge, taking them out to him. He was already looking through the DVDs.

"Find anything good?" she asked.

"Not much to choose from," he replied.

She fetched her own dinner and the chocolates he'd brought her and joined him.

"Looks like you already got chocolate," he said, nodding to the couch, where she'd set the box Seth had given her.

"When we run out of the ones you brought, we can eat those," she said. "What did you find?"

"Not much. We need some James Bond."

She set down her plate and picked up a DVD from his stack of discards. *Under the Tuscan Sun*. "This is a classic."

He looked at it dubiously. "Looks like a chick flick to me."

"So you can get in touch with your feminine side," she said, taking it out of its jewel case.

He grunted but took a seat.

"Yep, chick flick," he said in disgust after they were barely into the movie. "I'm out of here."

It was pretty female-centric, she had to admit. And he'd finished his sandwich and eaten half the candy in the box he'd given her.

"Thanks for the chocolate," she called after him as he left the room.

She opened Seth's box, dug out a chocolate caramel and popped it in her mouth. Aaah, lovely. Candy, a movie— what else could a woman want?

Oh, ha ha.

But by the end of the movie Jenna was feeling a little less depressed. Maybe even hopeful. Like the heroine of that cinematic tale, she, too, could find a good life. Who knew? Maybe someday some handsome stranger might come to town looking for a room and...

He wouldn't be Brody. He wouldn't be Seth.

She dug out a dark chocolate brittle. There was more to life than men. Who needed 'em?

She scowled at the box and shoved it to the far side of the couch.

Happy Valentine's Day. Bah, humbug.

Twenty-Three

Spring finally arrived, bringing daffodils and tulips for the deer to eat. Tyrella was complaining once more about the deer when the Friday night bunch gathered in Jenna's living room.

"I wish the city council had shipped them all back to the forest," she said.

"We didn't and they're here to stay so you may as well get used to them," Jenna said.

She was getting heartily sick of how ungrateful the Moonlight Harbor citizenry were. People showed up at meetings or stopped council members in the store to complain, but nobody ever thanked them for their hard work.

No one had thanked her when she finally climbed out of the black hole she'd fallen into to pull together her research on the benefits of a convention center. She'd had plenty of plusses to point out in her presentation to the council. A convention center would attract conventioneers, trade shows and more tourists. They could host events in all kinds of weather if they had a large covered area. There was the good news. Her fellow council members had zeroed in on the not so good news—centers could run up to twenty-five million dollars.

"But we wouldn't spend that much," she'd argued. "We're talking about a much smaller scale than a city like Seattle."

The time hadn't been right and Parker had tabled the idea. Afterward Jenna had gotten an earful from one of the longtime residents, a self-proclaimed watchdog who had no desire to see the town grow. Convention center, indeed. They didn't need the town overrun with outsiders all year round. What had Jenna been thinking?

And now here was Tyrella, complaining again about the deer when that problem had already been addressed. "The deer bring in tourists and the tourists keep our local economy humming," Jenna said. Okay, maybe not in her sweetest voice. Maybe she wasn't cut out to be a public servant.

"You're right," Tyrella said, holding up a staying hand. "My big bad."

"Sorry I got snippy," Jenna said. "I think I'm going through a bitchy phase." Hmm. It seemed like that phase had been lasting for some time. When did a phase stop becoming a phase and turn into the new you?

"You're allowed," Tyrella assured her.

Jenna smiled gratefully at her. "Thanks. Anyway, the way things are heating up with your new man, you may not even be here that much longer."

"New man? This is news," said Cindy Redmond. "Do tell."

They didn't have to twist Tyrella's arm. She was happy to rhapsodize over Darrell. "He's never been married. Can you believe it?"

"What is he, a monk?" Courtney asked.

"Just been busy in the Lord's service. He is eight years younger than me though," Tyrella said.

"There's nothing wrong with being with a younger man. Just ask my mom," said Jenna.

"Anyway, you look like you're thirty," Nora added. "That gorgeous skin—not a wrinkle anywhere."

"I'm jealous," said Cindy. "My Irish skin is a wrinkle magnet. It's trying to age me overnight."

"Age is just a number," Jenna told her. "That's what Aunt Edie would say."

Aunt Edie would have been so excited to see how her mother's romance with Ellis had bloomed. Their wedding date was right around the corner.

Courtney was busy making wedding plans, too.

"Have you set a date?" Patricia asked her.

"Weekend after the Fourth. We're getting married on the fire truck."

"I love that idea," Patricia said. "And I assume you're designing your wedding dress."

"I am. It's going to be red, and instead of a veil I'm wearing a fire hat."

"You are going to be too cute," Tyrella gushed.

"We decided to have the reception at Good Times and we're doing sundaes."

"Way to support local business," Nora said with a smile.

"And the party favors are going to be net bags filled with saltwater taffy," Courtney continued.

"Gee, I wonder who's providing that," Tyrella said, and winked at Cindy.

"Sorry, Jenna and Patricia, but we won't be staying in Moonlight Harbor for the honeymoon, so I can't give you any business."

"Have you decided where you want to go for your honeymoon?" Patricia asked.

"We're still kicking around ideas," Courtney said. "But I think it's going to involve a cabin somewhere in Canada. We're looking at Banff. They've got hot springs, and biking and hiking."

"Since when do you like to hike?" Cindy wanted to know.

"Since I met Jonas. I don't care where we go, really. It's all about being together. So, this year Banff, next year a resort on Grand Cayman."

"Something for everyone," Patricia murmured. "It's lovely to have wedding bells ringing in Moonlight Harbor. So much happiness. You have to be thrilled about your mother and Ellis," she said to Jenna.

"I am. He's perfect for her."

Her mother's happy ending was sewed up, and life was good with Celeste. At least that was two out of three of the Jones women. Three out of four, if you counted Sabrina.

Although who knew if things would last with Scotty? They were both so young. "Don't be in a hurry," Jenna kept telling her daughter. "You want to get it right the first time." *Unlike your mother.*

She hadn't gotten it right the first or the second time. The third time was supposed to be the charm, but with her luck, she wasn't buying that.

She could be glad for her mother, though. Mel and Ellis got married on the first Saturday in May. Between his family and friends and hers—both the ones she'd made in Moonlight Harbor and the ones who had come down from Lynwood—the church was packed. Ellis wore a white tuxedo and Mel had looked beautiful in a blush-colored tulle-draped calf-length dress Courtney designed and made for her. She'd accented it with her mother's pearls and a pearl bracelet Jenna and Celeste had bought her. Jenna, Celeste and Sabrina served as her bridesmaids, and all four women had their hair done by Moira at Waves—her wedding gift to the bride.

Ellis had insisted on hiring Annie to cater the event, and the tables in the church addition that had been built for such events were filled with guests enjoying salmon, Caesar salad, and one of Annie's pasta salads. Sunbaked, everyone's favorite bakery, had provided a four-tiered cake frosted with fondant in turquoise and white and decorated with sugar clam shells and starfish.

Mel was beaming as she and Ellis drove away in his classic car, heading for Sea-Tac airport, where they'd catch a plane for Paris. Another well-deserved reward for a life of kindness and sacrifice, Jenna thought, watching them drive off.

Tyrella, who was standing next to her, pointed to the bouquet Jenna had tried not to catch. "Girl, it looks like you're next."

"Don't hold your breath," Jenna said.

That whole bouquet thing had been embarrassing. Celeste had shoved her into the group of giggling single women. She'd edged away, but her mother had proved she really did have eyes in the back of her head by throwing it right at her. It would have been rude not to catch it, but both Mom and Celeste would hear about that when Mom returned from her honeymoon.

"Now it's your turn," Celeste told her.

There was no one left to take a turn with. Seth was his usual elusive self, and she was still struggling with her feelings about Brody.

Forgiveness, she was learning, wasn't an easy thing.

She still had days when she wished she could toss him in the ocean and use him for crab bait. Those days alternated with ones when she made an effort to pry her fingers off the grudge she was carrying, tried to put herself in his shoes. For reasons known only to herself, Aunt Edie had left the Driftwood Inn to him and he was merely honoring her final wishes.

Still, it felt wrong of him to keep the place. He should have offered to deed it over to her once it came to him. If he really loved her he would have. The fact that he was paying her so well to manage the place felt more like a sop to his conscience than a generous offer, and it frustrated and angered her that he put her off every time she tried to pin him down about buying the inn.

Her thoughts circled around like a whirlpool. She was ungrateful and being emotional and unreasonable. No, he was a selfish bastard. Where did the truth lie in all that? She still wasn't sure. All she knew was, what they'd been building between the two of them had gotten torn down. If he let her buy the inn, maybe they could at least build a bridge that would help them find their way back to friendship. She missed that. Missed him.

Oh, well, the single life wasn't so bad. Soon she'd be rid of Damien the leech and actually have a little money to spend on herself. Maybe she'd get a total makeover at Waves. For sure, once she had her freedom, she was going to throw a big party.

But first there was a dog park to dedicate. It had rained the week before, but on the big day, the sun burst through the clouds as if Aunt Edie had pushed them aside. The park had been built with loving care and it sported plenty of lawn and a doggie wading pool. It also had an area with doggie obstacles for agility practice and bright red fire hydrants at every corner, as well as a couple of doggie drinking fountains. The sign was wood with Aunt Edie's name burned into it and was held up by two thick wooden posts.

Before the ribbon could be cut, there had to be speechifying, and Parker was happy to do that. But she did let Jenna have the honor of cutting the ribbon, which she did, to much applause. Then owners and dogs rushed in to enjoy the new park. Jenna remembered her earlier conversation with her sister when Nemo did his part by lifting his leg and leaving a calling card at the base of the sign.

Parker scowled and Jenna chuckled. *Well, Aunt Edie, you should have been nicer to him.*

A week after the dog park opened, Jenna got her freedom. She called her sister. "I'm free! No more spousal support."

"All right. Come over for dinner tonight and we'll celebrate," Celeste said. "I've got a bottle of champagne I've been saving for the occasion."

"Champagne sounds good, but no toasts in front of Sabrina. After all, he is her father and I don't want to upset her."

"Yeah, I guess that wouldn't be cool. I bet he's not celebrating now that the gravy train has stopped running."

"About time," Jenna said.

"You are going to have that party to celebrate, right?" Celeste asked as she and Jenna laid out the side dishes to go with the meat Henry was barbecuing.

"For sure," Jenna said. "As soon as Mom gets back from her honeymoon."

"I'll help you plan it. We can burn Damien in effigy."

The idea appealed, but, "Somehow, I don't think that would go over well with Sabrina. How about we set off fireworks instead?" Jenna suggested.

"To celebrate your Independence Day. I like it. Let's do it Memorial Day weekend. Mom will be back by then."

Sabrina came in from the back deck with a plate of ribs, and Celeste's face flushed. Jenna could feel the heat on hers as well. What a guilty-looking pair!

"We're talking about having a beach party Memorial Day weekend," Jenna said.

Sabrina nodded but didn't say anything.

The two sisters exchanged looks. *You think she heard?*

She did. Later that evening, when it was the two of them back at the house, raiding the fridge for lemonade, she asked, "You don't mind if I don't come to your party, do you?"

"So you heard." Busted.

"I know you've been mad at Daddy and, um, him needing money."

Needing money. Way to whitewash the truth. Damien had probably had a hand in that.

"I promise, we're not going to burn your father in effigy or any other tacky thing. We're just going to have a party and celebrate my new beginning. But I'm sure you and Scotty and the gang would rather find somewhere else to party that day."

"I do want you to be happy," Sabrina said. "I know it's been hard, and I know Daddy's not perfect."

There was the understatement of the century. "None of us are," Jenna said. "Except you, my darling daughter, come pretty close. Come here." She held out an arm, and Sabrina tucked herself under it and hugged her. "Even though things didn't work out between your father and me, we still did one thing right, and that was you."

"I hope you find somebody like Aunt Celeste and

Grammy did," Sabrina said. "But don't take as long as Grammy," she added.

No guarantees there.

Oh, well. Onward and upward. With the date set, Jenna passed out invites at the next Friday night gathering at her house.

"We'll be happy to help you celebrate," Nora told her. "I'll bring the champagne, and some sand pebble ice cream bars."

"I'll bring champagne, too," Courtney said. "I have a feeling we'll go through a lot of it."

"I'll bring cookies," offered Annie.

A latecomer suddenly burst through the door. It was Tyrella and she was in tears. "I hit a deer!" she cried as she came into the living room. She fell onto the nearest chair, crying and waving her hands around as if she could brush away the memory.

"Did you kill it?" Cindy asked.

"No. It ran away but it was limping. Oh, Lord. What should I do?"

"Be sorry you didn't take it down?" suggested Courtney. "Aren't you the biggest deer hater in Moonlight Harbor?"

"I don't want to kill one," Tyrella howled.

Jenna remembered some very interesting comments to the contrary. But this was no time to rub that in.

She fetched some wine and handed over the glass. "Here, drink this. It'll help." Hopefully. In movies an upset heroine was always given a snifter of brandy. Jenna didn't have any of that. White wine would have to do.

Tyrella downed a gulp and coughed. "Should I call the police? Animal control?"

"Not much they can do if it ran away," Courtney said.

"Yes, but you probably should file a police report," said

Nora. "And take pictures of the car for your insurance company."

"How's your car?" asked Cindy.

"I don't know. I couldn't look." Tyrell said on a sob. She swiped at her nose and Nora found her a tissue. "I feel terrible," she said. "It jumped right in front of my car. One minute I was driving down the street and the next... Oh," she wailed.

"That happens sometimes," Nora said. She pulled out her cell phone and made the call to the Moonlight Harbor Police Department.

Moments later, Victor King, who was on duty that night, showed up and took the necessary information and even gave Tyrella a comforting hug. Jenna snapped the necessary pictures for Tyrella on her cell phone. She had a dent on her left front fender. And some blood. After Jenna had gotten the pictures, she cleaned it off. If Tyrella saw it she'd probably faint. Jenna wasn't sure who she felt more sorry for, the deer or Tyrella.

The deer, she decided. Tyrella would recover. The poor animal would probably walk with a limp for the rest of its life.

Things finally settled down and the women (all except Tyrella) were able to enjoy the rest of the evening. Everyone left with hugs for Jenna and promises to help her celebrate her financial freedom.

"I'm sorry I ruined your big announcement," Tyrella said as she was leaving. "It was just so traumatic. That poor deer."

"I know, and your trauma was more important than my moment of victory. I'll have plenty of time to celebrate at the party."

"We'll all make it a good one," Tyrella promised, and

hugged her. "I've got some tiki torches for sale at the store. I'll bring them."

"Great idea," Jenna said.

Things shaped up quickly for her big party and she found herself getting excited. New beginnings celebrated with good food and good friends. Oh, yes!

Speaking of good friends. She made a special trip to Seth's new house to invite him. She found him and a couple other men she'd seen at The Drunken Sailor busy putting on a new roof. He wore jeans and work boots and was shirtless, and his dark hair was in need of a cut. He should have been on a calendar.

"Hello up there," she called.

He turned at the sound of her voice, stood, and started walking across the roof. Fearlessly. Heights. Eew. It gave her the creepy crawlies to watch him.

He smiled down at her and called back, "Hey, there."

"You're making progress," she observed.

"Slow, but that's okay. What's up?"

"A party. I'm done with my spousal support and throwing a bash. I need a guitar player so we can sing 'Girls Just Want to Have Fun.'"

She called up the particulars, he gave her a thumbs-up, and that was that. She smiled as she walked away. It would be good to have him there.

She realized it would be the first beach party since her arrival where Brody wasn't present, and her smile got a little sick. New beginnings, she reminded herself.

Mel returned from her honeymoon beaming and bearing gifts—scarves for her girls, along with Madeleines de Commercy for Sabrina and jars of violet confit for both Jenna and Celeste. She also had a big to-do list as she and

Ellis would be combining two houses' worth of things into one.

But she was more than willing to make time to help Jenna with her party preparations, and the day before, she, Jenna and Celeste were busy in Jenna's kitchen, baking cupcakes and brownies and making deviled eggs, as well as Aunt Edie's famous baked beans. Henry was dispatched to buy hot dogs, buns, chips and pop.

"You're finally free of him," Celeste said on the big day as they started packing all the goodies into boxes and baskets to haul to the beach.

"Sort of. I'll still have to see him when Sabrina finally graduates from college, and I'm sure he'll think he needs to walk her down the aisle the day she gets married."

"Sick and wrong," Celeste said.

"He is her dad, even if he is a poor excuse for one, and they've managed to have some kind of relationship," said Jenna.

"I guess something is better than nothing."

"You've done what was required of you and you've weathered these five years beautifully," Mel said. "I'm proud of you, darling."

"You know what? I'm proud of me, too," Jenna said. "It's been a struggle."

"And totally unfair," Celeste added, full of indignation on her sister's behalf.

"But I did it. Now with money not so tight I feel like I can breathe again."

Except when she thought about not managing the Driftwood anymore. She'd given her notice, and asked Brody again about the possibility of buying it. He'd been evasive and that had been the writing on the wall. The place was now beyond her grasp. It was time to cut the cord.

"You have a bright new future stretching ahead of you," Mel told her.

"I hope so," she said.

If that future meant being alone, so be it. There were worse things. Like being married to a loser. Or marrying a user.

Pete and Henry hauled the boxes of supplies and two ice chests for drinks to the beach, and Seth showed up in time to help them. The three men gathered wood and Seth got the beach fire going.

Guests arrived bearing not only the promised champagne and cookies but makings for s'mores as well. And gifts. Lots of gift bags and envelopes with gift cards.

Tyrella led them in singing an old gospel song, "Oh Happy Day," and once the champagne was poured, Courtney made a toast.

"To Jenna Jones, who has and always will triumph over trouble. You're our hero."

"Yes, she is," put in Celeste. "And now we need to sing her new theme song." She grabbed Jenna by the arm and hauled her up to stand next to her. "Okay, ladies, you know what it's got to be. Hit it, Seth."

Seth started strumming his guitar and they all began singing "Girls Just Want to Have Fun," raising champagne glasses, sloshing champagne everywhere.

It was a good moment in time. Jenna was giddy and laughing, enjoying herself vastly. Until she saw the man coming across the dunes toward them. Who had invited him? Certainly not her.

Twenty-Four

The singing faded to a stop and an awkward silence fell as Brody approached. He wore jeans and a T-shirt, flip-flops on his feet. The breeze was ruffling his hair. Once upon a time he would have been a lovely sight to behold.

"Want me to get rid of him?" Pete asked, puffing up his scrawny chest.

"No, I'll take care of it," Jenna said. "Guys, we've got a lot more food to eat. Don't let me down."

She started across the sand to meet Brody halfway, her friends' concerned murmurs following her. He stopped and waited, letting her approach him. Good, they'd be out of earshot. She could say whatever she wanted.

Although she wasn't sure what she wanted to say. *Why are you here? You're not welcome. What happened to us?*

He was the first to speak. "Your mom told me where you'd be."

Thanks, Mom. "Why did you want to see me?"

"Maybe because I've missed being with you."

They'd spent little enough time face to face, even after Brody took possession of the Driftwood. Jenna had made sure she kept the business of running the place to direct deposits and emails (including her offers to buy it) to ensure as little personal contact as possible. No texts. Brody was no longer in her list of contacts.

He was as handsome as ever, and even if that gorgeous Brody smile was looking a little tentative, it still had the same kilowatt power.

It just didn't have any power over her.

She stood there, mute. All she could do was shake her head sadly. Look what they'd come to.

He held out a large envelope. "Congrats on winning your freedom."

"Thanks." She took it but didn't open it. Whatever kind of apology it was, it was too late.

"Open it."

"I'll look at it later. Right now I've got company."

She turned to go and he caught her arm. "You need to see what's in there. I've gone long enough without you knowing the truth."

The truth? "I know the truth."

"No, you don't. Open it."

She opened the envelope and pulled out something very official-looking. She blinked. She had to be hallucinating.

"What's this?" she said in shock.

"It's a quitclaim deed."

She looked up at him, confused. "I don't understand."

"I've been holding the Driftwood in trust for you ever since Edie died. Now it's yours."

"What?" This didn't make any sense.

"She knew her time was almost up, and her biggest worry was what would happen if she left you the place and your ex found out and came after you for more money before the time for your spousal support was over. It's been known to happen and she didn't want to take a chance on it happening to you so she asked me to help her. The Driftwood was mine, but only until such time as you were free. Then I was to deed it over to you."

"She trusted you to do that," Jenna said in a small voice.

She wanted to cry. Aunt Edie had been thinking of her all along and Brody hadn't betrayed her. And she'd been angry at both of them. More than angry with Brody. Downright bitter. There were sand fleas on the beach bigger than her.

"Why on earth didn't she tell me what she was going to do? Why didn't you tell me what was going on?"

All that wasted anger, their ruined relationship. She felt ill.

"Another fail-safe. It was better that you didn't know. We were basically hiding a very big asset. You couldn't look complicit in that. You can honestly say you knew nothing. Now you're free of your obligations and I'm free to give the place to you."

"And so you let me think the worst of you. Oh, Brody, how can I ever apologize enough? I'm so sorry."

"I don't blame you. I know how it looked. I'd have probably felt the same if I was you."

His words didn't make her feel any better. He wasn't a user, he was a hero. And she'd thought the worst of him and treated him like a villain.

He took her hand. "I hope we're friends again."

"Oh, Brody."

It was all she could seem to say. The tears were flooding her eyes so fast she felt as if she was looking at him from underwater. The overflow raced down her cheeks.

"Hey, it's okay," he said, wiping them away. He studied her a moment. "I don't suppose…" he began.

She knew where he was going. They could pick up the

broken pieces of their relationship and start again. She could put the ring back on.

But no. It wouldn't be fair to him.

She shook her head. "I was wrong not to trust you. I'd be just as wrong to get back together with you. I think Aunt Edie saved us from making a big mistake. There was a reason I dragged my feet for so long. I see that now."

He sighed. "It's because of Waters, isn't it?"

Stupid because nothing was happening between her and Seth, but there it was. She nodded.

He smiled. The smile had lost some of its wattage. "I guess it's time for me to be a good loser, then. And I will."

"Thank you," she said, and hugged him. "You are a true friend."

"Always," he said. He hugged her back, then disentangled himself. "I'm not going to be his best man. I'm not that damned noble. But I will come to the wedding." He leaned down and kissed her damp cheek. "Be happy, Jenna."

"You really are a hero," she said.

"Yeah, yeah," he said, blowing off the compliment. "Now go back to your party."

"You could join us."

"Next time," he said, and walked away.

She watched him go and felt sad. But she knew she was feeling sad because of her lack of trust and the needless hurt they'd both suffered, not because the romance was forever over between them.

She turned back to the party to see Seth packing up his guitar, a sure sign he was leaving. What had he thought when he saw her hug Brody? All the wrong things.

"What was that all about?" Celeste demanded as soon as Jenna had rejoined the circle around the bonfire.

"It was Brody, giving me the Driftwood. Hey, everyone," she announced, "it looks like we've got even more to celebrate. Brody Green has been holding onto the Driftwood for me all this time, protecting it from greedy ex-husbands. It's officially mine now."

"Darling, that's wonderful," said Mel.

"That sounds more like him," said Ellis.

Courtney added, "I'm glad he turned out not to be the jerk he looked like for a while there."

"I was wrong to ever think he was," Jenna said, tucking the important document inside one of the picnic baskets.

"It's understandable, though, darling, considering what you've been through with Damien," Mel told her. "It can be hard to trust people when someone has broken your trust."

"Now I won't have to beat him up," Pete said, and it was all Jenna could do not to laugh.

Once congratulations were over, conversation around the campfire settled back into the easy chatting of old friends. Jenna grabbed a can of pop, settled on a log, and pretended to be fully present.

It was hard to do. She looked down the beach at the lone figure carrying his guitar case. He was getting farther away with each step. Like her, he had his share of scars. Darn it all, look what they were doing to him. To them.

Celeste plopped down next to her. "So, what about you and Brody? Since he's not here I take it you're not getting back together."

"Just friends. That's all we were meant to be." Jenna took a sip of pop and tried not to look in Seth's direction.

"Speaking of meant to be, why are you sitting here like a lump letting Seth go wandering off by himself? We can party on just fine without you, you know."

Jenna frowned. "What's the point?"

"The point is you want to be happy and he needs to be."

Celeste went to one of the ice chests and dug out a bottle of champagne. She returned to where Jenna sat and held it out to her. "Enough postponing the inevitable already. Scram, and don't come back until it's empty. In fact, don't come back at all. Mom and I can take care of cleanup."

Still, Jenna hesitated. "He's too stubborn. It would be a waste of time."

"Oh, come on. You saved the Driftwood, rebuilt your life, became a council member. You ought to be able to figure out a way to get one stubborn man who's in love with you to commit."

Yes, darn it all, she should. She was tired of being miserable and she wanted to have sex again before she died. She wanted to grow old flying kites on the beach and enjoying evening bonfires with her soul mate. She'd been through enough storms. She was going to get that rainbow her mother was always talking about.

She took the champagne bottle and started off down the beach.

"Where's she going?" she heard Pete ask Celeste.

"She's going after her happy ending," Celeste said.

Yes, she was, whether Seth Waters liked it or not. She took off at a run.

She caught up with him as he was going up the back steps of his beach house. The place was looking good with its new roof and paint job. He'd replaced the rotting boards on the deck and steps and all they needed was to be stained.

He frowned at the sight of her. "What are you doing here? You've got a party going on."

"A party you left." She followed him up the steps and onto the back deck.

"You had the house peddler. You didn't need me."

"Yes, I do. And he was only there to give me back the Driftwood."

That stopped Seth in his tracks. He set down his guitar case and turned to face her. "Yeah?"

"Yeah. Aunt Edie asked him to hold on to it for me until I was done with my spousal support. She was afraid Damien would get wind of it and come after me for more money."

Seth nodded, taking that in. "Pretty noble of him. I'm glad for you, Jenna. So, congrats. Now you two can get back together."

She shook her head. "No, we can't. He'll always be my friend, but he's not the man for me. There's only one man I want to spend the rest of my life with and I think you know who that is."

"Don't be stupid," he said, and added a scowl for good measure.

But he'd put it on too late. She'd seen the look of hope cross his face.

"Oh, no you don't," she said. "We are not going there. Stupid is being with the wrong person. I'm done with that and I'm tired of wasting time, aren't you?" She held out the champagne bottle. "Now, are you going to help me drink this or not?"

His jaw jutted out. "Not. Go back to the party."

Stubborn, irritating man! "Give me one good reason why we can't be together."

"You know why. I'm an ex-con."

"Who took the blame for a crime he didn't commit to protect a messed-up sister. Thanks to you she got her life together." Jenna moved closer. "I want to get my life the rest of the way together. The only way that's going to happen is if I'm with you," she added softly.

He took a step back, shook his head. He looked as miserable as he was making her feel. "I'm trying to protect you."

"Protect me from what?" she challenged. "Heartbreak? Because this is sure not the way to do it. Unless, of course, you really don't want me as much as I want you. Is that it? Have I just been imagining you care about me? You really don't want me?"

"Are you kidding? Of course I want you. Shit, Jenna, I've been in love with you from the first time I met you."

"Good. Then that settles it."

He exhaled a frustrated breath and clawed his hands through his hair. "No, it doesn't. You can't just ignore my past."

Now it was her turn to scowl. "To heck with your past. Everyone has a past. Who cares? It's the present and the future that count."

"You deserve a better life than I can give you. I'm never going to be successful like Green."

"There's more than one way to measure success, and I don't want him, not the way I want you. I never really did."

"You could have a good life with him."

"But I wouldn't have my best life."

He gave a disgusted snort. "I'm not the right choice for that. I'm never going to be more than what I am now."

"You don't need to be. You're already more than enough. For crying out loud, you're noble and self-sacrificing, always there when someone needs you. Do you know how amazing that makes you?"

There came the blush again. She could see the rosy tint under his swarthy skin.

"Jeez, Jenna," he said helplessly.

"Look, I almost made a big mistake with Brody. I am so over making mistakes. I'm done playing games, and you're done being a martyr. Life's too short. So quit talking about what I deserve. You make me happy, and I want to spend the rest of my life making you happy, and that's what I deserve." She slipped her arms around his neck and pressed herself against him so closely she could feel his heart beating. It was going as fast as hers. She saw the longing in his eyes.

He let out a breath. "You're killing me here."

"I just might if you don't put your arms around me."

He shook his head in resignation, slid his hands along her waist. "Jenna." It came out as whisper.

"It's time for a new beginning. For both of us. I love you, Seth Waters."

He wrapped his arms completely around her. "I can't keep fighting this. I don't want to."

"I sincerely hope not," she said with a smile. "Now, are we going to drink that champagne before or after I seduce you?"

He smiled back at her, a half smile at first. Then he tightened his hold and gave her a smile that about sent her heart up in flames. "I think we'd better talk to Pastor Paul first. If you're determined to jump off the cliff we're gonna do it right."

"So, we have a deal, a future together? You may as well come right out and say yes because I'm not leaving until you do. In fact, I may not leave at all. Celeste told me not to come back."

"Are you sure? Last chance, Jenna."

"Don't be stupid," she said with a grin.

"Okay, then, a future together. I love you, Jenna, and I'm tired of trying to live without you," he said and kissed her.

Judging from the kiss, which had even higher wattage than that pirate smile of his, she knew it was going to be a spectacular future.

They Do

Once more, Jenna caught the bridal bouquet, this time when Courtney threw it. Right at her, as planned. And the next month, Jenna was the one carrying her own bouquet.

It was a simple wedding, held on the beach. The bride wore her mother's wedding gown, special both because Mel had worn it and because her friend Courtney had designed it. Celeste acted as Jenna's matron of honor, and Sabrina as her bridesmaid. Seth's sister, who Jenna finally got to meet, came up from California for the wedding, bringing his mother, who happily cried through the whole ceremony. Seth's brother brought his family down, and he stood as Seth's best man while Ellis West served as his other groomsman. Nemo the dog was a well-behaved ring bearer.

Tyrella and her new man sang at the wedding, and Jenna walked to her groom as they sang "Amazed" by Lonestar. After the I-do's, they sang "When God Made You" by NewSong as Jenna and Seth poured white and blue sand, the colors of the Driftwood Inn, into a heart-shaped ceremony glass, and Jenna felt the tears slipping down her cheeks. Finally, after a long, hard year, tears of joy.

Once the ceremony was over the party began, with a hundred people finding seats at the tables that had been set up under a white wedding tent or helping themselves to Annie's champagne punch, her gift to the bride and groom. Two long serving tables were loaded with all kinds of picnic food, including a batch of Aunt Edie's famous baked beans, and a smaller table offered a cupcake bar with every imaginable flavor of cupcake, lovingly baked by her mother and sister and daughter.

Brody, true to his word, came to the wedding. "Just so

I could kiss the bride," he teased, making Seth frown. "If you ever get tired of him…" he began.

"She won't," Seth said, his frown turning into a smirk as he looked back at Jenna. Maybe those two could be friends at last.

Brody took Jenna's hands in his and kissed her cheek. "I'm happy for you."

"Thank you," she murmured. "For everything."

It was a bittersweet moment. She did love Brody and would always be grateful for his friendship and all he'd done to help her. But much as she loved him, she loved Seth more.

"Where will you two live?" Nora asked later as they visited with her.

Seth and Jenna exchanged smiles and Jenna replied, "In Aunt Edie's house." Seth already had his place set up as a beach rental and was more than happy to share the house where Jenna had made so many good memories. Together they would pack in more.

Sunset finished the day with a blaze of orange and red. Darkness slipped in, and as the moon made her appearance, Celeste lit the miniature starfish candles that had been set out on the tables, and Tyrella lit the tiki torches she'd supplied and put around the party spot. The scene turned magical. Soon everyone was dancing to the music of a local all-girls band called The Mermaids.

The bride and groom had opted out of dancing their first dance as husband and wife for all the world to watch, preferring to have their special moment among the sea of well-wishers.

"Happy?" Seth asked as he snugged her up against him.

"Beyond happy. And you?"

He smiled at her with that dark pirate smile that had attracted her the moment she met him. "Happy doesn't even come close. You're the best thing that ever happened to me. I can't believe you chose me."

"For life," she warned him. "This is my happy-ever-after, so you can't ruin it for me."

"Trust me. I never will," he promised, and she knew she could believe him.

Anxious to enjoy their own private party, the newlyweds didn't linger long at the reception after the dancing had begun. Annie caught the bouquet, and Jenna hoped it was a sign that, somewhere down the road, she, too, would find love.

Jenna and Seth honeymooned at the Driftwood Inn, and as he carried her over the threshold into the same room he'd once rented, she felt sure that Aunt Edie was looking down on her and smiling.

* * * * *

Your Friends from
Moonlight Harbor
Are Sure You'll Be Smiling
When You Try These Recipes

Annie's Portuguese Doughnuts

Makes 3 dozen

Ingredients:
2 cups biscuit mix
1 cup milk
1 egg
½ tsp lemon or almond extract
1 Tbsp granulated sugar
4 slices of bread cut in 36 pieces
Oil for frying
Extra granulated sugar for coating

Directions:

Heat oil (2–3 inches) to 375 degrees in a deep fryer (or you can also use a tall pot). Stir together biscuit mix, milk, egg and extract and beat until smooth. Dip bread pieces into batter and fry until golden brown. Drain and roll in granulated sugar.

Tyrella's Macaroni Salad

Serves 6–8

Ingredients:
2 cups small elbow macaroni
3 stalks celery, finely chopped
½ cup finely chopped onion
½ cup finely chopped orange or red bell pepper
3/4 cup chopped black olives
1 cup cooked shrimp, chilled and chopped
2 Tbsp sweet relish
1 tsp dill weed
½ tsp salt
2 Tbsp finely chopped cilantro
¼ cup Asiago cheese, grated
¼ cup medium cheddar cheese, grated
¼ cup mayonnaise
*(you might want to add a little more if your salad turns
out drier than you like)*

Directions:

Cook macaroni according to package directions, then rinse, drain and cool. Add other ingredients and mix well. Allow to set up in the fridge for an hour before serving.

Nora's Potato Salad

Serves 6

Ingredients:
1½ pounds baby Dutch yellow potatoes
½ cup chopped sweet onion
½ cup chopped celery
½ cup chopped black olives
1 3-oz package crumbled bacon bits
Generous ½ cup ranch dressing

Directions:

Quarter and boil potatoes until just tender (about 10 minutes). Drain and cool, then place in refrigerator to chill. As potatoes are chilling, chop onion, celery and black olives. Add to potatoes once they're chilled, along with bacon bits and dressing.

From Aunt Edie's Recipe Box

There's something about family recipes that is so special. Ah, the memories they trigger when you find them!

Jenna was going through Aunt Edie's recipe box and found some more favorite recipes she'd like to share. (They bear a striking resemblance to some of the old classics from Sheila's family recipe box. Hmm. Is that a coincidence?)

Aunt Edie's Orange Cream Pie

Ingredients:
1 baked pie shell
Mandarin oranges for topping

For filling:
2 cups milk
½ cup sugar
½ tsp salt
3½ Tbsp cornstarch
1 Tbsp flour
2 large slightly beaten egg yolks
1 Tbsp butter
1 tsp orange extract

Directions:

Combine milk, sugar, salt, cornstarch, and flour in a medium saucepan and cook over moderate heat, stirring constantly until mixture thickens and begins to boil. Remove from heat. Slowly stir half of mixture into egg yolks, then blend into the rest of the mixture in the saucepan. Cook

1 minute more, stirring constantly. Remove from heat. Blend in butter and orange extract. Pour into pie shell and let stand for 10 minutes, then refrigerate. Allow to set 2 hours before serving. Serve topped with sliced mandarin oranges and whipped cream flavored with orange extract.

Streusel-Filled Coffee Cake

Note: I like to make this when I'm having a friend over for morning coffee.

Ingredients for cake:
¾ cup sugar
¼ cup butter
1 ½ cups flour
2 tsp baking powder
½ tsp salt
1 egg
½ cup milk

For streusel:
½ cup brown sugar
2 tbsp flour
2 tsp cinnamon
½ cup chopped walnuts

Directions:

In a large bowl, cream together sugar and butter, then add egg and mix well. Sift together dry ingredients in a separate bowl, then add to the creamed butter mixture in batches, alternating with the milk. Spread half of the batter on a greased 9 x 9 inch pan. In a medium bowl, combine streusel ingredients. Sprinkle half the streusel evenly over the batter in the pan. Add remaining batter, then sprinkle top with remaining streusel. Bake at 350°F for 25 minutes or until a toothpick inserted in the center comes out clean.

Tuna Roll-Ups

*My friends often request this when
I'm hosting a luncheon.*

Ingredients for rolls:
1 batch of biscuit dough

For tuna filling:
1 small can tuna, drained
½ cup minced celery
1 egg

For sauce and garnish:
1 can cream of mushroom or cream of celery soup
2 tbsp chopped parsley

Directions:

Roll out biscuit dough into a 12-inch square, then cut into
9 squares. In a medium bowl, mix together the tuna, celery
and egg. Spread 2 tbsp of the filling on each square and

roll up as for a jelly roll. Seal and place sealed side down on an ungreased baking sheet. Bake at 400°F for 20 to 25 minutes. Serve hot with hot soup (undiluted) as sauce and topped with parsley.

Pea Salad

This is always a hit at potlucks.

Ingredients for salad:
20 oz package petite frozen peas, thawed
2 cups finely chopped celery
1 cup finely chopped green pepper
½ cup sliced green onion
½ pound cooked bacon, crumbled
¾ cup sunflower seeds

For dressing:
½ cup each of mayonnaise and sour cream

Directions:

Mix all ingredients together in a large bowl and serve immediately.

Fruit Cocktail Dessert

This is scrumptious and should always be served with whipped cream.

Ingredients:
1 cup flour
1 cup sugar
1 tsp baking soda
½ tsp salt
1 egg, beaten
1 tsp vanilla
1 medium can (15 ounce) fruit cocktail,
omitting 2 tbsp juice
1 cup brown sugar
½ cup chopped pecan or walnuts

Directions:

Sift together the flour, sugar, baking soda and salt into a large mixing bowl. Add the beaten egg, vanilla and fruit cocktail, and mix. Pour into a lightly greased 9 x 9 inch baking pan, sprinkle with brown sugar and nuts, and bake at 350°F for 30 minutes or until firm and golden brown.

Carrot Cookies

This was the only way I could get Ralph to eat carrots!

Ingredients for cookies:
½ cup shortening
½ cup butter
¾ cup sugar
2 eggs
1 cup cooked mashed carrots
2 cups flour
2 tsp baking powder
½ tsp salt
¾ cup shredded sweetened coconut

For orange icing:
3 tbsp butter, softened
1 ½ cups powdered sugar
1 tsp grated orange zest
1 tbsp orange juice

Directions:

In a large bowl, cream together shortening, butter, sugar and eggs, then add carrots and mix. Sift in dry ingredients and mix well, then stir in coconut. Drop dough by small spoonfuls onto a lightly greased cookie sheet and bake at 350°F for 8 to 10 minutes. Cool cookies. For orange icing, cream butter and powdered sugar together in a medium bowl, then mix in orange zest and orange juice. If the icing is too thick, add a few more drops of orange juice. Decorate cooled cookies with orange frosting.

Strawberry Pizza

This is always a hit!

Ingredients for crust:
½ cup powdered sugar
1 cup flour
½ cup butter, softened

For filling:
8 oz cream cheese
½ cup powdered sugar

For topping:
1 quart strawberries
1 jar strawberry glaze
Whipped cream for serving

Directions:

In a large bowl, mix together powdered sugar, flour and butter. Pat into a 13-inch pizza pan. Bake at 325°F for 10 to 15 minutes. Let cool. In a large bowl, mix cream cheese and powdered sugar well, then spread on cooled shell. For topping, slice strawberries and spread over cream cheese mixture. Top with ¾ of the jar of glaze. Refrigerate. Serve topped with whipped cream.

Acknowledgments

I am so grateful for all the wonderful people who help me turn those stories in my head into a book someone can read and, hopefully, enjoy. Writing may be a solitary pursuit, but in the end it takes many hands. A big thank you to Cheron Wittman PA-C for sharing her medical expertise with me. Even though I've personally been on both sides of some medical events, the facts tend to blur and some of them are deliberately forgotten. Anything I still didn't get right on these pages is my own fault. Thank you also to my fabulous editor April Osborn for her insight, guidance and continued kindness, and to my incredible agent and friend Paige Wheeler who always works so hard on my behalf. All I can say to editorial and art department and marketing departments at Mira is that you are all fabulous and I'm grateful to be working with you. Lastly, thank you to my street team who give me so much support. Hope you'll find this tale worthy of your enthusiasm.

Get 4 FREE REWARDS!

We'll send you 2 FREE Books plus 2 FREE Mystery Gifts.

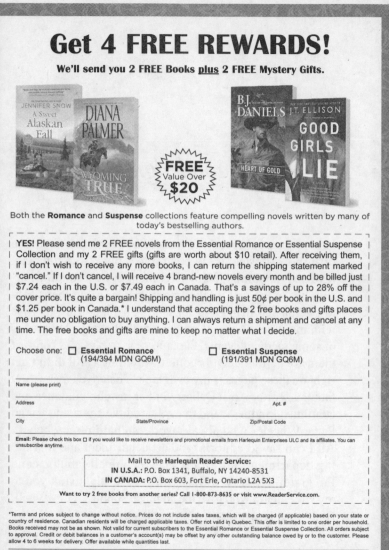

FREE Value Over **$20**

Both the **Romance** and **Suspense** collections feature compelling novels written by many of today's bestselling authors.

YES! Please send me 2 FREE novels from the Essential Romance or Essential Suspense Collection and my 2 FREE gifts (gifts are worth about $10 retail). After receiving them, if I don't wish to receive any more books, I can return the shipping statement marked "cancel." If I don't cancel, I will receive 4 brand-new novels every month and be billed just $7.24 each in the U.S. or $7.49 each in Canada. That's a savings of up to 28% off the cover price. It's quite a bargain! Shipping and handling is just 50¢ per book in the U.S. and $1.25 per book in Canada.* I understand that accepting the 2 free books and gifts places me under no obligation to buy anything. I can always return a shipment and cancel at any time. The free books and gifts are mine to keep no matter what I decide.

Choose one: ☐ **Essential Romance**
(194/394 MDN GQ6M)

☐ **Essential Suspense**
(191/391 MDN GQ6M)

Name (please print)

Address   Apt. #

City   State/Province   Zip/Postal Code

Email: Please check this box ☐ if you would like to receive newsletters and promotional emails from Harlequin Enterprises ULC and its affiliates. You can unsubscribe anytime.

Mail to the **Harlequin Reader Service:**
IN U.S.A.: P.O. Box 1341, Buffalo, NY 14240-8531
IN CANADA: P.O. Box 603, Fort Erie, Ontario L2A 5X3

Want to try 2 free books from another series! Call 1-800-873-8635 or visit www.ReaderService.com.

*Terms and prices subject to change without notice. Prices do not include sales taxes, which will be charged (if applicable) based on your state or country of residence. Canadian residents will be charged applicable taxes. Offer not valid in Quebec. This offer is limited to one order per household. Books received may not be as shown. Not valid for current subscribers to the Essential Romance or Essential Suspense Collection. All orders subject to approval. Credit or debit balances in a customer's account(s) may be offset by any other outstanding balance owed by or to the customer. Please allow 4 to 6 weeks for delivery. Offer available while quantities last.

Your Privacy—Your information is being collected by Harlequin Enterprises ULC, operating as Harlequin Reader Service. For a complete summary of the information we collect, how we use this information and to whom it is disclosed, please visit our privacy notice located at corporate.harlequin.com/privacy-notice. From time to time we may also exchange your personal information with reputable third parties. If you wish to opt out of this sharing of your personal information, please visit readerservice.com/consumerschoice or call 1-800-873-8635. **Notice to California Residents**—Under California law, you have specific rights to control and access your data. For more information on these rights and how to exercise them, visit corporate.harlequin.com/california-privacy.

STRS21MAXR